Professor

MORIARTY

THE HOUND OF THE D'URBERVILLES

Also by Kim Newman from Titan Books:

ANNO DRACULA

ANNO DRACULA: THE BLOODY RED BARON (APRIL 2012)

Professor

MORIARTY

THE HOUND OF THE D'URBERVILLES

KIM NEWMAN

TITAN BOOKS

Professor Moriarty: The Hound of the D'Urbervilles
Print edition: ISBN: 9780857682833
E-book edition ISBN: 9780857686015

Published by
Titan Books
A division of Titan Publishing Group Ltd
144 Southwark St
London
SE1 0UP

First edition: September 2011
3 5 7 9 10 8 6 4 2

Visit our website: www.titanbooks.com

Did you enjoy this book? We love to hear from our readers. Please email us at readerfeedback@titanemail.com or write to us at Reader Feedback at the above address.

To receive advance information, news, competitions, and exclusive Titan offers online, please visit our website: www.titanbooks.com

A CIP catalogue record for this title is available from the British Library.

Printed and bound in the United States.

For Barry Forshaw

PREFACE

Even during the global crisis which broke more famous financial institutions, the failure of Box Brothers was noisy. The private bank collapsed shortly after the arrest of Dame Philomela Box, Chief Executive Officer, on charges of fraudulent dealing. A warrant was also issued for her nephew, Colin Box. Press speculation that he had done a runner ended when his body was discovered in the boot of a burned-out Volvo on Havengore Island, Essex. Autopsy determined that Colin's head had been sawn off and used as a football. No one has ever been charged with his murder, or those of two other bank officers found dead in the next six weeks.

Only after the CEO's indictment could Box Brothers be called in print what it was, and always had been: the criminals' bank. Founded in 1869, the family-owned business maintained premises in Moorgate, Gibraltar and Bermuda [1]. For nearly a century and a half, Box Brothers provided financial services (no questions asked) to law-breakers great and small. Their client list ranged from underworld gangs (and, from the 1960s on, terrorist cells) with enormous turnovers to conceal to lowly smash-and-grab merchants with bloodied cash deposits to make. As their still-live website euphemistically has it, Box Brothers' twenty-first-century speciality was 'offshore wealth management' – which is to say, getting the loot out of the country. The house's oldest service was the most confidential and secure storage facility in the City of London – which is to say, a box to keep the jewels or paintings (or, in several cases, people) out of sight until the heat died down.

At the time of writing, the Moorgate premises remain under twenty-four-hour armed guard as suits and countersuits regarding access to the safety deposit vault (where it is rumoured the trophies of several famous, unsolved thefts are to be found) are argued. Or not… since it seems the management were not above dipping into the till to pay for Dame Philomela's passion for airships or Colin's white rap label [2]. Lawrence and Harrington Box, the founders, would have been aghast at the decline from the standards set in their day. Their simple philosophy was scrupulous honesty. Clients were expected to set aside their habitual larceny in dealing with the bank, just as the brothers made no moral judgement about business brought to them.

Before the crash, my dealings with Box Brothers were limited.

While my *A History of Silence: Victorian Crimes Against and By Women* [3] was in proof, my cat went missing. When I left for work, Crippen was locked in the flat. When I came home, the flat was still locked but Crippen was gone. The next day, my Female Serial Killers seminar was interrupted by a special messenger making a recorded delivery of a lawyers' letter which suggested I delete any mention of Box Brothers from my forthcoming book. I first read 'if the offending material is not removed, no further legal action will be taken' as a mistyping. Then I saw 'no further legal action' did not mean 'no further action'. When I got home, Crippen was back, with a triangle snipped out of her ear. The offending reference consisted of a footnote in a chapter about nineteenth-century brothelkeepers [4]. I made the edit.

When Box Brothers fell, several hastily researched articles about the bank's history appeared in the papers. Evidently, the bank no longer had the wherewithal to put pressure on journalists and historians. I assumed – not without *Schadenfreude* – that their in-house catnappers were busy avoiding larger, more dangerous animals. Widows and orphans and pension funds and small businessmen with accounts in Iceland run screaming to the government when their savings are in peril, but the sort of customer who banks with Box Brothers takes more direct action.

In July, 2009, I took a call in my office at Birkbeck College from Philomela Box's private secretary, Henry Hassan.

'Ms Temple, are you free to come into Dame Philomela's office this afternoon for a consultation?'

'On what?' I asked.

'Historical documents,' he said.

Considering Crippen's snipped ear, I was of a mind to tell Hassan where to file his historical documents. And to tell him it should be *Professor* Temple.

But it had been a boring week. The long summer vac was filled with faculty meetings about budget cuts. The only interesting PhD student I was supervising [5] was off working as a tour guide in Barcelona. So I agreed to visit the City.

Dame Philomela's office was not in Holloway Prison. She was still in Moorgate. Windows smashed by an angry mob were boarded up. The building was guarded both by uniformed policemen and helmeted private security. A faction of anti-capitalist enthusiasts mounted a cosplay protest which had thinned over the months since the credit crunch started to bite. Ghost-masked young folks wore loose pyjamas decorated with broad arrows, and dragged about Jacob Marley chains of ledgers and strongboxes. Their slogans suggested they didn't see Box Brothers as more criminal than any other bank.

Mr Hassan, the last loyal retainer, met me in a cavernous, dim reception room. Dustsheets were draped over the furniture. Loose wires showed where computers had once been plumbed in. Unfaded oblongs on the plush wallpaper marked the spots formerly taken by pictures which had walked out with suddenly unemployed staff. A cleaner had been arrested legging it down Silk Street with two Vernets and a Greuze in a Budgens 'Bag for Life'.

I was ushered into an inner office.

A tall, thin woman came out from behind a desk to shake my hand. A red light flashed on her ankle bracelet.

'Henry, get us espresso… if the plods haven't taken the last of it along with every bloody thing else,' said Dame Philomela. 'I'll have gin in mine, but the professor won't, I'm sure.'

Mr Hassan retreated, backing out like a nervous courtier.

Dame Philomela's office was hung with airship mobiles. She had a framed print of *The Hindenburg* disaster. On bookshelves where most bankers display leatherbound tomes of financial lore she had a complete set of Jeffrey Archer first editions. She was evidently a bit of a fan: in a photograph, she and Lord Archer wore matching flying helmets and her smile showed half a skull. I assumed he'd give her tips on how to get by in prison.

Dame Philomela was sixty. From experience with postgraduate students, I knew at once she was a functioning anorexic. She wore a tailored dark suit with a short skirt. Her long, straight black hair had a white streak – she must dye twice for the effect. Her only items of visible jewellery were a lapel-brooch in the shape of a dirigible and a discreet silver nose-stud.

The newspapers had made a lot out of Dame Philomela's resemblance to a Disney cartoon villainess. I wondered if she didn't cultivate the effect.

Her computer was gone. The Fraud Squad were going through thousands of Zeppelin .jpgs and .avis while looking for evidence. A brass-hinged wooden box stood on her desk where the monitor would have been.

'Sit,' she ordered.

I complied. She stood by her desk, long fingers on the box.

'Do you know the legal status of items left undisturbed in safety deposit for, oh, eighty years?'

'No,' I said.

'Neither do I,' Dame Philomela admitted. 'That was Colin's area. Bloody idiot. Anyway, I can tell you what we do with them here... it hardly matters any more. We use a master key our depositors don't know about to open the box, and divvy up the contents if obviously valuable... or stick them in a sub-basement junk room if not. That started before my day. A necessity, with new clients coming in and needing secure space. There's a waiting list – or, rather, there *was* – for our vault. Rather than go to the trouble of getting new boxes put in, it was easier to clear out lost causes and move on. Contrary to what you read in those awful rags, it's not all crown jewels and wodges of banknotes. If you want a giggle, I've a collection of musty old letters used to blackmail people who've been dead so long no one could possibly care about their sad old secrets. Have you heard of Sebastian Moran?'

'Yes,' I said. 'He was a minor Victorian. A soldier and explorer, big-game hunter. Implicated in something called the "Bagatelle Card Club Scandal". He was caught cheating by a man called Adair, who was later shot dead. Moran was arrested for the murder, but didn't hang... no one is quite sure how he got off, though he did go to prison for a few years. The only reason he's remembered is because the Adair case was the first solved, after the so-called "great hiatus", by...'

'Good, yes, fine, you know your scoundrels,' Dame Philomela interrupted. 'Now, don't go on, woman. Showing off is all it is. Anybody can Wikipedia this stuff now, so there's no need to have it all up in your head to be spat out again. Very unattractive, it is. I've no earthly interest in the old dead bastard, anyway. Except for this.'

She took the box from her desk and gave it to me.

On the lid was a brass plate, inscribed: 'Col. Sebastian Moran, 1st

Bangalore Pioneers, Conduit Street.'

'It's not locked,' said Dame Philomela.

Inside was a manuscript. Two separate sheafs, which I guessed were different drafts of the same material: a longhand version, neatly written on lined paper, and a typescript, with crossings-out and emendations in ink.

'Is it authentic?' she asked.

'I couldn't possibly say without closer examination.'

Dame Philomela looked annoyed. That cracked her tight face and brought out her inner hag.

'Well then, you silly bitch, examine closely,' said Dame Philomela.

I thought about leaving.

Mr Hassan came back with the espresso. It was criminally strong. I decided to stay, for a while.

'I want to know if there's money in this,' said Dame Philomela. 'And how quickly I can get it.'

'I'll have to take this away and have it looked at. Besides analysing the text, tests can be done on the paper and ink to get an estimate of the age.'

'I should cocoa,' snorted Dame Philomela. 'This stays here. You can read it in the next room. Then tell me what I've got. And how much it's worth.'

I took the typescript out of the tin, and riffled through it. It was a book-length manuscript, with numbered pages, divided into chapters. There was no title page, or author credit.

On the first few pages, someone had carefully inked out a recurring name and written in 'Mahoney' above the black patches. Then, the same hand scribbled 'sod it, can't be bothered!' in the margin, and gave up on the pretence of concealing identity.

The name someone had thought briefly to hide was Moriarty.

'Professor Moriarty?' I asked.

'Yes,' Dame Philomela said. 'I dare say you've heard of *him*.'

'A client of Box Brothers?'

'One of the originals. So was Moran.'

'He left a safety-deposit box?'

'Yes. Inside was a pornographic deck of Edwardian playing cards I've put on eBay, a string of pearls I'm keeping for my old age, and this. Now, do you want to read it or not?'

I did. I have. And, with minimal editorial alteration, this is it.

Dame Philomela didn't and doesn't care if it's an authentic memoir, though she was keen to establish that if it's fake, it's at least an old fake. No living author will come forward to claim royalties.

Tests were done. I confidently assert that this is the work of Colonel Sebastian Moran. Vocabulary and syntax are consistent with his published books, *Heavy Game of the Western Himalayas* (1881) and *Three Months in the Jungle* (1884)... though his tone in these memoirs is considerably less guarded. He incidentally settles a long-standing academic dispute by identifying himself as the anonymous author of *My Nine Nights in a Harem* (1879) [6]. The undated longhand pages were written between 1880 and 1910. Different paper and inks indicate the author worked intermittently, writing separate chapters over twenty years. It is probable sections were drafted in Prince Town Prison, where Moran was resident for some time after 1894.

Internal evidence suggests Moran intended to publish, perhaps inspired by the commercial success of others whose memoirs – many overlapping events he recounts – had already appeared. Of course, those authors did not confess to capital crimes in print, an issue which might have given Moran second thoughts. He was considering publication as late as 1923–4, when the typescript was made. We cannot definitively identify the person or persons who typed his manuscript for him [7], but can be sure it was not Moran – though the annotations are in his handwriting.

Without a research project which Dame Philomela, who is now serving a seven-year sentence in Askham Grange open prison, is unwilling to fund, a full assessment of the veracity of Moran's memoirs is impossible. Given that the author characterises himself as a cheat, a liar, a villain and a murderer, we are entitled to ask whether he was as dishonest in autobiography as he was in everything else. However, it seems he felt – perhaps later in life – a compulsion to make an accurate record. Few in his time thought Sebastian Moran anything but a rogue, but his famous associate saw straight away that he was what we might now diagnose as an adrenalin junkie. When age kept him from more active pursuits, perhaps writing a book which could lead to him being hanged was a substitute for the thrill of hunting tigers or breaking laws. However, he was in healthy middle age when he began writing up the crimes of Professor Moriarty – and was in fact busy helping commit them. Where dates, names and places that can be checked are given, Moran is a reliable historian – more so than some of his less crooked contemporaries.

On the text: I have made few corrections to Moran's spelling or syntax, except for consistency. He did go to Eton, after all. Some contemporaries took him for a fool, but he was an educated, well-read, intelligent man and articulate when he chose to be. The manuscript is overrun with hyphens and dashes which are pruned to some extent in the typescript, and have been pruned further by me. Moran held to nineteenth-century conventions ('cow-boy', 'gas-light', 'were-wolf') which would distract the modern eye. I have resisted a temptation to cut digressions or offhand references which raise tantalising matters upon which no further information is available. A thorough search of the vaults of Box Brothers has turned up no other Moran manuscripts – so we're unlikely to find out more about the 'Mystery of the Essex Werewolf' or the 'Affair of the Mountaineer's Bum'.

Perhaps surprisingly, given his candour, Moran exercised a degree of self-censorship. Make no mistake, the Victorians could be as foul-mouthed as we are. Moran won an Army–Navy swearing contest held in Bombay in 1875, outlasting 'the vilest bosun in the Fleet' by a full half-hour of obscene profanity without repetition or hesitation, but with a great deal of deviation. However, in his manuscript, he blots out swear words. Some pages look like heavily redacted CIA intelligence reports. The typescript is clearer, but still tactful ('c--t', 'f--k', etc.). Where necessary, I have kept that archaism.

I have chosen not to include several passages which would prove offensive or stultifying to modern readers. Some material (dealing with race, sex or politics) exists in manuscript but not typescript, suggesting Moran himself had second thoughts. As a sometime pornographer, Moran's accounts of sexual encounters run to dozens of detailed, unedifying pages; he writes about big-game hunting, horse-racing and card games in an identical manner. Where not directly germane to the narrative, I have trimmed paragraphs on these subjects. They are only of academic interest and this academic wasn't especially interested – *Heavy Game of the Western Himalayas* has been out of print for over a hundred years for good reason. If Moran had been only a tiger hunter and libertine, he would be forgotten. As he admits, if he is remembered at all, it is because he was Moriarty's lieutenant. In this edition of his memoirs, I have concentrated on that association, sparing the reader aspects of his life and times which now make Moran seem more appalling a human being than his inclinations towards larceny, duplicity and homicide.

Professor Christina Temple, BA, MA, PhD, FRHistS.
School of Social Sciences, History and Philosophy,
Department of History, Classics and Archaeology
Birkbeck College, London.
February 2011.

Contents

Chapter One: A Volume in Vermilion   19

Chapter Two: A Shambles in Belgravia   67

Chapter Three: The Red Planet League   85

Chapter Four: The Hound of the D'Urbervilles   137

Chapter Five: The Adventure of the Six Maledictions 221

Chapter Six: The Greek Invertebrate   311

Chapter Seven: The Problem of the Final Adventure   375

Chapter One: A Volume in Vermilion

I

I blame that rat-weasel Stamford, who was no better at judging character than at kiting paper. He later had his collar felt in Farnham, of all blasted places. If you want to pass French government bonds, you can't afford to mix up your accents *grave* and your accents *acute*. Archie Stamford earns no sympathy from me. Thanks to him, I was first drawn into the orbit, the *gravitational pull* as he would have said, of Professor James Moriarty.

In 1880, your humble narrator was a vigorous, if scarred, forty. I should make a proper introduction of myself: Colonel Sebastian 'Basher' Moran, late of a school which wouldn't let in an oik like you and a regiment which would as soon sack Newcastle as take Ali Masjid. I had an unrivalled bag of big cats and a fund of stories about blasting the roaring pests. I'd stood in the Khyber Pass and faced a surge of sword-waving Pathans howling for British blood, potting them like grouse in season. Nothing gladdens a proper Englishman's heart – this one, at least – like the sight of a foreigner's head flying into a dozen bloody bits. I'd dangled by a single-handed grip from an icy ledge in the upper Himalayas, with something huge and indistinct and furry stamping on my freezing fingers. I'd bent like an oak in a hurricane as Sir Augustus, the hated pater, spouted paragraphs of bile in my face, which boiled down to the proverbial 'cut off without a penny' business. Stuck to it too, the mean old swine. The family loot went to a society for providing Christian undergarments to the Ashanti, a bequest which had the delightful side effect of reducing my unmarriageable sisters to boarding-house penury.

I'd taken a dagger in the lower back from a harlot in Hyderabad and a pistol-ball in the knee from the Okhrana in Nijni-Novgorod. More to the point, I had recently been raked across the chest by the mad, wily old she-tiger the hill-heathens called 'Kali's Kitten'.

None of that was preparation for Moriarty!

I had crawled into a drain after the tiger, whose wounds turned out to be less severe than I'd thought. Tough old hellcat! KK got playful with jaws and paws, crunching down my pith helmet like one of Carter's Little Liver Pills, delicately shredding my shirt with razor claws, digging into the skin and drawing casually across my chest. Three bloody stripes. Sure I would die in that stinking tunnel, I was determined not to die alone. I got my Webley side arm unholstered and shot the hell-bitch through the heart. To make sure, I emptied all six chambers. After that chit in Hyderabad dirked me, I broke her nose for her. KK looked almost as aghast and infuriated at being killed. I wondered if girl and tigress were related. I had the cat's rank dying breath in my face and her weight on me in that stifling hole. One more for the trophy wall, I thought. Cat dead, Moran not: hurrah and victory!

But KK nearly murdered me after all. The stripes went septic. Good thing there's no earthly use for the male nipple, because I found myself down to just the one. Lots of grey stuff came out of me. So I was packed off back to England for proper doctoring.

It occurred to me that a concerted effort had been made to boot me out of the subcontinent. I could think of a dozen reasons for that, and a dozen clods in stiff collars who'd be happier with me out of the picture. Maiden ladies who thought tigers ought to be patted on the head and given treats. And the husbands, fathers and sweethearts of non-maiden ladies. Not to mention the 1st Bangalore Pioneers, who didn't care to be reminded of their habit of cowering in ditches while Bloody Basher did three-fourths of their fighting for them.

Still, mustn't hold a grudge, what? Sods, the lot of them. And that's just the whites. As for the natives… well, let's not get started on them, shall we? We'd be here 'til next Tuesday.

For me, a long sea cruise is normally an opportunity. There are always bored fellow passengers and underworked officers knocking around with fat notecases in their luggage. It's most satisfying to sit on deck playing solitaire until some booby suggests a few rounds of cards and, why just to make it *spicier*, perhaps some trifling, sixpence-a-trick element of wager. Give me two months on any ocean in the world, and I can fleece everyone aboard from the captain's lady to the bosun's second-best bumboy, and leave each mark convinced that the ship is a nest of utter cheats with only Basher as the other honest hand in the game.

Usually, I embark *sans sou* and stroll down the gangplank at the destination, pockets a-jingle with the accumulated fortune of my fellow voyagers. I get a warm feeling from ambling through the docks, listening to clots explaining to the eager sorts who've turned up to greet them that, sadly, the moolah which would have saved the guano-grubbing business or bought the Bibles for the mission or paid for the wedding has gone astray on the high seas. This time, tragic to report, I was off sick, practically in quarantine. My nimble fingers were away from the pasteboards, employed mostly in scratching around the bandages while trying hard not to scratch the bandages themselves.

So, the upshot: Basher in London, out of funds. And the word was abroad. I was politely informed by a chinless receptionist at Claridge's that my usual suite of rooms was engaged and that, unfortunately, no alternative was available, this being a busy wet February and all. If I hadn't pawned my horsewhip, it would have got some use. If there's any breed I despise more than natives, it's people who work in bloody hotels. Thieves, the lot of them, or, what's worse, sneaks and snitches. They talk among themselves, so it was no use trotting down the street and trying somewhere else.

I was on the point of wondering if I shouldn't risk the Bagatelle Club, where, frankly, you're not playing with amateurs. There's the peril of wasting a whole evening shuffling and betting with other sharps who a) can't be rooked so easily and b) are liable to be as cash-poor as oneself. Otherwise, it was a matter of beetling up and down Piccadilly all afternoon in the hope of spotting a ten-bob note in the gutter, or – if it came to it – dragging Farmer Giles into a sidestreet, splitting his head and lifting his poke. A comedown after Kali's Kitten, but needs must…

'It's "Basher" Moran, isn't it?' drawled someone, prompting me to raise my sights from the gutter. 'Still shooting anything that draws breath?'

'Archibald Stamford, Esquire. Still practising auntie's signature?'

I remembered Archie from some police cells in Islington. All charges dropped and apologies made, in my case. Being 'mentioned in despatches' carries weight with beaks, certainly more than the word of a tradesman in a celluloid collar you clean with India rubber. Six months jug for the fumbling forger, though. He'd been pinched trying to make a withdrawal from a relative's bank account.

If clothes were anything to go by, Stamford had risen in his profession. Tiepin and cane, dove-grey morning coat, curly brimmed topper, and good boots. His whole manner, with that patronising hale-fellow-snooks-to-you tone, suggested he was in funds – which made him my long-lost friend.

The Criterion was handy, so I suggested we repair to the bar for drinks. The question of who paid for them would be settled when Archie was fuddle-headed from several whiskies. I fed him that shut-out-of-my-usual-suite line and considered a hard-luck story trading on my status as hero of the Jowaki

Campaign – though I doubted an inky-fingered felon would put much stock in far-flung tales of imperial daring.

Stamford's eyes shone, in a manner which reminded me unpleasantly of my late feline dancing partner. He sucked on his teeth, torn between saying something and keeping mum. It was a manner I would soon come to recognise as common to those in the employ of my soon-to-be benefactor.

'As it happens, Bash old chap, I know a billet that might suit you. Comfortable rooms in Conduit Street, above Mrs Halifax's establishment. You know Mrs H.?'

'Used to keep a knocking-shop in Stepney? Arm-wrestler's biceps and an eight-inch tongue?'

'That's the one. She's West End now. Part of a combine, you might say. A thriving firm.'

'What she sells is always in demand.'

'True, but it's not just the whoring. There's other business. A man of vision, you might say, has done some thinking. About my line of trade, and Mrs Halifax's, and, as it were, yours.'

I was about at the end of my rope with Archie. He was talking in a familiar, insinuating, creeping-round-behind-you-with-a-cosh manner I didn't like. Implying that I was a tradesman did little for my ruddy temper. I was strongly tempted to give him one of my speciality thumps, which involves a neat little screw of my big fat regimental ring into the old eyeball, and see how his dove-grey coat looked with dirty great blobs of snotty blood down the front. After that, a quick fist into his waistcoat would leave him gasping, and give me the chance to fetch away his watch and chain, plus any cash he had on him. Of course, I'd check the spelling of 'Bank of England' on the notes before spending them. I could make it look like a difference of opinion between gentlemen. And no worries about it coming back to me. Stamford wouldn't squeal to the peelers. If he wanted to pursue the matter I could always give him a second helping.

'I wouldn't,' he said, as if he could read my mind.

That was a dash of Himalayan melt water to the face.

Catching sight of myself in the long mirror behind the bar, I saw my cheeks had gone a nasty shade of red. More vermilion than crimson. My fists were knotted, white-knuckled, around the rail. This, I understand, is what I look like before I 'go off'. You can't live through all I have without 'going off' from time to time. Usually, I 'come to' in handcuffs between policemen with black eyes. The other fellow or fellows or lady is too busy being carried away to hospital to press charges.

Still, a 'tell' is a handicap for a card player. And my red face gave warning.

Stamford smiled like someone who knows there's a confederate behind the curtain with a bead drawn on the back of your neck and a finger on the trigger.

Libertè, hah!

'Have you popped your guns, Colonel?'

I would pawn, and indeed have pawned, the family silver. I'd raise money on my medals, ponce my sisters (not that anyone would pay for the hymn-singing old trouts) and sell Royal Navy torpedo plans to the Russians… but a man's guns are sacred. Mine were at the Anglo-Indian Club, oiled and wrapped and packed away in cherrywood cases, along with a kitbag full of assorted cartridges. If any cats got out of Regent's Park Zoo, I'd be well set up to use a hansom for a howdah and track them along Oxford Street.

Stamford knew from my look what an outrage he had suggested. This wasn't the red-hot pillar-box-faced Basher bearing down on him, this was the deadly icy calm of – and other folks have said this, so it's not just me boasting – 'the best heavy game shot that our Eastern Empire has produced'.

'There's a fellow,' he continued, nervously, 'this man of vision I mentioned. In a roundabout way, he is my employer. Probably the employer of half the folk in this room, whether they know it or not…'

He looked about. It was the usual shower: idlers and painted dames, jostling each other with stuck-on smiles, reaching sticky fingers into jacket pockets and up loose skirts, finely dressed fellows talking of 'business' which was no more than powdered thievery, a scattering of moon-faced cretins who didn't know their size-thirteens gave them away as undercover detectives.

Stamford produced a card and handed it to me.

'He's looking for a shooter...'

The fellow could never say the right thing. I am a sportsman, not a keeper. A gun, not a gunslinger. A shot, not a shooter.

Still, game is game...

'...and you might find him interesting.'

I looked down at the card. It bore the legend 'Professor James Moriarty', and an address in Conduit Street.

'A professor, is it?' I sneered. I pictured a dusty coot like the stick-men who'd bedevilled me through Eton (interminably) and Oxford (briefly). Or else a music-hall slickster, inflating himself with made-up titles. 'What might he *profess*, Archie?'

Stamford was a touch offended, and took back the card. It was as if Archie were a new convert to papism and I'd farted during a sermon from Cardinal Newman.

'You've been out of England a long time, Basher.'

He summoned the barman, who had been eyeing us with that fakir's trick of knowing who was most likely, fine clothes or not, to do a runner.

'Will you be paying now, sirs?'

Stamford held up the card and shoved it in the man's face.

The barman went pale, dug into his own pocket to settle the tab, apologised, and backed off in terror.

Stamford just looked smug as he handed the card back to me.

II

'You have been in Afghanistan, I perceive,' said the Professor.

'How the devil did you know that?' I asked in astonishment.

His eyes caught mine. Cobra eyes, they say. Large, clear, cold, grey and fascinating. I've met cobras, and they aren't half as deadly – trust me. I imagine Moriarty left off tutoring because his pupils were too terrified to con their two times table. I seemed to suffer his gaze for a full minute, though only a few seconds passed. It had been like that in the hug of Kali's Kitten. I'd have sworn on a stack of well-thumbed copies of *The Pearl* that the mauling went on for an hour of pain, but the procedure was over inside thirty seconds. If I'd had a Webley on my hip, I might have shot the Professor in the heart on instinct – though it's my guess bullets wouldn't dare enter him. He had a queer unhealthy light about him. Not unhealthy in himself, but for everybody else.

Suddenly, pacing distractedly about the room, head wavering from side to side as if he had two dozen extra flexible bones in his neck, he began to rattle off facts.

Facts about me.

'…you are retired from your regiment, resigning at the request of a superior to avoid the mutual disgrace of dishonourable discharge; you have suffered a serious injury at the claws of a beast, are fully recovered physically, but worry your nerve might have gone; you are the son of a late Minister to Persia and have two sisters, your only living relatives beside a number of unacknowledged half-native illegitimates; you are addicted, most of all to gambling, but also to sexual encounters, spirits, the murder of animals and the fawning of a duped public; most of the time, you blunder through life like a bull, snatching and punching to get your own way, but in moments of extreme danger you are possessed by a strange serenity which has enabled you to survive situations that would have killed another man; in fact, your true addiction is to *danger*, to fear – only near death do you feel alive; you are unscrupulous, amoral, habitually violent and, at present, have no means of income, though your tastes and habits require a constant inflow of money...'

Throughout this performance, I took in Professor James Moriarty. Tall, stooped, hair thin at the temples, cheeks sunken, wearing a dusty (no, *chalky*) frock coat, sallow as only an indoorsman can be; yellow cigarette stain between his first and second fingers, teeth to match. And, obviously, very pleased with himself.

He reminded me of Gladstone gone wrong. With just a touch of a hill-chief who had tortured me with fire ants.

But I had no patience with his lecture. I'd eaten enough of that from the *pater* for a lifetime.

'Tell me something I *don't* know,' I interrupted...

The Professor was unpleasantly surprised. It was as if no one had ever dared break into one of his speeches before. He halted in his tracks, swivelled his skull and levelled those shotgun-barrel-hole eyes at me.

'I've had this done at a bazaar,' I continued. 'It's no great trick. The fortune-teller notices tiny little things and makes dead-eye guesses – you can tell I gamble from the marks on my cuffs, and was in Afghanistan by the colour of my tan. If you spout with enough confidence, you score so many hits the bits you get wrong – like that tommyrot about being addicted to *danger* – are swallowed and forgotten. I'd expected a better show from your advance notices, "Professor".'

He slapped me across the face, swiftly, with a hand like wet leather.

Now, I was amazed.

I knew I was vermilion again, and my dukes went up.

Moriarty whirled, coat-tails flying, and his boot-toe struck me in the groin, belly and chest. I found myself sat in a deep chair, too shocked to hurt, pinned down by wiry, strong hands which pressed my wrists to the armrests. That dead face was close up to mine and those eyes horribly filled the view.

That calm he mentioned came on me. And I knew I should just sit still and listen.

'Only an idiot *guesses* or *reasons* or *deduces*,' the Professor said, patiently. He withdrew, which meant I could breathe again and become aware of how much pain I was in. 'No one comes into these rooms unless I know *everything* about him that can be found out through the simple means of asking behind his back. The public record is easily filled in by looking in any one of a number of reference books, from the *Army Guide* to *Who's Who*. But all the interesting material comes from a man's enemies. I am not a conjurer, Colonel Moran. I am a scientist.'

There was a large telescope in the room, aimed out of the window. On the walls were astronomical charts and a collection of impaled insects. A long side table was piled with brass, copper and glass contraptions I took for parts of instruments used in the study of the stars or navigation at sea. That shows I wasn't yet used to the Professor. Everything about him was lethal, and that included his assorted bric-a-brac.

It was hard to miss the small kitten pinned to the mantelpiece by a jack-knife. The skewering had been skilfully done, through the velvety skinfolds of the haunches. The animal mewled from time to time, not in any especial pain.

'An experiment with morphine derivatives,' he explained, following my gaze. 'Tibbles will let us know when the effect wears off.'

Moriarty posed by his telescope, bony fingers gripping his lapel.

I remembered Stamford's manner, puffed up with a feeling he was protected but tinged with terror. At any moment, the great power to which he had sworn allegiance might capriciously or justifiably turn on him with destructive ferocity. I remembered the Criterion barman digging into his own pocket to settle our bill – which, I now realised, was as natural as the Duke of Clarence gumming his own stamps or Florence Nightingale giving sixpenny knee-tremblers in D'Arblay Street.

Beside the Professor, that ant-man was genteel.

'Who *are* you?' I asked, unaccustomed to the reverential tone I heard in my own voice. '*What* are you?'

Moriarty smiled his adder's smile.

And I relaxed. I *knew*. My destiny and his wound together. It was a sensation I'd never got before upon meeting a man. When I'd had it from women, the upshot ranged from disappointment to attempted murder. Understand me, Professor James Moriarty was a hateful man, the most hateful, *hateable*, creature I have ever known, not excluding Sir Augustus and Kali's Kitten and the Abominable Bloody Snow-Bastard and the Reverend Henry James Prince [1]. He was something man-shaped that had crawled out from under a rock and moved into the manor house. But, at that moment, I was *his*, and I remain his forever. If I am remembered, it will be because I knew *him*. From that day on, he was my father, my commanding officer, my heathen idol, my fortune and terror and rapture.

God, I could have done with a stiff drink.

Instead, the Professor tinkled a silly little bell and Mrs Halifax trotted in with a tray of tea. One look and I could tell she was *his*, too. Stamford had understated the case when he said half the folk in the Criterion Bar worked for Moriarty. My guess is that, at bottom, the whole world worked for him. They've called him the Napoleon of Crime, but that's just putting what he is, what he *does*, in a cage. He's not a criminal, he is crime itself, sin raised to an art form, a church with no religion but rapine, a God of Evil. Pardon my purple prose, but there it is. Moriarty brings things out in people, things from their depths.

He poured me tea.

'I have had an eye on you for some time, Colonel Moran. Some little time. Your dossier is thick, in here...'

He tapped his concave temple.

This was literally true. He kept no notes, no files, no address book or appointment diary. It was all in his head. Someone who knows more than I do about sums told me that Moriarty's greatest feat was to write *The Dynamics of an Asteroid*, his magnum opus, in perfect first draft. From his mind to paper, with no preliminary notations or pencilled workings, never thinking forward to plan or skipping back to correct. As if he were singing 'one long, pure note of astro-mathematics, like a castrato nightingale delivering a hundred-thousand-word telegram from Prometheus.'

'You have come to these rooms and have already seen too much to leave...'

An ice-blade slid through my ribs into my heart.

'...except as, we might say, *one of the family.*'

The ice melted, and I felt tingly and warm. With the phrase, '*one of the family*', he had arched his eyebrow invitingly.

He stroked Tibbles, who was starting to leak and make nasty little noises.

'We are a large family, many cells with no knowledge of each other, devoted to varied pursuits. Most, though not all, are concerned with money. I own that other elements of our enterprise interest me far more. We are alike in that. You only think you gamble for money. In fact, you gamble to lose. You even hunt to lose, knowing you must eventually be eaten by a predator more fearsome than yourself. For you, it is an emotional, instinctual, sensual thrill. For me, there are intellectual, aesthetic, spiritual rewards. But, inconveniently, money must come into it. A great deal of money.'

As I said, he had me sold already. If a great deal of money was to be had, Moran was in.

'The Firm is available for contract work. You understand? We have clients who bring problems to us. We solve them, using whatever skills we have to hand. If there is advantage to us beyond the agreed fee, we seize it...'

He made a fist in the air, as if squeezing a microbe to death.

'...if our interests happen to run counter to those of the client, we settle the matter in such a way that is ultimately convenient to us, while our patron does not realise precisely what has happened. This, also, you understand?'

'Too right, Professor,' I said.

'Good. I believe we shall have satisfaction of each other.'

I sipped my tea. Too milky, too pale. It always is after India. I think they put curry powder in the pot out there, or else piddle in the sahib's crockery when he's not looking.

'Would you care for one of Mrs Halifax's biscuits?' he asked, as if he were the vicar entertaining the chairwoman of the beneficent fund. 'Vile things, but you might like them.'

I dunked and nibbled. Mrs H. was a better madame than baker. Which led me to wonder what fancies might be buttered up in the rooms below the Professor's lair.

'Colonel Moran, I am appointing you as head of one of our most prestigious divisions. It is a post for which you are eminently qualified by achievement and aptitude. Technically, you are superior to all in the Firm. You are expected to take up residence here, in this building. A generous salary comes with the position. And profit participation in, ah, "special projects". One such matter is at hand, and we shall come to it when we receive our next caller, Mister – no, not Mister, *Elder* – Elder Enoch J. Drebber of Cleveland, Ohio.'

'I'm flattered,' I responded. 'A "generous salary" would solve *my* problems, not to mention the use of a London flat. But, Moriarty, what is this *division* you wish me to head? Why am I such a perfect fit for it? What, specifically, is its business?'

Moriarty smiled again.

'Did I omit to mention that?'

'You know damn well you did!'

'Murder, my dear Moran. Its business is murder.'

III

Barely ten minutes after my appointment as Chief Executive Director of Homicide, Ltd., I was awaiting our first customer.

I mused humorously that I might offer an introductory special, say a garrotting thrown in gratis with every five poisonings. Perhaps there should be a half-rate for servants? A sliding scale of fees, depending on the number of years a prospective victim might reasonably expect to have lived had a client not retained our services?

I wasn't yet thinking the Moriarty way. Hunting I knew to be a serious avocation. Murder was for bounders and cosh-men, hardly even killing at all. I'm not squeamish about taking human life: Quakers don't get decorated after punitive actions against Afghan tribesmen. But not one of the heap of unwashed heathens I'd laid in the dust in the service of Queen and Empire had given me a quarter the sport of the feeblest tiger I ever bagged.

Shows you how little I knew then.

The Professor chose not to receive Elder Drebber in his own rooms, but made use of the brothel parlour. The room was well supplied with plushly upholstered divans, laden at this early evening hour with plushly upholstered tarts. It occurred to me that my newfound position with the Firm might entitle me to handle the goods. I even took the trouble mentally to pick out two or three bints who looked ripe for what ladies the world over have come to know as the Basher Moran Special. Imagine the Charge of the Light Brigade between silk sheets, or over a dresser table, or in an alcove of a Ranee's Palace, or up the Old Kent Road, or... well, anywhere really.

As soon as I sat down, the whores paid attention, cooing and fluttering like doves, positioning themselves to their best advantage. As soon as the Professor walked in, the flock stood down, finding minute imperfections in fingernails or hair that needed rectifying.

Moriarty looked at the dollies and then at me, constructing something on his face that might have passed for a salacious, comradely leer but came out wrong. The bare-teeth grin of a chimpanzee, taken for a cheery smile by sentimental zoo visitors, is really a frustrated snarl of penned, homicidal fury. The Professor also had an alien range of expression, which others misinterpreted at their peril.

Mrs Halifax ushered in our American callers.

Enoch J. Drebber – why d'you think Yankees are so keen on those blasted middle initials? – was a barrel-shaped fellow, *sans* moustache but with a fringe of tight black curls all the way round his face. He wore simple, expensive black clothes and a look of stern disapproval.

The girls ignored him. I sensed he was on the point of fulminating.

I didn't need one of the Professor's 'background checks' to get Drebber's measure. He was one of those odd godly bods who get voluptuous pleasure from condemning the fleshly failings of others. As a Mormon, he could bag as many wives as he wanted – on-tap whores and unpaid skivvies corralled together. His right eye roamed around the room, on the scout for the eighth or ninth Mrs Drebber, while his left was fixed straight ahead at the Professor.

With him came a shifty cove by the name of Brother Stangerson who kept quiet but paid attention.

'Elder Drebber, I am Professor Moriarty. This is Colonel Sebastian Moran, late of the First Bangalore...'

Drebber coughed, interrupting the niceties.

'You're who to see in this city if a Higher Law is called for?'

Moriarty showed empty hands.

'A man must die, and that's the story,' Drebber said. 'He should have died in South Utah, years ago. He's a murderer, plain and flat, and an abductor of women. Hauled out his six-gun and shot Bishop Dyer, in front of the whole town. A crime against God. Then fetched away Jane Withersteen, a good Mormon woman, and her adopted child, Little Fay. He threw down a mountain on his pursuers, crushing Elder Tull and many good Mormon men [2]. Took away gold that was rightful property of the Church, stole it right out of the ground. The Danite Band have been pursuing him ever since...'

'The Danites are a cabal within the Church of Latter-day Saints,' Moriarty explained.

'God's good right hand is what we are,' insisted Drebber. 'When the laws of men fail, the unworthy must be smitten, as if by lightning.'

I got the drift. The Danites were cossacks, assassins and vigilantes wrapped up in a Bible name. Churches, like nations, need secret police forces to keep the faithful in line.

'Who is this, ah, murderer and abductor?' I asked.

'His name, if such a fiend deserves a name, is *Lassiter*. Jim Lassiter.'

This was clearly supposed to get a reaction. The Professor kept his own council. I admitted I'd never heard of the fellow.

'Why, he's the fastest gun in the South West. Around Cottonwoods, they said he struck like a serpent, drawing and discharging in one smooth, deadly motion. Men he killed were dead before they heard the sound of the shot. Lassiter could take a man's eye out at three-hundred yards with a pistol.'

That's a fairy story. Take it from someone who knows shooting. A side arm is handy for close work, as when, for example, a tiger has her talons in your tit. With anything further away than a dozen yards, you might as well *throw* the gun as fire it.'

I kept my scepticism to myself. The customer is always right, even in the murder business.

'This Lassiter,' I ventured. 'Where might he be found?'

'In this city,' Drebber decreed. 'We are here, ah, on the business of the Church. The Danites have many enemies, and each of us knows them all. I was half expecting to come across another such pestilence, a cur named Jefferson Hope who need not concern you, but it was Lassiter I happened upon, walking in your Ly-cester Square on Sunday afternoon. I saw the Withersteen woman first, then the girl, chattering for hot chestnuts. I knew the apostate for who she was. She has been thrice condemned and outcast...'

'You said she was abducted,' put in the Professor. 'Now you imply she is with Lassiter of her own will?'

'He's a Devil of persuasion, to make a woman refuse an Elder of the Church and run off with a damned Gentile. She has no mind of her own, like all women, and cannot fully be blamed for her sins...'

If Drebber had a horde of wives around the house and still believed that, he was either very privileged or very unobservant.

'Still, she must be brought to heel. Though the girl will do as well. A warm body must be taken back to Utah, to come into an inheritance.'

'Cottonwoods,' said Moriarty. 'The ranch, the outlying farms, the cattle, the racehorses and, thanks to those inconveniently upheld claims, the fabulous gold mines of Surprise Valley.'

'The Withersteen property, indeed. When it was willed to her by her father, a great man, it was on the understanding she would become the wife of Elder Tull, and Cottonwoods would come into the Church. Were it not for this Lassiter, that would have been the situation.'

Profits, not parsons, were behind this.

'The Withersteen property will come to the girl, Fay, upon the death of the adoptive mother?'

'That is the case.'

'One or other of the females must be alive?'

'Indeed so.'

'Which would you prefer? The woman or the girl?'

'Jane Withersteen is the more steeped in sin, so there would be a certain justice...'

'...if she were topped too,' I finished his thought.

Elder Drebber wasn't comfortable with that, but nodded.

'Are these three going by their own names?'

'They are not,' said Drebber, happier to condemn enemies than contemplate his own schemes against them. 'This Lassiter has steeped his women in falsehood, making them bear repeated false witness, over and over. That such crimes should go unpunished is an offence to God Himself...'

'Yes, yes, yes,' I said. 'But what names are they using, and where do they live?'

Drebber was tugged out of his tirade, and thought hard.

'I caught only the false name of Little Fay. The Withersteen woman called her "Rache", doubtless a diminutive for the godly name "Rachel"...'

'Didn't you think to tail these, ah, varmints, to their lair?'

Drebber was offended. 'Lassiter is the best tracker the South West has ever birthed. Including Apaches. If I dogged him, he'd be on me faster'n a rattler on a coon.'

The Elder's vocabulary was mixed. Most of the time, he remembered to sound like a preacher working up a lather against sin and sodomy. When excited, he sprinkled in terms which showed him up for – in picturesque 'Wild West' terms – a back-shooting, claim-jumping, cow-rustling, waterhole-poisoning, horse-thieving, side-winding owlhoot son of a bitch.

'Surely he thinks he's safe here and will be off his guard?'

'You don't know Lassiter.'

'No, and, sadly for us all, neither do you. At least, you don't know where he hangs his hat.'

Drebber was deflated.

Moriarty said, 'Mr and Mrs James Lassiter and their daughter Fay currently reside at The Laurels, Streatham Hill Road, under the names Jonathan, Helen and Rachel Laurence.'

Drebber and I looked at the Professor. He had enjoyed showing off.

Even Stangerson clapped a hand to his sweaty forehead.

'Considering there's a fabulous gold mine at issue, I consider fifty thousand a fair price for contriving the death of Mr Laurence,' said Moriarty, as if putting a price on a fish supper. 'With an equal sum for his lady wife.'

Drebber nodded again, once. 'The girl comes with the package?'

'I think a further hundred thousand for her safekeeping, to be redeemed when we give her over into the charge of your church.'

'Another hundred thousand pounds?'

'Guineas, Elder Drebber.'

He thought about it, swallowed, and stuck out his paw.

'Deal, Professor...'

Moriarty regarded the American's hand. He turned and Mrs Halifax was beside him with a salver bearing a document.

'Such matters aren't settled with a handshake, Elder Drebber. Here is a contract, suitably circumlocutionary as to the nature of the services Colonel Moran will be performing, but meticulously exact in detailing payments entailed and the strict schedule upon which monies are to be transferred. It's legally binding, for what that's worth, but a contract with us is enforceable under what you have referred to as a Higher Law...'

The Professor stood by a lectern, which bore an open, explicitly illustrated volume of the sort found in establishments like Mrs Halifax's for occasions when inspiration flags. He unrolled the document over a coloured plate, then plucked a pen from an inkwell and presented it to Drebber.

The Elder made a pretence of reading the rubric and signed.

Professor Moriarty pressed a signet ring to the paper, impressing a stylised M below Drebber's dripping scrawl.

The document was whisked away.

'Good day, Elder Drebber.'

Moriarty dismissed the client, who backed out of the room.

'What are you waiting for?' I said to Stangerson, who stuck on the hat he had been fiddling with and scarpered.

One of the girls giggled at his departure, then remembered herself and pretended it was a hiccough. She paled under her rouge at the Professor's sidelong glance.

'Colonel Moran, have you given any thought to hunting a *Lassiter*?'

IV

A jungle is a jungle, even if it's in Streatham and is made up of villas named after shrubs.

In my coat pocket I had my Webley.

If I were one of those cowboys, I'd have notched the barrel after killing Kali's Kitten. Then again, even if I only counted white men and tigers, I didn't own any guns with a barrels long enough to keep score. A gentleman doesn't need to list his accomplishments or his debts, since there are always clerks to keep tally. I might not have turned out to be a pukka gent, but I was flogged and fagged at Eton beside future cabinet ministers and archbishops, and some skins you never shed.

It was bloody cold, as usual in London. Not raining, no fog – which is to say, no handy cover of darkness – but the ground chill rose through my boots and a nasty wind whipped my face like wet pampas grass.

The only people outside this afternoon were hurrying about their business with scarves around their ears, obviously part of the landscape. I had decided to toddle down and poke around, as a preliminary to the business in hand. Call it a recce.

Before setting out, I'd had the benefit of a lecture from the Professor. He had devoted a great deal of thought to murder. He could have written the *Baedeker's* or *Bradshaw's* of the subject. It would probably have to be published anonymously – *A Complete Guide to Murder*, by 'A Distinguished Theorist' – and then be liable to seizure or suppression by the philistines of Scotland Yard.

'Of course, Moran, murder is the easiest of all crimes, if murder is all one has in mind. One simply presents one's card at the door of the intended victim, is ushered into his sitting room and blows his or, in these enlightened times *her*, brains out with a revolver. If one has omitted to bring along a firearm, a poker or candlestick will serve. Physiologically, it is not difficult to kill another person, to perform outrages upon a human *corpus* which will render it a human *corpse*. Strictly speaking, this is a successful murder. Of course, then comes the second, far more challenging part of the equation: *getting away* with it.'

I'd been stationed across the road from The Laurels for a quarter of an hour, concealed behind bushes, before I noticed I was in Streatham Hill *Rise* not Streatham Hill *Road*. This was another Laurels, with another set of residents. This was a boarding house for genteel folk of a certain age. I was annoyed enough, with myself and the locality, to consider potting the landlady just for the practice.

If I held the deeds to this district and the Black Hole of Calcutta, I'd live in the Black Hole and rent out Streatham. Not only was it beastly cold, but stultifyingly dull. Row upon monotonous row of The Lupins, The Laburnums, The Leilandii and The Laurels. No wonder I was in the wrong spot.

'It is a little-known fact that most murderers don't *get away with it*. They are possessed by an emotion – at first, perhaps, a mild irritation about the trivial habit of a wife, mother, master or mistress. This develops over time, sprouting like a seed, to the point when only the death of another will bring peace. These murderers go happy to the gallows, free at last of their victim's clacking false teeth or unconscious chuckle or penny-pinching. We shun such as *amateurs*. They undertake the most profound action one human being can perform upon another, and *fail to profit* from the enterprise.'

No, I had not thought to purchase one of those penny-maps. Besides, anyone on the street with a map is obviously a stranger. Thus the sort who, after the fact, lodges in the mind of witnesses. 'Did you see anyone suspicious in the vicinity, Madam Busybody?' 'Why yes, Sergeant Flat-Foot, a lost-looking fellow, very red in the face, peering at street signs. Come to think of it, he *looked* like a murderer. And he was the very spit and image of that handsome devil whose picture was in the *Illustrated Press* after single-handedly seeing off the Afghan hordes that time.'

'Our business is murder for profit, killing for cash,' Moriarty had put it. 'We do not care about our clients' motives, providing they meet the price. They may wish murder to gain an inheritance, inflict revenge, make a political point or from sheer spite. In this case, all four conditions are in play. The Danite Band, represented by Elder Drebber, seek to secure the gold mine, avenge the deaths of their fellow conspirators, indicate to others who might defy them that they are dangerous to cross, and see dead a foeman they are not skilled enough to best by themselves.'

What was the use of a fanatical secret society if it *couldn't* send a horde of expendable minions to overwhelm the family? These Danite Desperadoes weren't up there with the Thuggee or the Dacoits when it came to playing that game. If the cabal really sought to usurp the governance of their church, which the Professor confided they had in mind, a greater quantity of sand would be required.

'For centuries, the art of murder has stagnated. Edged weapons, blunt instruments and bare hands that would have served our ancient ancestors are still in use. Even poisons were perfected in classical times. Only in the last hundred and fifty years have fire arms come to dominate the murder market place. For the cruder assassin, the explosive device – whether planted or flung – has made a deal of noise, though at the expense of accuracy. Presently, guns and bombs are more suited to the indiscriminate slaughter of warfare or massacre than the precision of wilful murder. That, Moran, we must change. If guns can be silenced, if skills you have developed against big game can be employed in the science of man-slaying, then the field will be revolutionised.'

I beetled glumly up and down Streatham Hill.

'Imagine, if you will, a Minister of State or a Colossus of Finance or a Royal Courtesan, protected at all hours by professionals, beyond the reach of any would-be murderer, vulnerable only to the indiscriminate anarchist with his oh-so-inaccurate bomb and willingness to be a martyr to his cause. Then think of a man with a rifle, stationed at a window or on a balcony some distance from the target, with a *telescopic device* attached to his weapon, calmly drawing a bead and taking accurate, deadly shots. A *sniper*, Moran, as used in war, brought to bear in a civilian circumstance, a private enterprise. While guards panic around their fallen employer, in a tizzy because they don't even know where the shot has come from, our assassin packs up and strolls away untroubled, unseen and untraced. That will be the murder of the future, Moran. The *scientific* murder.'

Then the Professor rattled on about airguns, which lost me. Only little boys and poofs would deign to touch a contraption which needs to be pumped before use and goes off with a sad *phut* rather than a healthy *bang*. Kali's Kitten would have swallowed an airgun whole and taken an arm along with it. The whiff of cordite, that's the stuff – better than cocaine any day of the month. And the big bass drum thunder of a gun *going off*.

Finally, I located the right Laurels.

Evening was coming on. Gaslight flared behind net curtains. More shadows to slip in. I felt comfy, as if I had thick foliage around me. My ears pricked for the pad of a big cat. I found a nice big tree and leaned against it.

I took out an instrument Moriarty had issued from his personal collection, a spyglass tricked up to look like a hip flask. Off came the stopper and there was an eye piece. Up to the old ocular as if too squiffy to crook the elbow with precision, and the bottom of the bottle was another lens. Brought a scene up close, in perfect, sharp focus.

Lovely bit of kit.

I saw into the front parlour of The Laurels. A fire was going and the whole household was at home. A ripening girl, who wore puffs and ribbons more suited to the nursery, flounced around tiresomely. I saw her mouth flap, but – of course – couldn't hear what she was saying. A woman sat by the fire, nodding and doing needlework, occasionally flashing a tight smile. I focused on the chit, Fay-called-Rachel, then on the mother, Helen Laurence-alias-Jane Withersteen. I recalled the daughter was adopted, and wondered what that was all about. The woman was no startler, with grey in her dark hair as if someone had cracked an egg over her head and let it run. The girl might do in a pinch. Looking again at her animated face, it hit me that she was feeble-witted.

The man, Jonathan Laurence-né-Jim Lassiter, had his back to the window. He seemed to be nodding stiffly, then I realised he was in a rocking chair. I twisted a screw and the magnification increased. I saw the back of his neck, tanned, and the sharp cut of his hair, slick with pomade. I even made out the ends of his moustache, wide enough to prick out either side of the silhouette of his head.

So this was the swiftest *pistolero* west of the Pecos?

I admit I snorted.

This American idiocy about drawing and firing, taking aim in a split-second, is stuff and nonsense. Anyone who wastes their time learning how to do conjuring tricks getting their gun out is likely to find great red holes in their shirt-front (or, in most cases, back) before they've executed their fanciest twirl. That's if they don't shoot their own nose off by mistake. Bill Hickok, Jesse James and Billy the Kid were all shot dead while unarmed or asleep by folk far less famous and skilled.

Dash it all, I was going to chance it. All I had to do was take out the Webley, cross the road, creep into the front garden, stand outside the window, and blast Mr and Mrs Laurence where they sat.

The fun part would be snatching the girl.

Carpe diem, they said at Eton. Take your shot, I learned in the jungle. Nothing ruddy ventured, nothing bloody gained.

I stoppered the spyglass and slipped it into my breast pocket. Using it had an odd side effect. My mouth was dry and I really could have done with a swallow of something. But I had surrendered my proper hip flask in exchange for the trick telescope. I wouldn't make that mistake again. Perhaps Moriarty could whip me up a flask disguised as a pocket watch. And, if timekeeping was important, a pocket watch disguised as something I'd never need, like a prayer book or a tin of fruit pastilles.

The girl was demonstrating some dance now. Really, I would do the couple a favour by getting them out of this performance.

I reached into my coat pocket and gripped my Webley. I took it out slowly and carefully – no nose-ectomy shot for Basher Moran – and cocked it with my thumb. The sound was tinier than a click you'd make with your tongue against your teeth.

Suddenly, Lassiter wasn't in view. He was out of his chair and beyond sight of the window.

I was dumbfounded.

Then the lights went out. Not only the gas, but the fire – doused by a bucket, I'd guess. The womenfolk weren't in evidence, either.

One tiny click!

A finger stuck out from a curtain and tapped the windowpane.

No, not a finger. A tube. If I'd had the glass out, I could confirm what I intuited. The bump at the end of the tube was a sight. Lassiter, the fast gun, had drawn his iron.

I had fire in my belly. I smelled the dying breath of Kali's Kitten.

I changed my estimate of the American. What had seemed a disappointing, drab day outing was now a worthwhile safari, a game worth the chase.

He wouldn't come out of the front door, of course.

He needn't come out at all. First, he'd secure the mate and cub – a stronghold in the cellar, perhaps. Then he'd get a wall behind his back and wait. To be bearded in his lair. If only I had a bottle of paraffin, or even a box of matches. Then I could fire The Laurels: they'd have to come out and Lassiter would be distracted by females in panic. No, even then, there was a back garden. I'd have needed beaters, perhaps a second and third gun.

Moriarty had said he could put reliable men at my disposal for the job, but I'd pooh-poohed the suggestion. Natives panic and run, lesser guns get in the way. I was best off on my tod.

I had to rethink. Lassiter was on his guard now. He could cut and run, spirit his baggages off with him. Go to ground so we'd never find him again.

My face burned. Suddenly I was afraid, not of the gunslinger but of the Prof. I would have to tell him of my blunder.

One bloody click, that was all it was! Damn and drat.

I knew, even on brief acquaintance, Moriarty did not merely dismiss people from the Firm. He was no mere theoretician of murder.

Moran's head, stuffed, on Moriarty's wall. That would be the end of it.

I eased the cock of the Webley shut and pocketed the gun.

A cold circle pressed to the back of my neck.

'Reach, pardner,' said a deep, foreign, marrow-freezing voice. 'And mighty slow like.'

V

My father always said I'd wind up with a noose around my neck. Even Sir Augustus did not predict said noose would be strung from a pretentious chandelier and attached firmly to a curtain rail.

I was stood on a none-too-sturdy occasional table, hands tied behind my back with taut, biting twine. Only the thickness of my boot heels kept me from throttling at once.

Here was a 'how-d'you-do?'.

The parlour of The Laurels was still unlit, the curtains drawn. Unable to look down, I was aware of the people in the room but no more.

The man, Lassiter, had raised a bump on my noggin with his pistol butt.

I had an idea this was still better than an interview with a disappointed Professor Moriarty.

On the table, by my boot toes, were my Webley, broken and unloaded, the flask-glass, my folding knife, my (emptyish) notecase, three French postcards and a watch which had a sentiment from 'Violet, to Algy' engraved inside.

'Okay, Algy,' drawled Lassiter, 'listen up…'

I didn't feel inclined to correct his assumption.

'We're gonna have a little talk-like. I'm gonna ask questions, and you can give answers. Understand?'

I tried to stand very still.

Lassiter kicked the table, which wobbled. Rough hemp cut into my throat.

I nodded my understanding, bringing tears to my eyes.

'Fine and dandy.'

He was behind me. The woman was in the room too, keeping quiet, probably holding the girl to keep her from fidgeting.

'You ain't no Mormon,' Lassiter said.

It wasn't a question, so I didn't answer.

The table rocked again. Evidently, it *had* been a question.

'I'm not a Mormon,' I said, with difficulty. 'No.'

'But you're with the Danite Band?'

I had to think about that.

A loud noise sounded and the table splintered. A slice of it sheared away. I had to hop to keep balance on what was left.

My ears rang. It was seconds before I could make out what was being said.

'Noise-some, ain't it? You'll be hearin' that fer days.'

It wasn't the bang – I've heard enough bangs in my time – it was the smell, the discharged gun smell. It cleared my head.

The noose at my throat cut deep.

I had heard – in the prefects' common room at Eton, not any of the bordellos or dives I've frequented since those horrible days – that being hanged, if only for a few seconds, elicits a peculiar physiological reaction in the human male. Connoisseurs reckon this a powerful erotic, on a par with the ministrations of the most expert houri. I was now, embarrassingly, in a position to confirm sixth-form legend.

A gasp from the woman suggested the near-excruciating bulge in my fly was externally evident.

'Why, you low, disgustin' snake,' said Lassiter. 'In the presence of a lady, to make such a...'

Words failed him. I was in no position to explain this unsought, involuntary response.

Arbuthnot, captain of the second eleven, now active in a movement for the suppression of licentious music hall performance, maintained this throttling business was more pleasurable if the self-strangulator dressed as a ballerina and sucked a boiled sweet dipped in absinthe.

I could not help but wish Arbuthnot were here now to test his theory, instead of me.

'Jim, Jim, what are we to do?' the woman said. 'They know where we are. I told you they'd never give up. Not after Surprise Valley.'

Her voice, shrill and desperate, was sweet to me. I knew from the quality of Lassiter's silence that his wife's whining was no help to him.

I began to see the advantages of my situation.

I had been through the red rage and fear of peril and come to the cold calm clearing.

'At present, Mr and Mrs Lassiter,' I began in somewhat strangulated voice, giving them their true names, 'you are pursued only by foreign cranks whose authority will never be recognised by British law. If your story were known, popular sympathy would be with you and the Danites further frustrated. Those I represent would make sure of that.'

'Who do you represent, Algy?'

That was the question I'd never answer, not if he shot all the legs off the table and let me kick. Even if I died, Moriarty would use spiritualist mediums to lay hands on my ectoplasm and double my sufferings.

'If I step off this table, your circumstances will change,' I said. 'You will be murderers, low and cowardly killers of a hero of the British Empire...'

Never hurts to mention the old war record.

'Under whatever names you take, you will be hunted by Scotland Yard, the most formidable police force in the world...'

Well, formidable in the size of the seats of their blue serge trousers...

'All hands will be against you.'

I shut up and let them stew.

'He's right, Jim. We can't just kill him.'

'He drew first,' Lassiter said.

'This isn't Amber Springs.'

I imagined the climate was somewhat more congenial in Amber Springs, wherever that might be. The community's relative lack of policemen, judges, lawyers, gaolers, court reporters and engravers for the *Police Gazette* – which in other circumstances would have given it the edge over Streatham in my book – was suddenly not a point in its favour.

Even with my ringing ears, I heard the *click*. Lassiter cocked his gun.

He walked around the table, so he could at least shoot me to my face. It was still dark, so I couldn't get much of a look at him.

'*Jim*,' protested Jane-Helen.

There was a flash of fire. For an instant, Lassiter's fiercely moustached face lit orange.

The table was out from under me, and the noose dragged at my Adam's apple.

I expected the wave of pain to come in my chest.

Instead, I fell to the floor, with the chandelier, the rope-coil and quite a bit of plaster on top of me. I was choking, but not fatally. Which, under the circumstances, was all I could ask for.

A tutu and a sweetie would not have made me feel more alive.

Lassiter kicked me in the side, the low dog. Then the woman held him back. That futile boot was encouraging. The fast gun was losing his rag.

Gaslight came up. Hands disentangled me from the brass fixtures and the noose, then brushed plaster out of my hair and off my face.

I looked up, blinking, at a very pink angel.

'Wuvvwy mans,' said the glassy-eyed girl, 'Rache want to keep um.'

VI

Though still tied – indeed, with my ankles bound as well – I was far more comfortable than I had been.

I was propped up on a divan in the parlour of The Laurels. Rache – the former Little Fay – was playing with my hair, chattering about her new pet. She must have been fifteen or sixteen, but acted like a six- or seven-year-old. I remembered to smile as she cooed in my ears. Children can *turn* suddenly, and I had an idea this child-minded girl could be as deadly as her foster father if prodded into a tantrum.

She introduced me to her doll, Missy Surprise. This was a long-legged, homemade, one-armed ragdoll with most of her yellow wool hair chewed off. She got her name because there was a hiding place in her tummy, where Rache kept her 'pweciousnesses' – cigar-tubes full of sweets.

The 'Laurences' were still undecided about what to do with me.

It's all very well being a gunslinger, but skills that serve in the Wild West – or the jungle, come to that – need to be modified in Streatham. At least, that was the case if you were a fair-play fathead like Jim Lassiter.

These were truly good, put-upon people. That made them weak.

Rache kissed my ear, wetly.

'Stop that, darling,' said her mother.

Rache stuck out her lower lip and narrowed her brows.

'Don't be a silly, Rache.'

'Rache *not* a silly,' she said, knotting little fists. 'Rache *smart*, 'oo knows it.'

Jane-Helen melted, and pulled the girl away from me, hugging her.

'Not so tighty-tight,' protested Rache.

Lassiter sat across the room, gun in hand, glowering.

Earlier, he had been forced to tell a deputation of concerned neighbours that Rache had dropped a lot of crockery. No one could possibly mistake gunshots for smashing plates, but they'd retreated. Blaming the girl had put her in a sulk for a moment, and inclined her even more to take my part.

This blossoming idiot was heiress to a fabulous gold mine.

'We could offer him money,' Jane-Helen said, as if I weren't in the room.

'He won't take money,' Lassiter said, glumly and – I might add – without consulting me for an opinion.

'You, sir, Algy...' began the woman.

'Arbuthnot,' I said, '*Colonel* Algernon Arbuthnot, Fifth Northumberland Fusiliers...'

A right rabble, that lot. All their war wounds were in the bum, from running away.

'Hero of Maiwand and Kandahar...'

I'd have claimed Crécy and Waterloo if I thought they'd swallow it.

'*Victoria Cross.*'

''Toria Ross,' echoed Rache, delighted.

'Colonel Arbuthnot, what is your connection with the Danite Band?'

'Madam, I am a detective. Our agency has been on the tracks of these villains for some months, with regards to their many crimes...'

She looked, hopeful, at Lassiter. She wanted to believe the rot, but he knew better.

'...when we were alerted to the presence in London of dangerous Danites, well off their usual patch as you'll agree, we made a connection. Of course, we knew you were here under an alias. We had no reason to bother you, but the movements of incognito Americans – possessed of fabulous riches, but content to live in genteel anonymity – are noticed, you know. If we could find you, so could they. We've had men on you round the clock for two weeks…'

That was a mistake. Lassiter stopped listening. Anyone who could hear a cocking pistol through a window and across the road would have noticed if he were being marked.

'…if I'm not at my post when my replacement arrives, the agency will know something is amiss.'

Jane-Helen looked hard at me. She hadn't bought it either.

Still, in the short term, my story would be hard to *dis*prove. I had introduced a notion that would snag and grow. That I was to be *relieved*, that confederates would be arriving soon.

Lassiter's sensitive ears would be twitching.

Every cat padding over a garden wall or tile falling off an ill-made roof would sound like evidence of a surrounding force to our rider of the purple sage.

'Algy wants to see Rache 'utterflee dance now,' announced the girl.

She fluttered dramatically about the room, trailing ribbons, inflating sleeves and lifting skirts. One of her stockings was bagged around her ankle.

''Utterflee 'utterfly, meee oh myyy,' she sang.

Lassiter's face was dark and heavy. I was quite pleased with myself.

I snuck a peek at the clock on the mantel and made sure I was noticed doing it.

''Utterfly 'utterflee, look at meee…'

Lassiter chewed his moustache. Jane-Helen seemed greyer. And I was almost starting to enjoy myself again.

Then the front window smashed in and something black and fizzing burst through the curtains.

I saw a burning fuse.

VII

Lassiter got his boot on the fuse, killing the flame.

'That's not dynamite,' I said, helpfully. 'It's a smoke charge. They want you to run out the front door. Into the line of fire.'

I didn't mention that I'd thought of something similar.

'Jim, they're out there,' Jane said.

'Asty mans,' Rache said, peeved by the interruption.

There was a crack. More glass broke behind the curtains. A ragged hole appeared in the velvet. I'd not heard the shot. Another shattering and the curtain whipped with the impact. And again.

'Untie me and I can help,' I said.

Lassiter wasn't sure but Jane fell for it. She did my hands while Rache unpicked the knots at my ankles. I took my Webley from the floor, shaking off the flakes of plaster. Of course, it was empty.

The curtain rail, rope still attached, fell off the wall as another silent fusillade came. Cold wind blew through the ruined window. More panes were shot out.

The neighbours would be around again soon. This was not the thing for a respectable street.

Bullets ploughed into the floor, rucking the carpet, and the opposite wall.

Our sniper had an elevated position.

I waved my gun, to attract Lassiter's attention.

He dug into his pocket and brought out a handful of bullets, which he poured into my palm. I loaded and closed the revolver. I noticed Lassiter noticing how practiced I was. Algy Arbuthnot, VC, was an old soldier and daring detective so that shouldn't be too much of a surprise.

'Where is the gunman? Top floor of the house on the corner?'

Lassiter shook his head.

'Tree on the other side of the road?'

Lassiter nodded.

I'd been behind that tree earlier. It had been twilight when Lassiter conked me and was full dark now. No one was about when I took my watching spot; now, there were armed hostiles.

'How many?'

Lassiter held up four fingers, steadily. Then another three, with a wriggle at the wrist. He *knew* there were four men – Danites? – out there, and *felt* there might be another three besides.

I've come through scrapes with worse odds. From Moriarty's background check, I knew Jim Lassiter had too.

'This might be a moment for one of your famous rockslides,' I ventured.

Lassiter cracked a near-smile.

'Yup,' he said.

As Drebber had mentioned, Lassiter was once chased up a mountain by a mob and precipitated a rocky avalanche to sweep them away. His history was studded with such dime-novel exploits.

Was Drebber out there? And Stangerson? With other guns?

My suspicion was that, weighing up their contract with Moriarty & Co., the Danites decided £205,000 was a mite steep for an evening's work. They had come to us in the first place not because they were leery of doing their own murdering but because this wasn't their city and they didn't have any idea how to track Lassiter and his women to their hole. The Professor had come straight out and announced where they were to be found, to show off how bloody clever he was. No thought as to whether Basher might get caught 'twixt the guns. My only consolation was that Moriarty undoubtedly meant what he said about Higher Law. For breaking the deal, he'd probably exterminate the Danite Band to the last man (their horses and dogs too), then arrange a cholera outbreak in Salt Lake City to scythe through the Latter-day Saints.

I, of course, would still be dead.

Lassiter and I were either side of the window, just peeking out at a sliver of night.

Another shot.

I heard a rattling about from one of the nearby houses. A spill of light lay on the street as a front door opened. In that illumination, I glimpsed a figure in rough work clothes. A pointed red hood covered his entire head, big circles cut out for the eyes, gathered at the neck by a drawstring. Our shy soul froze a moment in the light and stepped back, but Lassiter plugged him anyway, reddening one of his eyeholes. He collapsed like an unstrung puppet.

An irritated, bald man in a quilted dressing gown came out of his house, to make further complaint about the infernal racket. He was surprised to find a masked gunman lying dead over his front gate, obscuring the 'no hawkers or circulars' sign. The neighbour looked around, astonished.

'What the devil…'

Someone shot him. Oops, it might have been me. I was always one to blaze away without too much forethought.

Lassiter looked disapproval at me.

A great many curtains fell from fingers in nearby houses.

The neighbour was only winged, but made a noise about it. The fellows who had accompanied him on his earlier deputation put cotton in their ears and went back to bed.

So my shot had accomplished something.

Lassiter looked out of the window, searching for another target.

From where I was, I could easily shoot him in the stomach and try to hold Drebber to coughing up the agreed fee.

Evidently he could hear the wheels turning in my head.

'Algy,' he drawled, gun casually aimed my way, 'how'd you like to go through the winder and draw their fire?'

'Not very much.'

'What I reckoned.'

Another bomb sailed through the window, without meeting any obstruction, and rolled on the carpet, pouring thick, nasty smoke. They'd let the fuse burn down before lobbing this one.

'Is there a back door?' I asked.

Lassiter looked at me, pitying.

Upwards of four men could surround a villa, easily.

Jane looked at Lassiter like a pioneer wife who trusts her man to save the last three bullets to keep the women out of the clutches of Injuns. I always wondered why those covered wagon bints didn't backshoot their pious pas and learn to sew blankets and pop out papooses, but I'm well known for my shaky grasp of morality.

Bullets struck the piano, raising strangulated chords.

'This is London, England,' Jane said. 'We left all this behind. Things like this don't happen here.'

Lassiter looked at me.

We both knew *everywhere* was like this, herbaceous border in the back garden and 'Goodbye, Little Yellow Bird' sheet music propped on the piano or no. He'd have done better going to ground in the Old Jago or Seven Dials, where life was more obviously like this – those rookeries had well-travelled rat runs and escape routes.

The smoke was getting thick and the carpet was on fire.

I saw an empty bucket lying by the grate. The water had been used earlier to douse the fire. That was my fault.

Lassiter chewed his moustache. That was his 'tell', the sign he was about to 'go off'.

'I'm goin' out the front door,' he said.

'You'll be killed for sure,' Jane pleaded.

'Yup. Maybe I can take enough of 'em with me so's you and Little Fay can get away clean. You're a rich woman, Jane. Buy this man, and men like him, and keep buyin' them. Ring yourself with guns and detectives. The Danites will run dry afore the gold.'

I peeked into the road again. The groaning neighbour was doubled over on the pavement, but the dead Danite had been dragged off.

Fire was coming from at least two points. Just harrying, not trying to hit anyone.

There was someone on the roof. We could tell by the creaking ceiling.

Lassiter filled his guns. He had two Colts with fancy-dan handles. He ought to have had holsters to draw from, but would have to carry them both. Twelve shots. Maybe seven men. He'd get hit several times, no matter how good he was. I might even be able to put a couple in his spine as he strode manfully down the path of The Laurels and claim it was a fumble-fingered accident.

He was an idiot. If it'd been me, I'd have picked up Jane and tossed her, in a froth of skirts, through the window. She was the one they wanted, heiress to the Withersteen property. At the very least, she'd be a tethered goat to draw the big game into range.

I was cold and clear and clever again. The Professor would have been proud.

'They can't afford to kill the women,' I said. 'That's why they didn't throw dynamite. They want someone alive to inherit, someone they can rob through Mormon marriage.'

Lassiter nodded. He didn't see how that helped.

'Stop thinking of Jane and Rache as your family,' I said. 'Start thinking of them as hostages.'

If he didn't take umbrage and shoot me, we might have a chance.

VIII

'We're coming out,' I announced. 'Hold your fire.'

Rache giggled. I held the baggage round the waist, gun in her ear, and stood in the doorway.

To the girl, it was a game. She had Missy Surprise hugged to her chest.

Lassiter and Jane were more serious, but desperate enough to try.

They had objected that the Danites would never believe their man would harm his beloved wife and daughter. I told them to stop thinking like their upright, moral, tiresome selves and put themselves in the mind-skins of devious, murderous, greedy blighters. Of course they'd believe it – they'd do the same thing with their own wives or daughters. Unspoken but obvious was that I would too.

Indeed, here I was – ready to spread a pretty little idiot's brains on the road.

It'd be a shame, but I've done worse things.

I took a step out into the garden. No one killed me, so I took another step down the path.

Lassiter and Jane came after me, backwards. The Danite perched on the roof wouldn't have a shot that didn't go through the woman.

Hooded men came out of the shadows. Five of them, carrying guns. All their weaponry was kitted out oddly. The barrels were as long again as they ought to be, and swelled into thick, ceramic Swiss-roll shapes. Silencers. I'd heard of the things, but never seen them. Cut down the accuracy, I gathered. The cat couldn't hear you firing, but you'd probably miss. I'd rather use one of Moriarty's airguns than a ridiculous contraption like that.

'Parley,' I said.

The leader of the band nodded, silly hood-point flopping.

The funny thing was that the hood was useless as disguise. Most masks are. You remember faces first of all, but people are a lot more than their eyes and noses – hands and legs and stomachs and the way they stand or hold a gun or light a cigar.

I was facing Elder Enoch J. Drebber.

I assumed our agreement was voided.

'You don't want these lovely ladies harmed,' I said.

'I only need one,' Drebber responded, raising his gun.

At this range, he could plug Rache in the breast and the shot would plough through her and me, killing us both.

'Rache not like mans,' she said. 'Rache poo on you!'

Drebber's eyes widened in his hood-holes. Rache held up Missy Surprise, and angled the rag-doll, her fingers working the hard metal inside the soft toy.

Lassiter's second gun went off and Missy Surprise's head flew apart.

The Danite on Drebber's right fell dead.

'You're next,' I told Drebber.

I was sure she'd been aiming at him in the first place, but he wasn't to know that.

The man on the roof decided it was time to take his shot. His finger had probably been itching all evening. I've had trouble with fools like that on safari, so keen on not coming home without having cleaned the barrel, they need to fire an elephant gun at the regimental water bearer just so they could say they've killed *something*.

Lassiter was quicker than a Bhishti, and not struggling with a ridiculously overweighted yard-and-a-half of rifle.

The keen rifleman tumbled dead into the flowery bower around the front door.

Seven, minus three. Four.

'Drop the ironmongery, Elder,' I ordered.

Rache blew a loud raspberry.

Drebber was shaking. He nodded, and guns fell onto the road.

'All of them,' I said.

Hands went to belts and inside pockets and boots and special compartments and a variety of hold-out single-shots and throwing knives rattled down as well.

'Now, take your dead folks and scarper.'

The four surviving Danites did as they were told. The fellow in the bower was a sixteen-stone lump of his many wives' cooking and it took two to lift him.

They had a carriage down the road, and it trundled off.

Not a bad night's work, I thought. Providing it was over.

Rache was dancing around, and I thought it a good idea to relieve Missy Surprise of her .45 calibre insides. I gave the doll back and the girl loved it none the less for not having a head.

Jane was looking at me with something like rapt gratitude. Usually a good moment to make a proposition. I doubted my currency with Jim Lassiter stood as high as that.

'Colonel Arbuthnot, what can we ever do to repay you?'

'You can die,' said a voice I recognised. 'Yes, die.'

IX

I was fuming.

Moriarty didn't deign to explain, but I had caught up on it.

Of course, he knew the Danites would try to save the fee and go for the kills on their own.

Of course, he had mentioned the Laurence address deliberately, to prompt fast action.

Of course, he had followed me and watched my travails all evening long, not intervening until the danger was over.

Of course, he had found a way to profit.

He strolled up the street, head bobbing. He was dressed all in black, for the night-time. He also had a carriage parked nearby, with Chop, his Chinese coachman, perched up on the box. He enquired solicitously after the neighbour, who was still making a performance of being slightly shot. Somehow, the man got the notion he had been saved by my intervention from a conspiracy of high-ranking Masons who wanted him dead over some imagined slight. It would be a risky proposition to complain officially about such well-connected villains since they owned the police. He bustled inside and drew his curtains, hoping to hide from inescapable doom under his coverlets.

Then Moriarty applied himself to the murders.

I was not privy to the arrangements the Professor made with Lassiter and Jane. I had to be in the still-smoky parlour, while Rache – excited to be up long past her bedtime – banged at the gutshot piano while singing more verses of her butterfly song.

At the conclusion of negotiations, Moriarty was proud owner, through hard-to-trace holding companies, of the Surprise Valley Gold Mine. Amusingly, he was now a major employer in Amber Springs, Utah.

Jim Lassiter/Jonathan Laurence, Jane Withersteen/Helen Laurence and Little Fay Larkin/Rachel Laurence were dead, burned to crackling in the smoking ruins of The Laurels, Streatham Hill Road. It was the gas mains, apparently. And the neighbours had some stories to tell.

What amazed me most was that the Professor had the corpses ready. Chop and I had to wrestle them into beds before the fatal match was struck. I suspected three strangers of the right ages had been 'burked', but Moriarty assured Jane the substitutes were 'natural causes' paupers rescued from anatomists' tables. She believed him, and that's what counts with women like her.

He had a satchel full of documents: passports, birth certificates, twenty-year-old letters, used steamer tickets, bank books, even photographs. If the Lassiter/ Laurences wanted to assume other identities, they should have come to him in the first place – when it would have cost less than a gold mine. He let Mr and Mrs Ronald Lembo of Ottowa keep a private fortune of, amusingly enough, £205,000, deposited at Coutts. Not unlimited wealth, but most people should be able to live comfortably on the interest. I'd run through it inside a week.

Jane said the Professor was a wonderful man, but Lassiter knew better. He went along, but knew he'd been bushwhacked. I now think Moriarty even contrived for Drebber to come across the Laurences in the first place. For him, a fugitive in possession of a fabulous gold mine is someone who needs their exile life turned upside down.

Rache was afraid of the man. She wasn't stupid, just different. She would have to learn a new name, Pixie, and address her parents as Uncle and Aunt, but they'd adopted her in the first place.

Along with the evidence of full lives lived from birth up to this minute, the Lembos found that they had been staying – in a suite at Claridge's! – in London for several days. Travelling trunks, including entire wardrobes, were ensconced there. I had no doubt the staff would recognise them and they'd be offered their 'usual' at breakfast the next day. The family were on a long, leisurely world tour and had tickets and reservations for Paris, Strelsau, Constantinople, and points east. Eventually they would fetch up in Perth, Australia.

In the coach on the way back to Conduit Street, I asked about Drebber and Stangerson.

'If anyone deserves to be murdered,' I said, 'it's those splitters.'

The Professor smiled. 'And who will *pay* us for these murders?'

'Those two I'd slaughter for free.'

'Bad business, giving away what we charge for. You won't find Mrs Halifax bestowing favours "on the house". No, if we were to take steps against the Danites, we would only expose ourselves to risk. Besides, as you know, giving out an address is often a far more deadly instrument than a gun or a knife.'

I didn't understand and said so.

'Elder Drebber mentioned another enemy of the Danites, one Mr Jefferson Hope. Not a fugitive, in this case, but a pursuer. A man with a deadly grudge against our clients which dates back to a business in America which is too utterly tiresome to go into at this late hour.'

'Drebber was half expecting to run across Hope,' I said.

'More like he was expecting Hope to run across him. This is even more likely now. I've sent an unsigned telegram to Mr Hope, who is toiling as a cab driver in this city. It mentions a boarding house in Torquay Terrace, Camberwell, where he might find Drebber and Stangerson. I gather they will try to get a train for Liverpool soon, and a passage home, so I impressed on Hope that he should be swiftly about his business.'

Moriarty chuckled.

If you read in the papers about the Lauriston Gardens murder, the Halliday's Private Hotel poisoning and death 'in police custody' of the suspect cabman, you'll understand. [3] When the Professor sets abut tidying up, slates are wiped clean, broken up and buried under a foundation stone.

So, at the end of it all, I was in residence at Conduit Street, part of the family. I was the Number Two in the Firm, the Man in Charge of Murder, but had a sense of how far beneath the Number One that position ranked. I had been near-hanged and shot at, but – most of all – kept out of the grown-ups' business. Like Rache, good enough to spring the big surprise but otherwise fondly indulged or tolerated, I wasn't party to serious haggling, just the bloke with the gun and the steady nerve.

Still, I knew how I would even things. I began to keep a journal. All the facts are set down, and eventually the public shall know them.

Then we'll see whose face is red. No, vermilion.

CHAPTER TWO: A SHAMBLES IN BELGRAVIA

I

To Professor Moriarty, she is always *that bitch*.

Irene Adler arrived in our Conduit Street rooms shortly after I undertook to assist my fellow tenant in enterprises of which he was the pre-eminent London specialist. In short, sirrah, *crime*.

The old bread and honey came into it, of course [1]. The Professor had me on an honorarium of six thousand pounds *per annum*. Scarcely enough to make anyone put up with Moriarty, actually, but it serviced my predilection for pursuits the naïve refer to as 'games of chance'. However, I own that the *thrill* of do-baddery attracted me, that blood-running *whoosh* of fright and delight which comes from cocking repeated snooks at every plod, beak and turnkey in the land. When a hunting man has grown bored with bagging tigers, crime can still jangle the nerves and keep up the pecker. The bloodless Moriarty got *his* jollies in the abstract, plotting felony the way you might play a hand of patience. I've heard him say the business of committing the crime itself is but a tiresome necessity, the practical proof of a theorem already solved to his satisfaction.

That morning, the Professor was thinking through two problems. A portion of his brain was calculating the timings of solar eclipses observable in far-flung regions. Superstitious natives can sometimes be persuaded that a white man has power over the sun and needs to be given handy tribal treasures if *bwana sahib* promises to turn the light on again. Bloody good trick, if you can get away with it [2]. The greater part of his attention, however, was devoted to the breeding of wasps.

'Your bee is a law-abiding soul,' he said, in his reedy lecturing voice, 'as reverent to their queen as the clods of England, dedicated to the production of honey for the betterment of all, buzzing about promiscuously pollinating to please addle-minded poets. They only defend themselves at the cost of their lives, for they sting but once. Volumes are devoted to the care of bees, and apiculture exists to exploit their good nature. Wasps do nothing but sting. Persistently venomous, they fly from one assault to the next. Unwelcome everywhere. Thoroughly nasty sorts. We are *not* bees, Moran.'

He smiled, a creepy thing for a man with lips as thin as his. His near-fleshless head moved from side to side. I couldn't follow Moriarty's drift, but that was usual. I nodded and hoped he would come, eventually, to a point. A schoolmaster before taking to villainy, his rambles tended to wind towards some inverted moral.

'Summer will be upon us soon,' he mused, 'the season for picnicking in the park, for tiny fat arms to go bare, for governesses to sit and gossip unveiled, for shop girls and their beaux to spoon in public. This will be a bumper year for our yellow-and-black-striped friends. My first generation of *polistes pestilentialis* is hatching. The world is divided, Moran, between those who sting and those who are the stingees.'

'And you would be the sting-*ers*,' shrilled that *voice*.

The American Nightingale had been admitted by Mrs Halifax.

'Miss Irene Adler,' acknowledged Moriarty. 'Your Lucia di Lammermoor was acceptable, your Maria Stuarda indifferent and you were perhaps the worst Emilia di Liverpool the stage has ever seen.' [3]

'What a horrible man you are, James Moriarty!'

His lips split and sharp teeth showed.

'My business is being horrible, Miss Adler. I make no effort at sham or hypocrisy.'

'That, I must say, is a tonic.'

She smiled full-bore and arranged herself on a divan, prettily hiking her hemline up over well-turned ankles, shifting her décolletage in a manner calculated to set her swanny mams a-wobble. Even Moriarty was impressed, and he could keep up a lecture on the grades of paper used in the forgery of high-denomination Venezuelan banknotes while walking down the secret corridor with the row of one-way mirror windows into the private rooms where Mrs H.'s girls conducted spectacularly indecent business day and night.

I still maintain all would have been well if only I'd shown the Adler minx what was what straight off, tossed her skirts over her head, plonked her fizzog-down on the reception room rug (a tiger whose head snarled as if he still bore a grudge from that tricky shot I made bringing him down) and administered one of my famous Specials. Had I but properly poked that Yankee popsy, she might have broken the habit which eventually set all manner of odd bods scurrying around trying to clear up her confounded messes.

Irene Adler had the face of an angel child, the body of a full-grown trollop and a voice like a steel needle slowly sliding into your brain. Even warbling to an audience of tone-deaf Polish, she hadn't lasted as prima donna. After her Emilia flopped so badly the artistic director of the Warsaw Opera had to blow his brains out, the company cut her adrift, leaving her on the loose in Europe to the disadvantage of several ruling houses.

And here she was on our settee.

'You are aware that the services I offer are somewhat unusual?' the Professor said.

She fixed Moriarty with a steely glint that cut through all the sugar.

'I am a *soprano* from New Jersey,' she began, pronouncing it 'Noo Joisey'. 'I know what a knob crook looks like. You can figure all the sums you like, Professor, but you're as much a *capo di cosa nostra* as the Moustache Petes in the back room of the Burly-Cue. Which is dandy, because I have a job of burglary that needs doing urgently. *Capisce?*'

The Professor nodded.

'Who's the red-faced gent who hasn't taken his glims off my teats for the last minute and a half?'

'Colonel Sebastian Moran, the heavy-game shot.'

'Good with a gun, eh? Looks more like a shiv-man to me.'

She pointed her index fingers at her cleavage, which she thrust out, then angled her fingertips up to indicate her face.

'That's better. Look me in the lamps, Colonel.'

I harrumphed and paid attention. If she hadn't wanted fellows to ogle, she shouldn't have worn that dress. There's no reasoning with women.

'Here's the thing of it,' she said. 'Have you heard of the Duke of Strelsau?'

'Michael Elphberg, so-called "Black Michael", third in line to the throne of Ruritania.'

'That's the fellow, Prof. Things being slow this season, I've been knocking around a bit with Black Mike. They call him that because of his hair, which is dark where the rest of his family's is flame-red. He's a gloomy, glowering type as well so it suits him on temperamental grounds too. As it happens, photographs were taken of the two of us in the actual pursuit of knocking around. Artistic studies, you might say. Six plates. Full figures. Complete exposures. It would ruin my reputation should they come to light. You see, *I'm being blackmailed!*'

Her voice cracked. She raised a kerchief to her eye to quell a tear, then froze, a picture of slighted maidenhood. Moriarty shook his head. She stuffed the hankie back into her sleeve and snorted.

'Worth a try just to keep my hand in. I'm a better actress than critics say, don't you know? Obviously, I'm *not* being blackmailed. Like you said, there are stingers and stingees. We are stingers.'

'And the stingee?'

'Another bloody colonel. Colonel Sapt. Chief of the Ruritanian Secret Police. Which has been a dozy doddle for the last thirty years, since it's one of the most peaceable, least-insurrection-blighted spots on the map. Not so much as a whiff of dissent since forty-eight. When, admittedly, the mob burned down the old White Palace. There are very scenic gardens on the site. Anyway, intrigue stirs. King Rudolf is getting on, and there's some doubt about who gets the throne next. Rudolf the Red, the Crown Prince, is set on shoring up his case by marrying his cousin, Princess Flavia. Where do they get these names? If you put them in an opera, you'd be laughed off stage. Rudolf is fond of a tipple and a tumble, and Black Michael would like to paint himself as the more responsible, conscientious brother. He hopes, for some bizarre reason, to appeal to the people and be acclaimed a worthy sovereign if Rudolf trips up a few more times and does something silly like not arriving at his own coronation. Sapt is loyal to Rudolf, and dead set against Michael. Lord knows why, but there you are. Some people are like that. He's also a keen appreciator of the aesthetic worth of a fine photo.'

'I see,' I said, 'this Sapt thinks to blacken Michael's name – further blacken, I suppose – so the duke will never be king.'

Irene Adler looked at me with something like contemptuous pity.

'Horse feathers, Colonel of the Nuts. If those pics were seen, Black Mike'd be the envy of Europe. He'd be crowned in a wave of popularity. Everyone loves a randy royal. Look at Vicky's brood. No, Sapt wants the photographs *off* the market, so Mikey can be nagged into marriage by Antoinette de Mauban, his persistently pestering mistress. Which would scupper any chance he might have with Flavourless Flavia.'

'You said *Rudolf* was engaged to the princess?'

She made a gesture, suggesting the matter was in the balance. 'Whichever Elphberg marries Flavia is a cert to be king. She's second in line. Black Michael is scheming to cut his half-brother out. Are you following this?' [4]

Moriarty acknowledged that he was.

'Why do you want those photographs?'

'Sentimental value. I come off especially well in Study No. 3, where the light catches the fall of my hair as I lower my... No? Not convinced? Rats, I must work on this acting lark. Obviously, I want to blackmail *everyone* – Colonel Sapt, Black Mike, Red Rudi, Mademoiselle Toni, the princess... With half of Ruritania paying me to keep quiet and the other half to speak up, I should be able to milk the racket for a good few years – at least, until succession is settled – and secure my comfortable old age.'

She could not have been more than twenty-five.

'And where might these "artistic studies" be found?' Moriarty asked.

She dug into her reticule and produced a paper with a map drawn on it.

'The Ruritanian Embassy in Belgravia,' she said. 'I have a collector's interest in floorplans, schedules of guards, and the like.'

'What's this?' the Professor indicated a detail marked with a red circle.

'A safe, hidden behind the portrait of Rudolf III, in the private office of Colonel Sapt. If I had the key, I wouldn't be here. I've been driven to associate with criminals by the need for skills in cracksmanship. You come highly recommended by Scotland Yard.'

Moriarty sniffed haughtily. 'Scotland Yard have never heard of Professor Moriarty.'

'For someone as crooked as you, I call that a recommendation.'

Moriarty's head started bobbing again. He was thinking the thing through, which meant I had to look after practicalities.

'What's in it for us, missy?' I asked.

'A quarter of what I can screw from the Elphbergs.'

'Half.'

'That's extortion!'

'Yes,' I admitted with a wink. 'We're extortion men, you might say. Half.'

She had a little sulk, made a practiced moue, shimmied her chest again, and bestowed a magnificent smile which warmed my insides. At some point in this business, I knew the old BMS would be required.

'Deal,' she said, sticking out a tiny paw to be shaken.

I should have shot her then and there.

II

The Ruritanian Embassy is a mansion in Boscobel Place. Belgravia fairly crawls with embassies, legates and consulates. The streets throng with gussied-up krauts strapped into fancy uniforms, tripping over swords they wouldn't know what to do with if a herd of buffalo charged them. I've no love for your average Johnny Native, but he bests any Frenchy, Sausage-Eater or Dutchman who ever drew breath. 'Never go into the jungle with a Belgian,' that's my motto.

If Irene Adler had gone to a run-of-the-mill safe-breaker like that cricket-playing fathead [5], the caper would have run to after-midnight window-breakage and a spot of brace-and-bit boring, with perhaps a cosh to Colonel Sapt's dome as an added extra.

Moriarty scorned such methods as too obvious and not sufficiently destructive.

First, he wrote to the *Westminster Gazette*, which carried his angry letter in full. He harped on about the sufferings of the slum-dwellers of Strelsauer Altstadt – some of which weren't even made up, which is where the clever part came in – and labelled Ruritania 'the secret shame of Europe'. More correspondence appeared, not all from the Professor, chiming in with fresh tales of horrors carried on under the absolute monarchy of the Elphbergs.

A long-nosed clergyman and an addle-pated countess formed a committee of busybodies to mount a solemn vigil in Boscobel Place. The protest was swollen by less dignified malcontents – Ruritanian dissenters in exile, louts with nothing better to do, crooks in Moriarty's employ.

Hired ranters stirred passers-by against the vile Ruritanian practice (invented by the Professor) of cleaning the huge cannons of Zenda Castle by shoving little orphan girls into the barrels and prodding them with sticks until their wriggling wiped out the bore. A few of the Conduit Street Comanche – that tribe of junior beggars, whores, pickpockets and garrotters whose loyalty the Professor had bought – got themselves up as Zenda Cannon Girls, with soot on their faces and skirts, and threw dung at anyone who so much as dared step outside the Embassy.

After typical foreign bleating and whining, Scotland Yard sent two constables to Boscobel Place to rap truncheons against the railings and tell the crowd to move along quietly. To the Comanche, a bobby's helmet might as well have a target painted on it. And horse dung is easily come by on the streets of London.

So, within three days, there was the makings of a nice pitched battle outside the Embassy. Moriarty and I took the trouble to stroll by every now and then, to see how the pot was boiling.

Hawk-eyed, the Professor spotted a face peering from a downstairs window. 'That's Sapt,' he said.

'I could pot him from here,' I volunteered. 'I've a revolver in my pocket. It'd be a dicey shot, but I could make it.'

Moriarty's head wavered. He was calculating odds.

'He would only be replaced. We know who Sapt is. Another secret police chief might not be such a public figure.'

My right hand was itching and I had a thrill in my water.

I had a notion to haul out and blast away, just for sport and hang the scheme. There were enough bearded anarchists about to take the blame. Sometimes an idea takes your fancy, and there's nothing to do but give in.

Moriarty's bony hand was on my wrist, squeezing. Hard.

His eyes shone. Cobra eyes.

'That would be a mistake, Moran.'

My wrist hurt. A lot. The Professor knew where to squeeze. He could snap bones with what seemed like a pinch. He let me have my hand back.

Moriarty rarely smiled, and then usually to terrify some poor victim. The first time I heard him *laugh*, I thought he had been struck by deadly poison and the stutter escaping through his locked jaws was a death rattle. That day's *Times* report from Ruritania solicited from him an unprecedented fit of shoulder-shaking giggles. He wound his fingers together like the claws of a praying mantis.

The prompt for this hilarity was Black Michael's vow to free the Zenda Cannon Girls.

'Let us wish him luck in finding them,' the Professor said. 'How delicious that the duke should be our staunch ally in this enterprise. Then again, Queen Victoria has also expressed sympathy for our imaginary orphans.'

Flashes came from the Embassy. My hand was on my revolver.

'More photographs,' the Professor said. 'Colonel Sapt's hobby.'

Sapt's face was gone, but a box-and-lens affair was pressed against the window. Moriarty and I had coats casually pulled up over our faces, against the wind.

'The Secret Police Chief likes to know his enemies, Moran. A man in his position collects them.'

'Why's Sapt in London anyway? Shouldn't he be cracking down on bomb-throwers on his home turf?'

Moriarty pondered the question. 'If we are to believe Miss Adler, Sapt can best serve his cause here.'

'His cause?'

'Up the Red, down the Black. But the Elphberg brothers are halfway across Europe. So, Sapt's attention is directed here on subtler business.'

'The woman?'

Moriarty's shoulders lifted and dropped.

'The old goat probably hopes she'll give him a tumble to get her snaps back,' I suggested. 'I'll wager he pulls the pics out of the safe every night and gives 'em a proper looking over.'

'If that were the case, she wouldn't have engaged us. Miss Adler does not strike me as a lady who likes to share. Yet she has willed over half the earnings of a profitable enterprise to us.'

'No choice, Moriarty. Who else could get her what she wants?'

The Professor tapped his teeth. 'No one but us, Moran. Evidently.'

Moriarty's fingers went to his watch pocket. In my years of association with the Professor, I never saw him pull out the timepiece I presume anchored the chain across his flat middle. Once an associate understood the import of timekeeping, everything went to schedule. Otherwise, there might have been *consequences*.

He had barely stroked his chain when Filthy Fanny dashed from the crowd and began kicking the police guard.

Fanny had been successfully presenting herself as a ten-year-old waif for a full two decades without anyone being the wiser. It was down to the proper application of dirt, which she arranged on her face with the skill other tarts devote to the use of paints and powder.

Now, Filth wore the sooty skirts of a Zenda Cannon Girl. And heavy shin-kicking clogs.

She harangued in backslang ('Reggub the Esclop!') that sounded mighty like Ruritanian, or whatever heathen tongue they use. [6]

After some painful toe-to-shin business, the plod got his truncheon out.

With a command of the dramatic that would put a Drury Lane tragedienne to shame, Filth tumbled down the Embassy steps, squirting tomato juice from a sponge clapped over her eye.

Moriarty handed me a cobblestone and pointed.

I threw the stone at the gawking copper, and fetched off his helmet. I'd once brought down a Bengal tiger with a cricket ball in exactly the same manner.

Then, the mob rose and rushed the Embassy. Moriarty hooked me with an umbrella handle and we milled in with the crowd.

The front doors caved, and the first rush of intruders slid about on the polished marble foyer floor like drunken skaters. Three guards tried to unscabbard sabres, but the Comanche set about stripping them – and the environs – of anything redeemable. Pawn-shop windows would soon display cuirasses, plumed helms and other items stamped with the Elphberg Seal.

Sapt poked his head out of his door. Moriarty signalled. A couple of bruisers laid hands on the Secret Police Chief.

The Professor sidled next to the anarchist with the biggest beard and suggested he draw up a list of demands, phrasing it so the fellow would think the whole thing was his idea.

Sapt looked about furiously, moustache twitching. Dirty hands held him fast.

A bunch of keys rattled on Sapt's belt. Moriarty pointed them out, and an urchin brushed past, deftly relieving Sapt of the keys.

'Give him a taste of what the Cannon Girls get,' I shouted.

We left the mob happily shoving the Police Chief feet-first up the nearest chimney. The anarchist had posted lookouts at the doors, and was waving an ancient revolver at the still-surprised constables.

'You can't rush us,' Comrade Beard said. 'This Ruritanian territory is claimed by the Free Citizens' Committee of Strelsauer Altstadt. Any action against us will be interpreted as a British invasion.'

The average London crusher [7] isn't qualified to cope with an argument like that. So they bullied someone into making them tea, and told the anarchist to hang fire until someone from the Foreign Office turned up. In return, Beard promised not to garrotte any hostages just yet.

Sapt, it appeared, had got stuck.

With all this going on, it was a simple matter to slip into Sapt's private office, take down the portrait and open the safe. It contained a thick, sealed packet – and, disappointingly, no cash box or surplus crown jewels. Moriarty handed me the goods, and looked about, brows knit in mild puzzlement.

'What? Too easy?'

'No, Moran. It's just as I foresaw.'

He locked the safe again.

There was a clatter of carriages and boots outside. Boscobel Place was full of eager fellows in uniform.

'They've called out the troops.'

'Time to leave,' the Professor said.

Back in the foyer, Moriarty gave the nod. Our Comanche confederates left off pilfering and detached themselves from those still intent on making a political point.

Sapt had fallen head first out of the chimney, sooty as a sweep. The Professor arranged the surreptitious return of his keys.

We left the building as we came, through the front door.

The Comanche melted into another crowd.

I came smack face to face with a junior guards officer, who was about to set diplomacy aside and invade. I stiffened my neck and snapped off a salute, which was smartly returned. Once you've worn the colours, they never wear off.

'Carry on, Lieutenant,' I said.

'Yes, sir,' he responded.

As often, Moriarty had contrived not to be noticed. Like those lizards who can blend into greenery, he had the knack of seeming like a forgettable old stick, someone who has got off the omnibus two stops early and wandered into a bloodbath which was none of his doing.

We strolled away from the battle. Shouts, shots, thumps, crashes and bells sounded. Nothing to do with us.

A cab waited on the corner.

III

Moriarty was in a black thinking mood. He chewed little violet pastilles of his own concoction – a substitute for the cigarettes which had yellowed his fingers and teeth but were now abandoned because he'd taken it into his head to deem tobacco a threat to human health – and paced his room, hands knotted in the small of his back, brow set in a crinkled frown.

I was still full of the thrill of jizzwhackery, and minded to pop downstairs to call on Flossie or Pussie or whatever the tiny blonde with the lazy eye said she was called. After the hunting grounds, the *boudoir*. I'd learned that in India, along with how to keep an eye on your wallet in the back of your trousers while they're draped over a chair. Fifi. Her name was Fifi. She really was French. And she had a friend. Véronique.

But the Professor was preoccupied.

The evening papers were in, along with tear-sheets of fuller reports that would be in tomorrow's editions. Sapt was claiming that dangerous Ruritanian revolutionary movements needed to be exterminated. He called upon Great Britain, Ruritania's ancient ally, to join the crusade against insurrection, alleging that the assault upon the Embassy (and his person) had been equally an insult to Victoria and Rudolf. Typical foreign sod, wanting us to fight his battles for him.

Back in Streslau, there had been street skirmishes between Michaelists and Rudolfites. Many arrests had been made and Sapt was expected to return to his country with information which would lead to a complete sweep of the organised troublemakers.

The packet of photographs lay on our bureau. It seemed that reclaiming this property of a lady had interesting side effects. Moriarty's imaginary revolution had genuinely to be put down.

'I hope the blasted country don't go up in flames before Irene can cash these chips, Moriarty. She'll get no blackmail boodle out of 'em if they're hanging from lamp posts in the public gardens.'

Moriarty growled. He left the room, and closeted himself in the dark, buzzing space where he raised his wasps and plotted the courses of heavenly bodies.

Speaking of heavenly bodies, my eyes went to the packet.

The seal was nice and red and heavy and official.

I remembered the line of Irene Adler's throat, the trim of her calves under silk, the swell of…

No one had said anything about not examining the merchandise.

I listened out: Moriarty was whistling to his wasps, likely to be absorbed for hours; there was no tread on the stair and Mrs Halifax was ordered to keep all callers away. So, no chance of interruption.

I sat at the bureau, and turned up the gas lamp to illuminate the blotter.

With a deft bit of penknifery, I lifted the seal intact so it could be re-attached with no one the wiser. My mouth was dry, as if I'd been in a hide for hours, watching a staked-out goat, awaiting the pad of a big cat. I poured a healthy snifter of brandy, an apt accompaniment to this pleasurable perusal.

With a warm pulse in my vitals, I slid the contents out of the packet.

It was like iced water tipped into my lap.

There were photographs. Views of Zenda Castle, with figures on the battlements. One wore a gauzy hat with a dead bird stuck to it, the other a comic opera uniform. Even at distance, I'd recognised the lovebirds. Irene Adler and Colonel Sapt.

'Disgusting,' I blurted.

A sheet of paper was slipped into the sheaf of photographs.

> *My Dear Col. Moran,*
>
> *I knew you'd not be able to resist a peek at these 'artistic studies'. Sorry for the disappointment.*
>
> *For what it's worth, you may keep all monies which can be raised from them. If b———l proves unprofitable, I suggest you license them to a manufacturer of postcards.*
>
> *My very best to the Prof. I knew I could rely on him to toss a pebble in the pond, sending out ripples enough to make a maelstrom. An ordinary workman would just have secured the package and been done with it. Only a genius on the level of a Bonaparte could turn a simple task into the prompt for turmoil raised across a whole continent.*
>
> *Please convey the thanks of another colonel. Being Chief of Secret Police in 'one of the most peaceable, least-insurrection-blighted spots on the map' was not a career with a future. The Elphbergs were intent on retiring him, but now – I fancy – he'll be kept on with an increase in salary.*
>
> *I expect you to retain the last figure for sentimental reasons, and I remain, dear Colonel Moran, very truly yours,*
>
> *Irene Adler*

I flipped through several more entirely innocent tourist photographs of picturesque Ruritania, until – at the bottom of the stack – I beheld the full face of the American Nightingale. In this final, studio-posed photograph she wore the low-cut bodice she'd affected on her visit to Conduit Street, somewhat loosened and lowered, though – dash it! – artistic fogging around the edges of the portrait prevented complete immodesty. Through the fog was scrawled her spidery autograph, 'as ever, Irene'. Even thus frozen, she looked like the sort who would be much improved by a Basher Moran Special. I gulped the brandy, and chewed my moustache for a few moments, contemplating this turn of events.

Behind me, a door opened.

I swivelled in the chair. Moriarty looked at me, eyes shining – he had thought it through, and was unhappy. When the Professor was unhappy, other creatures – animals, children, even full-grown men – tended to learn of it in extreme and uncomfortable manners.

'Moriarty,' I began, 'I'm afraid we've been stung.'

I held up Irene's photograph.

He spat out a word.

And that was how a great shambles broke out in Belgravia, shaking the far-off kingdom of Ruritania, and how the worst plans of Professor Moriarty were exploited by a woman's treachery. When he speaks of Irene Adler, or when he refers to her photograph, it is always as *that bitch*.

Chapter Three: The Red Planet League

✦

I

Professor Moriarty excelled in *two* fields of human endeavour.

Mathematics, for one. Never was such a fellah as the Prof for chalking up sums. Or the rigmarole with more squiggles than numbers. Equations. Did 'em in his head, for fun… damn his eyes.

I would wager several pawn tickets held on the family silver that you lot have little or no interest in fractional calculus or imperfect logarithms. You'd all be best pleased if I yarned up the *other* field in which James Moriarty was top of the class.

Crime. Just the word gets you tingly, don't it?

Well, tough titty… as the house captain who tried to roger me when I was a whelp at Eton used to say. Because this story is *all about* mathematics. I got my penknife to the house capt's goolies, by the way. Preserved my maidenly virtue, as it were. Blighter is Bishop of Brichester these days. That's beside the point: maths is the thing!

Get your thinking caps on, because I might put in some sums. Make you show your workings in the margin and write off for the answers. It will cost an extra 3d and a stamp just to find out if you're as clever as you think you are. Probably, you ain't. Most fellahs (including – I'm not ashamed to admit it – me) aren't as clever as they think they are. Moriarty, though, was *exactly* that clever, a rare bird indeed. More dodos are around than blokes like that. According to Mr Darwin, that's good joss [1] for the rest of us. Elsewise, we'd have long since been hunted to extinction by the inflated cranium people.

Drifting back to the subject in hand, Professor Moriarty was Number One Heap Big Chief in both his vocations. Which meant there was something he was even better at than complicated number problems or turning a dishonest profit – making enemies.

Over the years and around the world, I've run into some prize-winningly antagonistic coves. I recall several of that species of blood-soaked heathen who bridle under the yoke of Empire and declare war on 'the entire White Christian Race'. Good luck to 'em. Pack off a regiment of curates and missionaries led by Bishop Bum-Banger to meet their savage hordes on the field of carnage and see if I care. In India, some sergeants wear armour beneath the tunic because no soldier serving under them can be trusted with a clear shot at their backs. I've also run into confidential police informants, which is to say: grasses. Peaching on one's fellow crims to escape gaol is guaranteed to get you despised on both sides of the law. Fact is: no bastard born earned as many, as various, and as determined enemies as Moriarty.

First off, other crooks *hated* him. Get your regular magsman or ponce on the subject of Professor Jimmy Bleedin' Moriarty, and you'll expand the old vocabulary by obscenities in several argots. Just being a bigger thief than the rest of them was enough to get their goats. What made it worse was villains were often forced to throw in with him on capers, taking all the risk while he snaffled the lion's share of the loot. If they complained, he had them killed. That was my job, by the by – so show some bloody respect or there's a rope, a sack and a stretch of the Thames I could introduce you to. To hear them tell it, every cracksman in the land was *just about* to work out a foolproof plan to lift the jewels from Princess Alexandra's knickers or riffle the strongboxes in the sub-basement of the Bank of England when Professor Moriarty happened by some fluke *to think of it first*. A few more tumblers of gin and their brilliant schemes would have been perfected – and they wouldn't have to hand on most of the swag to some evil-eyed toff just for sitting at home and drawing diagrams. You might choose to believe these loquacious, larcenous fellahs. Me, I'll come straight out and say they're talking through a portion of their anatomy best employed passing wind or, in certain circumstances, concealing a robin's egg diamond with a minimum of observable discomfort.

Then there were coppers. Moriarty made sure they had no earthly notion who he might be, so they didn't hate him quite as *personally* as anyone who ever met him – but they sure as spitting hated the *idea* of him. By now, you've heard the twaddle… vast spider squatting in the centre of an enormous web of vice and villainy… Napoleon of Crime… Nero of Naughtiness… Thucydides of Theft, et cetera, et cetera. Detectives of all stripe loathed the unseen King of Krooks, and blubbed to their mummies whenever they had to flounder around after one of his coups. 'Scotland Yard Baffled', as if that were news. Hah!

One man above all hated Professor Moriarty. And was hated by him.

Throughout his dual career – imagine serpents representing maths and crookery, twining together like a wicked caduceus – the Prof was locked in deadly *survival* for supremacy – nay, for survival – with a human creature he saw as his arch-enemy, his eternal opposite, his *nemesis*.

Sir Nevil Airey Stent.

I don't know how it started. Stent and Moriarty were at each other's throats well before I became Number Two Big-ish Chief in the Firm. Whenever the Stent issue was raised, Moriarty turned purple and hissed – and was in no condition to elucidate further. I know they first met as master and pupil: Moriarty supervised young Nevil when the lad was cramming for an exam. Maybe the Prof scorned the promising mathematician's first quadratic equation in front of the class. Maybe Stent gave him an apple with a worm in it. Upshot is: daggers drawn, eyes ablaze, lifelong enmity.

Since this record might be of some academic interest, here are a few facts and dates I've looked up in back editions of the *Times*:

1863 – Boyish twenty-three-year-old Nevil Stent, former pupil of James Moriarty, rocks the world of astronomy with his paper 'Diffractive Properties of an Object-Glass with Circular Aperture'. Not a good title, to my mind – which runs more to the likes of *Heavy Game of the Western Himalayas* or *My Nine Nights in a Harem* (both, as it happens, written by me – good luck finding the latter: most of the run was burned by order of the crown court and the few extant volumes tend to be found in the collection of the judge who made the ruling).

1869 – Stent appointed to the Lucasian Chair of Mathematics at Cambridge University, succeeding brainboxes like Isaac Newton, Thomas Turton and Charles Babbage. Look 'em up – all gems, so I'm told. If said chair were a literal piece of furniture, it would be hand-carved by Chippendale and covered in a three-inch layer of gold flake. The Lucasian Professorship comes complete with loads of wonga, a free house, all the bowing and scraping students you can eat and high tea with the dean's sister every Thursday. Stent barely warms the Lucasian with his bottom before skipping on to occupy an even more exalted seat, the Plumian Chair of Astronomy and Experimental Philosophy. It's only officially a chair – everyone in Cambridge calls it the Plumian *Throne*.

1872 – The book-length expansion of 'Diffractive Properties' lands Stent the Copley Medal of the Royal Society. This is like the VC of science. Wear that little ribbon and lesser astronomers swallow their chalk with envy when you walk by.

1873 — Stent publishes again! *On an Inequality of Long Period in the Motions of the Earth and Venus* so radically revises the Solar Tables set out a generation earlier by Jean Baptiste Joseph Delambre that the Delambre Formulae are tossed into the bin and replaced by the Stent Formulae. JB is dead or Moriarty would have had to queue up behind him for the job of Nev's arch-enemy, methinks.

1878 — Stent knighted by Her Majesty, Queen Victoria — who couldn't even count her own children, let alone calculate an indice of diffraction — and is therefore universally hailed the greatest astronomical mathematician of the age. Rivals choke on their abacus beads. Naturally, Sir Nevil is also appointed Astronomer Royal and allowed to play with all the toys and telescopes in the land. Gets first pick of which bits of the sky to look at. Can name any cosmic bodies he discovers after his cats. The AR position comes with Flamsteed House, an imposing official residence. Greenwich Observatory is tacked onto it, rather like a big garden shed. Lesser mortals have to throw themselves on the ground before Sir Nevil Airey Stent if they want to take so much a shufti at the man in the moon.

Cast your glims over that little lot, and consider the picture of Sir Nevil in the rotogravure. Tall, fair-haired, eyes like a romantic poet, strong arms from working an altazimuth mount, winning little-boy smile. Mrs Sir Nevil is the former Caroline Broughton-Fitzhume, second daughter of the Earl of Stoke Poges, reckoned among the beauties of the age. Tell me you don't hate the swot right off the bat.

Now… imagine how you'd feel about Stent if you were a skull-faced, reptile-necked, balding astronomical-mathematical genius ten years older than the Golden Youth of Greenwich Observatory. Though recognised as a serious brain, that 'European vogue' for your 'Treatise on the Binomial Theorem' is but a faded memory. Your career has scarcely stretched beyond being ousted from an indifferent, non-Plumian chair – no more than a stool, they say – at a provincial university few proper dons would toss a mortarboard at. Officially, you're an army coach – cramming sums into the heads of dimwit subalterns who need to pass exams before haring off to do daring deeds (or die of jungle fever) in far distant quarters of the Empire. No one knows about the coups and triumphs of your *other* business. And Stent is a hero of the world of science, a veritable comet zooming through the night sky. If you aren't grinding your teeth with loathing, you probably lost them years ago.

Stent. It's even a horrible name, isn't it?

All the *Dictionary of National Biography* business I found out later. When Professor Moriarty, tense as a coiled cobra and twice as venomous, slithered into the reception room brandishing a copy of *The Observatory* – trade journal for astronomers, don't you know – I'd have been proud to say I had never heard of the flash nob who was giving that evening's lecture to the Royal Astronomical Society in Burlington House.

My understanding was that my flatmate and I were due to attend an exclusive sporting event in Wapping. Contestants billed as 'Miss Lilian Russell' and 'Miss Ellen Terri' in the hope punters might take them for their near look-alikes Lillian Russell and Ellen Terry were to face off, stripped to drawers and corsets, and Indian-wrestle in an arena knee-deep in custard. My ten bob was on Ellen to shove Lilian's face into the yellow three falls out of four. I was scarcely best pleased to be informed that our seats at this cultural event would go unclaimed. We would be skulking – in disguise, yet – at the back of the room while Sir Nevil Stent delivered his latest crowd-pleasing lecture.

His title: '*The Dynamics of an Asteroid*: A Comprehensive Refutation'.

II

'Has it not been said that *The Dynamics of an Asteroid* "ascends to such rarefied heights of pure mathematics there is no man in the scientific press capable of criticising it"?'

Sir Nevil Stent smiled and held up a thick volume.

I was familiar with the blasted book. At least a dozen presentation copies were stuffed into the shelves in our study. It was the Professor's magnum opus, the sum total of his knowledge of and contribution to the Whole Art of Mathematical Astronomy. In rare moments of feeling, Moriarty was wont to claim he was prouder of these 652 pages (with no illustrations, diagrams or tables) than of the Macao-Golukhin Forgery, the Bradford Beneficent Fund Swindle or the Featherstone Tiara Theft.

'Of course,' Stent continued, 'we sometimes have our doubts about "the scientific press". More sense can be found in *Ally Sloper's Half Holiday*.' [2]

A tide of tittering ran through the audience. Stent raised his eyebrows, and shook the book in humorous fashion, as if hoping something would fall out. Chuckles ensued. Stent tried to read the book upside down. Something which might be diagnosed as a guffaw erupted from an elderly party near us. Moriarty turned to aim a bone-freezing glare at the old gent – but was thwarted by his disguise. He wore opaque black spectacles and held a white cane in order to pass himself off as a blind scholar from Trinity College, Dublin.

Stent slammed the book down on the lectern.

'No, my friends, it will not do,' he said. 'Being beyond understanding is of no use to anyone. Astronomy will never progress from simple stargazing if we allow it to be dominated by such... and I don't hesitate to use the term... *piffling tripe* as Professor Moriarty's pound and a half of waste paper. It would be better titled *The Dynamics of a Haemorrhoid*, for its contents are *piles* of nonsense. This copy was taken by me this afternoon from the library of the Greenwich Observatory. As you know, this is the greatest collection of publications and papers in the field. It is open to the finest scholars and minds on the planet. Let us examine this *Dynamics of an Asteroid*, and see what secrets it has to tell...'

Stent picked up the book again and began to leaf through it. He showed the title page. 'A *first*, and indeed *only*, edition!' Then, he turned to the opening chapter, and drew his finger down the two-columned text, turned the page, and did the same, then turned the page and...

'Aha,' he exclaimed. 'After twenty pages, we find that the next leaf is uncut. As are all remaining leaves. What can we deduce from that? This book has been in the library for six years. I have a list of academics, students and astronomers who have taken it out. Seventy-two names. Many I see before me this evening. It seems no one has managed to read beyond the first *twenty pages* of this masterwork. Because I am not averse to suffering for my field, I *have* read the book, cover to cover, 652 pages. I venture to say I am the only man in the room who can claim such a Herculean achievement. Is there any comrade here, to whom I can extend my condolences, with whom I can share my sufferings? In short, has anyone else managed to finish *The Dynamics of an Asteroid*? Hands up, don't be shy. There are worse things to admit to.'

The handle of the Professor's cane snapped. He'd been gripping it with both knotted fists. The sound was like a gunshot.

'So you *have* joined us, James,' Stent said. 'I rather thought you might.'

A sibilance escaped Moriarty's colourless lips.

'We shall have need of you later,' Stent said, producing a long thin knife – which he proceeded slip into the book, cutting at last its virgin leaves. 'You can take off those ridiculous smoked glasses. Though, if you have suffered some onset of blindness which has not been reported in the press, it would explain a great deal. Gentlemen of the Royal Society of Astronomers, it is my contention that no man who has ever looked through a telescope with sighted eyes would ever be able to make the following statement, which I quote from the third paragraph of page one of *The Dynamics of an Asteroid...*'

Stent proceeded to dissect the book, wielding words like a scalpel, and flicking blood in Professor Moriarty's face. It was a merciless, good-humoured assassination. Entertaining asides raised healthy laughter throughout the evening.

The sums were well above my head, but I snickered once or twice at the amusing way Stent couched his refutations. I should have kept a stonier face: the next day, Moriarty had Mrs Halifax despatch Véronique, my second favourite French dollymop, to Alaska as a mail-order bride. Fifi, my first choice, was too good an earner to waste, but I'd learned a lesson.

At every point, Stent invited a response from Moriarty. None came. The Professor sat in silence as his theorems were shredded, his calculations unpicked, his conclusions burst like balloons.

Sir Nevil Airey Stent had no idea that the Professor's interests extended beyond equations. Blithely, the Astronomer Royal continued his lecture. Though I knew only too well what the clot was getting into, I could scarcely blame him for digging his own grave in public.

No one would have believed, in the next-to-last years of the nineteenth century, that his lecture was being watched keenly and closely by an intelligence greater than his own; that as he blathered on and on he was scrutinised and studied, perhaps almost as narrowly as a berk with a microscope might scrutinise the tiny wriggly bugs that swarm and multiply in a drop of water. With infinite complacency, Stent read from his little sheaf of notes, serene in the assurance that he was royalty among astronomers.

Yet, across the gulf of the lecture hall, a mind that was to Stent's as his was to those of the beasts that perish, an intellect vast and cool and unsympathetic, regarded the podium with envious eyes, and slowly and surely drew his plans against him.

'In brief, sirs,' Stent said, wrapping things up, 'this asteroid is off its course. Heavenly bodies being what they are, this cannot be allowed. Stars are inexorable. The laws of attraction, gravity, propulsion and decay are immutable. An asteroid does not behave in the manner our colleague alleges it does. This august body will fall prey to… to *men from Mars*, with three legs, eyes the size of saucers and paper party hats… before the asteroid will deviate one whit from the course I have charted. I would wager five pounds that Professor Moriarty can say no different. James?'

The pause stretched on. Moriarty said nothing. It was summer, but I felt a chill. So did the rest of the audience.

The silence was broken by Markham, the adenoidal twit who had introduced Sir Nevil. He stood up and called for a round of thunderous applause, then announced that the gist of the speech was now available as a pamphlet at the cost of 6d. There was a rush for the stall outside the lecture room, where a brisk trade was done.

Moriarty remained in his seat as the room emptied.

'James,' Stent said cheerfully from the podium as he gathered his notes, 'it's pleasant to see you in such evident health. There's actually some colour in your cheeks. I bid you a respectful good night.'

The Professor nodded to his nemesis. Stent left by a rear door.

Moriarty didn't move from his chair. I wondered if he even could.

Stent had set out to murder Moriarty the Mathematician. He didn't suspect his victim had another self. An unmurdered, unmerciful enemy.

'Moran,' he said, at last, 'tomorrow, you will call on The Lord of Strange Deaths in Limehouse. [3] The Lord is out of the country, but Singapore Charlie will act for him. You remember the Si-Fan [4] were able to import the swamp adder we supplied for Dr Grimesby Roylott [5]. I wish to place an order for a dozen *vampyroteuthis infernalis*. That is not yet an officially recognised genus of *coleoidea*, but specimens come on the exotica market from time to time.'

'Vampyro-whatsit?'

'*Vampyroteuthis infernalis*. Hellish vampire squid. Often mistaken for an octopus. Don't let Singapore Charlie palm you off with anything else. They are difficult to keep alive above their spawning depth. Pressurised brass containers will be necessary. Von Herder can manufacture them, reversing the principle of the Maracot Bell. Use the funds from the Hanway Street jeweller's, then dip into the reserve. Expense is immaterial. I must have my *vampyroteuthis infernalis*.'

I pictured what a hellish vampire squid might be. And foresaw unpleasant experiences for Sir Nevil.

'Now,' the Professor said, 'there is just time to catch the last falls. Would you be interested in making haste for Wapping?'

'Rath-er!'

III

The next few weeks were busy.

Moriarty dropped several criminal projects, and devoted himself entirely to Stent. He summoned minions – familiar fellahs from previous exploits, like Italian Joe from the Old Compton Street Café poisonings, and new faces nervous at being plucked from obscurity by the greatest criminal mind of the age. 'PC Purbright', a rozzer kicked off the force for not sharing his bribe-takings, was one such small fish. A misleadingly strapping, ferocious-looking bloke and something of a fairy mary, PCP specialised in dressing up in his old uniform and standing lookout for first-floor men. He had a sideline as a human punching bag, accepting a fee from frustrated criminals (and even respectable folk) who relished the prospect of giving a policeman a taste of his own truncheon. If you paid extra, he'd turn up while you were out with your darby girl and pretend to make an arrest – you could beat him off easily and impress the little lady with your fightin' spirit. Guaranteed a tumble, I'm told. He came out of the Professor's study with wide eyes, roped into whatever bad business we were about.

I was sent out to make contact with reliable tradesmen, all more impressed by the colour of Moriarty's gelt than the peculiarity of his requests. Paul A. Robert, a pioneer of praxinoscopes, was paid to prepare materials in his studio in Brighton. According to his ledgers, he was to provide 'speculative scientific educational illustrations' in the form of 'rapidly serialised photograph cells from nature and contrivance'. Von Herder, the blind German engineer, bought himself a weekend cottage in the Bavarian Alps with his earnings from the pressurised squid tanks and something called a burnished copper parabolic mirror. Singapore Charlie, acting for the mad Chinaman who had cornered the market in importing venomous flora and fauna, was delighted to lay his hands – not literally, of course – on as many squid as we could use.

The pets were delivered promptly, by Chinese laundrymen straining to lift heavy wicker hampers. Under the linens were Herder Bells, which looked like big brass barrels with stout glass view-panels and pressure gauges. A mark on the gauge showed what the correct reading should be, and a foot-pump was supplied to maintain the cosy deep-sea foot-poundage the average h.v.s. needs for comfort. If this process was neglected, they blew up like balloons. Snacks could be slipped to the cephalopods through a funnel affair with graduated locks. The Professor favoured live mice, though they presumably weren't usually on the *vampyroteuthis* menu.

Mrs Halifax supplied a trembling housemaid – rather, a practiced harlot who *dressed up* as a trembling housemaid – to see to the feeding and pumping. Pouting Poll said she'd service the entire crew of a Lascar freighter down to the cabin boy's monkey rather than look at the ungodly vermin, so hatches were battened over the spheres' windows at feeding time. Not wanting to follow *ma belle* Véro to Frozen Knackers, Alaska, Polly did her duty without excessive whining. The Prof spotted the doxy and promised her a promotion to 'undercover operative' – which the poor tart hadn't the wit to be further terrified by.

The squid were quite repulsive enough for me, but Moriarty decided their pale purplish cream hides weren't to his liking and introduced drops of scarlet dye into their water. This turned them into flaming red horrors. The Professor, cock-a-hoop with the fiends, spent hours peering into their windows, watching them turn inside out or waggle their tentacles like angry floor mops.

Remember I said other crooks hated Moriarty? This was one of the reasons. When he was on a thinking jag, he couldn't be bothered with anything else. Business as usual went out the window. While the Professor was tending his squid and sucking pastilles, John Clay, the noted gold-lifter (another old Etonian, as it happens), popped round to lay out a tasty earner involving the City and Suburban Bank. He wanted to rope in the Professor's services as consulting criminal and have him take a look-see at his proposed scam, spot any trapfalls which might lead him into police custody and suggest any improvements that would circumvent said unhappy outcome.

For this, no more than five minutes' work, the Firm could expect a healthy tithe in gold bullion. The Professor said he was too busy. I had thoughts about that, but kept my mouth shut. I'd no desire to wake up with a palpitating hellish vampire squid on the next pillow. Clay went off in a huff, shouting that he'd pull the blag on his lonesome and we'd not see a farthing. 'Even without your dashed Professor, I shall get away clean, with thirty thousand! I shall laugh at the law, and crow over Moriarty!'

You know how the City and Suburban crack worked out. Clay is now sewing mailbags, demonstrating the finest needlework in all Her Majesty's prisons. [6] A flash thief, he'd been an asset on several occasions. We'd never have got the Rajah's Rubies without him. If Moriarty kept this up, we wouldn't have an organisation left.

One caller the Professor deigned to receive was a shifty-eyed walloper named George Ogilvy. I took him straight off for a back-alley shiv-man, but he turned out to be another bally telescope tosser. First thing he did was whip out a well-worn copy of *The Dynamics of an Asteroid* (with all its leaves cut) and beg Moriarty for a personal inscription. I think the thing the Professor did with his mouth at that was his stab at a real smile. Trust me, you'd rather a *vampyroteuthis infernalis* clacked its beak – buccal orifice, properly – at you than see those thin lips part a crack to give a glimpse of teeth.

Moriarty got Ogilvy on the subject of Stent, and the astronomer poured forth a tirade. Seems the Prof wasn't the only member of the We Hate N.A. Stent Society. I drifted off during the seventh paragraph of bile, but – near as I can recollect – Ogilvy felt passages of *On an Inequality of Long Period* owed a jot to his own observations, and that credit for same had been perfidiously withheld. It was apparent that, as a breed, mathematician-astronomers were more treacherous, determined and murder-minded than the wounded tigers, Thuggee stranglers, card-sharps and frisky husband-poisoners who formed my usual circle of acquaintance.

Ogilvy happily signed up as the first recruit for the Red Planet League and left, clutching his now-sacred *Dynamics*.

I ventured a question. 'I say, Moriarty, what *is* the Red Planet League?'

His head oscillated, a familiar mannerism when he was pondering something dreadful. He looked out of our window, up into the pinkish-brown evening sky over London.

'The League is a manufacturer of paper hats,' he said. 'Suitable apparel for our cousins from beyond the vast chasm of interplanetary space.'

Then Moriarty laughed.

Pigeons fell dead three streets away. Hitherto-enthusiastic customers in Mrs Halifax's rooms suddenly lost ardour at the worst possible moment. Vampire squid waved their tentacles. I quelled an urge to bring up my mutton lunch.

Frederick Nietzsche witters on about 'how terrible is the laughter of the *Übermensch*' – yes, I have read a book without pics of naked bints or big game! – and establishes there is blood and ice in the slightest chuckle of these superior beings. If Fathead Fritzi ever heard the laugh of Professor Moriarty, he would have shat blood, ice and sauerkraut into his German drawers.

'Yes-s-s,' he hissed. 'Paper hats-s-s.'

IV

From the Diary of Sir Nevil Airey Stent.

September 2

Notices are in! My lecture – an unparalleled triumph! *The Dynamics of an Asteroid* – in the dustbin! Moriarty's hash – settled for good! I may draw a thick black line through the most prominent name on the List.

Now – on to other things.

Remodelling of Flamsteed House continues. All say it's not grand enough for my position. Workmen have been in all week, installing electric lamps in every room. In my position, we must have all the modern, scientific devices. Lady Caroline fears electricity will leak from the wiring and strike dead the servants with indoor lightning. I have explained to her why this is impossible, but my dear featherhead continues to worry and has ordered the staff to wear rubber-soled shoes. They squeak about the place like angry mice.

Similarly, the Observatory must expand, keep apace, draw ahead.

THE HOUND OF THE D'URBERVILLES

At ninety-four inches, our newly commissioned optical-reflecting telescope shall be the biggest in the world! The 'scopes at Birr Castle and the Lick Observatory will seem like tadpoles! I almost feel sorry for them. That's two more off the List!

Kedgeree for breakfast, light lunch of squab and quail eggs, Dover sole and chipped potatoes for supper. Congress with Lady C. – twice! Must eat more fish.

Reviewing my life and achievements on this, my forty-fifth birthday, I concede myself well-satisfied.

All must admire me.

Looking to the planets and stars, I feel I am surveying my domain. My Queen has her Empire, but she has gifted me the skies for conquest.

Mars is winking at me, redly.

September 6: A curious happening.

Business took me to the lens-grinders' in Seven Dials. Old Parsons' work has been indifferent lately, and I made a personal visit to administer a metaphorical boot to the seat of his britches.

After the booting was done, I left Parsons' shop and happened to notice the premises next door. Above a dingy window was a sign – 'C. Cave, Naturalist and Dealer in Antiquities'. The goods on offer ran to dead birds, elephant tusks, shark maws, fossils and the like. I'd thought this site occupied by a bakery, but must be misremembering. Cave's premises had plainly stood for years, gradually decaying and accumulating layers of dust and dirt.

My attention was drawn to the window by a red flash, which I perceived out of the corner of my eye. A stray shaft of light had reflected off an odd object – a mass of crystal worked into the shape of an egg and brilliantly polished. It might do for a paperweight if I were in need of such a thing, which I was not.

Then, I heard voices raised inside the emporium. One was known to me – that upstart Moriartian Ogilvy. Alone among the fraternity of astronomers, he has written in defence of *The Dynamics of an Asteroid*. His name was on the List.

I stepped back into the doorway of Parsons', but kept my ears open. Og was haggling with an old man – presumably, C. Cave himself – over the crystal lump, for which the proprietor was asking a sum beyond his purse. An opportunity.

Casually, I wandered into the shop.

Cave, a bent little fellow with egg in his stringy beard and a tea cosy on his head, had the odd mannerism of wobbling his head from side to side like certain snakes. I thought for a moment that I knew him from somewhere, but must have been mistaken. He smelled worse than many of his antiquities. I say, that's rather good – must save the line for my next refutation.

Og was going through his pockets, scraping together coins to up his offer.

Upon seeing me, Og said 'Stent, how fortunate that it's you,' with undue familiarity as if we were the closest of friends. 'Could you extend me a small loan?'

'Five pounds,' insisted Cave. 'Not a penny less.'

Og sweated like an opium addict without funds for his next pipe. Most extraordinary thing. I hadn't thought he had the imagination to be so desperate.

'Of course, my dear fellow,' I said. His face lifted, and his palm came out. 'But first I must conclude my own business.

My good man, I should like to purchase that curious crystal in your window.'

Og looked as if he had been punched in the gut.

'Five pounds,' Cave said.

'Stent, I say, you can't… well, that is… I mean, dash it…'

'Yes, Ogilvy, was there something?'

I drew out my wallet and handed over five pounds. Cave entered the sale in an ancient register, then fussed about extracting the object from the window.

I looked at Og. He tried unsuccessfully to cover fury and disappointment.

'Now about that loan,' I said, wallet still open.

'Doesn't matter now,' he said – and left the shop, setting the bell above the door a-jangle.

Another name off the List!

Cave came back with the object, cradled in black velvet. It struck me that I need only say I'd changed my mind to reclaim my outlay. But Og might creep back and get the blessed thing after all. Couldn't have that.

Cave held up the crystal and said something about 'the inner light'. Strange phrase. He meant the refraction, of course, but a lecture on optics would have been out of place in this circumstance. No fee would be forthcoming, and it doesn't do to cheapen the currency of scholarship by dishing out lectures gratis.

I took the thing away with me. Perhaps I can use it as a paperweight after all.

Roast boar with apricots at the Lord Mayor's. Congress with Lady Caroline in the carriage on the way home. Top-hole!

September 7: An odd day.

Luncheon at Simpson's in the Strand with Jedwood, my publisher. Cream of turbot, hock of ham, peppered pear. An acceptable Muscadet, porter, sherry. The *Refutation* pamphlet is shifting briskly, and J. is eager for more. Pity Moriarty hasn't fired other literary clay pigeons I could blast. J. proposes a collection of *Refutations* and suggests I consider expanding the arena of combat, to launch my intellectual ballista against other so-called great minds of the age. J. is a dolt – he doesn't understand the List, or that it is as important to choose the proper enemies as the proper friends. Nevertheless, I'm tempted. Tom Huxley, Darwin's old bulldog, could do with having his ears boxed for a change. And I didn't care for the way George Stokes hovered over Lady Caroline at the last Royal Society formal. Those Navier–Stokes equations have their tiny little cracks.

Most extraordinary thing. As J. and I were leaving the restaurant, a wild-haired, sunburned fellow accosted us in the street, gabbling 'the Martians are coming, the Martians are coming!' Ever since Schiaparelli put about that nonsense about canals, there has been debate about how one should address the notional inhabitants of the planet Mars. I am firmly of the belief that 'Marsian' is the only acceptable term. I took the trouble to correct the moonatic on this point, but he was in no condition to listen. He grabbed my lapels with greasy fingers and breathed gin in my face. He called me by name, which was discomforting. 'Sir Nevil,' he said, 'keep watching the skies! Look to the Red Planet! Look into the crystal egg!'

J. summoned a hefty constable, who laid a hand on the madman's shoulder. The fellow writhed in the grasp of the law, and a look of heightened terror passed over his face. It is no wonder men of his stripe should fear the police, but the extent of his pantomime of fright struck me as excessive even for his situation. Curiously, the constable seemed humpbacked, tailored uniform emphasising rather than concealing a pronounced lump on one shoulder. I assumed the Metropolitan Police imposed strict physical requirements on their recruits. Perhaps this fellow's condition has worsened in recent years? Something was not quite right about his hump, which I could swear wobbled like a jelly on a plate. His eyes were glassy and his face pale – indeed, our lawful officer was evidently in as poor a shape as our degenerate semi-assailant.

'Don't let them take me,' begged the madman, 'they wraps round you… and they bites… and they sucks your brains… and you ain't you no more. I've seen it!'

'Let's… be… 'avin… you… my… lad,' said the policeman, voice like a prolonged death rattle, monotonous and expressionless. 'You… don't… want… to… be… a-… botherin'… these… gentlemen…'

The madman's face contorted in a silent scream.

There was something peculiarly hideous about the constable's voice, as if he were a music hall dummy manipulated by a wicked ventriloquist.

'Mind… 'ow… you… go… sirs!'

The policeman lifted the madman – not a small individual, by the way – one-handed. He marched off stiff-legged, bearing his whimpering prisoner down the Strand. As he walked, his hump seemed to *shift* under blue serge as if it were a separate entity. I had a sense of evil eyes cast at me.

J. asked me if I had any idea who the maniac was.

He had something of a military mien, I thought – though come down in the world, perhaps having frazzled his brains out in some sunstruck corner of the Empire. It came to me that I had seen him before – perhaps in the audience at one of my many popular lectures, perhaps skulking on the street waiting for the chance to accost me. J. pointed out that he had known who I was, but – of course – everyone in England knows the Astronomer Royal.

'It should definitely be "Marsian",' I insisted. 'The precedents are many and I can recall them in order...'

J. remembered he had forgotten another appointment and left before I could fully convince him. Must send him my monograph on planetary possessives. Some still rail against 'Mercurial' and 'Jupiteric', though a consensus is nearly reached on 'Moonian' and 'Venutian'. By the end of this century, we shall have definitively colonised the sunnar system for proper naming!

September 7: later.

I had thought to dispel completely the unpleasant memory of this afternoon's strange encounter... but the words of the madman resounded.

By some happenstance, this was literally true.

The long-necked cabbie who conveyed me back to Greenwich bade me a jovial farewell with 'keep watching the skies, sir.' An unusual turn of phrase to hear twice in one day, perhaps – but a sentiment naturally addressed to a famous astronomer in the vicinity of the biggest telescope in the land.

Galvani, the Italian foreman of the gang who have completed – at last! – the electrification of Flamsteed House, handed me a sheaf of wiring diagrams marked 'for the attention of the householder' and clearly said *look to the Red Plan, et... es* essential for to understan' the current en the house'. There was, indeed, a red plan in the sheaf, but it seemed to me he had stressed the first part of his sentence, which echoed the words of the madman, and thrown away the second, which conveyed his particular meaning.

Then, before supper, I was passing the kitchens and happened to overhear Mrs Huddersfield, the new housekeeper, tell the butler to 'look into the crystal', referring to our fresh stock of Waterford glassware, a scant instant before Polly, the new undermaid, exclaimed 'egg!' in answer to a question about the secret ingredient of the face paste which keeps her complexion clear. To my ears, these separate voices melded to produce a single sentence, the madman's 'look into the crystal egg'.

Lady Caroline is at her sister's. I dined alone, unable to concentrate on supper. Every detail of the business on the Strand resurfaced in my mind.

I was shocked out of my reverie only by the sweetness of dessert – and looked down into a crystal bowl to see a quivering scarlet blancmange, with a curiously eye-like glacé cherry at its summit. In its colour, the dish reminded me of the planet Mars, and, in its movement, the somehow unnatural hump of the strangely spoken police constable.

Only then did I remember the paperweight snatched out from the grasp of the odious Ogilvy yesterday.

A mass of crystal, in the shape of an egg!

A crystal egg! Could the madman of the Strand have been referring to this item of bric-a-brac?

Unable to finish my dessert for thinking.

September 7: Still later. A great discovery!

After supper, I repaired to my study, where I keep my collection of antique and exotic optical and astronomical equipment: telescopes, sextants, orreries and the like. Signor Galvani's men have disturbed them greatly while seeing to the electrification of the room.

A new reflecting telescope arrived this morning, a bulky cabinet affair on trestles, with an aperture where a separate lens must presumably be attached. It is an unfamiliar design – a presentation, in honour of my achievements in mapping the night skies, from an august body who call themselves the Red Planet League. I have had my secretary respond with an autographed photograph and a note of thanks. Entering the study, I saw at once that the workmen had mistaken this gift for a species of lamp, and wired it up to the mains. I would be inclined to chide Galvani most severely, had this error not nudged me on the path to discovery.

I unwrapped the supposed paperweight and made close examination of it under the steady illumination of the electric lamps. Cave, the vendor, had mentioned an 'inner light' – a phenomenon I soon discovered for myself. It is a trick of the optics, of course – if held up to the light, the interior of the crystal egg coruscates, seeming to hold multiple refractions and reflections.

By accident, when Polly reached into the room and turned off the lights at the wall switch, I discovered the crystal had the unusual property of retaining luminosity even when the light source was gone. I did not measure the time of glow-decay, because the undermaid was fussing and apologising for not seeing I was still in my study when she plunged me into darkness. She whimpered that these newfangled inventions were not like proper gas. I fear Lady Caroline's 'indoor lightning' theory has infected the servants with irrational terror.

'What's that egg?' exclaimed the maid, meaning my crystal. 'And why's it lit up?'

I ventured to explain something of the laws of refraction, but saw my learning was wasted on this simple soul. Nevertheless, it is to Polly that I owe my next, most extraordinary discovery. She picked up the crystal egg, rather boldly for a person in her position I might say.

'Doesn't it go here, sir?' she said, slipping the egg into an aperture of the Red Planet League's reflecting telescope. It was a perfect fit. Before I could chide her, Polly had fiddled with a switch which triggered an incandescent lamp inside the cabinet – projecting a beam through the crystal, which diffracted out into the room. Suddenly, the opposite wall was covered by a swirling, swarming red cloud. Polly yelped, and fled – but I hadn't the heart to pursue and chastise her.

I was transfixed by the pictures on the wall.

Yes, pictures! Pictures that move! With a faint flicker, accompanied by a definite whirring from inside the reflecting telescope. I had never before seen the like.

At once it came to me that my crystal egg was in fact a crystal lens. When light passed through it just so, the crystal egg – by some means as yet undetermined by science – transmitted images from its interior.

The process was astounding, but I was more overwhelmed by the picture. It was as if I were looking out of a window which floated high over a ruddy desert far from Greenwich. Faintly visible above the horizon were familiar stars, skewed in the sky – as observed not from our home world, but from a body which must be considered (on a cosmic scale) our near neighbour. I perceived the tiny blue-green circle of Earth, and knew with utter certainty that this window looked out onto the plains of Mars.

The Red Planet.

All the tiny incidents of the last two days impelled me, inch by inch, towards this discovery.

I knew the subject of my next lecture, my next book. Indeed, the remainder of my career could be devoted to this. I am Master of Mars. No other can come close. Og must have had some inkling, but this is to be Stent's triumph – not Ogilvy's. From henceforth, this acreage of red dust will be Stent's Plain. In the distance, I saw slumped, worn hills, more ancient than the sharper peaked mountains of Earth – the Caroline Range! A deep channel grooves across the landscape, flowing with a thick, red, boiling mud – Polly's Canal, to commemorate the child whose unknowing hand urged me to this discovery! Nearby, a gaping pit was scraped raw like a bloody gouge in the Martian soil. I named this Victoria Regina Chasm in honour of the gracious lady who has bestowed so many honours on my name.

Inside VR Chasm, something stirred. My heart stopped, I am sure, for long, long seconds. Pads like large leaves, a richer scarlet than the crimson of the desert dirt, flopped over the rim and anchored in the soil. These were the tips of sinewy tentacles, which held fast and contracted as *a Marsian being* hauled itself out of its hole.

What manner of men might inhabit the Red Planet? Not men at all, it seems – but creatures beyond classification.

I saw its bulging, filmed-over eyes. Its beak-like mouth. Its mess of limbs. Its swelling carapace.

The thinner atmosphere of Mars and a colder, drier climate have shaped that planet's ruling species differently from us. I had no doubt that I was looking at a Man of Mars, not a brute animal. All around were signs of an intelligent species, a civilisation perhaps older than our own.

There were structures – a Marsian factory, perhaps, or a school. The Marsian hauled itself across metal frames, fighting the pull of its planet, and came closer to the window.

I confess to a moment of stark, irrational fear. As I could see the Marsian, could it see me? Did the crystal egg have a twin on Mars?

With no earthly object for comparison, it was difficult to get a sense of scale. The Marsian could be the size of a puppy or an elephant.

It wriggled closer to the 'window'. Its features grew gigantic on the study wall. I could see the wallpaper, the bookshelves and pictures through its phantasmal image. Then, suddenly, it shut off. There was a flapping sound, and a brief burst of bright, blank light – that died too, along with the incandescent bulb inside the Red Planet League's reflecting telescope.

How ironic that a body named after Mars should provide the

device which lead me to gain such an unprecedented view of our planetary neighbour!

I turned the switch on and off, and I fiddled with the crystal in its aperture, trying to reopen the line of communication. But the window closed as mysteriously as it had opened.

Still, I am too excited to be frustrated. I am certain that the phenomena shall be repeated.

Otherwise, I fear I have a head cold coming on. It may be the turn in the weather. I took a solution of salts in lemon and barley water. Though especially prepared by Mrs H. from her own curative recipe, this concoction served only to exacerbate my condition. I passed an indifferent night, with frequent recourse to the cp and my handkerchief.

September 8: Invasions!

That confounded cold has set in, in my head and chest. The servants have been lax in tending draught-excluders. Or else Signor Galvani's foreign crew have imported alien bacteria into the household – for which they will be reprimanded. I am known for my good health. These minor ailments do not normally afflict me.

Breakfast – porridge, honey-glazed gammon, courgettes, preserved pears. More of Mrs H.'s vile (and inefficacious) home remedy. It'll get worse before it gets better, I am assured – which is scarce comfort. I have instructed the housekeeper to dispense with her brews, and procure proper medicine from the chemist's.

My digestion was incomplete when Flamsteed was impertinently invaded. In my study, making a start on notes for my Marsian Announcement, I became aware of a great ringing on the bell and knocking at the door. My first thought was that barbarians were at the gates. This proved to be the case – though, a singular barbarian, the opprobrious Ogilvy, rather than a horde.

I ventured out into the hallway and found Mrs Huddersfield in the process of calling the stableboy to throw Og off our front step. Much as it would have pleased me to see the inky git tossed into the gravel and given a good kicking, it occurred to me that he should be consulted. Plainly, he had some dim perception of the importance of the crystal egg. It would be best to find out what he knew.

I instructed Mrs H. to let Og into the house. She stood aside and I had momentary pause about my decision. Having run across a superfluity of madmen in recent days, I saw at once that Og was one of their number. His collar was exploded and his cravat tied carelessly. The skirts of his frock coat bore singe marks as if he had jumped through a bonfire. There was a peculiar burned smell about him. He had no eyebrows left and a serious case of the sun. It had been overcast lately and I doubted Og was freshly returned from some tropical adventure.

'Brandy,' he insisted. 'Brandy, for God's sake, Stent.'

Mrs H. frowned, but I told her to send Polly to fetch decanter of the third-best brandy. No sense in wasting the good stuff on a hysteric. I'll need it to fight off this cold.

In my study, Og saw the egg, still fitted into the aperture of the new telescope.

'So you know what it is?' he exclaimed.

'Indeed.'

'A window – a portal – to the Red Planet. Have you seen the Martians?'

'Marsians,' I corrected.

'Their tripod machines? Their firing pit? Their heat devices? Have you determined their purpose, Stent? Their hideous purpose?'

The fellow was ranting, but I expected as much.

'I have made notes of my findings,' I told him. 'I will reveal my conclusions when I am ready to publish.'

'Publish! Who will there be to typeset, print and bind your conclusions, Stent? Who to read them? Do you hope to amuse our new masters with your book? They don't seem the types to be great readers, but I suppose you never know…'

Og was laughing, now – bitterly, insanely, irritatingly. Polly arrived, and Og snatched the decanter from her tray. He drew a mighty quaff, then wiped his mouth with the back of his hand. Never the most savoury of characters, he had apparently decided to become a wild Indian.

'There were four eggs,' he said. 'As far as we can tell.'

'We? Of whom are you speaking?'

'The Red Planet League,' he said. 'What there is left of it. When you took the final egg, we had this telescope delivered to you. I am loathe to admit it, but you are the greatest astronomical mind of the age…'

'True, true…'

'…and if anyone has a chance of cracking the egg's secrets, it is you.'

'No doubt.'

I fancied I caught a slight smirk from Polly. I told her she could be about her business. She left.

'It must have been fate that brought you to Cave's emporium. Cave is dead, by the way. The police report says "spontaneous combustion", if you can credit it. There has been a rash of such phenomena. Almost an epidemic. Colonel Moran and I had a brush with the heat weapons, two nights back. We were separated afterwards. His nerve snapped. Terrible thing when a brave man's nerve goes. He's faced tigers and native rebels and charging elephants, but that flash from the copper tube boiled away all his heart. You saw Moran yesterday, I believe – before *they* caught up to him.'

'I saw no one yesterday.'

'In the Strand, outside Simpson's. Moran would have seemed, ah, irrational. Lord knows, we all act like cuckoos. With what we have in our heads. It's only to be expected. A big man, Moran. Red-complected…'

I remembered. The madman who was taken away by the hump-backed policeman.

'Moran brought me into the League. He's a big-game hunter and adventurer. He found the first of the eggs, in a temple in India. It was the eye of an idol worshipped by an obscene cult. When the light fell into the temple on certain days of the year, the portal opened and the cultists saw their "gods". You know what they really saw, Stent. The men of Mars. Those tentacles, those eyes, those mouth parts! Another crystal was looted from the collection of the Emperor of China, carved into a goblet. I would not drink from that goblet for all the tea in its rightful owner's dominions, would you? A third was found fresh, among the hot fragments of a new-fallen meteorite in the California desert. All these came to the

KIM NEWMAN

League, and all have been *taken* – taken *back*, one might say.'

Og kept glancing at the crystal. I worried that he would snatch it from the telescope and flee the house.

'This one was sent here, to England. I don't know how Cave came by it. Dishonestly, I suppose.'

'It is mine,' I reminded him. 'Paid for and bought.'

He wasn't listening to me. 'Stent, have *they* seen *you*? The portal opens both ways. That we can see them is incidental, an accident, a flaw in the great plan. From the other side, from *Mars*, they spy us. Spy *on* us. It's what the eggs are for. They are taking our measure, making a study. Drawing plans. At first, the meteorites just brought the eggs. It's only recently that *they* have come. Just a few, but enough – for their purpose. Across millions of miles of empty space! What explorers they must be, what conquerors! They ready their armada, Stent, their fleet...'

I concede that Og was alarming me. A great deal of what he said struck me as fanciful drivel. Conquerors, indeed – what nonsense, as if creatures without hands or clothing could hope to stand up to the military might of Great Britain! But I worried there were eggs in other hands. Dangerous hands – other scientists eager to 'scoop' the Great Stent. If half of what Og said is true, someone else might publish first.

I cannot let that happen.

The doorbell rang. Mrs H. came into the study, and presented a *carte de visite*.

Colonel Sebastian Moran, Conduit Street.

'Your comrade in the League has extricated himself from the police,' I told Og.

The fellow looked further stricken, which was not what I

expected. I got little sense from him. I feared this would also be true of Moran – yesterday, he had been singing from the same hymn book.

'Don't let him in,' said Og, grabbing my lapel. 'In the name of all that's…'

'There's a policeman with the caller, sir,' said Mrs H. 'Constable Purbright.'

I could not have been more relieved. With all the ranting, raving and lapel grabbing, a policeman might be just what the doctor ordered. Clap these madmen in irons, and leave me to conclude my Marsian studies.

'Show them in,' I said.

'Very good, Sir Nevil. Don't you be straining yourself. Remember you're not a well man.'

Og threw himself into an armchair, in a pose of stark terror. Under his sunburn, he even went pale.

'Hullo… Sir… Nevil… Hullo… Ogilvy…'

It was the madman from the Strand, but much changed. His demeanour was more sober, respectable. His voice was uninflected, somehow metallic. And, since yesterday, he had grown a humpback. A long, red scarf wound around his neck, ends trailing down his back.

'Good… morning… gentlemen,' said the police constable beside Moran.

They could have been brothers, with the same shifting deformity, the same strange manner of speech.

'Keep them away from me,' shrieked Og 'They're… *them*!'

'Don't… make… a… fuss… old… chap.' Moran and Purbright spoke in unison, like a music hall turn. Their voices scraped the nerves. I was overcome by a powerful wish that all my visitors would leave. I could do with a medicinal tot and some peace.

The constable walked, stiff-legged, across the room, to the telescope. He laid a hand on the crystal egg.

'That's delicate scientific equipment,' I warned Purbright.

'Evidence... sir,' he said, twisting the egg free.

'I must protest...'

'Obey... the... law...' Colonel Moran said.

Moran was in my way. Beyond him, I saw the constable slipping the crystal egg into his tunic.

'I paid five pounds for that!'

'Stolen... goods...' Moran said.

I tried to strong-arm him out of the way, but he was immovable. My hand fell on his hump, and his long scarf unwound, showing where his jacket seam was split by the swelling. An angry, inhuman eye looked out from the hole! Sinewy, venous scarlet ropes wound around Moran's exposed neck. A beak-like barb was fixed to his throat, under the ear, blood dribbling from the conjunction.

A cowardly knee met my groin and I doubled over.

When I righted myself, Moran had rearranged his scarf. I knew what I had seen.

Og leaped up from the chair and flew at Moran.

From a pocket, Moran pulled a curious object – a tube with a burnished copper disc at one end. A beam of light seemed to project from this – and fell on Og, whose jacket started smoking. With a scream, Og fled from the room, down the hall, and out of the house. His clothes were on fire.

Moran turned to me. Purbright had also produced one of the heat-casting devices. Both were aimed in my direction.

I was in danger. But if the egg left the house, I would have no proof, no basis for my findings!

Og's screams still echoed.

'We... must... be... going...' Moran said.

'Not with my crystal egg.'

The copper discs were glinting at me. But I was resolute. No somnambulists, puppeteered by angry-eyed inhuman humps, would stand between me and recognition for my achievements.

'I am Sir Nevil Airey Stent, the Astronomer Royal,' I reminded them. 'I will thank you to return my property. On this world, sirs, I am not to be sneezed at.'

'Sneezed... at?' they both said.

At that inopportune moment, my cold struck again – and I had a sneezing fit.

This had the most peculiar effect on my threatening guests. They turned tail, in something like panic, and ran. Purbright dropped the egg which – mercifully – did not shatter. As they ran, they slumped over, arms dangling uselessly, heads lolling – as if they were piloted by their tentacular humps, who could no longer concentrate on even the semblance of normal conduct.

My sheer physical presence, and the dignity of my office, had overwhelmed these creatures.

But I did not doubt they would be back.

I took some brandy, for my chest and sinuses, and reflected over my triumph in this skirmish of the spheres.

Mrs H. called me to the garden. On the gravel driveway lay a human-shaped pile of ashes, already drifting in the wind. I don't have to worry about Ogilvy horning in on my findings any more…

Feeling much better, despite sniffles, I returned to my study.

In Lady Caroline's continued absence, attempted congress with Polly – but, for some reason, was thwarted. Have much on my mind.

D--- this cold!

September 8: Later. I capture a Marsian!

Mrs H. is has obtained a supply of a patent medicine, Dr Tirmoary's Infusion for Coughs, Colds and Wheezes. According to the label, it is mostly *diacetylmorphine hydrochloride*. The stuff burns in a basin, and is inhaled under a damp towel. I spent ten minutes breathing acrid fumes before supper – dressed Cornish crab, lamprey *surpris*, calamari, conger mousse, langoustines – and, finally, gained some measure of relief from congestion, sniffles and associated symptoms. Not only am I sneezing less, I am thinking more clearly.

After a fresh, post-prandial infusion of Dr Tirmoary's, I retired to my study, determined to tinker with the crystal egg until it yielded its secrets. But, light-headed and with a sense of fullness in my stomach and other parts, I fell into a doze in an armchair…

I was awakened by a whirring which I recognised as the sound of the telescope when the egg-portal is open. The room was bathed in a red, flickering light. The window to Mars!

Again, I saw Stent's Plain, the Victoria Regina Chasm, the Caroline Range. Now, there was great activity. Structures had changed, been erected or expanded. Many Marsian creatures could be seen, crawling about their purpose – which seemed to me to be the construction, within the Chasm, of a great cannon-like device. This could be aimed, I saw at once, at the tiny bluish speck on the Marsian horizon.

I recalled Og's ravings about a Marsian armada readying for a trip across the gulf of space.

Poppycock and nonsense!

My study door opened, and Polly came in. The possibility of renewed attempt at congress arose and I bound from my chair into the beam of egg-light. For a moment, I was distracted by my own silhouette, cast on the wall as images from Mars played across my body.

Something was amiss. Polly, hunched over, wore a heavy shawl – not suitable for indoors. She carried a wicker basket which I had not asked to be brought to me. Emboldened, I tore away her shawl. A red, wet creature pulsed on her shoulder, tentacles wound around her neck, face buried in her throat.

My maid was host to a Marsian!

I tripped over the carpet and fell back into the armchair. My nerve was resolute, but my limbs betrayed me – some side effect of Dr Tirmoary's, I'll be bound, for which the manufacturer will receive a stern letter. I could not stand. The room became a swirling red blur, as much Mars as Greenwich. I fancied the beings I saw working on their cannon could see me across the void and might crawl through the portal.

Polly set down the wicker basket.

She attempted a clumsy curtsey and craned her cheek against her Marsian master, stroking its slimy hide as if she were indulging a kitten. The creature, bereft of its native atmosphere, was in evident difficulty. I'll wager they can't last long among us. Susceptible to all manner of Earthly ailments, drowning in our alien air, boiling in what was to us a cool evening.

The lid lifted from the basket, and a curious contraption rose from within – like a brass diving bell, on three mechanical legs. Some sort of clockwork enabled it to 'stand', and 'walk'. A thick window showed the tentacle-fringed, scarlet face of a Martian. Within the sphere, it was comfortable – sustained by liquid atmosphere, doubtless rich with the nutrients of Mars.

This must be the chief of the Martians on Earth, leader of the expedition, the planet's most able diplomat. I looked it – him! – in the eyes, and began to introduce myself.

'We... know... who... you... are... Mr... Stent...'

The words came from a hooded figure who had slipped into the room. I realised at once that the superior creature in the bell could exert mental control over a human without the need for physical contact. This facility must be developed among the higher castes of the planet. The hooded figure was a meaningless person. His head bobbed from side to side like an imbecile's as the Martian Master spoke through him.

'It strikes me that you have not conducted yourselves in the proper manner,' I told him. 'You should have come to me first, not wasted your time with this ragtag Red Planet League.'

Meaningless syllables stuttered from the hooded puppet. The laughter of Mars!

'Well you may laugh, sir! A serious misunderstanding could have come about between our two great planets, as a result of your involvement with the likes of George Ogilvy. He holds no great office. Now you have come to the proper person, the Astronomer Royal. You are in communication with someone best placed to reveal your presence to the worthies of Great Britain. Treaties can be brokered, as trade agreements are being made in our world's Orient. If travel between planets is possible, we may send you missionaries, medical staff, advisers. We must form a limited company. Anglo-Marsian Trading. I perceive you get scant use from your famous canals, but a few Scots engineers will have a railway system up and running across your red sands in no time. You have a surfeit of coolies, I see.'

The syllables continued. Not laughter, I think – but song! A native hosanna at the prospect of deliverance from a state of ignorance and depravity.

I looked into the Marsian's huge, lidless eyes.

The hooded man spoke. 'I... speak... for... you... would... call... him... Roi... Marty... King... of... Mars.'

I was impressed that such an exalted personage should be my guest.

'And what service may I do the King of Mars?'

Polly and the hooded figure raised now-familiar copper tubes, which caught the red light from the telescope. I sensed Marsian treachery!

'You... can... *burn*...'

Then, things happened swiftly.

A sturdy broom scythed down on Polly's shoulder, squelching her alien master – which detached from her with a hideous shriek and flew across the room to explode against the mantelpiece, swollen organs bursting through its skin. The redoubtable Mrs Huddersfield was in my study, swinging her broom like a yeoman's quarterstaff. The hooded figure turned, and fire broke out on the wall where fell the beam from his copper tube. Mrs H. tripped him and he tumbled in a heap.

'Take that, you fiend from another world, you,' Mrs H. shouted, with some relish. 'I'll not have you botherin' the *Astronomer Royal*!'

Polly, bereft of a controlling mind, stood staring, still as a statue, angry weals on her neck and bosom. Mrs H. took to battering and sweeping the King of Mars' puppet, driving him from the room, and – indeed – out of the house.

The King's Bell began to move, edging away on its three legs. With all the skill of my days as a varsity three-quarter, I fell on the contraption, pinning it down, preventing its escape.

Robbed of its puppet, the King had no way to converse. Its eyes bulged in mute, frustrated fury.

'Your highness, you are captured!' I told it. 'You will surrender yourself to my authority.'

The spell of the crystal egg was broken. A last unsteady image held for a few moments, then bright red light replaced the vista of Mars. The whirring sped up after the picture was lost. Something flapped loosely inside the telescope before it shut off entirely.

Mrs H. returned, broom over her shoulder, and the puppet's hood in her grip. She reported that she had seen the puppet – a demented tramp, she believed – hightailing it down the drive. He was unimportant, I knew. No more than a set of vocal chords.

Polly was recovered from her upright faint, but still in a dazed state. She did not relish the memory of communion with the creature which lay dead in a jumble in the fireplace. All she could say was that its touch was slimy and sharp. I suggested a dose of Dr Tirmoary's, but she turned it down – she has promised her mother not to have truck with such potions, apparently. Mrs H. similarly passed up the opportunity to taste her own medicine, but I felt another dose would be restorative and invigorating. I am becoming quite partial to its effects. A certain gaiety is upon me after each infusion. Of course, I am in a heightened state of excitement just now, in the midst of these great events.

War is over before it is begun! I have captured the Marsian King!

Also, I have one of the copper tubes. A gun of Mars. I must find out how the hot-beam works. The burned patch on my study wall has a chemical smell, as if some reactive compound were smeared on the paper and left to ignite – but I sense the truth of the process is to do with transforming light into heat. I shall experiment with this device in safer, less expensively decorated premises.

The King squirms and writhes in his metal shell. The three legs are wired together, so it may not 'walk' free.

I have communicated by telegram with the Royal Society, setting a date three days hence for my Marsian lecture. I shall use the crystal egg and display the terrain and inhabitants of the Red Planet to those who would call themselves my scientific peers. I shall demonstrate the use of the copper tube – maybe singe the trousers of some of my more disbelieving colleagues, to make a point. Then, as the crowning moment, I shall present the King of Mars!

Surely, ennoblement must follow. I shall be Lord Flamsteed of Mars!

Considered congress with Mrs H. and/or Polly, but was persuaded instead to cap off the evening with another infusion of good old Dr Tirmoary's.

I am Conqueror of Mars!

V

Pah! Ever read such rot, eh? Believe me, those were the *interesting* pages. The rest of Stent's journal is fit only to start fires. His entries are stuffed with menus and 'congresses' and remarks about how brilliant, acclaimed, well loved and admirable he is. By my count, the Astronomer Royal penned 17,000 heated words about a controversial boot-scraper installed, removed, installed again, relocated by six inches and finally removed from outside the servants' door at Flamsteed House.

How did I get hold of the journal? Stole it, of course.

By pasting in these pages, I've saved myself a deal of penwork, which is all to the good. More time down the pub, rather than filling up an exercise book with this scribble.

Of course, you knew me at once when I turned up in Stent's narrative – doing my old 'madman' act, which has proved persuasive in many a tight spot. When I start frothing and raving, you wouldn't want to be around. Avoided being fed to crocodiles by throwing a similar wobbly. The queer… halting… voice… took more effort, and Moriarty had to coach us – me, PCP, Polly – in the proper hollow tones. We used Punch and Judy swizzles, as well. *That's the way to do it!*

As for the rest of it, the Professor only let us into as much of his grand scheme as he deemed necessary. Like his imaginary Squid King, Moriarty puppeteered his subjects, speaking words through us, chivvying Stent along until the fool fancied himself Conqueror of Mars. Of course, Ogilvy didn't know how flammable the gunk poured on his jacket really was. The cretin hopped around outside Flamsteed House, on fire from head to foot, until a bucket of merciful water was sloshed over him. By then, he was almost in as poor shape as the ash and cinder outline laid out on the gravel to represent his incinerated remains. Threw a sulk about that, he did. Still, can't make an omelette and all that. In Ogilvy's case, it's true. He lost the use of his hands and so literally can't make an omelette or perform many other everyday tasks. That's what you get for volunteering.

I've rarely had cause to remark upon Professor Moriarty's genius for disguise. There's good reason for that. Anyone less wholly shoved up his own bum than Sir Nevil Stent would have seen through Moriarty's beards and hoods and skullcaps and spectacles in a trice. That snake-oscillation mannerism always gave him away. He didn't list card-sharping among his favoured crimes, or he'd have known about 'tells' and taken steps to suppress his. On one occasion, I tried to raise the matter in as tactful a fashion as possible, venturing to suggest that the Professor moderate his 'cobra-neck tell' when incognito.

'What are you talking about, Moran? Have you been at the *diacetylmorphine hydrochloride* again?'

There was no sense in pressing the matter further. Genius or no, Moriarty truly didn't know about the thing he did with his neck. I wondered if he was unconsciously trying to make it difficult for the hangman. Probably not. It was just a habit. Other men scratch their balls, fiddle with their watch chains or chew their moustaches. That's when it's a good time to double up, throw the mortgage into the pot and slide an ace out of your cuff.

Nevertheless, Moriarty acquitted himself adequately in the multiple roles of 'C. Cave', filthy shopkeeper, 'long-necked cabbie', dispenser of jovially ominous sentiments, and 'Hooded Man of Mystery', mouth-piece of Martian Royalty. (Stent never did persuade anyone else to say 'Marsian'.) As you can tell from the diary, the worthy Mrs Halifax, pouting Polly, Italian Joe (Signor Galvani), PCP and some nobly self-sacrificing specimens of *vampyroteuthis infernalis* also strutted and fret their weary hours on the stage.

It's a shame there wasn't any money in it. The whole palaver cost the Firm a great deal, exhausting the proceeds of five good-sized blags, and sinking Moriarty into debts we had to work hard to pay off. I know we have a reputation as rotters and crooks and all, but it doesn't do to default on payments owed someone who likes to be called the Lord of Strange Deaths. Hellish vampire squid wouldn't have been the half of it.

For the Prof, the pay-off came at Stent's lecture.

VI

This time, the Royal Astronomical Society wasn't a grand enough platform for Sir Nevil, but we were back in Burlington House. The edifice is also HQ of *the* Royal Society, a body so sniffily superior it feels it doesn't even need to give you the full name – which, as it happens, is The Royal Society for the Improvement of Natural Knowledge – when you are expected to prostrate yourself before the hallowed altars of high science and furthermore purchase an illustrated souvenir program booklet to memorialise the hours you spent snoozing through a lecture. Chairman at the time of these occurrences was Thomas Henry Huxley, and you know what the Astronomer Royal thought of *him*. I don't doubt Huxley thought the same right back at Stent, who – for reasons which by now must be glaring – was not as popular with the general community of test-tube sniffers and puppy-vivisectors as he was with his home crowd of stargazing toadies.

Again, we took our seats. *Sans* disguises, on the assumption Stent wouldn't notice us in the crowd – at least, not until the crucial moment. The hall was packed, as if word had leaked out that Lola Montez would be tightrope-walking nude over the audience while Jenny Lind sang all eighty-six verses of 'The Ballad of Eskimo Nell'. Every branch of science was represented, for Stent had announced his lecture would radically affect all of them equally.

A lot of textbooks would need revising (or burning) after this one, the rumour-mill insisted. To me, the mob looked like an unkempt crowd of smelly schoolmasters on a spree, but the Prof clucked and tutted to himself, listing the great names who had shown up. Besides our home-grown brainboxes, there were yanks, frogs, krauts, eye-ties, dressed-up natives from far-flung lands and an authentic Belgian – all trailing more degrees, honours, doctorates and professorships than you could shake a stick at. It would have been humbling if they weren't mostly aged and chalk-covered. We had salted the room with a few of our own fellahs, who carried hat boxes or picnic hampers and were a bit fidgety in clean, respectable clothes. A squeaky-voiced draper's clerk tried to squeeze in on a platform ticket, but was properly ejected for being a lower-class bounder. [7]

This time, Stent went for dramatic effect.

The house lights dimmed, and a spot came up on the lectern. The Conqueror of Mars posed dramatically in a vestment-like long white coat.

'Gentlemen,' he began, 'we are not alone...'

He whipped a dust cloth from the 'reflecting telescope' which incorporated the 'crystal egg'. In the end, Polly had been forced to draw him a picture to show how she had 'accidentally' made it work. Between shows, someone had to reset or replace the strip of exposures inside the box and put in a new incandescent bulb – which meant getting Stent away from his toy. Fortunately, he'd quite a nose for Dr Tirmoary's Infusions and was often in a daze.

'I give you... the Planet Mars!'

Stent toggled a lever and electric current made a motor grind. Red images were cast on a white board erected on the platform. Squid crawled across a sandbox, gagging for water. There were gasps of awe, though a few coughs of scepticism too. A few sequences wound backwards, which gave an eerie, unnatural effect – as if pictures that moved weren't unnatural enough.

I'd seen some of these views 'taken' by Mr Paul A. Robert of Brighton.

Urchin assistants had to hand-colour the scenes, picture by picture. Robert has a glass-roofed studio under construction on the Downs. I had to be blindfolded and driven up and around country lanes before visiting it because he fears some Yankee swine is out to poach the process and present it as his own invention. Good luck to him, I say. Apart from making a fool of the Astronomer Royal, all Robert's whateveroscope is good for is giving anyone who stares too long at the stuttering pictures a blinding headache. There was still that damned whirring and flapping as exposures passed in front of the incandescent. The bloody racket is why Robert's Box Pictures in Motion will never 'catch on', if you ask me. They'll never replace the stereopticon. [8]

After the images from the crystal egg passed, Stent was assailed by questions. Some were about the creatures, but most were about Robert's Box – which several in the audience had heard of before. One or two had even seen the thing demonstrated while the inventor was soliciting funds for development of his annoying wonder of the age. When Stent repeated his assertion that the Box was a 'reflecting telescope', someone called him a 'blithering idiot'. He looked displeased. Several helpful souls shouted out the principles on which the Box worked. A couple of young fellahs got into a heated argument about 'persistence of vision' and 'Muybridge strips'. No one cared much about *what* they had seen (it could have been a chuffing train or a couple snogging, for all they cared) but many were intrigued by the process whereby moving images were cast on a board. Stent had caused a sensation, but not the way he expected.

Moriarty smiled to himself.

Seeing things not going his way, Sir Nevil hastened on to what would have been his grand finale.

'Sirs, men from Mars are among us! They have been here quite some time!'

Hoots, whistles, laughs.

Stent lifted another dust cloth from an exhibit.

'This is the King of Mars,' he announced.

There was sudden hush. The window in the bell had a magnifying effect, and the hideous red face of the creature trapped inside loomed. The buccal orifice clacked angrily.

For a moment, everyone was struck quiet and frozen. Swollen alien eyes, set in angry red facial frills, seemed to range over the assembled scientific multitudes, as if ready to direct a 'hot beam' across their ranks and wipe out the great minds of Earth before calling down a sky-fleet of bloodthirsty horrors. Red tentacles writhed, ready to crush human resistance before hauling up the Martian standard on the blackened ruins of Burlington House.

The Robert's Box was forgotten, and this new horror held the attention.

Stent, seeming to sense he was on the point of winning a few converts, radiated a certain smugness, as his thick hide recovered from the earlier pinpricks. His shirt front puffed out a bit, like a squid rising above its spawning depth, and he allowed himself to look on the audience with his old superior attitude. If this King of Mars could cow the Royal Society, then Stent might transfer his allegiance from the lesser, terrestrial monarch he had hitherto served. If his mighty brain went unappreciated on this poor planet, then perhaps he should look elsewhere for patronage...

Then, just as Stent was on the point of recapturing his audience, the Professor stood up and shouted, 'Where's his party hat?'

Stent was horror-struck at the sight of an enemy he'd thought bested. His mood turned. For a moment, I assumed he'd seen through the whole business and understood how he'd been gulled, but it was a passing doubt. The Astronomer Royal remained firm in his convictions. He believed what Moriarty had made him believe.

'I insist,' he said, holding up a copper tube, 'this is a visitor from another world.'

Seconds ago, he had been taken at his word. Now, the sceptics and rationalists – for is this not an age of doubt? – were inclined to get close to the old gift horse and pay close attention to his choppers.

An elderly Frenchman from the front row got up and took a closer look at the bell, squinting through pince-nez.

'This is a "hot beam" device,' said Stent, voice cracking. 'A weapon of Mars!'

He aimed it at the now-bewildered crowd, as if willing it to burst them into flame. Of course, we weren't smeared with the slow-acting chemical concoction which provided the fire when the pretend guns were used in Flamsteed House.

'This is a squid,' announced the Frenchman. 'Someone has cruelly dyed it red. An uncommon specimen, but not unknown.'

Some laughter was forthcoming. A paper dart, folded from a program, zoomed from the back of the room and sliced past Stent's head.

'This is the Marsian King,' Stent told the onion eater. 'Roi Marty. You, sir, are an unqualified dolt. You know nothing of alien worlds.'

'*Eh bien*, perhaps,' the Frenchman admitted. 'But I, *monsieur*, am Professor Pierre Arronax, greatest living authority on denizens of the deep. In debate about the courses of the stars, I would allow you are far more expert than I. However, in matters of marine biology, you are a child of five and I am an encyclopaedia on legs. This, I repeat, is a squid. An unhealthy squid.'

'I say, Stent, is that the sick squid you owe me?' brayed one wit.

'Here here,' shouted a vocal clique of Arronax supporters. 'A squid, a squid!'

Stent's world was collapsing. He knew not what to say. His mouth opened and closed, but no words issued forth. I saw he was desperate for an infusion of Dr Tirmoary's – damn fine stuff, let me tell you, though even I would caution against excessive use. The Astronomer Royal pressed his fists to his temples as if to shut out the catcalls and retreat into his own 'sunnar system'. There, many-limbed things crawled across the sands of Mars, intent on climbing into three-legged suits of armour, hurling themselves at the Earth to subjugate humanity for food and amusement.

Moriarty's facial tendons were tight as leather drum skin dried in the sun, making his face a skull-mask rictus of glee. His eyes lit up like Chinese lanterns. I'd wager every muscle in the old ascetic's stringy body was tight with sordid pleasure. He got like that when he had his way. Other fellahs might pop a bottle of fizz or nip down to Mrs H.'s for a turn with a trollop, but the Professor just went into these brain-spasms of evil ecstasy.

Huxley left the hall in disgust, followed by a dignified procession. Some of his colleagues, perhaps pettier, stayed to jeer. The draper's clerk poked his head in, and asked if he'd missed anything.

'Wait, don't leave,' Stent said, vainly. He viciously pressed a stud on his copper tube. No one caught fire. 'There's danger in disbelief. The Marsians are coming! You fools, you must listen. If you don't support me, you're next! They're here! The Marsians are among us!'

At that moment, Moriarty gave a signal.

Our people stood up in their seats – one or two were stationed 'backstage' – and lobbed struggling missiles at Stent. Out of water, the squid didn't last long – but they fought hard, as Polly and I can bear witness, getting tentacles around something convenient and squeezing madly while internal pressure blew them up like balloons. It was a sight to see, but most of the paying customers were gone.

A volley of squid fell upon Stent. He yelled and slipped, knocking over the lectern. Tentacles wound around his legs, his waist, one hand. A squid fixed to his lower face like a mask, beak thrust into his mouth in a ghastly kiss, shutting off his screams. Plastered with *vampyroteuthis*, he threw a full-on fit, back arching, limbs twitching. Eventually, attendants came and pried burst, dead creatures off him.

Arronax tried to lodge a protest at this mistreatment of rare specimens, but slipped into French to do it and was properly ignored. There are idiot Englishwomen (of both sexes) who would be generally happier to see children whipped, starved, laughed at, shot and mounted in the Moran den than brook any abuse of their 'furry or feathered friends' – but it was a rare crank, like Pop-eyed Pierre, who gave two hoots for anything with tentacles and a beak.

With all our wriggling shots fired, the Professor gave the nod – and our picked men melted into the crowds, well paid and frankly little the wiser for tonight's business. When Moriarty handed over coin and told you to bowl a squid at an astronomer, your wisest course was to ask 'over-arm or round-arm?' and get on with play.

As a strait-waistcoat was strapped around him, Stent begged for an infusion of Dr T.'s. He had the shakes, the sweats and the abdabs at the same time. All his strings were cut.

It so happened that the director of Purfleet Asylum – a far less pleasing official residence than Flamsteed – was in the audience, and well positioned to take the babbling madman off Lady Caroline's hands. I think she had papers already drawn up, assuming control of all Sir Nevil's estates and monies. Being the second daughter of an Earl doesn't come with much ready cash, but getting hold of the Stent fortune would do her for a while. I made a note to look her up.

The Astronomer Royal was carried from Burlington House, strapped to a stretcher.

We lingered in the imposing hallway, lined with portraits of past presidents. The attendants paused for a moment. Moriarty leaned over his now-broken nemesis.

Stent's eyes rolled upwards. His cheeks were striped red and dotted with horribly familiar sucker marks. He tried to focus on the face looming over him, the thin-lipped leering countenance of the author of *The Dynamics of an Asteroid*.

'I have, I think, made my point,' said Professor Moriarty. 'And you, Stent, have finally learned your lesson.'

Chapter Four: The Hound of the d'Urbervilles

I

As I entered our reception room, a slicing noise alerted me. A stick slashed at my head. I arrested its arc with a quick grab. As part of an unending 'testing process', Moriarty often tried to catch associates off guard. Some, not having my jungle-honed instincts, got broken heads.

I let the cane go and the Prof handed it to me.

Some lackwit had called while we weren't in. Mrs Halifax had turfed him out, but he'd left his stick behind. That foul October, London was full of fools tapping through vile, yellow fog. Angry blighters collided at every corner and laid about each other like Italian duellists. Pickpockets left watches, but snatched canes.

'Moran, what can you *deduce* about the owner of this item?'

Moriarty had picked up a craze for *deductions*. Don't know where he got it from. Don't bloody care. When I met him, he was set against guessing games. Still, when he was in a mood for ratiocination, it was best to humour him.

'Apart from that he's a forgetful sod, you mean?'

The Prof leered at my pleasantry.

I paced, swinging the stick, deliberately just missing scientific implements, pots of inestimable value and souvenirs of crimes past. Moriarty hissed as

KIM NEWMAN

prized fetishes were in peril. Served him right for the blasted 'testing process'. I seldom miss a shot, but confess I've sometimes missed *just missing*. A stuffed dodo under glass wobbled. Moriarty's eyes glowed like wreckers' lights. I stopped larking.

The stick was a specimen of the 'Calcutta Clobberer' or 'Chicago Good-Night'. A decent heft, solid lead handle and longer than usual. It had seen hard use. Stains dried to black; I knew my night-work – fresh, they'd been red.

I spouted my *deductions*.

'I should say this belongs to a chap who makes a habit of dashing the brains out of puppies, breaking the shins of beggars and throwing his weight around. A right bastard, I'll be bound. Oh, and taller than the average. Does that cover it?'

Moriarty's head craned from side to side. 'As it happens, our prospective client's legitimacy is in dispute.'

Hah! A client.

That wasn't much of a deduction. Visitors to our Conduit Street HQ either wanted a consultation or were dragged squealing into Mrs Halifax's basement with a flour sack over their heads. In basement cases, I'd often use my favourite cane – a flexible, steel-cored 'house prefect's coach-whip', relic of cherished boyhood days. Many conversations flow better if punctuated with thwacks.

'Anyone we know?' I asked.

Moriarty flicked a calling card at me, putting spin on it. As I bent down to pick it up, he showed teeth in a mirthless gurn.

JASPER STOKE, TRANTRIDGE, WESSEX.

In a long life spent at gaming tables, in brothels, up mountains and in the bush, I've gained valuable insights into human nature. Anyone called 'Jasper' is an arrogant, untrustworthy scoundrel. Anyone called 'Cedric' is liable to be worse. And anyone called 'Piers' should be shot on sight. Don't say you've never learned anything from my memoirs, for these are True Facts.

In the criminous line, arrogant, untrustworthy scoundrels might be valued customers. The Prof's reputation for ingenious mercilessness convinces Jaspers and Cedrics to modify their habits in one particular. Your slick wastrel thinks nought of running up sky-high tabs on the never-never with tradesmen. However, the most unreliable gadabout – even a *Piers* – understands that a bill from Professor Moriarty must be settled to the farthing the instant it falls due. Otherwise, the flour sack and the Eton whip are but the beginning of a hard education.

'Wessex,' I spat. 'Been through it on a train a time or two. Sheep-shagger country. Nothing worth shooting except wild ponies and potty parsons. Can't say I've heard of Jasper Stoke. Is Trantridge a village or a house?'

'Both. An estate of six thousand acres, it incorporates an ancient forest called The Chase. Trantridge Hall has been in the Stoke family since 1855. Properly, the tribe are the Stoke-*d'Urbervilles*. When the usurer Simon Stoke bought the property, he conjoined his humble name with that of a distinguished family thought extinct.'

'This Jasper is Old Simon's son?'

'Nephew. Simon's son and heir was killed over twenty years ago.'

'Oh ho! Did slippery Jasper ease his way to the fortune with grease on the back stairs or ground glass in the brandy butter?'

'Alexander Stoke-d'Urberville was murdered by his mistress, Theresa Clare. A stupid girl who, to complicate matters, claimed descent from the d'Urbervilles. She was hanged at Wintoncester. I despise amateurs, Moran. Murder is a calling. Few have the gift.' [1]

I wasn't surprised Moriarty could spout the facts. He committed volumes of the *Newgate Calendar* to memory, and had the lives of Jonathan Wild or Charley Peace off by heart. Reverting to the monotone drone which hampered his original career as a university lecturer, he would bore the

Conduit Street Comanche with lectures about ill-prepared, foolish fellows – or, as here, fillies – who ventured unwisely into the field of crime. These digressions were *Bedtime Stories for Bad Boys*: instead of 'Say your prayers and wash your hands or else nanny will give you a smack and your best tin soldier will be given to the poor children,' it was 'Scout your lay beforehand and eliminate your witnesses or else Sergeant Bigboots will truncheon your bonce and Jack Ketch will give you the Drop.'

'The slut muddied the waters of succession by birthing at least one bastard,' he continued. 'Her issue by Alexander might have inherited.'

'Don't hold with cousins breeding. The whelps always have withered arms or come out as giant frogs.'

'By most accounts, the child did not survive infancy.'

I looked again at the card. 'So Jasper don't want his family tree pruned?'

'All we know is that he has lived the greater part of his life in the Americas, North and South. He intends to take possession of his family seat and assume the life of a country gentleman.'

'You deduced this from his bloody walking stick?'

'No, I read this in the bloody *Times*.'

A three-month-old newspaper lay on the table. In quiet moments, Moriarty would clip unusual words and proper names out of headlines – they came in handy for anonymous letters of instruction, persuasion or revelation. The section on 'lately arrived' visitors debarking from ships included a notice: 'having lived the greater part of his life in the Americas, North and South, Mr Jasper Stoke now intends to take possession of his family seat and assume the life of a country gentleman'. I assumed that meant bouncing milkmaids, sheltering from sheets of rain in his leaky mansion, and pickling himself in poisonous Wessex 'scrumpy'.

Moriarty stood at the bay window.

'What d'you suppose Stoke wants with us?' I asked.

'I've no idea, Moran. But we shall find out soon enough. A man wearing an American hat is on the point of grasping our bell-pull.'

In Mrs Halifax's parlour, a bell jangled as someone yanked the chain in a frenzy. Usually, this signified the imminence of one of several regulars who paid to be secreted in a boudoir wardrobe with peepholes. For them, frenzied yanking was a way of life. I *deduced* this caller, coarsened by the Americas, was unfamiliar with civilised trappings like doorbells, roofs and trouser buttons.

The Professor whistled into a speaking tube, signalling Selden, the bruiser who kept the door, to admit our prospective client. The tintinnabulation ceased, succeeded by the clumping of heavy boots on our stairs. Our visitor can't have done much Indian fighting or buffalo hunting in the Americas. Anyone this noisy would soon be scalped or starved.

The door pushed open and a giant burst in. He wore a ten-gallon hat which might actually hold the full ten gallons. The norm is scarcely a single gallon and the orthography down to misapprehension of the Spanish for 'high gallant', don't you know? He snatched the stick from my hands, which stung for a day afterwards.

'There y'are, Gertie,' he exclaimed, hugging the cane like a long-missing gold coin. 'I was a-feared I'd lost yuh!'

'Mr Jasper Stoke?' enquired the Professor.

The giant looked perplexed. He wore an odoriferous fleece overcoat. His enormous, blue-stubbled jaw sagged, showing jagged brown teeth.

'No suh, I ain't a…'

'I am Jasper Stoke,' purred a smaller gent who made his way into the room in the giant's wake.

Neither Moriarty or I had thought to *deduce* that stick and card belonged to different people. I wasn't ashamed of the oversight, but it would rankle the Professor.

Stoke carried a curly brimmed topper and no stick. He could walk without support and had the giant on hand for cudgelling folk who got in his way. He was sharply dressed, with a deal of fancy braid on his waistcoat. Darkly handsome, if you care to know that sort of thing. He sported a double-dash of moustache, thin and oiled – with eyebrows to match. One cheek was faintly marred by parallel scars. Something clawed – a kitten or at least kittenish – had once had a go at him. His neat, white hands said 'card sharp' rather than 'cowboy'.

There I go, making *deductions* with the best of them. We may have theorised from the wrong stick, but I'd been spot on at 'right bastard'. Takes one to know one, as they say – before *they* get punched in the head for smugly spouting platitudes.

'This is my top boy, Dan'l,' Stoke said, indicating the stick cuddler. 'Known in three territories as Desperado Dan'l. There's a price on his head for killing a man…'

'T'ain't right, Mr Jass,' Dan'l said. 'Only white men I killed were shot fair and square in the front. That price ain't legal. Ain't no law against killing a Chinese in the back. Not accordin' to Judge Bean, and if'n it's his ruling in Texas, it's good enough for Arizona. Aye, and Engerland, too.' [2]

Moriarty was impatient with this legal footnote. 'What can we do for you, Mr Stoke-d'Urberville?'

One of Stoke's brows flicked up.

'Professor Moriarty, I want a dog killed.'

II

'No crime too small' was never exactly Moriarty's slogan, but the criminal genius would apply himself to minor offences if an unusual challenge was presented. To whit, if a sweetshop had a reputation for being impossible to pilfer from, he'd devote as much brainpower to a scheme for lifting a packet of gobstoppers as he would a plan for abstracting the Crown jewels from the Tower of London.

Before you ask – yes, Moriarty did ponder that particular lay. Rather than pull off the coup bungled by Thomas Blood [3], he negotiated quietly with a terrifying Fat Man in Whitehall. The plan was sold to HM government for a tidy sum, enabling the Yeoman Warders to institute countermeasures. Well-known objects are nigh impossible to fence at anything like list value, anyway. In 1671, the baubles were valued at £100,000, but Blood said he'd be lucky to get £6,000 for the mess of jewel-encrusted tat. The Professor was tempted to return annually to the well with improved schemes, but the prospect of getting further on the wrong side of the Fat Man gave even him pause.

Any rate, assassinating dogs was not generally in our line. On occasion, we had adversely affected the health of certain horses. If there were more lucre in fixing dog fights, we'd have applied similar methods to the odd pit bull.

But there isn't and we hadn't. In Russia, I'd hunted wolves with a Tartar war-bow – but that was sport, not business.

I doubted Jasper Stoke-d'Urberville was bothered by a neighbour's yapping pooch in darkest Trantridge. If that were the case, Dan'l could settle its hash. I'd already noted Gertie's suitability for puppy braining. With Dan'l's weight behind her, I dare say the stick could fell a prehistoric mastodon.

But our prospective client had brought his doggie problem to us.

'I am prepared to pay five thousand pounds,' Stoke said, 'for a pelt.'

Even at today's shocking prices, not a sum to be sniffed at, sneezed on or otherwise nasally rejected.

'Mr Stoke-d'Urberville,' said the Professor, rolling the name around like a sheik savouring a sheep's eyeball before popping it between his back teeth, 'whose recommendation brought you to our door?'

'I've had doings with Doctor Quartz of New York…'

The Professor flicked his fingers. Stoke knew enough to shut up.

Some said Jack Quartz, vivisectionist and educator, was to the Americas what Moriarty was to Britain. [4] You were well advised not to suggest the equivalence in either's earshot. I knew Quartz was still smarting over Moriarty's Surprise Valley Gold Mine coup, a foot set in his sphere of influence – though its fabulous output had run dry after a few months, leaving the Firm on the scout for prospects like Stoke-d'Urberville. Moriarty expressed concern that Yankee tentacles were feeling about the globe. Quartz had supposedly secret treaties with the Unione Corse and the Camorra in Southern Europe and Dr Nikola and the Si-Fan in Asia. Outwardly, Moriarty and Quartz maintained courteous, professional relations: each would refer petitioners departing for foreign shores to the other.

The Lord of Strange Deaths could sit at their table, should that mandarin deign to dine with beaky barbarians. The Grand Vampire, chief of Paris' *Les Vampires*, might have been admitted to the sewing circle, but no holder of that title had lived long enough in the office to take a hand in this Great Game.

Bet you didn't know the world was cut up like that.

'I am aware of Quartz,' conceded the Professor. 'Outline your situation, omitting no relevant detail.'

Stoke sat in the client's chair. He lit a cheroot and took his ease.

'I'll give you the straight of it, Professor,' he began. 'A year back, I reached an unwelcome conclusion. I was about to be run out of Tombstone, Arizona. That's a silver town. Previously, I made money in silver. Not digging it out of dirt, digging it out of miners. I operated saloons, gambling hells, rooming houses, some French girls. The real earner is baths. For the privilege of staying in business, everyone in Tombstone tithes to a brood of badged-up robbers. The Earps. Every damn brother holds some office. Federal marshal, town sheriff, tax collector. All want paying. Town has a shrinking economy. Mines are flooded. Silver's petering out. So the Earps saw no reason to let me retain the remainder of my income. They were set on discussing matters at a particular corral where financial disputes are oft-times settled with long rifles. I saw no profit in war, but the alternative was unprepossessing at best. Then, as providence has it, word came via telegraph. An estate is mine for the taking in a country where constables' hands might be out for pay-off but don't have Buntline Specials in them. I gathered my top boys and set out to stake my claim.'

'I got powerful sick on the boat,' put in Dan'l. 'Puked like to fill the wide ocean deep.'

Stoke shrugged.

'My spread is the Trantridge Estate, in Wessex. Uncle Si, who used to be called "Simon Screw-the-marks", bought it after a lifetime of squeezing pennies from widows. He didn't live long enough to enjoy his spread, but Auntie hung in there. On her deathbed for thirty years, by my reckoning. When she finally kicked the bucket, it turned out I'm the only living relative. I inherit the entirety of her holdings. The land, the village, a forest, a church, flocks of sheep, herds of cattle, fields of whatever muck they grow. Even a saloon. A *pub* they call it. The Old Red Dog. As Master of Trantridge, I own *people*… peasants, serfs, yokels. *Slaves.*'

In school, they say Wilberforce abolished slavery in the Empire and Lincoln freed the blacks in the Civil War. Abolition sounds impressive, doesn't it? It bears repeating that all the acts and decrees and petitions – plus the maintenance of an anti-slaving fleet off West Africa – didn't make slavery *go away*. Busybodies just made slavery *illegal* and, therefore, much, *much* more profitable. Pass a law against any endeavour and the honest merchants drop it. So who do you think takes over? Yes, *criminals*. There are laws against murder, theft or blackmail, but no windy politician or curate gets up and takes a bow for *abolishing* 'em. I've knocked about and seen plenty of human flesh bought, sold and put to work. The child purchased outright for six shillings in Piccadilly is as much a slave as any native on a block for ten dirham in Marrakech.

'Auntie kept a light rein on Trantridge,' continued Stoke. 'She never got over losing her sight, much less the cluster-hump with cousin Alec's murdering whore. A manager, Braham Derby, oversees rents, tributes and whatnot. This goof-off let the tenants misremember their situation, settle into a life of unearned ease and comfort. They're on d'Urberville property. All they keep from their labours is the gift of the master. *Id est*, me. With the old lady planted, the situation is in flux.

'On the trip over, while Dan'l was a-heaving, I read up German books on "economic models". Having just lost one business, I'm not about to be beggared again. Trantridge isn't like a silver town: big money for a few years, tailing out to nothing when the seam is exhausted, with the added drawback of thieving Earps. It's more akin to the big Texas cattle outfits or the old Southern cotton plantations: potentially big money forever, if the peons are ridden hard. The "economic model" can work, so long as malcontents are dealt with smartly.

'English landlords have sweated the paddies for generations. If the fighting Irish can be ground under by milksops, Wessexers ought to be a pushover, right? Hang a few, burn out a couple of hovels, cut some fences and they'll get an *understanding*. Then, I sit back and enjoy the life of a country gent. Buy a seat in parliament and a box at Toneborough Race Track.'

Stoke sat back and took a puff. I wondered when the dog would come into it. 'Economic models' are all very well, but if you put a dog at the beginning, there had damn well better be barking before act two.

'First priority is to explain to my tenants – as much my property as the sheep, chickens and crops – that I intend to exercise full rights. I had Derby, kept on in strictly advisory capacity, call a meeting at the Village Hall and make sure every man-jack turns up. So, this hubbub of smock-frock, fringe-beard straw-suckers sat on hard benches, wishing they were in the Red Dog. I kept 'em waiting a few hours.

'At last, I strode in. Place went hush. You could hear the tinkling of my silver spurs. My boys were stationed at strategic points, coat-tails folded back to show iron on their hips. In German economics, you learn to impose your will on a workforce through theatrical devices. Trantridgers have never seen the like of these *hombres*. Lazy-Eye Jack has been in a range war or two, Nakszynski the Albino once ate a Canadian mounted policeman's liver and Dan'l here fills a room without hardly trying.

'I delivered a speech, nothing too hard to follow. Two or three points, with pauses so the outraged babble could die down. What they considered theirs is mine. When the complaining went on too long, Lazy-Eye fired a slug into a beam. Shut everyone up. A roomful of clods stuck fingers in their ears. I awaited the inevitable. The point of giving the whole herd the bad news all at once is to stir the toughest, most resolute c---sucker into making a move. Then, you knock him down and the rest fall in line.'

Professor Moriarty, a follower of economic theory, nodded approval.

'So, who got up but Diggory Venn, a f---ing *startling* individual. Apache red in the face and hands. Owing to his former profession of peddling sheep-dye, if you can believe it. Nowadays, he wanders the lanes preaching dignity of labour and the rights of man. A veritable c--t. Venn isn't even a tenant. Just passing through. I counted on there being someone like him at the meeting. Venn aspired to go head-to-head about what I categorise as a "workable economic model" and he calls "bounden servitude". Of course, this wasn't a debate. This was an announcement.

'I gave the sign and Lazy-Eye and the Albino served the reddleman the way they treat sod-busters in Texas. Dragged onto the village green, tied to the village pump and given a village barbed-wire whipping. His back wound up matching his face and hands. The complaints stopped. Trantridge began to turn a profit… for me. Tenants might go a trifle hungry or have to patch up old coats rather than buy new, but that's how things are ordered in accordance with the property laws in Jolly Old England. Now, it's my turn to get comfortable… which I managed for about a fortnight.'

The Professor paid close attention.

'Venn is whipped. If he makes more trouble, I'll have him up at the assizes for sedition. Braham Derby has to listen to whining yokels and isn't exactly joyful, but keeps book smartly. Besides, I also shelter his sister Mod, the only poke-worthy baggage in the county.'

'Miss Mod's so purty,' Dan'l said, in tones which suggested Gertie had a rival. Stoke's expressive eyebrow twitched at his top hand's gush. Mod Derby was a tender point with him, which suggested she'd be worth meeting. Even a double-dyed Jasper can have a blind spot.

'Mod's a step up from her brothers, that's sure.'

'Brothers?' jabbed Moriarty.

'Besides Braham, who's useful enough when it comes to following milk yields and pig prices, there's Saul, a dreamy mooncalf.'

'I like Saul,' Dan'l said. 'He talks to me.'

'That's all you can say for Saul Derby,' conceded Stoke. 'He rubs along with Dan'l. He even cosies up reasonably with the Albino, who frightens most as much as… well, as much as you do, Professor.'

Moriarty smiled, not unpleased.

'The Derbys are like Injun scouts, you know. Injuns don't ever really go tame, but once they're beaten they see reason. Wessex, it transpires, is as fraught as the West. Adders in the fields. Mires on the moors. Dyed-red rabble-rousers. Escaped convicts from Prince Town Gaol. It's a marvel they don't have f---ing Earps, while they're at it. Though I'd rather be up against a Buntline Special than Parson Tringham's campfire bogey. You can backshoot even the fastest *pistolero*. With Tringham's dog, bullets don't take.'

'Who is Parson Tringham?' asked the Professor.

'Another unwelcome visitor. Breezed up one afternoon, eighty years old and babbling foolishness. I'd not underestimate the damage this mule head has done in a lifetime of sticking his prick into other people's compost. Makes a hobby of the d'Urberville family. Can you credit it? Preacher digs about in someone else's history for jollies. Even my daffy aunt knew better than let him cross her threshold. With her gone, Tringham wanted another stab at getting into "the archives". I should've had the Albino cut his throat and dump him in The Chase. Instead, Braham turned him away. He slunk to the saloon and told his tale of a dog.'

Now, we were getting to it.

'I had this later from Lazy-Eye. He's courting Car Darch, a local strumpet. They do their carousing in the Red Dog. Tringham came in, settled by the fire, ordered a pint of ole goat piss, and yarned to the starving serfs – they've tin enough in their pockets for drink, notice. He told 'em how their pub got its name…'

As he talked, Stoke leaned forward, voice low, cheroot-end burning bright, eyebrows like horns.

'My uncle bought the d'Urberville name outright. I couldn't tell you who his father… my grandfather… was, but I've a parchment listing d'Urbervilles all the way back to Sir Pagan, who came over in 1066. Simon Stoke was from no one out of nothing and laid out gelt for centuries of tradition. He bought *ancestors*. Also, the family seat, a pew in the church and a mess of ghost stories. A phantom coach heard when a d'Urberville is about to die. Just to confirm that Uncle Si got the family curse with the name, it was reported running to schedule when Cousin Alec was pig-stuck. Tess the Knife is supposed to haunt us too. Her spook can be recognised because her head lolls the wrong way, on account of vertebrae separating when she was hanged.'

'I seen the Brokeneck Lady,' Dan'l said. 'By The Chase, at night, net over her face, wailing…'

The giant shook in his fleece. Stoke was irritated by the interruption.

'You can set aside the phantom coach and the moaning murderess. It's the dog that's a bother. A great red hound. A big bastard beast. This is what I want killed. I want its hide above the fireplace in Trantridge Hall. I want its paws made into tobacco pouches. I want its teeth on a necklace for my fancy woman. I want its tail wound round the brim of my tall hat.'

Moriarty tapped his teeth with a yellow knuckle.

'This dog of yours…'

'He goes by "Red Shuck".'

'This "*Red Shuck*"? Am I to understand this is not a *living* animal but a *ghost*?'

Stoke stubbed out his cheroot and nodded grudgingly.

'Yes, it's supposed to be a ghost, but, answer me this… *Can a ghost rip out a strong man's throat*?'

III

I'm going to interrupt. I know, just as we'd got to *the dog*. So far, like Tristram Shandy, Red Shuck has barely figured in a story which purports to be all about him. Now, I'll tell you about the dog.

Stoke gave us the gist he had from Lazy-Eye Jack of what Tringham told the Trantridge soaks – which the parson, in turn, had gleaned from old Wessex wives. At the end of this chain of Chinese whispers, we got *great red hound… big bastard beast… said to be a ghost… ripped-out throat*. Very ominous and in line with Stoke's stated policy of theatrical effect, but scarcely useful intelligence. Moriarty had me pop round to the British Museum and look up our prospective quarry. The prime source on Sir Pagan d'Urberville is the *Historia Ecclesiastica of Orderic Vitalis* [5] and there's a chapter on Red Shuck in the Reverend Sabine Baring-Gould's *Book of Were-Wolves* [6].

So, herewith, the terrible tale of the 'Curse of the d'Urbervilles'. Read it by candlelight at midnight and be prepared to whiten your hair and soil your drawers.

As Stoke mentioned, Sir Pagan 'came over in 1066'. This signifies that, like many of the best families, the d'Urbervilles were founded by a bandit whose crown-snatching patron could bestow estates as he saw fit. During the Norman Conquest, Pagan was a sly, ginger-headed youth. How anybody could advance in a priest-ridden era with his name is beyond me! I imagine he spent his life trying to convince folk it was pronounced 'Pah-*ganne*'.

He was one of seventy-six Frenchmen who claimed to have put that fatal arrow into Harold at the Battle of Hastings. Several began the day fighting on the English side and three didn't even have right arms. An ancestor of the spotty prig who flogged me for misappropriation of buns at Eton shot the King from Calais. He claimed God's winds fetched his shaft straight into Harry's eye. This leads me to deem the typical eleventh-century frog no more trustworthy than today's nation of moustache musketeers, bedroom bandits and painted midgets. Sir Pagan, at least, was at the battle.

Having just taken over a whole country, the new king had a lot on his plate. For a start, he was on a tear to get everyone who'd scorned him as William the Bastard to hail him as William the Conqueror. Bill the Conk couldn't be bothered to sort through the claims, so seventy-six lying bowmen got knighted in a job-lot. After that, they felt literally entitled to claim their own fiefdoms. Sir Pagan d'Urberville's land-grab netted him a third of Wessex. He built himself a castle at Trantridge.

Titled and landed, Sir Pagan toadied less to the Conqueror, but knocked along with the Bastard's son, William Rufus. William I was an empire builder, a man with a mission; William II was an empire enjoyer, a pursuer of virile pastimes. Junior succeeded to the English throne in 1087 and grumbled that he would have preferred Normandy, which went to his older brother. With his pal crowned, Sir Pagan became eminent. After William Rufus remarked offhand that d'Urberville's forest offered the finest 'chase' in his kingdom, it became known as The Chase.

The new king was a fiend for hunting. His primary interest was any game animal which might provide horns, hide or tusks to decorate his castles. William II was killed by a close friend while they were out after deer. Something similar happened to a tiger-stalking crony of mine in India. It was said Walter Tyrell, William Rufus' slayer, was too good a bowman to make such a mistake. A like criticism was laid against me. I refer the interested reader to my earlier remark about how difficult it can be to *just miss* a shot.

With English game ripe to be brought down by Norman sports, Sir Pagan threw himself into the pursuit. Every huntsman has to have his dogs. The Trantridge kennels became famous. Though he cleans it up somewhat, Baring-Gould recounts a rumour that Sir Pagan d'Urberville himself sired the litter which became his hunting pack, getting puppies on a she-wolf imported from the Harz Mountains. The dogs came out big, hungry and red.

Even taking the she-wolf story with a pinch of the proverbial, Sir Pagan remained essentially French in his habit of tumbling anything which strayed past. You're aware of the custom of *droit de seigneur*, that the feudal lord is entitled – nay, obliged – to take first jump at any local bride on her wedding night? Pagan imported the custom to England. When grooms complained, he ruled that, to be impartial about it, he'd take his pleasure with them too. Extensive romping and riding to hounds made Sir Pagan a fine, rollicking fellow to lordly Norman chums and a bitterly hated tyrant to smelly Saxon underlings.

After a few years' happy hunting, Sir Pagan's dickybird got him into trouble. Comes to us all, I'm afraid. Sir Pagan, like several of his lineal and nominal descendents, came a cropper because he stuck it in the wrong hole – or at least the wrong hole-bearer.

Word got out that d'Urberville was regularly rogering peasant bridegrooms. Venic of Melchester, a Saxon monk, left his monastery to raise a fuss about such shocking behaviour. He turned up at Trantridge in the middle of a feast and had the poor judgement to deliver a fiery sermon against sodomy, fornication and the wicked habit of calling English meats by French names. Sir Pagan was a firm adherent of the philosophy that you could hunt or prod anything and often do both. He had Venic whipped and set off after the monk with his dogs. Baring-Gould doesn't go into what happened after Pagan ran down his prey in The Chase – but it's a fair bet Venic got served in the Bulgarian fashion and staggered away bow-legged. Don't see the attraction myself, but Mrs Halifax says it takes all sorts to butter a biscuit.

Aggrieved, Venic took a petition of complaint to the court, calling for the King's Justice upon Sir Pagan. When William Rufus laughed off his pal's high-spirited prankery, the monk went to the church and called for Heaven's Justice. The Bishops knew the king and his axeman lived closer to their palaces than the Pope in Rome, let alone God Almighty, and dismissed Venic as a crank. At this, he despaired. He swore aloud at a crossroads that he would deal with the Devil, if Hell's Justice were levelled against Sir Pagan d'Urberville…

Now pledged a monk for Satan, Venic returned to The Chase, where he lived wild, more beast than man. He harried Sir Pagan's men-at-arms, killed the livestock and raided foodstores. Sir Pagan made his own vow to kill Venic and – for months – set out regularly with his dogs. Even before Venic moved in, The Chase was reputedly haunted. Paths were ill mapped and changed from day to day. If you walked around the wood, it was no larger than a small-holding; if you walked through, it seemed the breadth of a kingdom. Still, Sir Pagan knew his woods and should have been able to catch Venic again.

Failing to bring back his monk's head, he grew moody. He let serfs go inviolate to their marriage beds. He failed to attend court and slid from Royal favour – making room for the rise of Walter Tyrell… and we all know how well that turned out.

He laid off hunting anything but the mad monk.

Cheated of regular prey, the pack became unruly, vicious, and fought among themselves. Soon, they were killing and eating each other. That's when Sir Pagan first noticed Red Shuck. Originally the runt of the she-wolf's litter, he grew stronger, surviving many battles. He grew wilder, redder even, as if taking on substance from dogs he killed, 'til he stood tall as a pony, long as a boat – with bloody froth about his mouth and fangs like daggers. Sir Pagan's remaining cronies cautioned him against the dog, but the Master was pleased with Red Shuck. He thought that only when it had consumed the hearts of the rest of the pack would it be able to root out Venic. At last, Red Shuck had the kennel to himself, as Sir Pagan was left alone with his servants by the desertion of his household. His wife and children removed themselves across Wessex and established the d'Urberville seat of Kingsbere.

Still, Venic was not found, no matter how knight and dog sought him. He would appear in the village, speaking against Normans in general and Sir Pagan in particular – but when d'Urberville and Red Shuck came, he was back in The Chase. This went on until Sir Pagan took it into his head to flush out his quarry by burning the forest to ash. In India, this is known as *hunquah*. It's a tricky practice, as likely to raze the village as flush out the tiger.

Hayricks were carted to a clearing and a fire started. It wouldn't spread, as if the breath of Hell kept it back. At sunset, Sir Pagan sensed his enemy nearby and sicced his dog. Red Shuck bounded from the clearing, intent on rending Venic apart. Fearful cries, human and animal, were heard. Sir Pagan's last servants abandoned him – except one page, necessary to recount the end of the story. Sir Pagan ranted at the trees, his failing fire and the skies. Then, who should step into the clearing but Venic of Melchester, wearing the bloody skin of Red Shuck.

Most versions of the tale throw in 'hold, varlet'/'Norman dog'/'Saxon swine'/'have at thee, sirrah' chatter out of *Ivanhoe*. I imagine the actual talk between mortal enemies ran to free exchange of Old English and French words not in Sir Walter Scott's vocabulary.

Sir Pagan reached for his sword. Venic wrapped the dog-hide around his shoulders, until it was tighter than his own skin. Then his eyes got big. He had more and longer teeth. He was covered in red fur. He was, in fact, Red

Shuck, walking on his hind legs like a man. Baring-Gould's version is that the dog was the monk all along, but *Orderic Vitalis* has it that Venic commingled with Red Shuck just as the top dog had taken on the strength of the pack – by consuming his flesh and spirit. At any rate, this thing which was both Red Shuck and Venic fell upon wicked Sir Pagan and tore out the knight's gullet. To finish off his meal, the big dog ate d'Urberville's still-beating heart.

Since that day, the legend goes, Red Shuck has lived in The Chase, snacking off lost children, feasting on d'Urberville meat whenever the family produces a tyrant or villain. Which, as you might expect, has happened often.

Over the centuries, dozens of dastardly d'Urbervilles have been killed in circumstances ambiguous enough to allow the legend of the avenging demon dog to enjoy periodic revivals. Few of the family died in bed – unless you count those stabbed by their popsies like Alec Stoke-d'Urberville or poisoned by impatient heirs like Puritan General Godwot d'Urberville. No wonder the true line was extinct when Shylock Si was rooting for a new name. It's a mystery the d'Urbervilles lasted as long as they did, considering an apparently hereditary predisposition to suspicious accident, outright homicide, unusual suicide (Sir Tancred d'Urberville arranged to be eaten by rooks), inexplicable mutilation and unsolved disappearance.

The phantom coach is a sixteenth-century addition to the family's spectral register, summoned by Lizzie d'Urberville to fetch her naughty children off to Hades. When you say 'naughty children', you mean broken crockery and pulled pigtails... when my sanctimonious pater said 'naughty children', he meant gambling debts and housemaids in the pudding club... when a sixteenth-century d'Urberville said 'naughty children', she meant violated churchyards, drowned schoolfellows and a castle burned to the ground.

Before and after the story of the coach was put about, the primary d'Urberville ghost was Red Shuck. However, upon examination of first-hand accounts, the spook tales mostly amount to a d'Urberville dying and within three months someone seeing a dog in the dark which might have been red but might equally not, or could also have been a large goat or a stile with a blanket thrown over it.

It's on record that, at various times, rashes of savage attacks on animals and people have taken place in or near The Chase. In the 1820s, the naturalist Dunstan d'Urberville advanced a theory that the legend of 'Red Shuck' related to some as-yet uncatalogued animal found only in the thick of the ancient woodland.

In clubrooms, I've run across the odd sportsman – Long John Roxton comes to mind – obsessed with hunting specimens which aren't in the books. Undeterred by the obituaries of predecessors who actually have pre-deceased them on the trail of monsters, they set out to bag Scotch lake serpents or the Beast of Gévaudan. Few of these Nimrods bring back trophies which don't look like they've been sewn together for a funfair. However, every year, in unexplored corners of the globe, new creatures are catalogued by intrepid men of science – shortly followed by intrepid men of sport, like yours truly. Sticking a Latin name on a lemur or warthog or dragonfly is all very well, but it can't compete with the honour of being the first to pot the marvel and mount it over the mantelpiece. As a veteran of a couple of go-rounds with the Abominable Snowman of the Himalayas, I know whereof I speak.

Duffer Dunstan posited the existence in The Chase of a large, unusually hardy wolf species which had survived the extinction of wolfkind in the rest of the British Isles. While tracking his 'Wessex Wolf', Dunstan tripped over a tree stump and broke his fool leg. He expired, without heir, of odoriferous gangrene and that was the last of the d'Urbervilles.

…Until Simon Stoke saved up his pennies.

IV

Having outlined the Red Shuck legend, as told by Parson Tringham in the Red Dog, Jasper Stoke continued his own story.

'Two nights later, there was a howling in The Chase. I've heard coyotes and I've heard Injuns pretending to be coyotes. This was different. You know that animal screech you hear after someone's been tortured a spell?… After the tough leather has gone out of a hard customer, but before the body's completely done for?… The deep-lungs scream that comes when the mind cracks like a walnut?'

Professor Moriarty nodded, with a tiny smile.

'Well, the howling was worse than *that*. The whole house stirred from their beds, or whoever's beds they were in, and clattered about in nightshirts and boots. We found guns and gathered in the great hall.'

'I fetched Gertie,' Dan'l said.

'Howling seemed to come from all around, as if it had got into the house like a draught. Nakszynski, the coolest of hands, let shot fly and pimpled a suit of armour. The maids quacked like geese. Saul, who isn't all there, sat by a window, gazing out at the bright moon. He looked like a ghost himself. He uttered "Red Shuck", which was the first I heard the name. I asked what he meant, but he was dreaming out loud. Mod stopped me from shaking an answer out of her brother, saying Saul always comes over queer on full-moon nights. Just one more piece of f---ing information calculated not to set the mind at ease.

'The howls were going on full-throat and the Albino firing a shotgun indoors hadn't soothed the ears any. Lazy-Eye Jack heard "Red Shuck" and dug up what he recollects of Tringham's yarn. The phrase "ghost dog" gave me a sudden insight. I was being fooled with by someone who wished ruin to my prospectus for Trantridge. I don't credit tales of infernal animals or a d'Urberville curse. I'm more inclined to lay my troubles on the corporeal, contemporary Diggory Venn. I suspected red-stained fingers in the puddle. I told the boys to track down the howling c--t and put it out of its misery.'

Dan'l looked sheepish at this.

'I expect a deal of smart snapping-to when I give out an order,' continued Stoke. 'On this occasion, there was general hesitation. Though Lazy-Eye hadn't seen fit to pass the parson's ghost story to me, he'd spread it round the bunkhouse, with embellishments to frighten superstitious, ignorant morons...'

He looked at Dan'l.

'Mod and her brothers knew the tale from childhood. So did the servants. I was the only prick to whom Red Shuck was fresh news. As master, it fell to me to venture out with my Winchester and see off the howling nuisance. Braham advised against it, and he's supposed to be the sensible, educated one in his family. Nakszynski was fired up to shoot something which would bleed. We stepped out the big front door. As soon as we were outside, the howling shuts off... and the rest of the yellow-livered curs joined us in the drive...'

'Was anyone absent?' asked the Professor.

'No,' responded Stoke. 'I counted heads and checked off names. I thought, like you, that it was an inside job. But we were all present. At sun-up, two maids and a stablehand gave notice and hared off as if there was an Earp price on their heads. One dolly didn't even stay to pick up her wages. The other said she'll be safer on the game in Casterbridge. Which gives you an idea of what I'm facing.'

'All this from a noise in the night?' I snorted.

'Something got into the chicken coops and tore apart the poultry...'

'Feathers and guts and beaks and eyes everywhere,' elaborated Dan'l. 'Like to put me off mah feed!'

'In daylight, Braham grew back his balls and concluded a fox or a weasel was the guilty party. Maybe a fox *and* a weasel, working together. Nasty critters, foxes and weasels. I ordered new wire fences around the coops, stouter timbers... and restocked the place. No fox-weasel is going to fright me off my land. I got more of the Red Shuck story from Lazy-Eye Jack and Mod. It isn't happenstance Trantridge Hall got raided and howled at. This was direct challenge to me and my position.

'Next night, there was howling again... further off from the house. I'd set night-guards, but they didn't see anything. I was all for charging into The Chase and killing whatever and whoever was behind the racket. Again, I was cautioned against this. After a moment, I saw Braham's right and I'm wrong. Not because a demon dog is waiting in the clearing where wicked Sir Pagan was devoured... but because I knew this was a trick to draw me into the wild woods where I could be done away with in such manner a ghost can take the blame. No law's ever hanged a ghost. So, I insisted we all go back to bed and ignore the rumuckus. I personally had a fine night's sleep.

'Next morning, one of the tenants, Git Priddle, was missing some sheep who'd bled a deal before being fetched off, but that's his problem. Payment was still due and, after the Albino knocked Priddle about a bit, was forthcoming. I know there is subterfuge round Trantridge and still suspect a red hand in it, though Venn hasn't been sighted since he took his back-stripes. I took advantage of the rent-collection round to have the estate entirely searched, prying into every barn and pen to conduct a census of livestock necessary for the accounts, and to see if anyone, or any creature, is concealed. We turned up beasts scurvy tenants were keeping off the rolls and clipped ears with wirecutters to discourage the practice. I'm in two minds about Git Priddle's famous black ram, which strikes me as more likely in hiding than done for, but it didn't show up. No trace of the reddleman either. And no Red Shuck.

'By day, I had The Chase searched, though that's the definition of futile endeavour. Next night, last of the full moon, I thought to get ahead of Red Shuck and frame my own trap. Leaving the Hall and grounds unguarded would be too obvious, so I had the boys sit up after dark, complaining loudly at the inconvenience, then slope off in the small hours as if shirking duty. Trick of it was that, well before sundown, without letting anyone else in on it, Lazy-Eye secreted himself by the coops under a blanket of twigs and leaves which makes him look, even *smell*, like a garbage heap. The old Injun fighter can lay still for days if need be. Among the aliases on his "Wanted – Dead or Alive" poster is "Ambush Jack". He had orders to shoot any c---sucker who showed face on the grounds. That night, there was no howling. I figured Ambush Jack trumps Red Shuck…

'Lazy-Eye wasn't at his post the next morning. His blanket was flung aside and tracks led into The Chase. Dan'l and I set out after him. Trail was plain even in the early morning mist. When we found Jack, in a clearing, he wasn't yet dead. Blood bubbled out of his throat. Air whistled through a hole. He died without saying anything. His holster was empty. We found the gun yards away, still in his hand – Jack's hand wasn't on the end of his arm any more. I'm no tracker, but I could tell something's been about from the broken bushes and trampled grass. In soft earth, we found this…'

From his coat pocket, Stoke produced an object wrapped in a red scarf. He passed it to Moriarty, who unwound the scarf.

'Your department, I think, Moran,' he said, and tossed it over.

I'd seen similar things. It was a plaster of Paris impression of a pawprint, or at least a dent in the ground made by something shaped like a big animal's foot. From the shape, the print was dog or a wolf, but the span suggested something the size of tiger or rhino.

'The detail which springs out of the foolishness of the legend,' continued Stoke, 'is that Red Shuck persecutes d'Urbervilles whenever one of the family is "a tyrant or villain". I'm not given to the vice of self-deception. My tenants view me as tyrant and villain. If that's their comfort, fine. So long as they work and pay and bow and scrape. My plan for Trantridge *depends* on me being tyrant and villain. My conviction, from study of German economics, is that what was once categorised as tyrannical and villainous is, in modern times, respectable and even necessary. That aside, it's my personal whim to play tyrant and villain. As Master of Trantridge, it is my lawful right. This is why I have brought my business to you...'

Moriarty nodded.

'Red Shuck may be a phantom and a fraud, but it's killed my top boy. I can't let that go. Word about Lazy-Eye Jack spread over the county afore noon. And suddenly everyone's talking up that damned Red Shuck. Already, Trantridgers grumble about paying rents and following orders. A few beatings, and even a barn-burning, and they're still not trodden down enough. They whisper that Venic of Melchester has come back in demon dog form to serve me as he served wicked Sir Pagan. This interferes with my affairs, do you understand? My position depends on the exercise of terror. By me, not against me. When I walk about, peasants must crap their britches. They must be in mind of Diggory Venn's bloody back, or Git Priddle's black eye, or the Kail lad's clipped ear, or the poorhouse hells they'll fetch up in if I turn them off the land. I cannot be seen to be afraid. I cannot be struck at without returning the blow *tenfold*. I had it from an old-time Georgia overseer: if one slave runs, hang ten. Most don't have the salt for it, not least because the ones you hang are your own property and their worth comes off your book. But once you do it, they tend their own pens, keep their own troublemakers in shackle.

'In Wessex, I might be able to hang a shepherd or two, but ten would be more trouble than they're worth. So, I pick a family at random, the Balls, and evict 'em, set to wander and beg on the roads and wind up destitute, derelict and, I fervently hope, dead. That's for Lazy-Eye Jack. But it's not enough. While the parson's ghost tale is going round, I can't press on with my economic plan. So there must be no more bedtime stories, no whispers that New Master will get his comeuppance, not even a *hope* of deliverance. You understand? The dog must be killed, even if it doesn't exist. I've come to you, Professor, because I need the *story* killed. Now, can you do that?'

The Professor pondered. Stoke glared intently, playing with his still-glowing cheroot stub.

'Your problem – though inherently absurd – has features of interest,' Moriarty said.

I was interested enough by the mention of £5,000 for a pelt.

Stoke let out breath. People aren't usually relieved when Moriarty involves himself in their affairs, but I suppose it has to happen from time to time.

'Legends of spectral avengers abound,' said the Prof, 'and encourage a persistent fiction that "evil-doers" who, by ingenuity and endeavour, evade human justice must answer to supernatural authority. Such fables are a hindrance to the Calling of Crime. By eliminating your Red Shuck, we chip away at the monument of this myth. I shall accept your commission…'

And the five thousand plums!

'… and replace the fairy tale of Virtue Triumphant with the brute fact of Wickedness Rewarded. A philosophical – nay, a *mathematical* – point must be proved. Your problem provides an opportunity to serve the cause of Higher Thought.'

Moriarty read his German economics too. It's all very well to theorise that wickedness, cruelty, self-interest and the whims of the few overriding the bleats of the many are essential to the furtherance of an efficient, modern society. But, to me, deep-thinkers like Moriarty, Nietzsche and Machiavelli miss an essential truth – *it's a lot of jolly good fun being an 'evil-doer'*. None of these coves seem to relish being a total rotter – though Moriarty, at least, did not confine his evil to theory like some of the windier philosophers. I believe that – in his tiny, shrivelled, eight-months-gone apple of a heart – the Professor got spasms of *enjoyment* from his crimes, for it's a sad rogue who strives his life long to increase the miseries of his fellow man without getting at least a warm feeling when he sees others beggared or dumped in unmarked graves on his account. Everyone knows I'm a sentimental soul.

Moriarty's head oscillated. Dan'l, alarmed, gripped Gertie as if he were worried the Prof was about to turn into a snake as old Venic turned into Red Shuck. I knew the Prof's habits – he was calculating…

'I am currently much involved,' he announced. 'Several crimes require my presence in London…'

This was news to me.

'…you will soon read of the Barrie-McTrostle disinheritance… the Clapham Gas House atrocities… and the Winklesworth & Company stock malfeasance…'

He was making this rot up, but Stoke's eyes goggled – imagining vast feats of inconceivable criminality. Moriarty was not above puffing up his feats by reference to imaginary crimes. Usually, he was deceiving someone about something and had a long game in mind, so I played along.

'There's the abduction of the Ranee of Ranchipur, too,' I put in.

The 'Ranee of Ranchipur' was the professional name of Molly Duff, one of Mrs Halifax's girls. She stained herself brown to pass as a Hindu princess.

Moriarty nodded sagely. 'Yes, an exacting proposition. The Ranee is to be taken from under the Rajah's nose and sold to a Scottish peer during her birthday party. That will require my personal attention.'

Stoke's wonderment was tinctured with dismay as he saw his own knotty problem sliding down the agenda and out of the door.

'However,' said the Professor, 'in this instance, I can with full confidence entrust your dog to my associate, Colonel Moran. He is known far and wide as the greatest hunter of the age. If an animal draws breath, he's killed it.'

The old chest fairly swelled with pride, though I knew the Prof was stroking the client while palming the job off on me.

'I know all about keeping natives under the lash,' I said. 'I doubt those of Wessex differ much from the heathens I ran into out East.'

'Moran will run down to Trantridge with you…'

'…bringing along my guns, what?'

'…suitably armed to bring down any Wessex Wolf. He will take stock of your situation, then act expeditiously to effect a satisfactory outcome.'

Stoke had the temerity to baulk at this.

'I've set a pile of money on the table, Professor… I was hoping for the boss of this outfit, not the top hand.'

'Mr Stoke-d'Urberville, when it comes to tramping through mud and muck after ferocious beasts, the Colonel has far more experience than I. Moran will set down observations and send me regular *communiqués* about his progress…'

This again was news to me, and not entirely welcome.

'A portion of my brain will be fully occupied with Red Shuck. Even if I am removed from the scene of your travails. If you are beset by a mysterious "do-gooder", he or she will be thwarted. On that, you have the word of Professor James Moriarty.'

Which, as far as it went, was impressive. If Moriarty promised to cut your throat or assault your sister and get away with it, you could be assured he'd follow through. Otherwise, his word was worth about as much as my promissory notes to tailors or cabbage-men… but Jasper Stoke, tyrant and villain though he might be, set much by hollow wordage from so distinguished a gent.

V

I packed guns for a trip west.

Impertinent reviewers of my *Heavy Game of the Western Himalayas* made waggish remarks about the Moran propensity for 'droning at length' about *guns*. I still hold those seventy-eight pages, with practical footnotes, on the rifle 'Prometheus' a worthwhile addition to the literature and essential to the understanding of later, more immediately exciting chapters. Discerning readers have given testimonials as to the *fascinating, educational* and *profoundly important* nature of these outpourings from my pen – which not a few rank higher than anything from Dickens or Shelley.

'Prometheus', custom-made by George Gibbs of Bristol, is sadly lost. Having served me better than any woman I've ever paid for, the rifle suffered tragically when pressed into service as a crutch as I hobbled out of an East African jungle on a broken leg. I laid the gun to rest in a grave with the three bearers who deserted me. I don't officially record those sammies, because close-up executions spat from an abused and spoiled weapon can't be set beside the true shots of the gun's great days. But they constituted the final bag. Had 'Prometheus' survived beyond publication of *Heavy Game*, I might have added a literary lion or two to its tally. Luckily, the

Eton coachwhip was to hand when opportunity came to answer my critics.

If you've a fancy to hang the antlers of a Grand Duke in your lodge, you might need a recoilless pistol which looks like a pair of opera glasses and doesn't make a noise louder than a round of applause. Then, Blind Herder's your man. Still, if Red Shuck was actual game, I needed a game rifle. Gibbs & Co. remained my preferred supplier. I'd not named a gun since 'Prometheus', but I'd a rack to choose from. Elephant, lion, tiger, bear, native and witness widows across the Empire could attest to their reliability. I took three rifles, including one calibrated for shots of up to three-quarters of a mile with an optical contraption for sighting purposes. My Webley had finally succumbed when I was forced to use its barrel as a jemmy and its handle as a hammer to extricate myself from the oubliette of Arnsworth Castle. So, I needed a side arm. Officially, Gibbs does not make a revolver – but, as a service to a valued customer, they furnished me a superbly crafted, teak-handled specimen superior to the job lots of shooting iron turned out by Yankee bodgers like Samuel Colt.

It was arranged that, three days after our first consultation, I would meet Jasper Stoke at Paddington Station and we would chuff-chuff west. Before leaving, I conferred with Moriarty in the windowless study where he experimented. He was not busy with other crimes, imaginary or genuine. He was dissecting a violin. An Amati of Cremona, if that means anything. He had secured it at auction for a fabulous sum – solely, I believe, to keep it from a rival bidder for whom he had a particular dislike. With dressmakers' scissors and a surgeon's scalpel, he anatomised his fiddle, snipping strings, sundering joins. Perhaps the Prof hoped to find out where the tunes came from.

Looking up from his labours, Moriarty saw me dressed for the country and raised a bony finger to signal I shouldn't leave just yet.

He pushed away from his workbench, rolling his chair on castors across uncarpeted floor towards a cabinet of many drawers. The Professor boasted that this contained a thousand unique methods of murder – though, when someone was to be got rid of, he usually left the mamba venom envelope gum and asphyxiating orchids to his oriental peer, relying instead on tried-and-true British bludgeoning or my own marksmanship. He pulled a drawer marked '58' and took out a small cardboard box.

'It's not a spider, is it, Moriarty? You know my opinion on arachnids!'

The Professor opened the box, which was full of apparently ordinary bullets. Moriarty plucked a rimmed .455 pistol cartridge. They make them by the thousand. But instead of dull lead, its nose gleamed sterling silver.

I whistled and commented, 'Pricey.'

'Indeed,' Moriarty said. 'Material is costly and manufacture complicated. But you lecture often on the importance of using the proper loads. The literature would have it that supernatural game such as Red Shuck requires a *silver* bullet. I shall want a precise account of every shot fired. Any rounds not discharged are to be returned when this matter is settled.'

I slipped the box into my pocket.

'Moriarty, do you give any weight to the notion that there's a ghost or goblin behind this business? Our client plainly doesn't...'

'Our client, though not unperceptive in some matters, is a *limited* man.'

'I've seen mysteries beyond explanation in the East, but run into many more which turn out to be some clever fakir trying to put one over on the white man.'

'Dullards would have you believe that once you have eliminated the impossible, whatever remains, however improbable, must be the truth... but to a mathematical mind, the impossible is simply a theorem yet to be solved. We must not eliminate the impossible, we must *conquer* it, suborn it to our purpose. Whatever remains, however dully probable, will satisfy earthbound thinkers, while we have the profit of the hitherto *inconceivable*. Besides, I daresay anyone with a silver bullet in his brains couldn't tell it from lead.'

From this, I knew Moriarty was playing his own game. When he rattled on, he was mesmeric. He could convince you *Alice's Adventures in Wonderland* – also the product of 'a mathematical mind', remember – made sound sense. Most criminals were so rapt by his phrases and his eyes and his snake-neck wobble they blithely did whatever he wanted without knowing why. I was not immune, but had been with the Firm long enough to know the Prof's tricks.

I left Moriarty to his musical experiments, and Chop drove me to the station.

VI

In our first-class compartment on the Great Western Railways train to Stourcastle, I quizzed Jasper Stoke about the layout at Trantridge. It's advantageous to know the territory before setting a foot there. I had conned maps, almanacs and gazetteers; now I drew Stoke out on things nobody thought to set down. You can *deduce* – to use the word of the week – a great deal from *smells*. Not a pleasant topic, especially when the odours of Wessex are under discussion, but revealing.

'The Chase stinks like Pennsylvania,' Stoke said. 'Open-cast mine country.'

'Is there any mining?' I asked.

'In the New Forest, towards Bramshurst, there are pits, but nothing in The Chase. I can't even say what the luciferous stench is. Chemicals in the ground? And something rotten. Like eggs gone off.'

Stoke filled up the compartment with fug, puffing on his cheroots. He gave a lot away when smoking. He tried to exhale confident clouds, Indian signals announcing himself as Big Chief, but chewed the stub, got leaf-bits stuck to his teeth and punctured the will-o'-the-wisp. A man for putting up a front, he couldn't keep it together. No wonder he'd been chased out of Tombstone by the improbably named Earps. He was buckling in Wessex, and – if he didn't get his dog-pelt soon – would probably be chased out of Trantridge too.

I can't say I took to Stoke. British-born, he might be – but American in his ways. Big-talking, craven, insensitive and miserly. In his terms, a compleat c---sucker. If he ever ran across Jim Lassiter, he'd be dead in the dust before he could clear his holsters. Still, at least he wasn't a bloody Mormon.

He didn't want to look yellow-livered, though – despite his tale of terror – and compensated with high-handed, down-the-nose lecturing. In advance of the promised five thou, a small sum had passed from his coffers to ours. He felt this entitled him to treat Moriarty & Moran as jobbing carpenters hired to put up shelves. He gave out German cant about 'payment by results' and it still rankled that the Professor wasn't personally in Wessex dancing to his tune.

Dan'l, the savage giant, was more forthcoming. From him, I picked up the fact that The Chase put folk in a funk even before the story of Red Shuck was revived. This stretch of ancient woodland had been the site of many crimes, it seems – now even the most daring poacher hesitated to trespass there. Dan'l wasn't that troubled by the beast which had done for Ambush Jack, which he said did less damage than a mountain lion. He'd killed mountain lions with Gertie, and showed me deep old scars to illustrate the yarn. I have a few of those too and we played a jolly game of pulling up sleeves and opening shirts to display manly badges. However, Dan'l was scared of the Brokeneck Lady. Something was done to Theresa Clare in The Chase which she didn't complain about at the time. It excited her spirit post-mortem, though. Dan'l said that, while taking his turn on guard, he'd seen her, veiled, head lolled to one side, creeping out of the woods.

'Put the fear in me, she did,' he said. 'Mountain lion's nothin', but there's no tellin' with a haint. All sorts of ways a haint can hex you.'

Stoke snorted, but I took note. There might be a bagful of spooks to deal with, though our client only laid bounty on the dog. Still, I had a box of silver bullets.

At Stourcastle, a covered trap waited.

It was, of course, raining.

VII

Moriarty asked me to set down my observations. Very well…

I have visited all the shitholes of the world and Wessex ranks with the worst of 'em. Whores smell better in Afghanistan. Weather is nicer in Tibet. Cuisine is more appetising in the Australian outback, where snakes count as a Sunday delicacy you look forward to all week. And the natives are more welcoming in the Andaman Island Penal Colony.

The dull, driving rain made me miss London's pea-souper.

Two bedraggled souls stood outside the station, sheltering under a lean-to which was near collapse.

'Where's the coachman?' barked Stoke.

This was addressed to a burly man with the puff gone out of him. A well-chewed moustache and creeping baldness betokened a tendency to fret and fuss.

'Come on, Derby,' continued Stoke. 'Out with it.'

Derby didn't elucidate, but his smaller companion – a reedy, floppy-haired, permanently smiling cove in a peculiar tweed singlet and dun-coloured hooded cape – piped up cheerily.

'Coachman fled the scene,' he said, with a strange whistling voice. 'Took fright. Not the only one. More maids quit. And the cook. And Chitty, the butler. Thring's taken his place. We'll have to make do as best we can, Mr Stoke. As best we can.'

Stoke, angry at the news, made no introductions. I gathered these were Braham Derby, Stoke's overseer, and his purportedly mad brother, Saul.

'You should have hired someone,' Stoke said. 'How does it look to have my manager doing scut-work like carriage-driving?'

Braham shrugged. 'No one's to be had, Mr Stoke. Not at any price.'

I understood. Besides the prospect of being ripped by Red Shuck, none of the locals wanted anything to do with fetching home the hated New Master. They'd be best pleased if Stoke caught a chill on the platform and died.

'Been more howling,' Saul said, almost cheerfully.

He turned to me, wide eyes darting up as if he glimpsed something high over my shoulder, swooping towards my back. When I cast an eye behind me, there was nothing. He caught me once and I resolved not to be fooled again. In turn, Stoke, Dan'l and even Braham – who ought to be used to his brother's ways – owl-twisted their necks and got rain in their faces. Saul whistled to himself, seemingly unaware. I had him down as either the village idiot or a genius wearing the cloak of lunacy.

Saul was snug in the carriage while Braham sat up on the seat in the wet and grimly drove us to Trantridge. Stoke said nothing to encourage it, but Dan'l – who evidently felt the mooncalf a kindred spirit – asked for news.

'Much disturbance among mammals,' said Saul. 'Hares and rabbits and rats and shrews and stoats. The Hall is plagued with their mischief. The creatures of The Chase are quitting their homes. The pink-eyed man shoots at them. But they get into the house and fight the cats. All nature is in an uproar. I have written to the press about the phenomenon.'

Stoke snorted. He didn't know what it means when small game flees. A bigger predator is about.

I was in tiger country.

VIII

Seen through a veil of drizzle, Trantridge Hall was what you'd expect – big front to impress the peasants, but boarded upper windows and fallen tiles suggested lack of care with the upkeep.

The drill for greeting the Master in the lesser great houses of the shire counties is standard. Even if the landowner has only popped into town to have a tooth pulled or purchase the latest number of *La Vie Parisienne*, he expects to come home and find the servants have left off whatever they were doing – or pretending to do – and lined up smartly on the front lawn, showing teeth in beaming smiles.

If it's wet, that's just hard cheese. Valets, maids and the like are too afraid of dismissal without references to come down with sniffles like high-born folk.

The showing outside the Hall was like inspection the morning after a skirmish. Gaps in the ranks betokened casualties or – most likely – desertions. Such smiles as were on display didn't pass muster. Here, dismissal in disgrace was early parole.

The carriage halted. An undersized menial advanced to open the door and lower the step, then offer Stoke the temporary shelter of an umbrella. Thring had a red splotch birthmark as if a ball of mud flung at his eye had spattered half his face. He was a jumped-up footman, filling the too-big tail-coat of the butler who'd taken flight.

'Welcome home, sir,' Thring said – as if he hated his Master enough to think he deserved a place like this.

Stoke grunted and stepped down, boots sinking into the miry, rutted drive. He paid no heed to the line of soggy servants, as if about to make an undignified dash for the front door. In the lea of the gothic door arch was a woman wrapped in oilskins. She took the prize for most convincing sham smile in the vicinity, and even fluttered flirty fingers.

From Dan'l's sigh, I gathered this was his favourite – Braham and Saul's sister Mod. I'd marked her down as 'of interest' because she was reputedly the finest piece on the estate. One would be hard-put to determine the yay or nay of that from her weatherproof bonnet and fishing gear, though she showed a pleasant, pink face.

Thring made no move for the house and Stoke deigned to look at the line. Some maids curtseyed, but most made no effort to pretend they weren't cold and miserable. A *snap* produced more snarling smiles.

Leaning against a wall was a pink-eyed, skull-faced apparition wrapped in a Yankee cowman's duster coat. He had cracked a whip to signal the respect due the Master. Dead-white hair straggled from under his broad-brimmed hat. Even a rank amateur deducer would peg him as Nakszynski the Albino, Stoke's surviving gunhand.

'Back to work, the lot of you,' shouted Stoke – in the circumstances, almost a kindly gesture. He didn't have to say it twice; the servants hurried out of the rain.

Under Thring's umbrella, Stoke trudged towards the door and the charms of Miss Derby.

I unbent myself out of the trap and looked about.

'Best get inside, Colonel,' Braham said. 'Get a hot toddy in you.'

Mod Derby opened her arms and spread oilskin bat wings as if to envelop Jasper Stoke.

Then another woman appeared, from behind a bush, and levelled a rifle at Stoke. He threw himself into the mud, squealing. The grim-faced harpy, dress front torn open and hair caked with dirt and twigs, stood over the Master of Trantridge and took surprisingly steady aim.

The Firm was on the point of losing a client before the job was half started.

The woman's weapon was a Brown Bess. The musket might have been a relic of Waterloo, kept for seventy years in a corner with the brooms. I doubted the would-be assassin had kept her powder dry.

Stoke fairly blubbed for his life. He crab-walked backwards three or four yards, making a muddy arse-and-boot-heel trail in the grass. No wonder he'd quit Tombstone. If an apparition with an antediluvian firearm reduced him to wailing terror, I could imagine the effect of a sharp-eyed Earp with a working Winchester.

'Mattie Ball, come away,' said Braham. 'Kill him and you'll swing for sure.'

The woman didn't take heed. With her thumb, she pulled back the cock.

I strode into the scene and interposed my chest, shoving up against the musket's cold barrelmouth.

'If you want to shoot someone,' I said. 'How about me? Got the sand for that, eh? I'm Colonel Sebastian Moran, of the First Bangalore Pioneers. I've cheated death in all corners of the world and don't fancy a Wessex grave. Not at all, my good woman. If you were in shooting mood, you'd already have discharged this antique.'

I recollected Stoke had turned a family named Ball off the estate. Mattie must be a survivor of the clan, demented by sufferings too sordid to dwell on.

She could fire her musket but once – if, indeed, it would fire. She'd not get a chance to reload, pack and take aim again. The avenging farmgirl wouldn't want to waste her shot on anyone but the author of her misfortunes.

Mattie Ball was demented, but I faced her down. I've done as much to men and beasts – and similarly bloodthirsty females – before. A moment of clarity, of *understanding*, decides the way the cards will fall. Such encounters are over with between the ticks of a clock… but the seconds stretch to hours while you're in it.

Thus far, the turn has always been in my favour.

Hesitation sparked in the woman. I made a grab for her gun, got a grip and forced the barrel upright. I slipped my gloved thumb into the lock, which bit as Mattie Ball jerked the trigger. The lock scarcely penetrated leather.

I wrenched the musket from her hands. The Albino, who should have kept better lookout, was suddenly there, holding Mattie from behind, spade-bladed Bowie to her neck. Not the proper tool for opening a throat, but it'd do.

Braham wanted to protest, but Nakszynski showed yellow teeth in pink gums which matched his eyes. He began a shallow, preliminary cut.

'Enough of that, Chalky,' I said. 'Miss Ball is just leaving.'

I wasn't having some bunny-eyed Johnny-come-lately Yankee Polack mule-skinner spoiling the moment. I'd shared something with Mattie Ball, more intimate than the usual mess between man and woman. I wasn't minded to let it go yet. The knife-touch pricked the woman's soul. Her eyes and teeth were set in defiance.

Nakszynski gave me a 'Who are you?' look, but didn't press on with his murdering.

Stoke, muddied all over, was helped up by Thring and Dan'l. Mod indicated she'd *like* to fuss over him, but held back because of the dirt.

'Hello Mattie,' Saul said. 'I was sorry to hear about your poor mama… and your brothers… and Granver Ball… and…'

I assumed Stoke would have need of Nakszynski's whip. Instead, he broke free of his aides and sloshed at Mattie. Squirting angry tears, he stuck a craven fist into her belly. She doubled, twisting out of the Albino's grip, and fell, retching. Stoke kicked her in the side, and rolled her over. He spat on her and kept kicking. Animal whining and growling came out of him. His kicks echoed inside her chest as if it were a tight drum.

I started to feel the pinch of the gun-cock.

I gently eased it back and removed my throbbing thumb. I was right about the musket's age, but it had either been cared for well over the years or recently restored.

Mattie curled, hugging her face, knees over her stomach. Stoke kept booting her spine. Thring stood by, umbrella raised over his Master's head. A little more rain could hardly put the self-declared tyrant and villain in a sorrier state.

In the spirit of experiment, I cocked the musket and pulled the trigger.

The blast caught everyone's attention. I'd like to say a far-off bird tumbled from the sky, but the ball went wild and fell spent. Brown Bess had a fine record in seeing off England's enemies, but only in the days when Jean François marched close enough for you to smell the garlic breath before you let fire. For accuracy at a distance, you were better off with a longbow.

The crack of the shot echoed.

Stoke froze in mid-kick and Mattie Ball scurried away, quick for someone who'd taken such punishment. She hared across Trantridge Hall's well-kept lawns towards tangled forest. The Chase. Mattie paused, tiny against the thick, tall trees, and raised a fist. Then she was gone.

No one was inclined to follow.

'Moran,' shouted Stoke, 'what the Devil do you think you're about?'

'Put a bounty on the pelt and I'll bring her down from here,' I said, raising Brown Bess as if to take aim. The gun, of course, was empty, though I judged Stoke in no state to distinguish a single-shot musket from a repeating rifle. 'But my understanding is that I'm here to hunt a dog. Anything else is out of season. Now, someone mentioned "hot toddy". It would behoove us to show the sense to get out of the f---ing rain...'

No one argued the point.

I strode to the door, where I encountered Mod Derby. She gave me a welcoming wink and hand squeeze.

'Colonel Sebastian Moran, ma'am,' I said, raising her hand to my lips.

'Welcome to Trantridge, gallant Colonel,' she said. Her smile put a dimple in her cheek, and I always appreciate a dimple. 'You have saved us all from murder.'

It was *possible* that, after putting her single ball in Stoke, Mattie Ball could have found a bayonet in her shawl, fitted it to the musket and skewered the entire household. I'd have laid odds against, though.

'I suppose I have,' I said, as if the thought of receiving thanks never entered my head. 'All in a day's work, ma'am.'

'Modesty,' she said. 'But you may call me Mod.'

As with Mattie, I shared a long moment with Mod in which things were settled. Again, my hand took a trick. Without words, something to our mutual benefit was decided.

Stoke, plastered with filth, barged past into his house. He took no notice of what had passed between me and his supposed fancy woman.

We all went into Trantridge Hall.

IX

In conduct under fire, Jasper Stoke had settled the question of the hue of his innards – a sickly custard-yellow. His hands, the servants and the Derby siblings knew it. Even simple Dan'l and fairy-feathered Saul. Having 'lost face', as the Celestials say, mine host kept the company waiting for supper. Another theatrical device, no doubt. Probably made sense in German economics.

We convened in a big gloomy room. Blazing logs raised steam from damp furnishings within a few feet of the fireplace. Cow-gum stink suggested wallpaper paste liquefying. Paintings above the mantel, warped by years of radiant heat, did not hang true. However, the warmth did not reach as far as the table. We might have sat in Siberia or Staines for all the good the fire did us.

Gussied up in regimental dinner jacket, displaying a shelf-load of gongs earned by bravery and homicide in the service of the Queen, I did my best to ignore the cold. Mod Derby had abandoned oilskins for more flattering dress, with the neck cut lower than is the London fashion – displaying one or two reasons for favouring counties over capital. She had a head of long, fine, flaxen hair. I was persuaded to recount anecdotes relating to my medals. Seated at my right, Mod jogged my memory by replenishing my goblet with wine from Simon Stoke's recently discovered cellar. Twittering Saul was to my left, grazing on plates of nuts and berries set out to keep stomachs from rumbling as the evening meal was delayed by the non-appearance of the Master of Trantridge.

Also present were Braham and Nakszynski. Dan'l evidently took his eats with the children or the cowboys. I was surprised to discover another guest at table: that same Parson Tringham who was the unwitting inspiration for Stoke's dog problem or else an active participant in the plot against him. If the old idiot were puzzled that Stoke – who'd turned him out on his ear the last time he attempted to call – should ask him to dine, it hadn't stopped him coming. Tringham nattered about long-dead d'Urbervilles as if anyone were interested. He was of our company because Stoke thought he should be grilled for further intelligence. After listening to his witterings, it seemed to me a happier outcome would be if the parson were simply grilled. The Albino had no compunctions about eating a mountie's liver. Surely, a clergyman's tongue would at least serve as an appetiser?

I ignored Tringham and maintained attentions to Mod. I had every reason to anticipate private entertainment from that direction.

It nagged, however, that Moriarty had charged me with making detailed observations. *Encomia* to Modesty Derby's teats would not interest the cold, sad maniac. No, the Professor would rather have the ramblings of a crackpot genealogist.

Tringham had long sought entry to the archives of the family – meaning the centuried d'Urbervilles, of course, not the jumped-up Stokes. The dinner invitation had persuaded him such was now within his grasp. Well past the age when any self-respecting Eskimo would have packed himself off on an ice floe, his enthusiasms – and his mouth – were unstilled. To be so close to a cherished objective pricked his bump of excitability, and he expostulated about every item in the room.

Of all things, Tringham started on about the paintings.

Over the fireplace was a full-length portrait of Simon Stoke-d'Urberville.

In a case of 'never mind the picture, look at the frame', an oblong of gilt curly flourishes and oak leaves surrounded the moneylender. The Shylock's hand rested on a stack of ledgers. The fizzog was bland – the sort you forget while you're looking at it – but the artist had worked on that long-fingered hand, giving the impression its usual placement was in someone else's pocket. To Simon's right, in an equally pretentious, equally twisted frame was a veiled young crone, posed in a bower. Birds perched on her head and arms as if she were a Christmas tree, chickens mixed in with robins and sparrows. This was the widow who'd lingered long abed upstairs before leaving the accumulated boodle to her remittance-man nephew. Being blind, she couldn't have known how hideous her picture was; being rich, I doubt she was troubled by anyone telling her.

Tringham called our attention to the third in the trinity above the mantel. The matching frame should have been inhabited by murdered Alexander, beloved sprog of Mr and Mrs Stoke-Parvenu. Instead, a red-bearded brute in armour skulked in the woods, a big red mastiff curled about his metal boots. The painting was old, dark and curling at the edges.

'Pagan Plantagenet d'Urberville,' the parson said. 'Circa 1660. Costumed as the original Sir Pagan. Born Percy d'Urberville, he took the names of his ancestors, provable and fancied. He believed secret marriages intermingled the blood of the d'Urbervilles with the line of the rightful kings of England. When the Interregnum ended, Pagan Plantagenet nominated himself as a truer heir to the throne than Charles. Few supported him. Lord Rochester ridiculed him as "Percy the Pretender". He spent a fortune on forged documents, muddying the waters of d'Urberville scholarship for centuries to come. It's a frightful bother when a scrap of Norman parchment might be a Restoration fake.'

'Looks a grim old swine,' I said. 'What happened to him?'

'He perished in a duel with a neighbour, Squire Frankland. He insulted the squire by shooting his terrier. In a manner of speaking, he was another victim of the legend of Red Shuck. While posing for this picture, he was bitten by the dyed mastiff used as a model for the original Red Shuck. This gave him an entrenched terror of dogs. He took to carrying a brace of pistols for protection from them. That's how he came to kill the squire's pet. As aggrieved party, Frankland had choice of weapons and picked rapiers. For all his Norman affectations, Pagan Plantagenet was a poor swordsman. But he shouldn't be here.'

'What d'you mean, Parson?' I asked. Tringham was agitated about some *wrongness*.

'His picture shouldn't hang in this spot. Certainly not in that horrible frame. The d'Urbervilles were long gone from Trantridge Hall in Pagan Plantagenet's time. His seat was Kingsbere-sub-Greenhill, as are the family tombs. Incidentally, it might amuse you to know I once had cause to alert John Durbeyfield – an offshoot, degenerate modern twig of the family – to the existence of those tombs. Later, to my astonishment, the wife and children of this peasant "Sir John" took up temporary residence among their ancestors, like Indian ghouls. What do you think of that?'

'Not much,' responded Mod – who, in a brief flash of teeth, indicated this footnote amused her not at all. I had come in on the last act of a play which was a long evening in the running, and couldn't hope to pick up all the plot threads.

'If Percy were fascinated by his ancestor,' I suggested, getting back to the portrait, 'wouldn't he have poked around here?'

'Much as you have,' added Mod, with a cutting tone which didn't cut the thick-skinned parson.

'Pagan Plantagenet was afraid of The Chase,' he answered. 'Red Shuck, you know, supposedly abides hereabouts. The painting is *Ecole de Lely*. Face and dog were executed by the commissioned artist at a sitting, the rest assigned to pupils. One would have done the armour, for instance, from an empty suit. A junior could have visited The Chase to put in the trees without the sitter having to come near the place. The mystery is how the picture comes to be at Trantridge not Kingsbere.'

'Him,' Mod said, pointing at Simon Stoke, 'he's your answer. He bought his ancestors in a job lot. He probably put the picture up. Hung so he himself seems superior. A sign of conquest, of his *swallowing* of the old d'Urbervilles.'

'My sister has a point,' Saul said. 'Stoke probably didn't know which Pagan he had, and took Percy the Pretender for the original.'

'It's not so much the picture that excites,' Tringham said, 'but the possibility Mr Stoke acquired other items along with it – documents, perhaps, or books. Pagan Plantagenet collected authentic items along with his fakes. Among his sins was the sacrilege of destroying them to provide raw materials – scraping manuscripts clean, so he had properly aged paper upon which to set out mendacious scrawls. If the cause of scholarship is just, Pagan Plantagenet d'Urberville might be judged the worst man in his family...'

'Might he now?' announced Jasper Stoke-d'Urberville, sweeping into the hall, scrubbed and scented, in evening clothes. A dramatic entrance, of course. The doors were held open by footmen. 'Might he indeed? I hope to contest that title, Parson.'

He sauntered to his place at head of table.

'I intend to go Mr Percy Pagan Plantagenet one better,' said the Master of Trantridge. 'When I have a dog shot, it'll be the right one.'

From this, I *deduced* Jasper had loitered outside, eavesdropping, awaiting the theatrical moment.

Suddenly, in another stage device, maids were hurrying about under Thring's direction, setting food on the table. They began with Jasper rather than, as tradition would dictate, the company's sole lady. I always advocate feeding a filly first, since such trifles make the dears more warmly inclined to one's *advances*. Scorning points of amatory order leads to nights in cold, lonely beds – even, nay *especially*, on the part of blokes who foolishly suppose they have proprietary interest in some delicate personage. Stoke had staked claim by referring to Mod Derby as his 'fancy woman'. Finely attuned as I am to feminine character, I could tell that if he expected a midnight visit after this day's work, he was out of luck.

Stoke dug into his grub without waiting for his guests to have plates in front of them. Tringham, served last, muttered needless grace over his mess of cabbage and boiled beef. No one else troubled the Divinity before scoffing.

With his mouth full, Jasper announced he had sent word to the constabulary, indicting Mattie Ball for attempted murder.

'I'll have the countryside against her,' he crowed. 'I'll post bounty on her, as you suggested, Moran. She'll not be taken alive. An example must be made. One deranged female won't stand in the way of progress.'

Mod and Braham Derby exchanged glances.

'It is not enough that the Ball woman failed in her murderous mission,' Stoke continued, warming to his subject, flecks of gravy marring his starched dickey. 'The story of her attempt, her *exploit*, must end in defeat and degradation. Matilda Ball must be despised and laughed at, not to suit my vanity, mind you, but in the spirit of *propaganda*. Her downfall will elevate my status as Master of Trantridge.'

I remembered sobbing, muddy Jasper Stoke kicking a defenceless damsel. I usually advocate kicking a man when he's down. What better time, indeed, to kick a man than when he's suitably arranged within boot distance? But for a passionate surge of victory, the tiger you bring down must have claws. I'd shared a moment with the musketeer maid. It rubbed the wrong way when Stoke, in his telling of the tale, got between me and her. I care not two hoots and a shit for prayer before meals. Food is brought to table by violence and drudgery or wanting because some other sod has skipped grace and eaten it first. God don't come into it. But Stoke's manner in talking of Mattie Ball was my idea of sacrilege.

Saul Derby took the conversation off on another tangent – a proposed study of badger runs in The Chase. He ventured they might be of more use than overgrown, broken and disused human paths.

Then, as the poet has it, there came a knocking. Not a gentle raven-tap at the window, but a hammering on the front door. This resounded through the foyer and thence to the dining room. I had noticed a great iron handle, suitable for raising such a racket, stuck to the front of Trantridge Hall.

Stoke ordered Thring to see who it was and tell them to piss off. Proving himself not a complete fool, he gave Nakszynski the nod to go with the butler. Even discounting ghosts, he had a superfluity of here-and-now enemies who would love a clear shot at him.

'Come now,' said Braham, as the Albino stood up. 'It's not like anyone who wants to kill Mr Stoke would just walk up the drive and knock on the door...'

That marked Braham Derby as an amateur. In point of fact, a murderer often knocks on the door – summoning a victim conveniently to the point of a knife or the end of a gun. I've paid such calls myself, tipped my hat to a cooling corpse, and walked off before hue and cry can be raised.

Stoke wavered and Nakszynski sat again.

The doors were flung wide again. The caller trumped the Master's strut with a genuine theatrical effect. A big man, dressed entirely in crimson from his shoes to his tall hat, he was bright scarlet in the face and hands. Across broad shoulders he carried a heavy, limp bundle. Completing the infernal effect, he whiffed of something like brimstone. Frankly, I've met subtler volcanic eruptions.

The Albino had a Colt .45 drawn. I kept my Gibbs out of sight, but equally out of my pocket. If needs be, I could fire under or through the table. Mod gave a little intrigued parp as my cold revolver brushed her thigh.

Diggory Venn, the red-dyed radical – for it could be no one else! – shrugged off Thring as the butler tried to lay hand on him. Venn heaved his bundle onto the table. It displaced the remains of the meal, and splayed before the Master of Trantridge.

As the bundle slid, wrapping came loose.

A white face showed, with a red hole beneath it. Mattie Bell was open-eyed in death, throat ripped out.

Before Stoke could blurt 'what is the meaning of this?' or somesuch, Tringham stood up, gulped, and fainted.

'Satisfied?' said the reddleman, directly addressing Stoke.

The Master was astonished and queasy. Blood dripped into his lap. Corpse-eyes looked up at him.

If you swear by Mrs Beeton, this was probably the wrong time for the maid to fetch in the port. But Jasper Stoke wasn't the only one among us glad of access to fortified spirits.

Pistol back in my pocket, I examined the body. I shut Mattie's eyes. My smell was still on her, but some other animal had taken what was rightly mine. That ticked me off and made this a personal matter. Hunter's honour, you know. I don't expect anyone to understand, but these things run deep.

I would skin that bloody Red Shuck.

X

I doubt anyone else at Trantridge Hall slept that night as soundly as I did. I know no one else breakfasted as heartily the next morning.

Even the Stoke-d'Urberville kitchens couldn't go far wrong with breakfast. We were served buffet fashion in the foyer. Mattie Ball was still laid out on the dining table, a drop cloth for a shroud. I had second helpings of poached eggs and devilled kidneys.

When setting off on a hunt – or a punitive military expedition – it's essential to be rested, refreshed and well fed, else you're halfway to failure before you've taken your first shot. I've the happy knack of being able to pinch out thoughts like a candle as soon as I bed down. No nightmares trouble the rest of Basher Moran. I run into enough while I'm awake.

Stoke, however, was red-eyed from a case of the horrors. He cuffed a maid who offered him toast. Braham Derby, if anything, looked worse. From Mod, I knew her brother and Mattie had once had an 'understanding' which didn't survive the New Master's German economics.

We'd forgotten Parson Tringham, and left him where he fell. Some time in the night, he'd roused to find himself alone with Mattie and quit the Hall.

Stoke was worried he'd be browbeaten into traipsing into The Chase. On that score, he had no concern. No use for a yellow liver in a hunting party.

I also recalled cases where the Firm lost a fee because a client happened to get killed before his bill was settled. So: five thousand reasons to keep Jasper Stoke among the living.

It fell to me, as ranking *shikari*, to pick beaters and bearers. From the Hall, I chose Nakszynski and Saul. I reckoned the Albino a stealthier accomplice than blundering Dan'l, and gathered he had experience in tracking and killing dangerous beasts and deadly men. The strange youth knew the wilds and paths of The Chase better than anyone alive. Practically raised in them. On first-name terms with the squirrels. Knew every tree to talk to. They have holy fools like that in India. Some make damn decent guides – they take you to where the tigers are, and no one is too put out if they get eaten.

Outside the Hall, Diggory Venn waited. He hadn't slept under Stoke's roof. The client still favoured shooting the reddleman, being three-quarters convinced he was in league with the demon dog. I saw his reasoning, but he was wrong. Stoke could have sacrificed an ally to deceive an enemy – a trick I'd essayed a time or two myself – but Venn, foolish fellow, rang true. He could no more slaughter an innocent than turn blue.

The beast had killed Mattie Ball *and* Lazy-Eye Jack, on opposite sides at Trantridge. Red Shuck was indiscriminate, as much a threat to the villagers as the Master. Venn, self-declared protector of downtrodden tenants, wanted it dead as much as Stoke, self-appointed oppressor of the unwashed.

Since his whipping, the reddleman had been living off the land. He had a lair in The Chase. He was careful not to say if anyone in the village or at the Hall helped him with the odd hot meal or mug of tea – though I'd swear he hadn't been abiding on nuts, berries and edible bark alone.

I quizzed him. He'd come across signs of a large animal or animals in the woods and heard nocturnal howling, but hadn't so much as glimpsed red hide through the trees.

'No ghosts then?'

'Didn't say that,' replied Venn. 'I seen the Brokeneck Lady. Or someone like. After I found Mattie, she were there – at edge of Temple Clearing, close by a tree. An *ululation* alerted I to her presence, such as no human nor animal tongue could make. First, I were 'suaded 'twas Mattie's spirit, gone from her mortal clay, lingering to see justice done. Then, I perceived this woman were garbed different. Long black dress, with shiny black buttons up the front. A thick veil, like twenty year of cobweb. Head kinked over to one side. From the hanging, they do say.'

'You think it was Theresa Clare?'

'Tess Durbeyfield as was?' he said, shrugging. 'Couldn't see this one's face through the veil. I never set eyes on Tess when she were living. Can't say who this were. She been seen hereabouts afore. I had little concern for her. Were Mattie Ball to think on.'

From concealment in The Chase, Venn had seen what happened at the Hall yesterday. When Mattie fled into the forest, he resolved to offer her shelter and succour. When he caught up with her, she was dead on the ground, eyes glassy. In his rage, Venn assumed Stoke responsible, just as Jasper blamed the reddleman for the death of Lazy-Eye Jack. Now, there was uneasy truce. A third party, set against both factions, was in play: Red Shuck, perhaps in league with this spectral lady.

I'd risen early, with a hunting thrill in my water and a stiff prick. It takes little to make me happy – something new to kill today, and someone new to bed tonight. Prospects fair in both categories, I judged.

Holstered under my arm, my revolver was loaded with silver bullets – which I hoped to conserve, though one or two might make souvenirs. I put my trust in plain lead and carried a rifle I reckoned almost equal to the late 'Prometheus'. The gun's bag ran to six tigers, nine lions, a few Welshmen and one Honourable Lord brought down in testing circumstances from the visitors' gallery to save the House from an excessively dull speech on the subject of Irish Home Rule. Never let it be said that Moriarty & Moran made no contribution to politics.

A drab, damp, cold October day. Sunrise about ten-thirty *ante meridien*; near full dark just after lunch. It had stopped raining. Thick strands of mist stirred at knee-height like ghost eels.

Venn and Saul, in a huddle, argued over the best path to take to the clearing where Mattie had been found. Venn looked even stranger under thin sunlight which brought out the peculiar, unrelieved redness of his entire person. He carried a stout straight stick which was a match for Dan'l's Gertie and held it as if he had some skill at the old English sport of quarterstaff. I've seen men with long sticks beat men with short swords, so I didn't care to underguesstimate the reddleman's martial prowess.

Saul was in a Norfolk jacket and knickerbockers, armed only with a bag for scientific specimens. He'd been responsible for the plaster cast Stoke had brought to Conduit Street and was silly enough to whimper that we should take Red Shuck alive since it might be an unknown species. I promised we'd name it *Canis Rufus Saulus*, but it'd be easier to stick on a label post-mortem.

Nakszynski wore a shaggy coat made from grizzly hide, tailored with pockets for concealed hold-out pistols and lengths of cheesewire. The lining sheathed sufficient knives to serve boneless duck and fish at a Lord Mayor's dinner and have enough left over to perform emergency amputations on a cartload of railway-crash wounded. He performed a familiar ritual – loading and checking guns, spitting on blades. His murder tools were in order, ready for use. Stoke stood by his man like a prize-fight trainer, happy to dispense advice on the theory of fisticuffs yet happier still not to be the fellow stepping into the ring to put the advice into practice while another bludgeon-fisted ape pounded on his head.

Most of the household were here to see off our expedition. Mod planted a crafty kiss on my cheek, and slipped a hand into my trousers to administer a secret squeeze. Stoke scowled at the intimacy he could see, but losing a poke-partner came a long way down his list of frets. I reckoned he'd retreat inside and have the Hall barricaded until we came home with Red Shuck hanging upside down from Venn's stave.

We set off across the lawn, and paused in the shadow of The Chase.

'This is a truly venerable tract of forest,' Saul announced, as if lecturing sightseers, 'one of the few remaining woodlands in England of undoubted primeval date, wherein Druidical mistletoe is still found on aged oaks. Enormous yew trees, not planted by the hand of man, grow as they did grow when they were pollarded for bows.'

He made a few more remarks about 'sylvan antiquity'. I disregarded them like the steam of his breath. The tall stark trees were more black than green. Within the woods, groundmist was waist high. The Chase showed its true self.

It was not a forest. It was an English jungle.

XI

Saul – smallest, least encumbered of the party – bent low and scurried through his famous badger runs. Venn, the Albino and I had to take less thorny paths through the dripping woods.

We could scarcely have got wetter if it were raining.

The morning mist didn't burn off, which made looking out for beast's spoor an iffy prospect. Exposed roots and the mouths of rabbit-warrens became mantraps. A sane hunter was exceedingly careful where he put his boots.

Sunlight was intermittent. Every step took us back in time. All Saul's rot about Druidical mistletoe and pollarding for bows brought to mind high old merrie England. Flagons of foaming mead and clots in armour gallantly clouting each other. This was more savage, cold and bloody uncomfortable. As Stoke had warned, it *stank* like a tannery.

'What is that smell?' I asked Venn.

'What smell?' he responded. His nostrils must have been burned senseless by living with the stench. In fact, now I came to think of it, the reddleman had the pong on him like the stain on his face.

I *like* jungle, but The Chase was a Pit of Hell on a wet Wednesday.

After an hour of slow going, we felt we had travelled ten hard leagues but might well have only penetrated a few hundred yards into the wood. Venn tapped his stave against an oak, signalling a halt. We had found an open space about fifty paces across. The trees were so tangled above, the clearing was like a leaky cathedral. Shafts of light poured down through a ceiling of woven wood.

'Here be the place,' the reddleman said.

'Temple Clearing,' Saul said, popping out of his badger-run. 'Where Venic turned and Red Shuck killed Sir Pagan. They found that Lazy-Eyed Jack fellow here with his gizzard gone.'

Venn walked slowly, stirring the mist with his stick.

'Mattie were here,' he said, 'lying on this.'

He knelt and waved mist away from a long, flat stone – the size of a table or a tomb. Hewn from rock, smoothed by time. Someone had taken the trouble to haul it here from a quarry.

'Scary Face Stone,' Saul said.

I looked at it several ways, but couldn't see it. Cracks in rock or knots in wood can pull a face, but this was featureless.

'The name is a corruption,' Saul went on. 'Originally, it was Sacrifice Stone. Old even in Sir Pagan's time. Our Palaeolithic ancestors used it. It's been washed over and over in blood.'

There were traces of blood on it now.

'You say the woman was lying here?' I addressed Venn. 'How? Arms and legs out, as if thrown away? Or tucked straight, as if on display?'

Venn thought about it, red brows knitting. 'The second way.'

'Her hands? Show me how her hands were. By her sides, or…?'

I made defensive claws, as if shielding my throat. Venn crossed his wrists, palms flat against his breast.

'Never known an animal arrange kill for a funeral,' I said.

Venn nodded. 'Only one do have such a habit. That be a human man. But a human man don't bite out a woman's throat.'

That showed how limited the reddleman's experience of the world was. As Moriarty and I learned during the Affair of the Hassocks Hobgoblin, some specimens of 'human man' have exactly that predilection. In this case, I'd seen Mattie's wound and concurred that no man had done that damage.

'Only a beast could have killed Mattie, but only a man would have laid her out,' said Saul. 'In the story of Red Shuck, Venic was sometimes man and sometimes beast.'

Nakszynski spat tobacco at Scary Face Stone, unimpressed.

I was conscious of my silver-loaded revolver. As if on cue, the howling started.

The others had heard this before, but all bristled. Even Nakszynski's white hair rose under his patched hat.

I don't know what men mean by fear. My nerves aren't plumbed in that way. But that howling – softer, more expressive than I'd imagined from reports – pricked an instinct I'd thought dead. It was as if a sail-maker's needle slid into the nape of my neck then drew down, scraping every bone-knob in turn. My wet skin crawled in disgust at myself, the others, the *noise*…

We looked around, but it was impossible to tell where the howling came from. I fancied it might be high up, in the trees – but dogs, no matter how big, don't climb. Red Shuck wasn't a cat – they scratch as well as bite and Mattie had no claw marks on her. Besides, I know cats. You can live with cats if you're wary, but you can't *use* them the way you can dogs. Red Shuck was being used.

Nakszynski, guns in his hands, wheeled about, scanning for movement. Venn stood slowly, in a fighter's stance – a double-grip on his stave. The howl died down. There was a noise of birds taking flight. The Albino aimed upwards, but didn't waste a shot.

Saul, not at all concerned, whistled shrilly.

It was a wonder Nakszynski didn't shoot him there and then. I knew at once what he was doing.

In answer to his trilling came another howl. Longer, and closer.

With the mist and the trees and the wet, even the best tracker wouldn't be able to run down Red Shuck in his own woods. But bringing the beast to us was easy. All we had to do was sound a dinner gong.

Saul whistled again.

XII

In the Carpathians, they say this about werewolves: there's always a tree between you and it, but never a tree between it and you.

I tugged off my right glove with my teeth and stuffed it in a pocket. I like a naked finger on the trigger, no matter the cold. I unslung my rifle and took a firing position, stock to shoulder. Beyond the gunsight, I saw only trees. Thick black pillars in white mist.

There was movement in the mist.

We could still hear howling, but Temple Clearing was confusion to the senses. The noise didn't seem to come from the moving shape.

I kept my gun up. Eddies and waves in the mist told me something big was coming, careening between trees, picking up speed. We heard crashes, saw lower branches shake. The thing was running blind.

Beats, like a galloping horse. It was coming fast and low, without regard for itself or us.

Another howl sounded, shrill and close and mocking, off to one side. *Not from the onrushing creature.*

I looked to the howling, bringing my aim round.

We were in The Chase with more than one beast.

I swung back to the more imminent threat, just as some big, black – not red! – and shaggy quadruped burst into the clearing, barrelling like a bull, snorting like a hog, foaming like a mad dog. I fired true and placed a shot in its skull. Momentum kept the thing coming. What was it? Venn whacked with his stave, which was snatched from his hands. I cleared my breech and reloaded. The Albino's guns went off, blasting fist-sized red gobbets out of a woolly hide.

The howling kept up. I didn't fire again. This might be a tactic to get us to waste our shots.

'It's Old Pharaoh,' shouted Saul.

It must be dead or dying, but still it tore around, head down, butting at us. Venn, off his feet, slammed into me. I fell backwards into damp mist and put out my hand – which jammed painfully against cold rock. I fell onto Scary Face Stone. My rifle hit me in the face.

'Git Priddle's prize black ram,' Saul explained.

I recalled the beast, which Priddle claimed was taken by Red Shuck. Stoke suspected Old Pharaoh was hidden from his tally-man, so the farmer could duck out of paying tax due.

Through agitated mist, I saw the ram was as big as some lions I've shot, humped like a buffalo, with curls of battered, hardened horn. Blood leaked from the hole I'd put in its bulbous forehead. Life was gone from saucer-sized eyes, but it took long moments for the message to reach the body.

Then, Old Pharaoh fell, dead.

Outside Temple Clearing, the howling abated.

I groped in the mist for my gun. Saul waded towards me – to help? His boot came down on my bare hand, crushing it against Scary Face Rock. Two or three fingers broke. Pain rushed up my arm.

I swore.

Saul tried to apologise. I kept swearing, at the pulsating hurt as much as the blundering idiot. Saul took me by the shoulders and helped me get my balance. I found the rifle on the ground, but agony hit again as I made a fist to pick it up.

I raised the gun in a rough aim, but could no more fit my snapped trigger-finger into the guard than you could thread a needle with a sausage. I threw the rifle down. My revolver was slung for a cross-draw. I had to reach into my coat and fish the gun out of my armpit with the wrong hand.

I laid against a bleeding wall of mutton, as if the dead ram were a pile of sandbags. Venn was beside me.

'Sheep be driven,' he said. 'By a dog.'

I'd worked that out by now.

Even though we'd all suspected human agency behind Red Shuck, no one at Trantridge – including yours truly – had thought it through. With my hand swollen and useless and the smell of just-dead sheep in my nose, I had a moment to wonder whether Moriarty had seen the truth and not troubled to mention it. It was the manner of smug trick he was given to, a refined version of his testing via sudden missile or sharp question.

From Stoke's story, I'd pictured a canny malcontent importing or discovering or raising some unknown species of canine and letting it prey on whom it might. This feint with Old Pharaoh bespoke more active agency. Our as-yet unknown enemy had Red Shuck *trained* as a sheepdog. Doubtless, the doggie was tutored in amusing tricks – fetch out the fellow's throat, jump up and bite, roll over and kill. In Wessex, it wouldn't even take a mastermind. A half-skilled shepherd could manage the trick, and the region was thick with the bastards. If I survived the afternoon I'd call on the Priddle hovel with harsh questions for a well-known ram-withholder.

I was still trying to make a fist, to control the knot of pain at the end of my arm.

Venn coughed blood. It smeared his chin, matching his skin. Even his teeth were red.

Saul, in the centre of the clearing, shrugged off his sample-bag, ears pricked. The Albino was by him, reloading. Besides Old Pharaoh, he had shot several trees – which bore fresh, white scars.

The howling stopped, but I didn't think the beast had gone away. It had been called to heel.

Saul whistled again, drawing out his trill.

I brought up my revolver. I'm a fair left-hand shot, and the pistol was best for close work anyway.

In answer to Saul's whistle came a low growl.

'Shuck be hungry,' Venn said.

'Chalky,' I called. 'It'll be under the mist. Can you shoot fish?'

The Albino nodded.

'If it comes into the clearing, blast it!'

I flapped my crushed hand, as if telling Nakszynski – and whoever else might be spying – I was out of the fight. My thought was to leave the sheepdog to the Albino and save my silver for the shepherd.

Saul whistled again, higher – as if trying out signals.

'Shut up, you damn fool,' I shouted. 'Dog knows we're here. Dog don't need a foghorn to find us.'

Saul swallowed and was silent. Who'd have thought such a fairy-footed fellow could do so much damage? My hand felt as if it'd been stamped on by an elephant in clogs.

I didn't like the way this expedition was going.

Either you bring back trophies or scars – often, both. I could claim Old Pharaoh's horns, but ram wasn't the game I'd set out for.

Unlike Old Pharaoh, our new caller came stealthily. The mist was all about like a smoking pool, thickening by the moment. I couldn't see my own boots. The ram's hump was barely an island. Saul was in it up to his chest. Nakszynski, furthest off, was almost a ghost.

THE HOUND OF THE D'URBERVILLES

I heard the dog. It might be a Wessex Wolf or a Trantridge Terrier, but it was a dog. Only dogs pant that way. Only dogs rattle spit as they contemplate din-dins.

We were supper on the hoof.

Though it was only early afternoon and less than a mile from Trantridge Hall, we were lost in nighted jungle, with monsters on all sides.

'Why be you smiling?' Venn asked.

'If you don't know, I can't tell you,' I said.

I might die in The Chase. The notion made me hot and angry. It rankled I was so ill-prepared as to find myself in this fix. But a curl of my brain – which everyone from the fulminating Sir Augustus to the calculating Professor Moriarty found fault with – was alive now as at no other time. Some chase women, some chase opium dragons, some chase pots of gold. Dammit, some chase postage stamps or currant buns. I chase these edge-of-life-and-death moments – when an animal or man tries to kill me, and I kill them instead. It's the surge inside – in the water, behind the eyes, in the loins. That's what Basher Moran's about. All the rest is fancy trimming. Nice enough to have, but not *real*. I'd protested when the Prof diagnosed my 'addiction to fear' on our first meeting, but had come to see he'd known me better than I knew myself in those innocent days.

There was that smell again. The Chase smell, vile to the nose and eyes. Old and faint on the reddleman, sharp and new on the dog.

Nakszynski was taken by a red devil which leaped up on his chest and bore him under the mist. I glimpsed eyes of flame and teeth like yellow knives. No point in firing wild. I guess the Albino dropped his guns and tried to get a grip on the neck of the thing with its fangs in his throat.

A long string of terrible Polish words came out of Nakszynski – the only speech I ever heard from him. I'd thought him mute. Then, with a liquid gurgle, his verbal torrent petered out.

'Saul, *run*,' I shouted.

He needed no further orders and bolted for one of his tunnel-paths. I looked for a red streak in the white – and took aim. If Saul Derby played hare to this hound, it might afford me a shot.

No movement.

I turned to Venn, to suggest he watch our backs. Red Shuck could come at us from any direction.

The reddleman's face was an open-mouthed mask of surprise. He saw something behind me. A whining, straining, inhuman sound assaulted my ears. I turned and brought up my gun. A heavy length of wood smacked into my skull.

A human figure rose out of the mist, head hung to one side. It was veiled, wore a long black dress and held Venn's stave.

I wondered if silver bullets were good for ghosts.

Before I could fire, the apparition swung. I took a whack to my head. Hot wet blood gouted from my ear and I went down. This time, I went out too.

XIII

I woke up in an earth-floored, flame-lit space. My cold, wet clothes were now hot, wet clothes. Blood crusted in my ear, under a field dressing. My fingers were splinted and bound.

I tried to sit up, which hurt.

Venn, bent over the fire, stirred a cauldron of broth. With his flame-lit, scarlet face, he could pass for a pantomime demon. The sulphurous smell was thick. Runic scratchings marked rock walls. Stick-figure men chasing big-mouthed, pointy-eared dogs twice their size.

'Where are we?' I asked.

Venn noticed I was awake. 'Red's Hole. Old, old place. Be my home, for now. Plenty live here afore me, back to Bible times.'

That was a comfort.

'It might sound ungrateful to ask, but why aren't we dead?'

'Brokeneck Lady. Drove off Shuck. Patched you up.'

I'd expected to be torn to pieces by the beast which brought down Nakszynski. Unconscious, I couldn't have put up a fight.

'Where is this spectral Flo Nightingale now?'

'Outways,' Venn said, jerking his thumb towards a woven curtain of vines.

'She have much to say?'

'Not so you'd note. Ghosts, generally, don't.'

My head hurt from more than the thwacking now. I'd failed to make the proper *deductions*...

By my watch, it was getting on in the evening. I still had my half-hunter, though my guns had been taken.

I was hungry enough to try the reddleman's soup.

The curtain rustled. A white, long-fingered hand gathered a fold and switched it aside. Into Red's Hole came the Brokeneck Lady...

A wet dress dragged on the ground. The veil hung to the waist on one side but almost up to the ear on the other. I've seen hanged men. Their heads loll just the same.

Venn glanced up, but kept stirring.

The ghost's head rolled, as if it were trying to set skull on spine like a cup and ball game. For a moment, the head was in its proper position. Then it inclined in the other direction. And back again. Then, evenly, it nodded from side to side. The veil swung.

I knew that cobra-neck wobble!

The veil was lifted.

'Moriarty,' I shouted. 'You f---ing c--t!'

Professor Moriarty showed teeth and hissed. His eyes were flint.

'What I mean to say is... damn it, what's the meaning of this?' I blustered. Few call the Prof a 'f---ing c--t' and live to write their memoirs. 'How? Why? What the...'

'Fair questions, Moran,' he said. 'They shall be answered.'

Moriarty unfastened his dress, pinching a row of little black buttons out of their eyelets. Underneath, he wore his town clothes.

I saw his dress and veil were shiny, waterproof material. More practical than unearthly. In his cocoon, the bastard kept snug and dry. Whereas I felt like shit. Wet shit that's been trodden in.

'You hit me,' I said. 'Twice!'

'You were about to waste silver, Moran.'

It was like him to be more concerned over expenses than the threat to his life. Even with my left hand, I'd have shot him square.

'One can learn more observing from concealment than out in the open,' he expounded. 'With you in the field, Moran, no one looked for me.'

So, *I'd* been the hare to flush out this hound. I wasn't surprised. Being used this way came with the position of Number Two. Everyone in his employ was expendable. I wasn't even angry he had acted according to his nature, just as I would to mine. That didn't mean I liked being so used, or would forget.

'How long have you been here?'

'I came down on the same train as you,' he said. 'In the next compartment. I overheard every word which passed between you and our client. Stoke, in fact, mentioned the significant point of the *smell* in The Chase...'

'Hold on a mo, Moriarty! You couldn't have got off at Stourcastle. We'd have seen you.'

'I travelled on to Sherton Abbas and made my way back to Trantridge via hired trap. I have been in The Chase ever since.'

I couldn't imagine the habitué of lecture halls and laboratories in the wild woods, even with his waterproof frock.

'Where did you sleep?'

'I did not sleep. I took an injection. Too much had to be found out and tested. I exploited rumours of the ghost of Theresa Clare to conceal my presence.'

He would never admit it, but I knew Moriarty derived some thin, watery thrill from 'dressing up'. Like his deduction craze, it came on him as if he were in a competition whose terms were set by another he wished to better. Usually, he was rotten at dissembling. He couldn't do voices and the snake-neck thing gave him away. This performance was well above his average. The Polish Jew in Irving's *The Bells* wasn't half as eerie.

'How did you make the noise? The ghost sound?'

The Professor's lips set in a tight line – his approximation of a smile. From his pocket, he produced a wooden box with a crank-handle. He worked it and a whine filled the cave. It set my teeth on edge.

'You don't imagine I would dismantle an Amanti on a whim? The violin was sacrificed to this invention.'

Mercifully, he shut the toy off.

'Wouldn't rattling a chain and going "woo-woo" have been a damn sight cheaper?'

'This is not for your ears, Moran. Nor any human ears.'

'Communicating with spirits now, Moriarty? I'd not take you for a table-rapper.'

'This instrument has nothing to do with ghosts. It is for dogs.'

XIV

It was full dark in The Chase.

Venn remained in his hole. He was not Red Shuck's master. Our commission was to kill the dog only. Therefore, we'd no quarrel with the radical reddleman.

Moriarty returned my guns. I could balance the rifle on my bandaged paw and pull the trigger with my left hand – but accuracy would be an issue.

'Saul has queered my game,' I complained. 'What happened to the idiot? Did Red Shuck get him?'

If Saul made it home, he'd be taken for the party's sole survivor. That would really put the wind up our client, who was panicky enough to start with.

Moriarty lead the way with a dark lantern, as if he knew The Chase as well as Saul. In his few hours as Weird Witch of the Woods, he'd explored thoroughly.

He stopped in his tracks and shone the beam at a thicket between two old tree trunks. Red scuffs showed on bark.

'Blood?' I asked.

'Reddle.'

'Venn?'

The Professor shook his head. 'Smell it,' he said.

I bent to sniff. That damn pong!

'I can't understand why Venn doesn't whiff this,' I said.

'He's lived in it for years,' Moriarty said. 'He no longer notices.'

I touched fingers to sludgy stains. Wet powder, not blood. That goes sticky and stops being red.

'Sheep dye,' Moriarty said. 'Not presently being used on sheep.'

He lifted aside the bushes, which were uprooted but tethered together. They disguised a gate fixed between the two trees. He unlatched it. We entered a concealed enclosure.

Moriarty shone his light around.

'What is this?' I asked.

'Originally, Venic of Melchester's hideaway. Recently, put back in use. Look...'

Iron animal cages were at present empty, gnawed animal bones strewn in the straw. Drinking bowls bore the marks of chewing. Posts set in the ground had iron rings and shackles.

'Red Shuck's lair,' Moriarty said. 'Here, our demon has been trained to viciousness. Here, he has been reddened...'

Under a tarpaulin, we found brushes and pots of dye.

'He?'

I counted six cages.

'Strictly speaking, *they*.'

I saw spoor on the dirt. Not the fantastic, elongated, claw-toed prints of the plaster cast, but tracks I was more familiar with. I'd seen enough in the snows of the Steppe.

'Wolf,' I said.

'White wolf,' concurred Moriarty. 'Large, not inexpensive. Imported from the Russias. I made enquiries with the usual importers of exotic animals about recent purchases of unusual canines. As a professional courtesy, Singapore Charlie was forthcoming. You know the Lord of Strange Deaths' fondness for spiders and such...'

I did – though that's not a story I want to go into now, or indeed ever.

'Some months ago, a customer paid cash for six white wolves, giving the name "Pagan Sorrow". Wolf fur is prized, but I fear dye makes these pelts unsaleable.'

'Except to Stoke. He'll be happy with fox-red tails, just so long as Red Shuck is brought down.'

Moriarty nodded in agreement.

'It's not just Red Shuck, though. Someone – this "Pagan Sorrow" – whistled up the doggies and sicced 'em on Stoke...' I continued.

'Indeed.'

'And tricked up the plaster cast? To sell the Red Shuck story?'

'Quite so.'

'Cunning bastard!'

Moriarty shrugged, allowing a neatness to the scheme.

'Moriarty, if these cages are empty... where are the wolves?'

The Professor looked at me. 'I'm sure we shall find them before they find us.'

With that comforting thought, we were on our way again.

XV

Outside Trantridge Hall we found Dan'l, standing guard, Gertie at the ready.

'Saul said you wuz done for. Et by a dog demon.'

'Saul's not the first and won't be the last to report my death. He's alive then?'

'Came back in a state. Said hounds of Hell were after him.'

'So they were.' I noted the plural.

Inside, we found the company in the dining room. A Guy Fawkes' Night bonfire roared and spit on the huge grate. A carved, bloody side of beef was hacked to the bone on a platter. Stoke, drunk and affrighted, sunk in an armchair. Mod, in a scarlet satin dress, poured for the Master. Braham paced in front of the fire. Thring stood by, with a trolley of bottles fetched up from the cellar.

Saul, it seems, had gone early to bed after an exhausting day.

Mod swarmed up at me in a froth of concern.

'Sebastian,' she cooed, 'it's such a relief you are living! We thought you'd perished in The Chase. Another victim of the Curse of the d'Urbervilles.'

'No, that was Nakszynski.'

She touched my bandaged head and kissed my cheek.

'You've been heroically wounded. Who did those splints for you? I'll change them properly. You'll take brandy, of course. And supper.'

I warmed under the spell of feminine attentions. Mod cocked her head, as if only just noticing I was not unaccompanied.

'This is Professor Moriarty,' I said. 'My associate.'

She curtseyed and extended a hand which the Prof did not take. He sized Mod up with a single watery-eyed glare.

Moriarty distrusted and disliked women. I only distrust them.

'Moriarty and Moran – f--kload of use you've been,' blustered Stoke from the depths of his chair. 'Nakszynski's dead, and the dog's not.'

Moriarty looked at our client.

'You will have your pelt,' he assured the craven sot. 'But, first, Mr – Derby is it? – would you fetch down the portrait which hangs above the mantelpiece? The one on the left. Yes, the fellow in the armour. I wish to examine it...'

Braham was surprised to be so addressed.

'Are you sure?' he responded. 'It's a dirty, ugly thing.'

'If I were not sure, I would not make the request. Now, in the name of your Master, please comply.'

In his sozzled fug, Stoke gave a shoulder hitch which indicated his manager should follow Moriarty's orders.

'It's Sir Pagan Plantagenet d'Urberville,' said Mod to the Professor. 'Last night, Parson Tringham told us...'

Moriarty waved her silent. She pouted, but recovered.

Braham carried a tall-backed chair close to the fire and stood on it. He had to stretch to heft the picture off its hooks. Flames licked at his trousers. He wobbled on the chair, finding his burden unwieldy. Sticky canvas parted from the frame in a curl.

'Careful, you shitbird,' shouted Stoke. 'That's my f---ing property!'

Braham stopped the music hall comedy turn and deliberately chucked the picture onto the fire. He reached into his jacket and pulled a pistol.

Making the most expensive left-hand shot of my life, I plugged Braham under the chin. Silver ploughed up through his skull. The top of his head spattered over Uncle Si's portrait. Braham dropped like a liquid turd from a loose-bowelled elephant.

I assumed my chances with his sister were up the chimney.

Moving fast, Moriarty fetched the picture off of the fire and laid it on the table. He blotted out flames with a napkin.

Mod had her hand in her mouth, stopping a scream.

Braham lay where he fell. No point even checking to see if he was dead. Still, I kicked his gun out of his hand, into a far corner of the room.

Stoke tried to focus. Dan'l hurried in, summoned by the shot.

Thring squeaked and ran. I drew a bead on his back as he made for the kitchen door.

'Let him go,' Moriarty said, still concerned with the painting. 'The butler has nothing to do with it.'

The Professor took the peeled-up corner of the portrait, then ripped the canvas from the frame. Pagan Plantagenet's picture had been glued over the portrait of a handsome, weak-faced young man.

'Remind you of anyone?' asked the Professor.

The hair was dark – otherwise, it was Saul Derby to the life.

This had to be Simon's son and intended heir, the rake who was too stupid not to turn his back on a woman when a knife happened to be within easy reach.

I felt a sharp pain in my back. Craning around, I saw a meat fork stuck out of my left shoulder. It had been pulled from the beef and put into me. Mod, less solicitous of my health than before, twisted the fork. Pain ran down my arm. My revolver fell from nerveless fingers.

I was no longer in a position to sneer at the late Alexander Stoke-d'Urberville.

From the foyer, a whistle sounded.

The doors opened. In walked Saul Derby, accompanied by four wolves.

The pack trotted in step with him – big mouths open, spit-ropes hanging from fangs, eyes bright, fur thick with reddle and gore.

One animal broke ranks and loped over to Braham to lick salty mess from his head. Saul whistled, sharply. The wolf sat up, alert.

Sauntering as if he owned the Hall, pets matching his pace, Saul came to the table. He admired the portrait as if looking in a flattering mirror. Then, he took notice of the picture's discoverer.

'Professor Moriarty, I presume,' he said, mildly.

Moriarty nodded and responded '…and you are "Pagan Sorrow". Sorrow Durbeyfield.'

Saul regarded the Prof with admiration.

'You could call yourself Sorrow Clare, if you took your mother's married name,' continued Moriarty. 'Or claim the name and estates of your father, variously called Alexander Stoke, Stoke-d'Urberville or plain d'Urberville.'

Saul touched his father's painted face. I suppose he was mad, but who in this room wasn't?

Moriarty lectured on what was doubtless the wolf-whistler's favourite subject: himself.

'You're supposed to have died in infancy, are you not? There's some tuppenny tears anecdote about an unbaptised babe refused the solace of a tiny grave in Marlott churchyard. Was that a trick or did you have a short-lived twin? No matter. You were raised discreetly with your mother's siblings. No one in Wessex keeps a name whole. Over centuries, D'Urberville became Durbeyfield. Clipping it to Derby was a recent expedient. This is your Aunt Modesty. That fellow cooling by the fire is your Uncle Abraham. Your aunt Elizabeth-Louise is around somewhere, hanging her head in shame for her impersonation of her sister's ghost. Did you huddle together in the d'Urberville tombs all those years ago, swearing to have your birthright and bring ruin to the perfidious Stokes?'

Saul-Sorrow shrugged. So did his wolves.

'It's a curious thing, when one parent murders the other. Clouds issues. And the inheritance.'

'Trantridge is mine, whichever way you look at it,' said Saul-Sorrow, who didn't seem so foolish now. 'Whether through the Stokes or the d'Urbervilles, I am true Master.'

'C---sucker!' rumbled Stoke from his chair. He'd drawn up his legs at the sight of so many Red Shucks. He must think he was seeing through the multiplying glass of drink. 'Whey-faced c--t!'

It was easy to forget Stoke was in the room. While Moriarty laid out the plot, I was more concerned with the pressing – not to say stabbing – matter of the fork in my back.

'There is another claimant,' Moriarty told Saul. 'My client.'

'That's for damn certain,' put in Stoke.

'I want no battle with you, Professor,' Saul said. 'I am an admirer. I daresay few appreciate your achievements as I do. What I've done has taken applied thought. It's not been rushed into like ordinary crime. It has been a scientific campaign.'

Moriarty's head oscillated. Someone was in trouble.

I wished the bloody fork out of my back. My hands were at present useless to me. Saul stepping on my gun-hand was no mistake but a strike in his campaign.

'I had to prime Tringham to revive the Red Shuck legend. I had to craft that plaster cast to sell the monster. I had to find, treat and train my pack. I had to harry away, not too quickly, removing all Stoke's comforts and aides. It's taken much to reach this pass. There have been sacrifices.'

We all stood or sat still, mindful of the beasts in the room. Mod, in theory of the wolves' party, was uncomfortable around them. Among Saul's 'sacrifices' had been his brother's former fiancée, I remembered. Aside from physical discomfort, I was rather cheered it was all now out in the open. You know where you are when you can see the animal's eyes. Or, in this instance, the animals' eyes.

'Whatever Stoke is paying you, I'll double,' Saul said to the Prof. 'Look at him. Your client. A useless, drunken, cowardly braggart. Practically an American! No fit Master of Trantridge. I have plans for the estate, Professor. Scientific plans. I intend to reintroduce the Wessex Wolf to England. I'll clear out the village, of course. People get in the way. But The Chase will be preserved. Do we have an understanding? *Double the fee!*'

Stoke whimpered, clutching an empty goblet. I believe he wet himself.

Moriarty's head continued its swaying.

'No, Mr Sorrow,' he said, at last. 'It will not do. I have taken a commission. Thus far, Mr Stoke-d'Urberville has kept his part of the bargain. I have a reputation to uphold.'

That was a laugh. He'd sold out clients for profit so often it was almost a habit – though he was careful to keep it quiet so as not to inhibit trade.

Stoke looked desperately hopeful.

'Have you ever seen anyone torn apart?' Saul asked. 'By wolves?'

'Not by wolves,' the Professor replied.

'It's most… *instructive*…'

Saul gave a short, shrill whistle. His wolves leaped…

XVI

Stoke screamed as Red Shuck – *four* Red Shucks! – swarmed all over him. Their teeth caught in his clothes. Cloth ripped.

Then, another noise assaulted my eardrums.

And the wolves laid off our client.

Moriarty had produced his crank-handle music box. Its thin, unearthly whine filled the dining room. Unpleasant to human ears, it was agony to canine senses. The wolves rolled over, choking on their froth, biting their own tails, pawing their skulls.

Saul was almost as sorely affected. The confidence went out of him. Dan'l got meaty arms around him and held him from behind.

I scraped the fork out of my back against a long-case clock. I felt a wet seepage inside my jacket. Better out than in, though.

Mod made a rush towards the Professor, but I tripped her – then put a boot on her head to keep her on the carpet.

The wolves' eyes rolled and bulged, as if their brains were boiling in their pans. Bloody tears started from their eyes. Red foam oozed from their nostrils.

My gold back teeth pained me.

At once, the Professor's gadget shut off, with the twang of a snapped string in its works. Its job was done, though. The demon dogs lay, heads leaking – dead as fur rugs.

Stoke uncurled from his ball of terror and stood. In a poor state, quivering like a recruit who's survived his first charge, he bled from a dozen scratches. Half his face was slack, skewing his villain's moustache to one side.

Swiftly, our client got his starch back. As he crossed the room, he stood taller, taking pleasure in having the upper hand and his enemies out in the open.

Mod writhed and kicked, but I kept her down with boot pressure. For skewering me, the minx deserved worse.

Stoke would serve his enemies as he saw fit.

He picked up Gertie, which Dan'l had dropped, and felt the stick's weight. I recalled my deduction that it had been used in night-work. Saul struggled in Dan'l grip, but had nothing to say for himself. He bled from the ears, showing kinship with his wolves.

Stoke fetched an enormous clout to Saul's face. Cheekbones gave way.

Let go, Saul fell to his knees. Stoke rained blows on his head and shoulders, then launched into kicks to the chest – with odd reverse heel-stabs which would have made sense if he were wearing spurs – and vicious jabs at the groin.

Our client kicked Saul from one side of the hall to the other. Saul's clothes soaked through until they were a match for Diggory Venn's.

Mod keened in frustration. I noted a sympathetic spasm on Dan'l's face. The big cowboy wasn't entirely with his boss in all this. He liked Saul and Mod and – despite what had happened in front of his face – his slow mind wouldn't change for a while yet…

Eventually, Stoke left off kicking and went to the table. He stuffed a thick slice of beef into his mouth and washed it down with a quaff of wine. Exercise had given him an appetite.

Saul rolled into a heap, among his dead wolves.

Stoke was drunk on the thrill of hurting someone helpless, aglow with the sudden change in his fortunes. He wasn't afraid any more. Despite the sorry state of his appearance, he was Master of Trantridge again.

'You'll join me in a drink, Moriarty? Moran?'

I needed to get a hellcat out from under my foot, but appreciated the offer.

'Just a tipple,' I said.

Mod thumped the floor.

'Our business is concluded,' Moriarty said, curtly – freezing Stoke as he reached for the bottle. 'There is the question of the agreed fee. Five thousand pounds for a pelt.'

Stoke grinned. 'Indeed. You've earned it right smartly, Professor. You and your little gimmick-box. That was your *angle*, of course. You could have just sold me the box and I'd not have needed your personal services. I'll not grudge you that. It's sound economics, one businessman to another.'

Stoke took a key from his waistcoat and opened a cabinet. Inside was a big, solid safe. Several gents of my acquaintance could have opened it quicker without knowing the combination beforehand than Stoke did working the wheel with excited, still-bloody fingers.

'Silver to your satisfaction?'

Stoke laid five weighty bars of Tombstone silver on the table.

Moriarty waited, making no move.

'What is it?' asked Stoke.

'We agreed five thousand pounds for a pelt… you have *four*. You do not need a Professor of Mathematics to tally that up as *twenty thousand pounds*. Silver is acceptable.'

The mobile half of Stoke's face fell to match the dead side… then he caught himself and managed a cracked chuckle. He brought up a finger in mock-accusing, would-be jovial fashion.

'Ah, a good one, Moriarty. A fine funny gag. You nearly had me there…'

Moriarty's head began to oscillate.

'Surely, *no*, you can't be serious?' said Stoke. 'That's... why, that's gross *extortion*. No, I'm grateful as all get-out, Moriarty. You've served me well, but what you ask is... ridiculous, out of the question, *unholy*. Contrary to all principles of sound business. No, five thousand is the limit. The price we agreed, and the price I'll pay.'

Stoke took a Gladstone bag from the cabinet, and transferred the silver to it under the vulture eye of Professor Moriarty.

'A fair sum for services rendered,' he said. 'I'll even throw in the bag.'

He tried to grin, though his face wasn't working yet.

A movement caught my eye. A pair of feet disappearing through the kitchen door. A bloody trail across the floor showed where Saul had dragged himself.

'Now,' said Stoke. 'There's the matter of another thrashing. Colonel, if you'd shift your boot...'

I did so. Mod gathered her skirts and stood. She spat in Stoke's face. He smiled.

'My family owes yours a murder,' he said. 'Yours won't be in the papers, though. You're for an unmarked grave in The Chase with your brother – nephew? – and his f---ing mutts.'

Moriarty picked up the Gladstone bag as if it were a specimen.

'Moran, our business here is done,' he said. 'We should leave Mr Stoke and Miss Durbeyfield to their discussions. I doubt they'll care for witnesses.'

'Hah,' Stoke said. 'You're a card after all, Moriarty. I'm glad to have known you, and no hard feelings. You've not done badly out of Trantridge.'

My wounds might argue, but I didn't.

Moriarty and I made for the door. Jasper reached for a carving knife.

Then Dan'l noticed there was one body missing from the pile of human and animal remains in the corner.

'Where's Saul?' he asked.

'What, eh, what?' Stoke said.

We left the dining room.

In the foyer, we saw Saul – reddled and torn from head to toe – on the stairs, supporting himself on a banister, trying to work his wrecked mouth.

There were *six* wolves. Only four bagged.

When he saw us, Saul's remaining eye shone with rage. He uttered strange, angry sounds.

Moriarty nodded polite acknowledgement to the bloodied heir of Sir Pagan and Red Shuck. We no longer had business with him.

Behind us, the dining-room doors opened again. Stoke charged out, waving Gertie.

'There you are, you c---sucker!' Stoke shouted at Saul. 'Prepare for a complete skull-f---ing!'

Saul managed a shrill screech. Two red wolves, larger than their slain comrades, charged down the stairs towards the Master of Trantridge. Their eyes shone, as if with nightshade drops.

Mod was at the dining-room doors. Dan'l held her back with tender restraint which suggested she'd suffer less at his hands than his employer's.

Saul sank to his knees, bleeding. His whistle became a rattling sigh. He kept trying to raise his hands. Stoke struck one of the red, snapping beasts with the stick, but the other was on him, forepaws to shoulders, jaws around his face. Gouts of gore sprayed the wallpaper.

Moriarty helped me out of the house and closed the door behind us.

Across the lawn, stepping out from The Chase, was a woman in a long black veil, head hung to one side. I lifted my splinted hand to wave at her, and she darted back into the trees.

From inside the house came a howling.

We walked away from Trantridge Hall, leaving claimants to settle disputes among themselves.

Chapter Five: The Adventure of the Six Maledictions

❦

I

Professor Moriarty did not readily admit his mistakes. Oh, he made 'em. Some real startlers. You were well advised not to bring up the Tay Bridge Insurance Fiasco in his gloomy presence. Or the Manchester and Provincial Bank Robbery (six months' brain work to set up, a thousand pounds seed money to pull off: seven shillings and sixpence profit). The Professor was touchy about failures. Indeed, he retained me to keep 'em quiet.

However, one howler he would own to.

He was ruminating upon it that morning, just as the sensational events I've decided to call 'The Adventure of the Six Maledictions' got going. Jolly good title, eh, what? Makes you want to skip ahead to the horrors. But don't… you won't fully appreciate the gut-slitting, dynamiting, neck-breaking, Rawhead-and-Bloody-Bones business without understanding how we got neck-deep in it.

In our Conduit Street rooms, we were doing the books, perhaps the least glamorous aspect of running a criminal empire. Once a mathematics tutor, Moriarty enjoyed balancing ledgers – as much as he could enjoy anything, the sad old sausage – more than robbing an orphanage trust fund or bankrupting a philanthropic society. He opened a leatherbound book and did that side-to-side snakehead thing which I've had cause to mention before. Everyone else who met him remarked on it too.

'I should not have taken Mr Baldwin as a client,' he declared, tapping a column of red figures. 'His problem was of minimal interest, yet has caused no little inconvenience.'

The uninteresting, inconvenient Ted Baldwin was a union 'organiser' in Pennsylvania coal country. As ever in America, you can't tell who were the worst crooks: the mine-owning robber barons or the fee-gouging workers' brotherhood. In our Empire, natives dig dirt, plant tea and fetch and carry for the white man. However, Red Indians don't take to the lash and the Yanks fought one of the century's sillier wars over whether imported Africans should act like proper natives.

Nowadays, America employs – which is to say, enslaves – the Irish for such low purposes. A sammy takes only so much field-slog before up and cutting your throat and heading into the bush. Your bog-trotter, on the other hand, grumbles for 700 years, holds rowdy meetings, then decides to get very, very drunk instead of doing anything about it.

On the whole, I prefer natives. They might roast you on a spit, but won't bore the teats off you by blaming it on Cromwell and William the Third. Yes, I know Moran is an Irish name. So is Moriarty. That comes into it later, too.

Our client Baldwin's union – the Vermissa Valley Scowrers (don't ask me what that means or if it's spelled properly) – were undone by a Pinkerton operative who, when not calling himself John McMurdo, went by the unbelievable name of Birdy Edwards. The Pinkerton Detective Agency is a disgrace to the profession of Murder for Hire. If you operate in a country where captains of industry and hogs of politics make murder legal so long as it's a union organiser being murdered, what's the point, eh? Moriarty never lobbied for laws to make it all right for him to thieve and murder and extort.

Posing as a radical, Edwards infiltrated the Scowrers. As a result, most of the reds wound up shot in their beds or hanged from mine-works, but our man Baldwin was left in the wind at the end of the bloodletting with a carpet bag full of union funds. In his situation, I'd blow the loot on women and cards, but Baldwin was of the genus *bastardii vindice*.

Just to rub it in, this Birdy flew off to England with Baldwin's sweetheart. Hot on the trail and under the collar, Baldwin came to London and called on the Firm. A wedge of greenback dollars hired us to locate the Pink, which we did sharpish. Sporting the more plausible incognito of John Douglas, Edwards was sunning himself at Birlstone, a moated manor.

An easy lay! Shin up a tree in the grounds and professionally pot the blighter through the leaded library window as he sits at his desk, perusing *La Vie Parisienne*. Aim, pull, bang… brains on the wall, 'Scotland Yard Baffled', notice in *The Times*, full fee remitted, thank you very much, pleasure to do business with you!

But, no, the idiot client got all het up and charged off to Birlstone to do the deed himself. Upshot: one fool face blown through the back of one fool head. Yes, sometimes they have guns too. A careful murderer is mindful of the risk inherent in turning up at a prospective victim's front door with a red face and a recital of grievances.

With the client dead, you might think we'd close the account and proceed to the next profitable item of deviltry. Not how the racket works. We'd accepted a commission to kill Edwards-McMurdo-Douglas. Darkly humorous remarks about persons not being dead when Professor Moriarty has been paid to polish them off were heard. Talk gets started, you lose face. Blackguards with inconvenient relatives take their business elsewhere. The Assassination Bureau, Ltd. or that Limehouse Chinese with the marmoset would be delighted to accommodate them.

So, at our own expense, we pursue Edwards, who has booked passage to

Africa. This is where you might remember the bounder. He – ahem – *fell* overboard and washed up on the desolate shore of St Helena. We could have shoved Birdy off the dock at Southampton and been home for tea and – ahem, encore – *crumpet* in Mrs Halifax's establishment for licentious ladies. Not obtrusive enough, though. Nothing would do for the Prof but that the corpse be aimed at the isle of Napoleon's exile. He spent hours with charts and tide-tables and a sextant to make sure of it. Moriarty was thinking, as usual, two or three steps ahead. There was only one place on Edwards' escape route anyone – specifically, anyone who scribbles for the London rags – has ever heard of. A mysterious corpse on St Helena gets a paragraph above the racing results. A careless passenger drowned before embarkation doesn't rate a sentence under the corset endorsements. Advertising, you see: Moriarty strikes! All your killing needs satisfied!

Still, it was Manchester and Provincial all over again. Baldwin's dollars ran out. On St Helena, the Professor insisted we take the sixpenny tour and poke around the eagle's cage. He acquired a unique, if ghastly, souvenir which figures later in the tale – this is another ominous intimation of excitements to come! The jaunt entailed five different passports apiece and seventeen changes of mode of transport across two continents. Expenses mounted. The account was carried in debit. [1]

'Politics will be the ruination of the fine art of crime,' Moriarty continued. 'Politics and religion…'

This is the moral, Oh My Best Beloved: never kill anyone for a 'Cause'.

For why not, Uncle Basher?

Because causes don't pay, Little Friend of all the World. Adherents expect you to kill just for the righteousness of it. They don't want to pay you! They don't understand why you want paying!

Not ten minutes after our return, malcontents were hammering at our door, soliciting aid for the downtrodden working man. Kill one Pinkerton and everyone thinks you're a bloody socialist! Happy to risk your precious neck on the promise of a medal in some twentieth-century anarchist utopia. I wearied of kicking sponging gits downstairs and chucking their penny-stall editions of *Das Kapital* into the street.

Reds fracture into a confusion of squabbling factions. The straggle-bearded oiks didn't even want us to strike at the adders of capital. That would at least offer an angle: rich people are usually worth killing for what they have about their persons or in their safes. No, these firebrands invariably wanted one or other of their comrades assassinated over hair's-breadth differences of principal. Some thought a Board of Railway Directors should be strung up by their gouty ankles on the Glorious Day of Revolution; others felt plutocrats should be strung up by their fat necks. Only mass slaughter would settle the question. If the GD of R has not yet dawned, it's because socialists are too busy exterminating each other to lead the rising masses to victory.

I think this circumstance gave the Prof a notion about Mad Carew's quandary. Which is where the blessed maledictions I mentioned earlier – you were paying attention, weren't you? – come in, and not before time.

II

Just after the Prof let loose his deep think about 'politics and religion', the shadow of a man slithered into the room. Civvy coat and army boots. Colonially tanned, except for chinstrap lines showing malarial pallor. Bad case of the shakes.

I knew him straight off. Last I'd seen him was in Nepal. He'd been plumper, smugger and without shot nerves, attached to the British Resident; attached to the fundament of the British Resident, as it happens. Never was a one for sucking up like Mad Carew. Everyone said he'd go far if he didn't fall off a Himalaya first.

Fellah calls himself 'Mad' and you know what you're getting. Apart from someone fed up of being stuck with 'Humphrey' and dissatisfied with 'Humph'.

There's a bloody awful poem about him... [2]

> He was known as 'Mad Carew' by the subs at Khatmandu,
> He was hotter than they felt inclined to tell;
> But for all his foolish pranks, he was worshipped in the ranks,
> And the Colonel's daughter smiled on him as well.

Reading between the lines – a lot more edifying that reading the actual lines – you can tell Carew knew how to strut for the juniors, coddle the men, sniff about the ladies of the regiment (bless 'em) and toady to the higher-ups. Officers like that are generally popular until the native uprising, when they're found blubbing in cupboards dressed as washerwomen.

Not Carew, though. He had what they call 'a streak'. Raring off and getting into 'scrapes' and collecting medals and shooting beasts and bandits in the name of jolly good fun. I wore the colours – not the sort of colonel with a daughter, but the sort not to be trusted with other colonels' daughters – long enough to know the type. Know the type, I was the type! I'm older now, and see what a dunce I was in my prime. For a start, I used to do all this for army pay!

'Mad' sounds dashing, daring and admirable when you hold the tattered flag in the midst of battle and expired natives lie all over the carpet with holes in 'em that you put there. 'Mad' is less impressive written on a form by a commissioner for lunacy as you're turned over to the hospitallers of St Mary of Bedlam to be dunked in ice water because your latest 'scrape' was running starkers down Oxford Street while gibbering like a baboon.

Major Humphrey Carew was both kinds of Mad. He had been one; now, he was close to the other.

'Beelzebub's Sunday toast fork, it's Carew!' I exclaimed. 'How did you get in here?'

The blighter had the temerity to shake his lumpy fist at me.

After a dozen time-wasting socialist johnnies required heaving out, Moriarty had issued strict instructions to Mrs Halifax. No one was admitted to the consulting room unless she judged them solvent. Women in her profession can glim a swell you'd swear had five thou per annum and enough family silver to plate the HMS *Inflexible* and know straight off he's putting up a front and hasn't a bent sou in his pockets. So, Carew must have shown her capital.

Moriarty craned to examine our visitor.

Carew kept his fist stuck out. He was begging for one on the chin.

Mrs Halifax crowded the doorway with a couple of her more impressionable girls and the lad who emptied the pisspots. None were immune to the general sensation which followed Carew about in his high adventures. Indeed, they seemed more excited than the occasion merited.

Slowly, Carew opened his fist.

In his palm lay an emerald the size of a tangerine. When it caught the light, everyone on the landing went green in the face. Avaricious eyes glinted verdant.

Ah, a gem! So much more direct than notes or coins. It's just a rock, but so pretty. So precious. So negotiable.

Soiled doves cooed. The pisspot boy let out a heartfelt 'cor lumme'. Mrs Halifax simpered, which would terrify a colour sergeant.

Moriarty's face betrayed little, as per usual.

'Beryllium aluminium cyclosilicate,' he lectured, as if diagnosing an illness, 'coloured by chromium or perhaps vanadium. A hardness of 7.5 on the Mohs Scale. That is: a gem of the highest water, having consistent colour and a high degree of transparency. The cut is indifferent, but could be improved. I should put its worth at...'

He was about to name a high figure.

'Here,' Mad Carew said, 'have it, and be done...'

He flung the emerald at the Professor. I reached across and caught it with a cry of 'owzat' which would not have shamed W.G. Grace, the old cheat. The weight settled in my palm.

For a moment, I heard the wailing of heathen worshippers from a rugged mountain clime across the roof of the world. The emerald sang like a green siren. The urge to keep hold of the thing was nigh irresistible.

Our visitor's glamour was transferred to me. Mrs Halifax's *filles de joie* regarded my manly qualities with even more admiration than usual. If my pisspot had needed emptying, I wouldn't have had to ask twice.

The stone's spell was potent, but I am – as plenty would be happy to tell you if they weren't dead – not half the fool I sometimes seem.

I crossed the room, dropped the jewel in Carew's top pocket, and patted it. 'Keep it safe for the moment, old fellow.'

He looked as if I'd just shot him. Which is to say: he looked like some of the people I've shot looked after I'd shot them. Shocked, not surprised; resentful, but too tired to make a fuss. Others take it differently, but this is no place for digressions.

Without being asked, Carew sank into the chair set aside for clients – spikes in the backrest could extrude at the touch of a button on Moriarty's desk, and doesn't that make the eyes water! – and shoved his face into his hands.

'Privacy, please,' Moriarty decreed. Mrs Halifax pulled superfluous spectators away, not forgetting to tug the pisspot boy's collar, and closed the door. Listeners at the keyhole used to be a problem, but a bullet hole two inches to the left indicated Moriarty's un-gentle solution to unwanted eavesdroppers.

Carew was a man at the end of his tether and possessed of a fortune. An ideal client for the Firm. So why did I have that prickle up my spine? The sensation usually meant a leopard prowling between the tents or a lady of brief acquaintance loosening her garter to take hold of a poignard.

Before he said any more, I knew how the story would start.

'There's a one-eyed yellow idol to the north of Khatmandu,' began Mad Carew...

Lord, I thought, here we go again.

III

Some stories you've heard so often you know how they'll come out. 'I was a good girl once, a clergyman's daughter, but fell in with bad men…' 'I fully intended to pay back the rhino I owed you, but I had this hot tip straight from the jockey's brother…' 'I thought there was no harm in popping in to the Rat and Raven for a quick gin…' 'I must have put on the wrong coat at the club and walked off wearing a garment identical to – but not – my own, which happens to have these counterfeit bonds sewn into the lining…'

And, yes, 'There's a one-eyed yellow idol to the north of Khatmandu…'

I've a rule about one-eyed yellow idols – and, indeed, idols of other precious hues with any number of eyes, arms, heads or arses. Simply put: hands off!

I don't have the patience to be a professional cracksman, which involves fiddling with locks and safes and precision explosives. As a trade, it's on a level with being a plumber or glazier, with a better chance of being blown to bits or rotting on Dartmoor – not that most plumbers and glaziers wouldn't deserve it, the rooking bastards! Oh, I have done more than my fair share of thieving. I've robbed, burgled, rifled, raided, waylaid, heisted, abducted, abstracted, plundered, pilfered and pinched across five continents and seven seas. I've lifted anything that wasn't nailed down – and, indeed, have prised up the nails of a few items which were.

So, I admit it – I'm a thief. I take things which are not mine. Mostly, money. Or stuff easily turned into money. I may be the sort of thief who, an alienist will tell you, can't help himself. I steal (or cheat, which is the same thing) just for a lark when I don't especially need the readies. If a fellow owns something and doesn't take steps to keep hold of it, that's his lookout. But even I know better than to pluck an emerald from the eye socket of a heathen idol… whether it be north, south, east or west of Kathmandu.

Ever heard of the Moonstone? The Eye of Klesh? The All-Seeing Eye of the Goddess of Light? The Crimson Gem of Cyttorak? The Pink Diamond of Lugash? All sparklers jemmied off other men's idols by fools who, as they say, 'Suffered the Consequences'. Any cult which can afford to use priceless ornaments in church decoration can extend limitless travel allowance to assassins. They have on permanent call the sort of determined, ruthless little sods who'll cross the whole world to retrieve their bauble and behead the infidel who snaffled it. That also goes for the worshippers of ugly chunks of African wood you wouldn't get sixpence for in Portobello Market. Pop Chuku or Lukundoo or a Zuni Fetish into your game bag as a souvenir of the safari, and wake up six months later with a naked Porroh man squatting at your bed-end in Wandsworth and coverlets drenched with your own blood.

Come to that, common-or-garden, non-sacred jewels like the Barlow Rubies, the Rosenthall Diamonds and the Mirror of Portugal are usually pretty poison to crooks who waste their lives trying to get hold of 'em. Remember the fabled Agra Treasure which ended up at the bottom of the Thames? [3] Best place for it.

Imagine stealing something you can't *spend*? Oversize gems are famous, thus instantly recognisable. They have histories ('provenance' in the trade, don't you know? – a list of people they've been stolen from) and permanent addresses under lock and key in the coffers of dusky potentates or the Tower of London where Queen Vicky (long may she reign!) can play with them when she has a mind to.

Even cutting a prize into smaller stones doesn't cover the trail. Clots who loot temples are too bedazzled by the booty to take elementary precautions. Changing the name on your passport doesn't help. If you're the bloke with the Fang of Azathoth on your watch chain or the Tears of Tabanga decorating your tart's décolletage, you can expect fanatics with strangling cords to show up sooner or later. Want to steal from a church? Have the lead off the roof of St Custard's down the road. I can more or less guarantee the Archbishop of Canterbury won't send implacable curates after you with scimitars clenched between their teeth.

Ahem, so, to return to the case in hand. Since the tale has been set down by another (one J. Milton Hayes – ever heard of anything else by him?), I'll copy it longhand. Hell, that's too much trouble. I'll shoplift a *Big Book of Dramatic and Comic Recitations for All Occasions* from WH Smith & Sons and paste in a torn-out page. I'll be careful not to use 'Christmas Day in the Workhouse', 'The Face on the Bar-Room Floor' or 'The Boy Stood on the Burning Deck (His Name Was Albert Trollocks)' by mistake. Among the set who stay away from music halls and pride themselves on 'making their own entertainment', every fool and his cousin gets up at the drop of a hat to launch into 'The Ballad of Mad Carew'. You've probably suffered Mr Hayes' effulgence many times on long, agonising evenings, but bear with me. I'll append footnotes to sweeten the deal.

There's a one-eyed yellow idol to the north of Khatmandu,
There's a little marble cross below the town;
There's a broken-hearted woman tends the grave of Mad Carew,
And the yellow god forever gazes down.

He was known as 'Mad Carew' by the subs at Khatmandu,
He was hotter than they felt inclined to tell;
But for all his foolish pranks*, he was worshipped in the ranks,
And the Colonel's daughter§ smiled on him as well.

* e.g.: setting light to the bhishti's turban, putting firecrackers in the padre's thunderbox… oh how we all laughed! – S.M.

§ Amaryllis Framington, by name. Fat and squinty, but white women are in short supply in Nepal and you land the fish you can get. – S.M.

He had loved her all along, with a passion of the strong,
The fact that she loved him was plain to all.
She was nearly twenty-one* and arrangements had begun
To celebrate her birthday with a ball.

* forty if she was a day. – S.M.

He wrote* to ask what present she would like from Mad Carew;
They met next day as he dismissed a squad;
And jestingly she told him then that nothing else would do
But the green eye of the little yellow god§.

* since they were at the same hill station, why didn't he just ask her? Even sherpas have better things to do than be forever carrying letters between folks who live practically next door to each other. – S.M.

§ that's colonel's daughters for you, covetous and stupid, God bless 'em. – S.M.

On the night before the dance, Mad Carew seemed in a trance*.
And they chaffed him as they puffed at their cigars;

But for once he failed to smile, and he sat alone awhile,
    Then went out into the night beneath the stars.

* kif, probably. It's not just the natives who smoke it. Bloody boring, a posting in Nepal.

– S.M.

He returned before the dawn, with his shirt and tunic torn,
    And a gash across his temple dripping red;
He was patched up right away, and he slept through all the day*,
    And the Colonel's daughter watched beside his bed.

* lazy malingering tosser. – S.M.

He woke at last and asked if they could send his tunic through;
    She brought it, and he thanked her with a nod;
He bade her search the pocket saying 'That's from Mad Carew',
    And she found the little green eye of the god*.

* if you saw this coming, you are not alone. – S.M.

She upbraided poor Carew in the way that women do*,
    Though both her eyes were strangely hot and wet;
But she wouldn't take the stone§ and Mad Carew was left alone
    With the jewel that he'd chanced his life to get.

* here's gratitude for you: the flaming cretin gets himself half-killed to fetch her a birthday present and she throws a sulk. – S.M.

§ which shows she wasn't entirely addle-witted, old Amaryllis. – S.M.

When the ball was at its height, on that still and tropic night,
    She thought of him* and hurried to his room;
As she crossed the barrack square she could hear the dreamy air
    Of a waltz tune softly stealing thro' the gloom.§

---

* the least she could do, all things considered. Note that M.C. being stabbed didn't stop her having her bally party. – S.M.

§ poetic license at its most mendacious. You imagine an orchestra conducted by Strauss himself and lilting, melodic strains wafting across the parade ground. The musical capabilities of the average hill station run to a corporal with a heat-warped fiddle, a boy with a Jew's harp and a Welshman cashiered from his colliery choir for gross indecency (and singing flat). The repertoire runs to ditties like 'Come Into the Garden, Maud (and Get the Poking You've Been Asking For All Evening)' and 'I Dreamt I Dwelled in Marble Halls (and Found Myself Fondling Prince Albert's Balls)'. – S.M.

His door was open wide*, with silver moonlight shining through;
    The place was wet and slipp'ry where she trod;
An ugly knife lay buried in the heart of Mad Carew§,
    'Twas the vengeance of the little yellow god.

---

* where were the guards? I'd bloody have 'em up on a charge for letting yak-bothering clod-stabbers through the lines. – S.M.

§ how much worse than being stabbed with a pretty knife, eh? – S.M.

There's a one-eyed yellow idol to the north of Khatmandu,*
    There's a little marble cross below the town;
There's a broken-hearted woman tends the grave of Mad Carew,
    And the yellow god forever gazes down§.

* yes, J. Milton skimps on his poetical efforts by putting the first verse back in again. When Uncle Bertie or the bank manager's sister read it aloud, they tend to do it jocular the first time, emphasising that rumty-tumty-tum metre, then pour on the drama for the reprise, drawing it out with exaggerated face pulling to convey the broken heartedness and a crack-of-doom hollow rumble for that final, ominous line. I blame Rudyard Kipling. – S.M.

§ Have you noticed the ambiguity about the idol? Is it only one eyed because M.C. has filched the other, or regularly configured like Polyphemus and now has its single eye back? Well, Mr Hayes was fudging because he plain didn't know. To set the record straight, this was always a Cyclopean idol. And the poet didn't hear the end of the story.

– S.M.

Oh, I know what you're thinking – if Mad Carew's emerald-pinching escapade led to a twit-tended grave north of Khatmandu, how did he fetch up unstabbed in our London consulting room, presenting a sickly countenance? Ah-hah, then read on...

IV

'I took the eye from the idol,' Carew admitted. 'I don't care what you've heard about why I did it. That doesn't matter. I took it. And I didn't give it away. I can't give it away, because it comes back. I've tried. It's mine, by right of… well, conquest. Do you understand, Professor?'

Moriarty nodded. If he understood, that was more than I did.

'I had to fight – to kill – to get it. I've had to do worse to keep alive since. They've not let up. They came for me at the hill station. Nearly had me, too. If letting them have the stone would save my hide, I'd wish it good riddance. But it's not the gem they want, really. It's the vengeance. Blighters with knives have my number. Heathen priests. That's an end to it – they think, at any rate. Some say they *did* get me, and I'm a ghost…'

I'd not thought of that. He didn't look like any ghost I'd run across, but, then again, *they* don't, do they. Ghosts? Look like what you're expecting, that is.

'I didn't just take this thing. I copped a fortune in other stones and gold doodads, too. Not as sacred, apparently. Though most folk who bought from me – chiselled at a penny in the pound, if that – are dead now. Even with miserly rates of fencing, I netted enough to buy out and set myself up for life. Thought I could do a lot better than Fat Amy Framington, I tell you.

'Resigned my commission, and left for India… with the little brown men after me. More of 'em than I can count. Some odd ones, too – brown in the face, but hairy all over. *White* hairy, more brute than man. There are a few of 'em left in mountain country. *Mi-go* or yeti or Abominable Snowballs. They're the trackers, when the priests let them off their leashes. They dogged me over India, into China… across the Pacific and through the States and the Northern Territories. Up to the Arctic with them after me on sledges… they have yeti in Canada too, Sasquatch and windigo. I heard the damned beasts hooting to each other like owls. Close scrape in New York. Had to pay off the coppers to dodge a murder charge. Steam-packet to Blighty.

'They nearly got me again in a hotel in Liverpool, but I left six of 'em dead. Six howling bastards who won't make further obeisance to their bloody little yellow god. Now I'm here, in London. The white man's Kathmandu. I've still got this green lump. Worth a kingdom, and worth nothing…'

'This narrative is very picturesque,' Moriarty said, 'though I would quibble about your strict veracity on one or two points. You could place it in the illustrated press. What I fail to perceive, Major Carew, is what exactly you want us to do?'

Carew's eyes became hooded, shifty. For the first time, he almost smiled.

'I heard of you in a bazaar in Peking, Professor. From a ruined Englishman who was once called Giles Conover…'

Him, I remembered. Cracksman, and a toff with it. Also enthusiastic about precious stones, though pearls were his line. Why anyone decided to set a high price on clams' gallstones is beyond me. Conover went for whole strings. Lifted the Ingestre Necklace from Scotland Yard's Black Museum to celebrate the centenary of the burning down of Mrs Lovett's Fleet Street pie shop. I'll wager you know that story. [4]

The Firm had done business with Conover. Before his spine got crushed.

'You are… what was Conover's expression… a consultant? Like a doctor or a lawyer?'

Moriarty nodded.

'A consulting criminal?'

'A simple way of stating my business, but it will suffice. Professionals – not only doctors and lawyers, but architects, detectives and military strategists – are available to any who meet their fees. Individuals or organisations have problems they have not the wits to solve, and call on those with expertise and experience to do so. Criminal individuals or organisations have problems too. If sufficiently interesting, I apply myself to the solution of such.'

'Conover said you helped him…'

'Advised him.'

'…with a robbery. You – what? – drew up plans he followed? Like an engineer?'

'Like a playwright, Major Carew. A dramatist. Conover's problem required a certain flamboyance. Parties needed to be distracted while work was being done. I suggested a means of distraction.'

'For a cut?'

'A fee was paid.'

The Prof was being cagey about details. We arranged for a runaway cab to collide with a crowded omnibus at the corner of Leather Lane and St Cross Street. This convenient calamity drew away night guards at Tucker & Tarbert's Gemstone Exchange long enough for Conover to nip in and abstract a cluster known as 'the Bunch of Grapes'. Nobody died except a drunken Yorkshireman, but seven passengers were handily crippled – including a Member of Parliament who couldn't explain why he was in the hansom with two tight-trousered post office boys and had to resign his seat. A fine night's work all round.

Carew thought about it for a moment.

'They are in London. The brown priests. The yeti. They mean to kill me and take back their green eye.'

'So you have said.'

'They nearly had me in Paddington two nights ago.'

The Professor said nothing.

'Consider this an after-the-fact consultation, Moriarty,' Carew said, taking a plunge. 'I don't need help in planning a crime. The crime's done with, months ago and on the other side of the world. I need your help in *getting away with it.*'

It became clear. The Professor ruminated. His head oscillated. Carew hadn't seen that before and was startled.

'You will be killed,' the Professor said. 'There's no doubt about it. In all parallel cases – you have heard of the Herncastle Heirloom, I trust [5] – the, as you call them, "little brown men" have prevailed. Unless some other ironic fate overtakes him first, the despoiler is routinely done to death by the cult. Did Conover tell you of the Black Pearl of the Borgias?'

'He said he'd lost the use of his legs and been driven from England because of the thing, and he didn't have it in his hands for more than a minute or two.'

'That is so,' Moriarty confirmed. 'There are differences between your circumstances, between your Green Eye and his Black Pearl, but similarities also. With the Borgia pearl, the attendant problem was not presented by brown men, but by a white man, if man he can truthfully be called. The Hoxton Creeper. He has haunted the pearl through its unhappy chain of ownership, breaking the backs of all who try to keep hold of it. He crushed Conover's bones to powder, though the prize was already fenced. I dare say the Creeper, a London-born Neanderthal atavism, is as abominable as any Himalayan snowman.'

Some in dire situations are gloomily happy to know others have been in the same boat. Not Carew.

'Hang the Creeper,' he exclaimed. 'There's only one of him. I've a whole congregation of Creepers, Crawlers and Crushers after me!'

'So, you must die and that's all there is to it.'

The last remaining puff went out of Mad Carew. He might as well change his daredevil nickname to Dead Carew and be done with it.

'...and yet...'

Now the Prof's eyes glowed, as other eyes glowed when the emerald was in view. His blood was up. Profit didn't really stir Moriarty. He loved the numbers, not the spoils they tallied. It was the problem. The challenge. Doing that which no one else had done, which no one else could do.

'All indications are that you must die, Carew. The raider of the sacred gem is doomed, irrevocably. Yet, why must that be? Are we not greater than any fate or superstition? I, Moriarty, refuse to accept any so-called inevitability. We shall take your case, Major Carew. Give Colonel Moran a hundred pounds as a retainer.'

Surprised and suspicious, Carew blurted out 'Gladly!' and produced a cheque book.

'Cash, old fellow,' I said.

'Of course.' He nodded glumly, and undid a money belt. He had the sum about him in gold sovereigns.

I piled them up and clinked them a bit. Sound. Coin, I can appreciate!

'You are to take lodgings in our basement. There is a serviceable room, which has been used for the purpose before. Meals are provided at eight shillings daily. Breakfast, dinner, supper. Should you wish high tea or other luxuries, make private arrangements with Mrs Halifax. I need not tell you only to eat and drink what comes to you from our kitchen. We must preserve your health. I prescribe Scotch broth.'

Now, he was talking like a doctor. The Moriarty Cure, suitable for maiden ladies and gentlemen of a certain age.

'One other thing...' he added.

'What? Anything?' Carew said.

'The Green Eye. Sell it to me for a penny down and a penny to pay at the end of the week, with the stone returned to you and the first penny forfeit if I fail to make the second payment. I shall have a legal bill of sale drawn up.'

'You know what that would mean?'

'I know what everything would mean. It is my business.'

'I've sold it before. It comes back, and the buyers… well, the buyers are in no position to come back. Ever.'

The Professor showed his teeth and wrote out a legible receipt.

'Moran, give me a penny,' he said.

Without thinking, I fished a copper from my watch pocket and handed it over. Seconds later, it struck me! I'd roped myself in along with Moriarty on the receiving end of the curse. Don't think the Prof hadn't thought of that, because – as he said – he thought of bloody everything.

Moriarty exchanged the coin for the emerald.

It lay on his desk like a malign paperweight.

So, we were all for the high jump now.

V

Our client was snug in the concealed apartment beneath the storerooms – a cupboard with a cot, where we stashed tenants best advised not to show their faces at street level. Mrs Halifax, alert to the clink of a money belt, supplied tender distractions and gin at champagne prices. When Swedish Suzette (who was Polish) went downstairs, Mrs H. called it a 'house call' and charged extra. If Mad Carew wasn't dead by the end of the week, he'd be dead broke.

Professor Moriarty disappeared into the windowless room where he kept his records. We were up to date on the *Newgate Calendar*, the *Police Gazette* and *Famous Murder Trials*. The Professor knew more about every pick-pocket and high-rip mobster than their mothers or the arresting officers. The more arcane material was in code or foreign languages, or translated into mathematics and written down as page after page of numbers. [6] He said he needed to look into precedents and parallels before deciding on a plan. I had an intimation that would be bad news for some – probably including me.

While the Prof was blowing the dust off press cuttings and jotting down cipher notes, I had the afternoon to myself. Best to get out of the flat and beetle about.

I decided to scratch an itch. On constitutionals through Soho, I had twice had my trouser cuffs assaulted by a pup in Berwick Street Market. The tiny creature's excessively loud yapping was well known. It was past time to skewer the beast. You could consider it a public service, but the truth is – and I don't mind if it shocks more delicate readers – killing an animal always perks me up. I'd prefer to stalk big game in the bush, but there's none of that in London except at the zoological gardens. Even I think it unsporting to aim between the bars and ventilate Rajah the Lion or Jumbo the Elephant, though old, frustrated guns have tried to swell their bags this way when gout or angry colonial officials prevent them from returning to the veldt.

A small annoying dog should take the edge off this hunter's bloodlust. The prey would be all the sweeter because it was the pet of a small annoying boy. I've a trick cane which slips out six inches of honed Sheffield steel at a twist of the knob. The perfect tool for the task. The trick was to stroll by casually and perform a *coup de grâce* in the busy street market without anyone noticing. In Spain, where they appreciate such artistry, I'd be awarded both ears and the tail. In London, there'd be less outrage if I killed the boy.

I swanned into the market and made a play of considering cauliflowers and cabbages – though drat me if I know the difference – while idly twirling the old cane, using it to point at plump veggies at the back of the stalls, then waving it airily to indicate said items didn't come up to snuff under closer scrutiny. The pup was there, nipping at passing skirts and swallowing tit-bits fed it by patrons with a high tolerance for noisome canines. The boy, who kept a tomato stall, was doting and vigilant, his practiced eye out for pilferers. A challenge! Much more than the fat, complacent PC on duty.

For twenty minutes, I stalked the pup. I became as sensible of the cries and bustle of the market as of the jungle.

Which is how I knew they were there.

Little brown men. Not tanned hop pickers from Kent. Natives of far shores.

I didn't exactly see them. But you don't. Oh, maybe you glimpse a stretch of brown wrist between cuff and glove, then turn to see only white faces. You think you catch a few words in Himalayan dialect amid costermongers' cries.

At some point in any tiger hunt, you wonder if the tiger is hunting you – and you're usually right.

I approached the doggie, *en fin*. I raised the stick to the level where its tip would brush over the pup's skull. My grip shifted to allow the one-handed twist which would send steel through canine brain.

From a heap of tomatoes, red eyes glared. I looked again, blinking, and they were gone. But there were altogether too many tomatoes. Too ripe, with a redness approaching that of blood.

The moment had passed. The pup was alive.

I rued that penny. Though not strictly the present possessor of the Green Eye of the Yellow God, I had financed the transfer from Carew to Moriarty. I was implicated in its purchase.

The curse extended to me.

I hurried towards Oxford Street.

The pup knew not how narrow its escape had been. I only left the market – where it would have been easy for someone to get close and slip his own blade through my waistcoat – because I was allowed to. The bill wasn't yet due.

Eyes were on me.

I used the cane, but only to skewer an apple from a stall and walk off without paying. Not one of my more impressive crimes.

Hastening back to our rooms by a roundabout route, I forced myself not to break into a run. I didn't see a yeti in every shadow, but that's not how it works. They let you know there is a yeti in a shadow, and you have to waste worry on every shadow. Invariably, you can't keep up the vigilance. Then, the first shadow you don't treat as if it had a yeti in it is the one the yeti comes out of. Damn strain on the nerves, even mine – which, as many will attest, are constituted of steel cable suitable for suspension bridges.

Only when I turned into Conduit Street, and spotted the familiar figure of Runty Reg – the beggar who kept lookout, and would signal on his penny whistle if anyone official or hostile approached our door – did I stop sweating. I flicked him a copper, which he made disappear.

I returned to our consulting room, calm as you like and pooh-poohing earlier imaginings. Professor Moriarty was addressing a small congregation of all-too-familiar villains. The Green Eye shone in plain sight on the sideboard. Had he summoned the most light-fingered bleeders in London on the assumption one would half-inch the thing and take the consequences?

'Kind of you to join us, Moran,' he said, coldly. 'I have decided we shall assemble a collection of Crown jewels. This emerald is but the first item. You might call this gem matchless, but I believe I can match it.'

He reached into his coat pocket and pulled out something the size of a rifle ball, which he held up between thumb and forefinger. It glistened, darkly. He laid it down beside the Green Eye.

The Black Pearl of the Borgias.

VI

Before Moriarty, the last person unwise enough to own the Black Pearl was Nicholas Savvides, an East End dealer in dubious valuables. Well known among collectors of such trinkets, he was as crooked as they come – even before the Hoxton Creeper twisted him about at the waist. When the police found Savvy Nick, his bellybutton and his arse crack made an exclamation mark. His eyes were popped too, but he was dead enough not to mind being blind and about-face.

The peculiar thing was that the Creeper didn't want the pearl for himself. He was the rummest of customers, a criminal lunatic who suffered from a glandular gigantism. Its chief symptoms were gorilla shoulders and a face like a pulled toffee. He lumbered about in a vile porkpie hat and an old overcoat which strained at the seams, killing people who possessed the Borgia Pearl, only to bestow the hard-luck piece on a succession of 'French' actresses. These delights could be counted on to dispose of the thing to a mug pawnbroker, and set their disappointed beau to spine twisting again. He'd been through most of the cancan chorus at the Tivoli, but – as they say – who hasn't?

The Creeper had been caught, tried and hanged by whatever neck he possessed, and walked away from the gallows whistling Offenbach. To my knowledge, he'd been shot by the police, several jewel thieves and a well-known fence. Bullets didn't take. Once, he'd been blown up with gelignite. No joy there. Something to do with thick bones.

I had no idea Moriarty had the Black Pearl. Since his arse was still in its usual place, I supposed the Creeper hadn't either. Until now. If the prize were openly displayed, the Creeper would find out. He lived rough, down by the docks. Eating rats and – worse – drinking Thames water. Some said he was psychically attuned to his favoured bauble. Even if that was rot, he had his sources. He would follow the trail to Conduit Street. As if we didn't have enough to worry about with the vengeance of the little yellow god.

Moriarty's audience consisted of an even dozen of the continent's premier thieves. Not the ones you've heard of – the cricketing ponce or the frog popinjays. Not the gents who steal for a laugh and to thumb their noses at titled aunties, but the serious, unambitious drudges who get the job done. Low, cunning types we'd dealt with before, who would do their bit for a share of the purse and not peach if they got nobbled. When we wanted things stolen, these were the men – and two women – we called in.

'I have made "a shopping list"', announced the Professor. 'Four more choice items to add lustre to the collection. It is my intention that these valuables be secured within the next two days.'

A covered blackboard – relic of his pedagogical days – stood by his desk. Like a magician, Moriarty pulled away the cloth. He had written his list clearly, in chalk:

1. The Green Eye of the Yellow God

2. The Black Pearl of the Borgias

3. The Falcon of the Knights of St John

4. The Jewels of the Madonna of Naples

5. The Jewel of Seven Stars

6. The Eye of Balor

Simon Carne, a cracksman and swindler who insisted on wearing a fake humpback, put up his hand like a schoolboy.

'You have permission to speak,' the Professor said. It's a wonder he didn't fetch his mortar board, black gown and cane. They had been passed on to Mistress Strict, one of Mrs Halifax's young ladies; she took in overage pupils with a yen for the discipline of their school days.

'Item three, sir,' Carne said. 'The Falcon. Is that the *Templar* Falcon?'

'Indeed. A jewelled gold statuette, fashioned in 1530 by Turkish slaves in the Castle of St Angelo on Malta. The Order of the Hospital of St John of Jerusalem intended it to be bestowed on Carlos the Fifth of Spain. It was, as I'm sure you know, lost to pirates before it could be delivered.'

'Well, I've never heard of it,' Fat Kaspar said A promising youth: his appetite for puddings was as great as his appetite for crime, but he'd a smart mind and a beady eye for fast profit.

'It's been sought by a long line of adventurers,' explained Carne. 'And not been seen in fifty years.'

'So some say.'

'You want it here *within two days*?'

Moriarty was unruffled by the objection.

'If there's no fog on the Channel, the Templar Falcon should join the collection by tomorrow morning. I have cabled the Grand Vampire in Paris with details of the current location of this *rara avis*. It has been in hiding. A soulless brigand enamelled it like a common blackbird to conceal its value.'

'The Grand Vampire is stealing this prize, and giving it to you?' Carne said.

I didn't believe that either.

'Of course not. In point of fact, he won't have to steal it. The Falcon lies neglected in Pére Duroc's curiosity shop. The proprietor has little idea of the dusty treasure nestling in his unsaleable stock. We have a tight schedule, else

I would send someone to purchase it for its asking price. If any of you could be trusted with fifteen francs.'

A smattering of nervous laughter.

'I have offered the Grand Vampire fair exchange. I am giving him something he wants, as valuable to him as the Falcon is to us. I do not intend to tell you what that is.'

But – never fear – I'll release the feline from the reticule. On our St Helena excursion, Moriarty took the trouble to validate a rumour. As you know, Napoleon's imperial bones were exhumed in 1840 and returned to France and – after twenty years of lying in a cardboard box as the frogs argued and raised subscriptions – interred in a hideous porphyry sarcophagus under the dome at Les Invalides. You can buy a ticket and gawp at it. However, as you don't know, Napoleon isn't inside. For a joke, the British gave France the remains of an anonymous, pox-ridden, undersized sailor. The Duke of Wellington didn't stop laughing for a month.

On the island, the Prof found the original unmarked grave, dug up what was left of the Corsican Crapper and stole Boney's bonce. That relic was now on its way to Paris by special messenger, fated to become a drinking cup for the leader of *Les Vampires*, France's premier criminal gang. A bit of a conversation piece, I expect. Les Vamps run to that line of the dramatic the Frenchies call Grand Guignol. Supposed to make their foes shiver in their beds, but hard to take seriously. Grand Vampires don't last long. There's a whole cupboard full of drinking cups made out of their skulls.

'Moran, you're au fait with the Jewel of Seven Stars.'

I had heard of item five. It was an Egyptian ruby with sparkling flaws in the pattern of the constellation of the plough, set in a golden scarab ring, dug out of a Witch Queen's Tomb. Most of the archaeologists involved had died of Nile fever or Cairo clap. The sensation press wrote these ailments up as 'the curse of the Pharaohs'. I knew the bauble to be in London, property of one Margaret Trelawny – daughter of a deceased tomb robber. [7]

Just for a jolly, while idly considering the locations of the most valuable prizes in London, I'd cased Trelawny House in Kensington Palace Gardens. Fair-to-middling difficult. But, see above, my remarks on famous gems: Thorny Problem of Converting Same into Anonymous Cash. Also, the place had a sour air. I'm not prey to superstition, but know a likely ambush from a mile off. Trelawny House was one of those iffy locations – best kept away from. Might I now have to take the plunge and regret the fancy of planning capers one didn't really wish to commit?

'The Jewels of the Madonna are of less intrinsic interest,' continued Moriarty. 'These gems – mediocre stones, poorly set, but valuable enough – bedecked a statue hoisted and paraded about Naples during religious festivals. I see I have your interest. A notion got put about that they were too sacred to steal. No one would dare inflict such insult on Mary – who, as a carpenter's wife in Judea, was unlikely to have sported such ornament in her lifetime.

'As it happens, the *real reason* no one tried for the jewels was that the Camorra decreed they not be touched. Italian *banditti* who would sell their own mothers retain a superstitious regard for Mother Mary. They wash the blood off their hands and present pious countenances at mass on Sunday. However, as ever, someone would not listen. Gennaro, a blacksmith, stole the jewels to impress his girlfriend. They have been "in play" ever since.

'Foolish Gennaro is long dead, but the Camorra haven't got the booty back. [8] At this moment, after a trans-European game of pass the parcel with corpses, the gems are hidden after the fashion of Poe's purloined letter. One Giovanni Lombardo, a carpenter whose death notice appears in this morning's papers, substituted them for the paste jewels in the prop store of the Royal Opera House in Covent Garden. Signorina Bianca Castafiore, "the Milenese Nightingale", rattles them nightly, with matinees Wednesday and Saturday, in the "jewel scene" from Gounod's *Faust*. It is of scientific interest that the diva's high notes are said to set off sympathetic vibrations which burst bottles and kill rats. I should be interested in observing such a phenomenon, which might have applications in our line of endeavour.'

'What about the eye-tyes?' asked Alf Bassick, a reliable fetch-and-carry man. 'They've been a headache lately.'

'Ah, yes, the Neapolitans,' the Professor said. 'The London address of the Camorra, as you know, is Beppo's Ice Cream Parlour in Old Compton Street. They present the aspect of comical buffoons but, by my estimation, the activities of their Soho Merchants' Protective Society have cut into our income by seven and a half per cent.'

The SMPS was a band of Moustache Petes selling insurance policies to pub-keepers and restauranteurs: don't agree to cough up the weekly payments and your place of business has trouble with rowdy, window-breaking customers; stop paying and you start smiling the Italian smile. That's a deep cut in your throat, from ear to ear; it really does look like a red clown's grin.

'Hitherto, the London Camorra has merely been an inconvenience. Now they know their blessed jewels are in the city, they will be more troublesome. It is a cardinal error to classify the Camorra as a criminal organisation, an Italian equivalent to *Les Vampires*...'

Or us, he didn't say. He liked to think of the Firm as an academic exercise: abstruse economics, *sub rosa* mathematics.

'...at bottom, the Camorra – and their Sicilian and Calabrian equivalents, the Mafia and the 'Ndrangheta – are a romantic, fanatic religious-nationalist movement, as remorseless and unreasonable as the priests of the yellow god. They care not about dying, as individuals. This makes them exceedingly dangerous.'

He let that sink in.

'Don Rafaele Corbucci, chief of chiefs of the Camorra, has vowed to return the jewels to the Madonna. He has taken an oath on the life of his own mother. He has personally followed the jewels across Europe and is presently in London. He paid a call on the late Signor Lombardo at his place of business yesterday. Measures must be taken to pluck the fruit before he can get his hands on it.'

To scare each other, criminals told stories about Don Rafaele. You can imagine how they run. It is said that when a devoted lieutenant thoughtlessly spit out a cigar end in church on a saint's day, the pious Don had him strangled with his only son's entrails. He took his culture seriously, too – and had a sense of humour. While infatuated with *that bitch* Irene Adler – yes, he's another of her leavings – he took against a critic who ridiculed her performance as Duchess Hélène in *I Vespri Siciliani*. The man wound up with his own ears cut off and a donkey's ears nailed onto his head in their place.

I was surprised to learn this monster had a mama. If it were a matter of keeping his word, Don Rafaele would personally sink the old biddy in the Bay of Naples.

'What about item six?' Carne chipped in.

'The Eye of Balor,' Moriarty said. 'A gold coin, named for a giant of Irish mythology, reputed to have been taken from a leprechaun's pot... Lately the "lucky piece" of "Dynamite" Desmond Mountmain, General-in-Chief of the Irish Republican Invincibles, which brought him only poor luck, since last week an infernal device of his own manufacture went off in his face when he thumped the table too hard at a meeting of his Inner Council of Immortals.'

I told you Ireland would come into it.

'The Eye of Balor is currently among Mountmain's effects, in the possession of the Special Irish Branch of Scotland Yard. Half a dozen sons, cousins and brothers would like to obtain the coin. It's said that, if "the wee folk" approve, the owner will ascend to the office of Mage-King of Ireland, whatever that means. The chief contestant for the position is Desmond's son, Tyrone.'

That was foul news. Another 'romantic, fanatic religious-nationalist movement'. Your paddy bomber though concerned with his own individual skin is too hot-headed as a rule to preserve it. Dynamite Des wasn't the first Fenian to blow himself up with his own blasting powder.

Tyrone Mountmain, the heir apparent, figured high on my list of people I hoped never to meet again.

So, now we had to worry about brown priests and marauding *mi-go*, the Hoxton Creeper, Mysteries of Ancient Egypt, the Knights Templar, the Naples Mob, the little people and the bloody Fenians! It was a wonder Malvoisin's Mirror, the Monkey's Paw, Cap'n Flint's treasure and Sir Michael Sinclair's Door were off the 'shopping list'.

How cursed did Professor Moriarty want to be by the end of the week?

VII

Recall my remarks re. nuisance value attendant on one little murder carried out in the service of a trade union?

Ask anyone who knows us (and is still in a position to talk) and you'll be told we are a mercenary concern. We kill anyone, of whatever political stripe or social standing. For a price. It's not true that money is all that interests us. The thrill of the chase is involved. If nothing else is on, I'd cheerfully pot someone or steal something just to keep my hand in.

Moriarty claims pure intellectual interest in the problem at hand, and can be inveigled into an enterprise if it strikes him as out of the ordinary. He feels pepper in the blood too, in the planning if not the execution. The moment of clear thrill which burns cold – as a perfect shot brings down a tiger or an archduke – is the closest I can get to the fireworks which go off in the Prof's brain when his reptile head stops oscillating… and he suddenly knows how an impossible trick can be brought off.

We have no cause but ourselves. We have no politics. We have no religion. I believe in Sensation. Moriarty believes in Sums. That's about as deep as it needs run.

It was an irritant when the misconception set in that we were in sympathy with the working man. That inconvenience was as nothing beside the notion that fellows with names like Moriarty or Moran must support Irish Independence.

From time to time – usually when an American millionaire who'd never set foot on the isle of his ancestors for fear of being robbed by long-lost cousins decided to fund the Struggle – one or other of the many branches of Fenianism secured our temporary services. If Desmond Mountmain weren't so all-fired certain he could handle his own bombmaking, he might have been buried in one piece. It takes a more precise touch to blow the door off a strongroom than the medals off a chief constable. Dynamiters on our books have names like 'Steady Hands' Crenshaw, not 'Shaky' Brannigan.

As a rule, Irish petitioners were much more trouble than they were worth.

Over the years, half a dozen proud rebels had tried to enlist us on the never-never in fantastic schemes of insurrection. You could separate the confidence men from the real patriots because simple crooks venture sensible-sounding endeavours like stealing cases of rifles from the Woolwich Arsenal. Genuine Irish revolutionaries run to crackpottery like deploying an especially made submarine warship to overthrow British rule in Canada. We decided against throwing in with that and you can look up how well it turned out. [9] Canada is still in the Empire last I paid attention, though I've no idea why. The place has nothing worth shooting (unless you count Inuit and Sasquatch which, at that, I might) and boasts 50,000 trees to every woman.

When a bold Fenian's proposal of an alliance – with our end of it providing the funds – is rejected, he acts exactly like a music hall mick refused credit for drink. Hearty, exploitative friendliness curdles into wheedling desperation then turns into dark threats of dire vengeance. Always, there's an appeal to us as 'fellow Irishmen'. If the Prof or I have family connections in *John Bull's Other Island*, we'd rather not hear from them. We've sufficient unpleasant English relatives to be getting on with.

It is possible the Professor is a distant cousin of Bishop Moriarty of Kerry, though rebels know better than to raise that connection. The Bishop – in one of the rare sensible utterances of a churchman I can recall – once declared: 'When we look down into the fathomless depth of this infamy of the heads of the Fenian conspiracy, we must acknowledge that eternity is not long enough, nor Hell hot enough to punish such miscreants.' Far be it from me to agree with anything said in a pulpit, but the Bish was not far wrong.

So: Tyrone Mountmain.

Here's why he wasn't at the meeting of the Inner Council of Immortals of the Irish Republican Invincibles which ended with a bang… he was the only man in living memory to devote himself with equal passion to the causes of Irish Home Rule and Temperance.

A paddy intolerant of strong drink is as common as a politician averse to robbing the public purse. An Irishman who goes around smashing bottles and barrels has few comrades and fewer friends. If he weren't a six-foot rugby forward and bare-knuckle boxer, I dare say Tyrone wouldn't have lasted beyond his first crusade, but he was and he had. Dear old Da, whose favoured tipple was scarcely less potent than the dynamite which did for him, could not abide a teetotaller in his home and exiled his own son from the Invincibles. They had a three-day donnybrook about it, cuffing each other's hard heads up and down Aungier Street while onlookers placed bets.

After the fight, Tyrone quit the Irish Republican Invincibles and founded the Irish Invincible Republicans. He attracted no followers except for his demented Aunt Sophonisiba, who advocated the health-giving properties of drinking from her own chamberpot, the tithing of two pennies in every shilling to establish an Irish Expedition to the Planet Mercury and (most ridiculous of all) votes for women.

Tyrone promulgated a plan for bringing Britain to its knees by dynamiting public houses. The Fenian Brigades would never countenance such a sacrilegiously un-Irish notion. With Desmond dead, Tyrone rallied the unexploded remnants of the IRI and folded them into the IIR. Claiming Aunt Soph was in touch with his Da on the ethereal plane, Tyrone relayed the story that if Dynamite Des hadn't been so annoyed at a wave of recent arrests made by the Special Irish Branch he wouldn't have hit the table so hard. That made Desmond a martyr to the Cause. Tyrone declared war on the SIB.

As has been said about any number of conflicts, including the Franco-Prussian War and the Gladstone–Disraeli feud, it's a shame they can't both lose.

Tyrone had a bee in his bonnet about the Eye of Balor.

Soph put it into his head that he must have the coin to rise to his true position. Desmond had thought it an amusing relic to show off to his drinking cronies. Tyrone, who had no drinking cronies, believed it possessed supernatural powers.

The only reason he hadn't yet tried to steal it back from Scotland Yard was that Soph said she knew from 'a vision' that if the Eye of Balor were not in the hands of its rightful owner, the 'little people' would bring about the ruination of anyone who had the temerity to hang onto it. So, the Irish Invincible Republicans were waiting for the Special Irish Branch to be undermined by leprechauns. I assumed they were all down the pub, against Tyrone's orders, leaving him home with only a vial of his own piddle, as recommended by potty aunts everywhere, to warm his insides.

Ireland! I ask you, was ever there such a country of bastards, priests and lunatics?

VIII

As promised, another item for our collection arrived first thing the next morning. Hand-delivered by an apache from Paris, who took one sniff at an English breakfast, muttered, '*Merde alors*', and hopped back on the boat train. Can't say I blamed her.

1. ~~The Green Eye of the Yellow God~~
2. ~~The Black Pearl of the Borgias~~
3. ~~The Falcon of the Knights of St John~~
4. The Jewels of the Madonna of Naples
5. The Jewel of Seven Stars
6. The Eye of Balor

The fabulous gold, jewel-encrusted Templar Falcon looked like a dull black paperweight. A label attached by string to one claw indicated decreasingly ambitious prices. Generations of Parisian tat connoisseurs had not nibbled. On principle, the Grand Vampire had stolen the bird – murdering three people, and burning the curiosity shop to the ground – rather than meet the asking price (which, I'm sure, Pére Duroc would have lowered yet again, if pressed). I trusted our esteemed colleague was enjoying his afternoon *anis* from the skull of the Emperor Napoleon.

'Are you sure there are jewels in that?' asked Fat Kaspar, who was trusted with dusting the sideboard.

Moriarty nodded, holding the thing up like Yorick's skull.

'What was the point of it again?' I enquired.

'After the Knights of St John were driven off Rhodes by Suleiman the Magnificent, the Emperor Carlos let the order make stronghold on Malta and demanded a single falcon as annual rent. He expected a live bird, but the Knights decided to impress him by manufacturing this fantastically valuable statue… which was then stolen.'

Fat Kaspar prepared a spot for the bird, and Moriarty set it down.

'What happened afterwards?' the youth asked.

'What usually happens when rent isn't paid. Eviction. The Templars were booted out of Malta. In shame. Later, they were excommunicated or disavowed by the Pope. In Spain and Portugal, they practiced "unholy" rites – the usual orgiastic behaviour such as you'd find in any brothel when the fleet's in, but with incense and chanting and vestments. Other orders made war on them, hunted them down. It is said the last of them were hung on cartwheels and left for the crows to peck out their eyes.

'But the Knights of St John still exist, and I am sure they wish the return of their property. I doubt the present Grand Master feels any obligation to deliver it to the Spanish Crown.'

'Who's this Grand Master wallah?' I asked.

'Marshall Alaric Molina de Marnac.'

'Never heard of him.'

'That would be why it's called a secret society, Moran. The Knights of St John have many other names in the many territories where they operate. In England, they are a sect of Freemasons, and have conjoined with several occult groups. Their Grand Lodge, in the catacombs under Guildhall, is abuzz with preparations for a visit from the Grand Master. The call has gone out and the Holy Knights will answer. De Marnac heard that the falcon had surfaced in Paris…'

'What little bird whispered that in his ear?'

Moriarty's thin lips approximated a sly smile. 'He set out by special train from the Templar fastness in Cadiz, but arrived too late… as the embers of the Duroc establishment were settling. A troop of men-at-arms, in full armour, clashed with *Les Vampires* in Montmartre. Lives were lost. I calculate they delayed the arrival of de Marnac on these shores by eighteen hours. The Grand Vampire will be less inclined to do us favours in the future. I had taken that into account – we shall have to do something about France when this present business is concluded.'

I did not think to remind him that our purpose was simply to save one rotten Englishman's hide. Moriarty had not forgotten Mad Carew. He was playing a much larger game, but the original commission remained.

Fat Kaspar looked at the falcon. He brushed its jet wings with his feather duster, and the thing's dead eye seemed to glint.

Something was going on between boy and blackbird.

Moriarty had already assigned the day's errands. Simon Carne was off in Kensington 'investigating a gas leak'. Alf Bassick was in Rotherhithe picking up items Moriarty had ordered from a cabinetmaker whose specialty was making new furniture look old enough to pass for Chippendale. Now, it was my turn for marching orders.

'Moran, I have taken the liberty of filling in your appointment book. You have a busy day. You are expected at Scotland Yard for luncheon, the Royal Opera for the matinee and Trelawny House for late supper. I trust you can secure the items needed to complete our collection. Take whoever you need from our reserves. I shall be in my study until midnight – calculations must be made.'

'Fair enough, Prof. You know what you're doing.'

'Yes, Moran. I do.'

IX

So, how does one steal a coin from a locked desk in Scotland Yard? A castle on the Victoria Embankment, full to bursting with policemen, detectives, gaolers and ruthless agents of the British State. An address – strictly, it's New Scotland Yard – lawbreakers would be well advised to stay away from.

Simple answer.

You don't. You can't. And if you could, you wouldn't.

For why?

If such a coup – a theft of evidence from the Headquarters of Her Majesty's Police – could be achieved, word would quickly circulate. The name of the master cracksman would be toasted in every pub in the East End. Policemen drink in those pubs too. Even if you left no clue, thanks to the brilliance of your foreplanning and the cunning of the execution, your signature would be on the deed.

Rozzers don't take kindly to having their noses tweaked. If they can't have you up for a given crime, they take you in on a drunk and disorderly charge, then tell anyone foolish enough to ask that you 'fell down the stairs'. Once inside the holding cells, any number of nasty fates can befall the unwary. When the Hoxton Creeper was in custody, the peelers got shot of seven or eight on their most-hated list by making felons share his lodgings.

No, you don't just breeze into a den of police with larcenous intent and a set of lock picks. Unless you've a yen for martyrdom.

You walk up honestly and openly, without trace of an Irish accent. You ask for Inspector Harvey Lukens of the SIB and *buy* whatever you want. Not with money. That's too easy. As with the Grand Vampire, you find something the other fellow wants more than the item they possess which you desire. Usually, you can cadge a favour by giving Lukens the current addresses of any one of a dozen Fenian troublemakers on the 'wanted' books. The Branch was constituted solely to deal with a rise in Fenian activity, specifically a bombing campaign in the eighties which got under their silly helmets – especially when the *pissoir* outside their office was dynamited on the same night some mad micks tried to topple Nelson's column with gunpowder.

Here's the thing about the Special *Irish* Branch: unlike their colleagues in the Criminal Investigation Department, they didn't give a farthing's fart about *English* crime. As far as Inspector Lukens was concerned, you could rob as many post offices as you like – abduct the postmistresses and sell 'em to oriental potentates if you could get threepence for the baggages – just so long as you didn't use the stolen money in the cause of Home Rule.

When it came to Surrey stranglers, Glasgow gougers, Welsh wallet-lifters, Birmingham burglars or cockney coshers, the SIB were remarkably tolerant. However, any Irishman who struck a match on a public monument or sold a cough drop on Sunday was liable to be deemed 'a person of interest', and appear – if he survived that far – at his arraignment with blacked eyes and missing teeth.

Shortly after luncheon – a reasonable repast at Scotland Yard, with cold meats and beer and tinned peaches in syrup – I left the building, frowning, and made rendezvous with a band of fellows. Thieves, of course. Not of the finest water, but experienced. *All* persons of special interest:

Michaél Murphy Magooly O'Connor, jemmy-man.

Martin Aloysius McHugh, locksmith.

Seamus 'Shiv' Shaughnessy, knife thrower.

Pádraig 'Pork' Ó Méalóid, hooligan.

Patrick 'Paddy Red' Regan, second-storey bandit.

Leopold MacLiammóir, smooth-talker.

They did not think to wonder what special attributes qualified them for this particular caper. The Professor was in it, so there'd likely be a payout at the end of the day.

'It's no go, the bribery,' I told them. 'Lukens won't play that game. So, it's the contingency plan, lads. The coin's in the desk, the desk's in the basement office. I've left a window on the latch. When the smoke bomb goes off and the bluebottles run out of the building, slip in and riffle the place. Take anything else you want, but bring the Professor his item and you'll remember this day well.'

Half a dozen nods.

'Ye'll not be regrettin' this at all at all, Colonel, me darlin',' Leopold said. His brogue was so thick the others couldn't make out what he was saying. He was an Austrian who liked to pretend he was an Irishman. After all, whoever heard of a Dubliner called Leopold? It's possible he'd never even been to the ould sod at all.

Ó Méalóid pulled out a foot-long knotty club from a place of concealment and Regan slipped out his favourite stabbing knife. McHugh's long fingers twitched. Shaughnessy handed around a flask of something distilled from stinging nettles. The little band of merry raiders wrapped checked scarves around the lower halves of their faces and pulled down their cap brims.

I left them and strolled back across the road. Pausing by the front door, I took out a silver case and extracted a cylinder approximately the size and shape of a cigar. I asked a uniformed police constable if he might have a lucifer about him, and a flame was kindly proffered. I lit the fuse of the cylinder and dropped it in the gutter. It fizzed alarmingly. Smoke was produced. Whistles shrilled.

My thieves charged across the road and poured through the open window. And were immediately pounced on by the SIB Head-Knocking Society.

The smoke dispelled within a minute. I offered the helpful constable a real cigar he was happy to accept.

From offstage came the sounds of a severe kicking and battering, punctuated by cries and oaths. Eventually, this died down a little.

Inspector Lukens came out of the building and, without further word, dropped a tied handkerchief into my hand. He went back indoors, to fill in forms.

Six easy arrests. That was a currency the SIB dealt in. Six Irish crooks caught in the process of committing a stupid crime. As red-handed as they were redheaded.

This might shake your belief in honour among thieves, but I should mention that the micks were hand-picked for more than their criminal specialties and stated place of birth. All were of that breed of crook who don't know when to lay off the mendacity... the sort who agree to steal on commission but think for themselves and withhold prizes they've been paid to secure. Dirty little birds who feather their own nests. Said nests would be on Dartmoor for the next few years. And serve 'em right.

It didn't hurt that they were of the Irish persuasion. I doubt any one of them took an interest in politics, but the SIB would be happy to have six more heads to bounce off the walls or dunk in the ordure buckets.

You might say that I had done my patriotic duty in enabling such a swoop against enemies of the Queen. Only that wouldn't wash. I've a trunkful medals awarded on the same basis. Mostly, I was murdering heathens for my own enjoyment.

I unwrapped the handkerchief and considered the Eye of Balor. It didn't look much like an eye, or even a coin – just a lump of greenish metal I couldn't tell was gold. In legend, Balor had a baleful, petrifying glance. On the battlefield, his comrades would peel back his mighty eyelids to turn his Medusan stare against the foe. Stories were confused as to whether this treasure was that eye or just named after it. Desmond Mountmain claimed it had been given to him during a faerie revel by King Brian of the Leprechauns. I suspected that the brand of pee-drinking lunacy practised by his sister ran in the family. It was said – mostly by the late Dynamite Des – that any who dared withhold the coin from a true Irish rebel would hear the howl of the banshee and suffer the wrath of the little people.

At that moment, an unearthly wail sounded out across the river. I bit through my cigar.

A passing excursion boat was overloaded with small, raucous creatures in sailor suits, flapping ribbons in the wind. The wail was a ship's whistle. Not a banshee. The creatures were schoolgirls on an outing, pulling each other's braids. Not followers of King Brian.

Ever since the tomato stall, I'd had my whiskers up. I was unused to that. This business was a test for even my nerves.

After a few moments, I carefully wrapped the coin again and passed it on to a small messenger – Filthy Fanny, not a bloody leprechaun – with orders to fetch it back to Conduit Street. Any temptation to run off with the precious item would be balanced by the vivid example of the six Irishmen. The professional urchin took off as if she had salt on her tail.

I summoned the not-for-hire cab I had arrived in.

'The Royal Opera House,' I told Chop, the Firm's best driver. 'And a shilling on top of the fare if we miss the first act.'

X

Some scorn opera as unrealistic. Large licentious ladies, posturing villains, concealed weapons, loud noises, suicides, thefts, betrayals, elongated ululations, explosions, goblets of poison and the curtain falling on a pile of corpses. Well, throw in a bag of tigers, and that's my life. If I want treachery, bloodshed and screaming women, I can get enough at home, thank you very much.

I dislike opera because it's *Italian*. The eye-tyes are the lowest breed of white man, a bargain-priced imitation of the French. All hair oil and smiling and back-stabbing and cowardice, left out in the sun too long.

This brouhaha of the Jewels of the Madonna of Naples was deeply Italian, and thoroughly operatic. The recitative was too convoluted to follow without music.

The gist: a succession of mugs across Europe got hold of the loot first lifted by Gennaro the Blacksmith, also known as Gennaro the Damned and Gennaro the Dead. The Camorra – a merciless, implacable brotherhood – was sworn to kill anyone who dared acquire the treasure, but no fool thought to return the loot and apologise. They all tried for a quick sale and a getaway, or thought to hide the valuables until 'the heat died down'. Under the jewels' spell, they forgot about the only institution ever to combine the adjectives 'efficient' and 'Italian'. The Camorra carries feuds to the fifth generation; there's little to no likelihood of anyone or their great-grandchildren profiting from Gennaro's impetuous theft.

As mentioned, the latest idiot to acquire the Jewels was Giovanni Lombardo, a propmaker for the Royal Opera. He'd received the package from an equally addled cousin, who expired from strychnine poisoning at a Drury Lane pie stall a few hours later. Lombardo had been victim of a singular, fatal assault in his Islington carpenter's shop. His head chanced to be trapped in a vice. Several holes were drilled in his brain-pan. A bloodied brace and bit was found in the nearby sawdust.

An editorial in the Harmsworth Press cited this crime as sorry proof of the deleterious effects of gory sensationalism paraded nightly in Italian on the stage, instead of daily in English in the newspapers as was right and proper. That *Faust* was sung in French didn't trouble the commentator. Generally, the French are to be condemned for license and libertinism and the Italians for violence and cowardice. When foreigners copy each other's vices, it confuses the English, so it's best to ignore the facts and print the prejudice.

The Harmsworth theory, which Scotland Yard was supposedly 'taking seriously', painted the culprit as a demented habitué of the opera, sensibilities eroded by addiction to tales of multiple murder and outrageous horror. No longer satisfied with the bladders of pig's blood burst when a tenor was stabbed or the papier maché heads which rolled when an ingénue was guillotined, this notional fiend had become entirely deranged. He doubtless intended to recreate gruesome moments from favourite operas with passing innocents cast in the roles of corpses-to-be. No one was safe!

This afternoon, a gaggle of ladies loitered outside the Royal Opera House with banners. One pinned a 'suppress this nasty foreign muck' badge on my lapel. I assured the harridan I'd sooner send my children up chimneys than expose their tender ears to the corrupting wailing of the so-called entertainment perpetrated inside this very building. If there were still profit in selling brats as sweeps, I'd be up for it. Only the mothers of my numberless darling babes, mostly dark-skinned and resident in far corners of the Empire, would insist on their cut of the purse and render such child-vendage scarcely worth the effort.

While chatting with the anti-opera protester, I cast a casual eye about Covent Garden. No more suspicious, olive-skinned loiterers than usual. Which is to say anyone in sight could – and perhaps would – turn out to be a Camorra assassin. One or two of the protesting ladies wore suspicious veils.

Lombardo's wounds consisted of two medium-sized holes, one small (almost tentative) hole and one large (ultimately fatal) hole. He had kept the secret of the jewels until that third hole was started. Then, the final hole was made to shut him up. All very Italian.

Lombardo had asked around London fences for prices on individual stones, so the spider in the centre of his web heard of it. Moriarty also knew the carpenter had been commissioned to provide props for the current production, and saw at once where the loot was hidden. In act three of *Faust*, Marguerite, the stupid bint who passes for a leading lady, piles on a collection of tat gifted her by the demon Méphistophélès and regards herself in a mirror. She gives vent to the 'Jewel Song' ('*Ah! Je ris de me voir si belle en ce miroir!*'), an aria which sets my teeth on edge even when sung in tune (which is seldom). It's about how much lovelier she looks when plastered with priceless gems.

Thanks to Moriarty's learned insight, we knew about the jewels. Thanks to strategic cranial drilling, Don Rafaele knew about the jewels. The Camorra could have saved some elbow-work if they'd read their Edgar Allan Poe. [10] The only person in the case – I dismiss Scotland Yard, of course – who didn't know about the jewels was Bianca Castafiore, the young, substantial diva enjoying a triumphant run in the role of Marguerite.

When the Milanese Nightingale performs the 'Jewel Song', the unkind have been known to venture she would look lovelier still with a potato sack over her head. However, la Castafiore had a devoted clique of ferocious admirers. I knew the type: several of Mrs Halifax's regulars couldn't get enough of the Welsh trollop known as Tessie the Two-Ton Taff.

As I entered the foyer of the Opera House, I thought the banshee associated with the Eye of Balor had pursued me. A wailing resounded throughout the building.

Then I recognised the racket as that bloody 'Jewel Song'.

A commissionaire was worried about a chandelier, which was vibrating and clinking. A small, crying boy was led out of the auditorium by an angry mama and a relieved papa. I swear they were bleeding at the ears. In the garden, dogs howled in sympathy. The silver plugs in my teeth hurt.

Vokins, the Professor's useful man at the opera, awaited me. Not an especially inspiring specimen: all pockmarks, bowler hat and whining wheedle. His duties, mostly, were to fuss around the petticoats of chorus girls who no longer believed they'd be whisked off and married by a baronet – usually, being whisked off and something elsed by a baronet put paid to that illusion – or could rise to leading roles by virtue of their voices. Alternative methods of employment were always available to such. A modicum of acting ability came in handy when seeming to be delighted at the prospect of an evening – or ten expensive minutes – with Mrs Halifax's more peculiar customers. Vokins, officially an usher, also scouted out the nobs in the boxes and passed on gossip… 'All part of the great mosaic of life in the capital,' Moriarty was wont to say.

First off, I asked if there'd been any break-ins or petty thefts lately.

'No more'n usual, Colonel,' he replied. 'None who didn't tithe to the Firm, at any rate.'

'Seen any remarkable Italians?'

'Don't see nothing else. The diva has a platoon of 'em. Dressers and puffers and the like.'

'Anyone very recently?'

'We've a 'ole new set o' scene-shifters today. The usual lot 'oo come with the company didn't turn up this morning. Took sick at an ice cream parlour, after hours. All of 'em, to a man 'ad cousins ready to step in. Seventeen of 'em. Now you mentions it, they are a *remarkable* bunch, for eye-talians. Oh, you can't mistake 'em for anythin' else, Colonel. To look at 'em, they're eye-tye through and through. Waxy 'taches, brown complexions, glittery eyes, tight trews, black 'air.

'But there's a funny thing, a *singular* thing – they don't squabble. Never met an eye-tye 'oo didn't spend all the hours o' the day shoutin' at any other eye-tye within earshot. Most productions, scene-shifters come to blows five or six times a performance. Someone storms out or back in. Elbow in the eye, knee in the crotch, a lot o' monkey-jabber with spitting and hand gestures 'oose meanin' can't be mistook.

'There's been woundin', cripplin', even, all over 'oo gets to pick up which old helmet. But this lot, the substitute shifters, work like clockwork. Don't say anythin' much. Just get the job done. No arguments. Management's in 'eaven. They wants to sack the no-shows, and keep this mob on permanent.'

So, the Camorra were already in the house.

They couldn't have the jewels yet, because the song was still going on, and it would last a while longer. The Castafiore clique would call at least two encores. The rest of the house might be impatient to get on with the story – especially the bit in act five where Marguerite is hanged – but the diva would milk her signature tune for all it was worth.

I peeped through the main doors. Marguerite's jewels sparkled in the limelight and her mirror kept flashing.

'When she goes offstage, what happens to her props?' I asked Vokins.

'A dresser takes the jewels and the mirror off her. 'Attie 'Awkins. She's took ill, too; must be somethin' goin' round. But 'er sister turned up with the others. Not what you'd expect, either. Funny that a yellow-'aired Stepney bit called 'Awkins 'as a sister called Malilella who's dark as a gypsy. I made 'umble introductions and proffered my card, enquiring as to whether she'd be interested in a fresh line of work. This Malilella whipped out one o' them stilletters and near stuck me Adam's apple. You can still see the mark where she pricked.' He pulled back his collar to show me a red welt. 'She's in the wings, waiting for the jewels.'

I saw where the snatch would be made. There was no time to be lost.

'Vokins, round up whoever you can bribe, and get 'em in the hall. I need you to reinforce the Castafiore clique. I must have as many reprises as you can get out of her – keep the "Jewel Song" going!'

'You want to 'ear it *again*?'

'It's my favourite ditty,' I lied. 'I want to hear it for twenty minutes or more.'

Enough time to get round to the wings, minding out for the girl with the stiletto and her seventeen swarthy comrades.

'No accountin' for taste,' Vokins said. I gave him a handful of sovereigns and he rushed about recruiting. Confectionary stalls went unmanned and mop buckets unattended as Vokins lured their proprietors into an augmented clique.

Bianca Castafiore, up to her ankles in flowers tossed by admirers, paused to take a bow after concluding her aria for the third time. Even she looked startled when the crowd swelled with cries of '*Encore, encore!*' Never one to disappoint her public, she took a deep breath and launched into it once again.

'*Ah! Je ris de me voir si belle en ce miroir...*'

Groans from less partisan members of the audience were drowned out, though more than a few programs were shredded or opera glasses snapped in two.

This is where the Moran quick-thinking came into it.

The situation was simple: upon her exit, the diva would surrender the

Jewels of the Madonna without knowing they were real. The valued new staff of the Royal Opera House would quit en masse.

So, why hadn't the jewels been lifted before the performance? Well, if Don Rafaele Corbucci held one thing almost as sacred as the Virgin Mary, it was opera. A once-in-a-lifetime opportunity to see the jewel scene performed with real jewels was an overwhelming temptation. He would be in one of the boxes, enjoying the show before fulfilling his obligation to avenge the indignity perpetrated by Gennaro. I hoped his brains had been boiled by la Castafiore's sustained high notes, for I needed him distracted.

Once the jewels were offstage, they were lost to me.

So, what to do?

Simple. I would have to seize them before they made their exit.

By a side door, I went backstage. In a hurry, I picked up items as I found them on racks in dressing rooms. When I told the story later, I claimed to have donned complete costume and make-up for the role of Méphistophélès. Actually, I made do with a red cloak, a cowl with horns and a half-facemask with a Cyrano nose.

I noticed several of the new scene-shifters, paying attention to the noise and the stage and therefore not much interested in me. I found myself in the wings just as la Castafiore, whose prodigious throat must be in danger of cracking, was chivvied into an unwise, record-setting seventh encore.

A little man with spikes of hair banged his fists against the wall and rent his shirt in red-faced fury, screeching 'Get that sow off my stage!' in Italian. Carlo Jonsi, the producer, had little hope his pleas would, like Henry II's offhand thoughts about a troublesome priest, be acted on by skilled assassins. Though, as it happened, the house was packed with skilled assassins.

The dresser's supposed sister Malilella – she of the stiletto – was waiting impatiently for her moment. I wouldn't have put it past her to fling her blade with the next jetsam of floral tributes and accidentally stick the star through one prodigious lung.

'Can't someone end this?' Maestro Jonsi shouted, in despair.

'I'll give it a try,' I volunteered, and made my entrance.

To give her credit, the Camorrista sister was swift to catch on. And her knife was accurately thrown, only to stick into a scenery flat I happened to jostle in passing. I boomed out the Barrack Room lyrics to 'Abdul Abulbul Amir', lowering my voice to deep bass and drawing out phrases so no one could possibly make out the words or even the language.

Marguerite was astonished at this demonic apparition.

Most of the audience, who knew the opera by heart, were surprised at the sudden reappearance of Méphistophélès but, after eight renditions of the 'Jewel Song', were happy to accept whatever came next, just so long as it wasn't a ninth.

'Those joooo-oooo-wels you muuuuu-ust give baaaa-ack,' I demanded. 'Your beau-uuuuu-ty needs no suuuu-ch adorn-meeee-ent!'

I picked up the prop casket in which the jewels had been presented and pointed into it.

With encouragement from Vokins' clique, who chanted 'Take them off!' in time to the desperately vamping orchestra, Bianca Castafiore removed the necklaces and bracelets and dropped them into the casket.

I was aware of commotion offstage. A couple of scene-shifters tried to rush the stage but were held back by non-Italians.

As the last bright jewel clinked into the casket, I looked at the woman in the wings. Malilella drew her thumb across her throat and pointed at me. I had added to my store of curses. Again.

There were Camorra in the wings. Both sides.

So I made my exit across the orchestra pit, striding on the backs of chairs, displacing musicians, knocking over instruments. I didn't realise until I was among the audience that I had trailed my cloak across the limelights and was on fire.

I paused and the whole audience stood to give me a round of applause.

Clapping thundered throughout the auditorium. Which is why I didn't hear the shots. When I saw holes appear in a double bass, I knew Don Rafaele was displeased with this diversion from the libretto.

I shucked my burning cloak and dashed straight up the centre aisle, out through the foyer – barging past a couple of scene-shifters on sheer momentum – and out into Covent Garden, where Chop awaited with the cab.

I tossed my mask and cowl out of the carriage as it rattled away.

Cradling the jewel casket in my lap, I began to laugh. The sort of laugh you give out because otherwise you'd have to scream and scream.

That is how I made my debut at the Royal Opera.

XI

After such a day, with two coups to the credit, many a crook would feel entitled to a roistering celebration. It's usually how they get nabbed.

Your proud bandit swaggers into his local and buys everyone drinks. Asked how he comes to be suddenly in funds, he taps the side of his hooter and airily mentions a win on the dogs. No track in London pays out in crisp, freshly stolen banknotes. Every copper's nark in the pub recalls a sick relative and dashes off into the fog to tap the plods 'for a consideration'.

So, in my case, no rest for the wicked.

However, before proceeding to the evening's amusement, I had Chop drive back to Conduit Street.

I chalked off the latest item myself.

1. ~~The Green Eye of the Yellow God~~
2. ~~The Black Pearl of the Borgias~~
3. ~~The Falcon of the Knights of St John~~
4. ~~The Jewels of the Madonna of Naples~~
5. The Jewel of Seven Stars
6. ~~The Eye of Balor~~

Moriarty emerged from his thinking room with sheets of paper covered in diagrams. Finding the celebrated circles and clown-smile squiggles named for the mathematician John Venn inadequate to the task, he had invented what he said – and I've no reason to doubt him – was an entirely new system for visually representing complex processes. He was delighted with his incomprehensible arrays of little ovals with symbols in them, stuck together by flowing lines interrupted by arrows.

Indeed, the diagrams excited him more than his latest acquisition. He waved aside the casket of jewels in his eagerness to show off a form of cleverness I was incapable of making head or tail of. If he hadn't been distracted, he might have taken steps to introduce his system to the wider world. Schoolboys destined for the dunce cap could curse him as the inventor of Moriarty Charts. As it is, Mr Venn rests on his inky laurels.

Mrs Halifax reported that Mad Carew was given to noisy spasms of terror. He was losing faith in the Professor's ability to save his hide. She'd sent Lotus Lei to the basement with a sixpenny opium pipe which would cost the client seven shillings, in the hope that a puff might calm his nerves. However, at the sight of the celestial poppet, the loon took to gibbering, 'The brown-skin monks of Nepal have slant eyes.' In the gloom of the basement, Lotus reminded him of the sect sworn to avenge the stolen eye.

'Funny thing is,' I remarked. 'The Chinese are about the only fanatic race we haven't offended this week.'

'I considered adding the Sword of Genghis Khan to our shopping list,' said the Professor. 'The hordes of Asia will rally to any who wield it, and I know where it can be found. The Si-Fan would certainly view it falling into Western hands as sacrilege. But the tomb in Mongolia would take months to reach. For the moment, it can stay where it is.'

That was a relief. I've reasons for not wanting to go back to Mongolia. Under any circumstances. It's a worse hole than Bognor Regis.

Discarded on the desk were the *cartes de visite* of Marshall Alaric Molina de Marnac, Don Rafaele Corbucci and Tyrone Mountmain, Bart. A wavy Nepalese dagger lay beside them, gift of the priests of the little yellow god. The Creeper didn't run to cards, but the broken-backed corpse left on our doorstep in a laundry basket probably served the same function. Runty Reg wouldn't be at his post from now on. So, I gathered the interested parties all knew their most precious preciouses were arrayed on our sideboard.

'I trust we've reinforcements coming,' I said.

The Professor arched an eyebrow.

'This little lot don't play tiddlywinks,' I continued. 'Runty's liable to be just the first casualty. Consider that stand which has just set up across the road, feller who's bawling "Get-a ya tutsi-frutsi ice-a cream-a," could be a noted opera lover dressed in a white hat and apron. The monks soliciting alms for the poor on the corner creak under their robes – steel jerkins and chain mail long-johns. The friends and relations of the Irishmen we handed over to the peelers this lunchtime are drunker and rowdier than usual in the Pillars of Hercules.

'It'll be the Battle of Maiwand out there soon. I doubt that Mrs Halifax standing on our doorstep looking stern will keep the blighters out long.'

Moriarty mused, making more calculations.

'Not quite yet, I think, Moran. Not quite yet. The constituent elements are volatile, but one more is required for combustion. Now, off with you to Kensington to fetch the Jewel of Seven Stars.'

He patted me warmly on the chest – a unique gesture from him, with which I was not entirely comfortable – and disappeared back into his den.

As few men, I had his trust. Which was terrifying.

Outside, I found Chop by his cab, just about to stick his tongue into an ice cornet freshly purchased from the furious Don Rafaele.

'Don't eat that,' I warned, dashing the cornet into the gutter. It fizzed surprisingly.

More than the usual amount of rubbish and rags were in the street. Some of the piles were shifting. I saw glittering eyes in the trash heaps. Our original Nepalese admirers remained foremost among the array of annoyed maniacs which came along with our Crown jewels.

I climbed into the cab, ignoring the gypsy death signs chalked on the doors, and we were away – for more larceny.

XII

The streetlamps were on, burning blue. Autumn fog gathered, swirling yellow. Chop's cab rattled down Kensington Palace Road, and drew up at a workman's hut erected beside a grave-sized hole in the gutter. Signs warned of a gas leak. Simon Carne had watched Trelawny House all day from inside the hut. He wore another of his disguises, as an old Irishman he called 'Klimo'. Dialect humour was superfluous to the simple lookout job, but Carne was committed.

Other residences on the street had stone roaring lions flanking their driveways. Trelawny House favoured an Egyptian motif: sphinxes stood guard at the gate, the columns beside the front door were covered in hieroglyphs, and a pyramid topped the porch.

Carne gave a brief report. This evening, Margaret Trelawny was entertaining. Carriages had come and gone, depositing well-dressed people who took care not to let their faces be seen. Their coaches were of quality, many with their distinctive coats of arms gummed over with black paper. Vaguely musical sounds and rum, spicy smells emanated from the house.

'I've managed to secure an invitation,' Carne said.

He led me into the hut, where two of our associates sat on a purple-faced fellow who was securely bound and gagged.

'Isn't that Henry Wilcox? The colossus of finance?' I asked.

At mention of his name, Wilcox writhed and purpled further, about to burst blood vessels. Known for sailing close to the wind in his business and personal life, he had just capsized. I kicked him in the middle. When an opportunity to boot the goolies of capital presents itself, only a fool misses it. Karl Marx said that, and it is the only socialist slogan which makes sense to me.

Carne's men had taken a gilt-edged card bearing the sign of the ram from their captive, and Wilcox's bag contained a long white robe and a golden mask with curly horns and a sheepish snout.

Obviously, this was my day for fancy dress.

I got into the ridiculous outfit and took the card.

Wilcox protested into his gag. Another kick quieted him.

I climbed back into the cab and Chop made great show of delivering me to the door of Trelawny House.

The knocker was in the shape of a green-eyed serpent. At a rap, the door was opened by a gigantic black prizefighter wearing harem pantaloons. His face and chest were painted gold. I handed over the ram card, which he dropped into a brazier. He stood aside.

I followed the noise and the – slightly intoxicating – smell. Through a hall filled with the usual clutter of elephant's foot umbrella stands and potted aspidistras gone to seed, down stone steps into a cellar, where scented oil-lamps cast odd shadows. People dressed like silly buggers gyrated to the plinkings of instruments I couldn't put names to. A proper knees-up.

The large cellar was decorated like an Egyptian tomb. I should say, decorated *with* an Egyptian tomb. All around were artefacts looted from the burial place of Queen Tera in the Valley of the Sorcerer. Each item cursed seven ways to sunset.

The guests were all of a type with Wilcox. Robes and masks didn't conceal thick middles, bald pates and liver-spotted, well-manicured hands. Well-to-do and well connected, I judged. Members of Parliament and the Stock

Exchange, commanders of manufacturing empires and shipping lines, high officers of the law and the armed forces, princes of the church and our ancient institutions of learning. More money than sense, more power than they knew what to do with.

So, the hostess was working a high-class racket. With marks like these on her lists, Miss Trelawny was well set-up.

Mixed among the robed, masked guests were professional houris of both sexes, immodestly clad in gold paint and little else. They sported Egyptian fripperies: hawk headdresses, golden snake circlets, ankhs and scarabs, that eye-in-the-squiggle design. Some might have been imported from Eastern climes, but I recognised a body or two from the city's less exotic vice establishments. Mrs Halifax had mentioned a few of her younger, prettier earners had gone missing lately; that mystery was now solved.

At the far end of the cellar was an altar. Two little black boys waved golden palm fronds at the high priestess of this congregation.

Margaret Trelawny dressed to show off her person, though she would stop traffic in a nun's habit. Already a tall girl, she towered well over six-and-a-half feet with the famous crown of Queen Tera set on her masses of jet-black hair. The headdress consisted of seven intertwined, jewel-eyed serpents with onyx-inlaid cheekguards.

As a connoisseur, I would venture her frontage – judged by size, firmness and 'wobble factor' – finer than Lily Langtry's… and, after a couple of gins, Lily could crack walnuts between her knockers. To display the goods, Miss Trelawny wore an intricate yet minimal bustier composed of interlinked gold beetles. A transparent skirt gathered in a knot under her bare belly. If tautness of tummy were your prime requirement in womanly form, she'd pass the bounce-a-sixpence-off-it test with flying colours.

A big sparkling ruby was set in a ring on her forefinger. The Jewel of Seven Stars looked like a congealed gobbet of blood. Her eyes had a mad, green-and-red lustre. Her commanding – indeed demanding – beauty was uncommon among the milk-and-water ladies of Kensington.

Miss Trelawny danced, which is to say undulated, in a shimmy which drew further attention – as if attention were required – to her broad hips, serpentine stomach and generous bosom.

Beneath an exotic arrangement, I recognised the tune her three-piece slave band was playing. 'The Streets of Cairo, or the Poor Little Country Maid'. You probably don't know the title – I had to ask a cocaine-injecting trumpet player from the Alhambra – but it's sung the world over by dirty-minded little boys. You can hear many, many variations on the rhyme 'oh, the girls in France/do the hoochy-koochy dance… and the men play druu-u-ums/on the naked ladies' buu-u-ums,' et cetera, et cetera.

For the moment, I entertained the possibility that Margaret Trelawny was – as she claimed – wicked Queen Tera reborn. She possessed at least one demonstrable supernatural power. In her presence, I suffered a prominent inconvenience in the trousers. I believe this condition was shared by not a few of the other gentlemen present.

I was drawn through the crowd, as if by magnetic attraction… or an invisible thread knotted about my gentlemen's parts. I was gripped by tantalising, almost painful desire. I had to concentrate on the real object of my visit – the ruby. Its redness grew large, tinting my whole view. I suspected there was something funny in the incense.

All about, houris were groped by guests and responded with a fair simulation of wild abandon. Divans were set aside for continuance of these activities, several already in use by knots of two or three – or, in one rather dangerous-looking conjunction, five – dedicated, conscience-free revellers.

Some masks had slipped. A prominent social reformer and a tiresomely staunch advocate of female emancipation were sandwiching a slave-boy; the maiden ladies who signed their petitions and wore their banners would probably disapprove. A magistrate known for harsh sentences was bent over a wooden horse, taking a spirited whipping from two Cleopatra-wigged tarts.

Jam jars of sweet, sticky cordial were passed around, suitable for drinking or smearing. I forgot myself and took a swallow of the stuff, which seemed laced with gunpowder.

I had a notion that Margaret Trelawny wouldn't give up her prize as easily as Bianca Castafiore.

The music rose in frenzied crescendo. The dancing – and other activity – in the room became faster and faster. Someone indeed played drums on the posteriors of unclad maidservants, slapping with more enthusiasm than skill.

I was near the altar-dais now, and the crowd was thicker. A girl with bared teeth and wide eyes tore at my robe, but I discreetly kneed her in the middle and threw her aside. She was pounced on by a provincial mayor who wore his chain of office and nothing else.

Miss Trelawny's exertions were extraordinary.

My inconvenience throbbed like a hammered thumb.

Then, a gong was struck, resounding throughout the cellar. Everything stopped.

Masks came off, en masse. I made no move to doff mine, but it was gone anyway.

Margaret Trelawny took a scimitar and lashed, precisely, at my head. I was unharmed, but unmasked. No, not quite unharmed. A line across my forehead dribbled blood. I clamped a hand to the wound.

My imperious hostess held a blade to my throat.

'Balls,' I said, with feeling.

XIII

I woke in darkness, wearing clothes not my own. Not even clothes, I realised as my senses crawled back. Tight wrappings which smelled of mothballs. I wriggled and found my legs tethered together and my arms bound to my chest. I was bandaged all over! I shifted my shoulders and banged against confining walls.

With a grinding sound, darkness went away. Something heavy shifted and I was looking up at Margaret Trelawny. Next to her stood a fork-bearded cove I didn't recognise, wearing a steel balaclava. I lay in an Egyptian sarcophagus, trussed like a mummy.

'Apologies for the "rush job", Colonel Moran,' my hostess said. 'Before wrapping, you should have had your heart, lights and liver removed to be placed in canoptic jars and your brains pulled out through your nostrils. Revival of the arts of Egypt proceeds slower than I would like.'

Why had they wrapped and entombed me, then taken the trouble to re-open the sarcophagus? Miss Trelawny must want something from me before I was buried for the archaeologists of 3,000 years' hence to exhume and put on display. I swear, the maledictions upon Moriarty's Crown jewels are a Sunday stroll compared to the curses I'll lay on those fellows. Beware the wrath of Basher Moran, you unborn tomblooters!

The party had broken up. I hoped not on my account.

I couldn't get that da-da-*daaaah*-da-da 'Streets of Cairo' whine out of my head. *Oh, the girls in France…*

'I'll be humming it for days,' I said. 'Don't you hate it when you get a tune stuck?'

Margaret sneered, magnificently. She still wore her queenly vestments. This angle afforded me a fine view of those excellent teats. With every breath, metal scarabs seemed to crawl over all that pink *poitrine*. My bandages stirred, which was all I needed. My hostess was less likely to be flattered by the response than swat the swelling with her scimitar.

She dangled a hand in front of my face. My eyes and mouth were free of bandages.

That bloody jewel loomed like the sun and the moon and – most particularly – the stars. I saw the sparkling flaws, in the shape of the constellation of Ursa Major. I've never been able to see the Plough or Bear in it, just seven dots which look like a saucepan with a too-long handle. Now I had cause to wish myself upon some far star, rather than in a Kensington basement at the mercy of this monumental (if decorative) cuckoo.

Maniac Marge took the Queen of Ancient Egypt business seriously. To her, it wasn't a racket, but a *religion*. Another lunatic, albeit more tempting… I've no idea why anyone would be willing to blow themselves up for Irish Home Rule or get their throat cut for the honour of a tatty Neapolitan statue, but a tumble with the fleshly incarnation of wicked Queen Tera might well be worth small discomfort. Though at this point, that was a distant prospect.

I tried to sit up, but had no joy. You think of mummy wrappings as rotten old things, but new linen bandages are stout stuff.

Then rough hands grabbed handfuls of bandage where my lapels would have been and hauled me half out of the coffin. The angry man beside Miss

Trelawny had lost patience. He snarled in my face. He wore iron gauntlets and a tabard with a crusader cross.

'Calm down, Marshall Alaric,' said our hostess, both soothing and commanding.

'He must be put to the Question! The Falcon must be recovered!' the man demanded fiercely.

I thumped back into my coffin, bumping my head on a stone pillow.

Margaret patted me on the chest. If the ring had a smell, it would have been in my nostrils.

I realised I'd just met Marshall Alaric Molina de Marnac, Grand Master of the Knights of St John. It should have come as no surprise these people knew each other. There were occult, Masonic ties between the Templars and Queen Tera's orgiastic cult. Rivalries, too, but a lot in common. They would have friendly competitions, like the Oxford–Cambridge boat race or the Army–Navy rugby match but with more sacrificed virgins and obscene oblations. Though – even after an evening in the basement of Trelawny House – it was hard to credit that Margaret could preside over *anything* more chaotically perverted than the piss-up which follows the Army–Navy brawl.

De Marnac, a foreigner, spat.

'I won't tell you where the Falcon is,' I swore – knowing that, realistically, I'd tell him before he got to the fingers of my right hand. I can stick more pain than most but I've tortured enough to know everyone talks in the end.

'It's on your Professor's sideboard, silly,' Miss Trelawny said. 'All London knows. Among other trinkets, you also have the Green Eye of the Yellow God and the Jewels of the Madonna of Naples. Once Moriarty took to collecting, word got round.'

Again, I should have known that would happen.

My hostess made a fist and pressed her ring to my forehead.

'I can't think what goes on in that head of yours, Colonel,' she said. 'Did you really believe you could just wander in here and take the Jewel of Seven Stars? It's the focus of aetheric forces which have enabled me to endure centuries in darkness and enter this shell to live anew. I was hardly likely to give it up.'

'You all say that...'

She slapped me, lightly.

'You are asking yourself why we're having this conversation. Why are you not screaming in a tomb, using up precious air?'

I did my best to shrug.

'While we were going through your clothes, an odd item came to light...'

I had French postcards in my wallet, but nothing likely to shock Queen Tera Redivivus. The two-shot pistol holstered in my sock, perhaps?

'Why was this in your waistcoat lining?'

She held up a shiny black oval. The Borgia Pearl. I remembered Moriarty patting me, and thinking it an odd gesture. Now, I realised he had slipped me one of his Crown jewels. However, I had no idea why...

'Swapsies?' I suggested.

Would she have the thing set in another ring? Wearing the Jewel of Seven Stars and the Black Pearl of the Borgias would be asking for double trouble... I'd been collecting cursed items for two days, and what had I got for it? Mummification and the prospect of burial alive.

The Marshall made an iron fist and aimed at my face.

'Steady on, old man,' I said, 'try not to lose your rag.'

Of course, that was calculated to inflame him further. I'd the measure of the Grand Master. Wrath was his presiding sin. He launched a punch. I shifted my head to the side of the sarcophagus. Metalled knuckles rammed the stone pillow. He swore in French and Spanish and bit his bluish beard.

'You mustn't let things get on top of you, chummy. Try whistling,' I suggested.

This time, he put his hand flat on my chest and pressed down. That hurt.

Quite a bit. I didn't consider whistling.

'You are a puzzle, Colonel,' Margaret said. 'I don't suppose you would consider… an arrangement?'

She pouted, prettily. The snakes set off her face.

In disgust, de Marnac left me alone. He had disarranged my bandages and, as I'd hoped, torn through a few. If you loosen one, you loosen 'em all. My sister Augusta knitted me a cardigan for my twelfth birthday which suffered from the same flaw. A tiny dropped stitch and the whole thing unravelled. I made a play of breathing heavily, expanding and contracting my chest inside the bandages. I fancied I'd be able to get my arms loose.

'Employment with me offers "benefits" I doubt you get from that dried-up maths tutor,' Margaret said, trailing fingers over my face. 'A desirable package is offered.'

Leaving Moriarty's employ wasn't as simple as she suggested. And, when working for him, I wasn't likely to be transformed into an ass simply by a wink and a shimmy. I knew myself well enough to know this would not be the case if I became an attendant to Queen Tera. When there's a woman in the crime, you always anticipate 'benefits' but get dirked in the arras. I speak from sorry experience, to whit: Irene 'that bitch' Adler, Mrs Sarah 'the Black Widow of Lauder' Stewart, Hagar 'Thieving Pikey' Stanley, et cetera, et cetera.

'The Falcon, the Falcon,' muttered the Marshall, obsessively. There was something about these objects. You set out to own them and they end up owning you. Tera Trelawny was a ring wearing a woman.

Above, outside, there was a crashing, and a drawn-out scream.

I hoped for Simon Carne leading an army of Moriarty's hand-picked roughs in a well-armed, brilliantly conceived frontal assault, intent on my rescue. But the quality of the screams suggested otherwise. No matter what disguise Carne wore, he wasn't *that* terrifying.

Margaret and de Marnac exchanged anxious looks. I managed to sit up, arms free under the bandages, and wasn't instantly slapped down.

'What is that?' said the Grand Master.

A huge shape blocked the doorway. A huge shape topped with a porkpie hat. A knocked-over lamp underlit a jowly, pig-eyed face which seemed to have melted. Big fists opened and closed.

De Marnac drew a sword.

The Hoxton Creeper tottered into the cellar, eyes fixed on Margaret, but not for the reason most blokes stared at her. In her open palm glistened the Black Pearl.

'Who are you?' demanded de Marnac.

The Creeper whistled the 'Barcarolle' from *Tales of Hoffman*. He had a tune in his head, too. As he advanced, he loomed bigger. His shadow grew.

'Here,' said Miss Trelawny, 'Grand Master, you'd better have this.'

She popped the pearl into the back of his tunic and it disappeared. He reached awkwardly for the back of his neck, but couldn't trap it. He wriggled, as if a bug were burrowing under his armour.

The Creeper wheeled about and stared at the Knight of St John. He raised his arms.

Margaret's black prizefighter, blood streaming from his broken face, came into the room and laid hold of the Creeper's shoulder, only to be shrugged off and thrown against the wall.

All the while, I was unpicking my bandages. I rose from the coffin. Bereft of jewels, I was of no interest to anyone.

De Marnac slashed at the Creeper, who blocked with his arm. The blade bit into the giant's knotted sinew like an axe in wood, then wouldn't come free. The Creeper got a hold of the Grand Master and twisted him round. The crack of spine snapping was louder than the squeak of scream he managed before the angry lamps went out in his eyes.

Something small, like a marble, rolled from his armour onto the floor.

Miss Trelawny looked at the dropped pearl. It fascinated her as she fascinated me – a nigh-irresistible urge to seize. The Creeper, too, sighted the object of his fixation.

I saw where this was going. And rooted around for the scimitar, which was lying on the altar. I doubted it'd be any more use against the Creeper than the sword he prised out of his arm.

The Creeper bent down and tried to take the Borgia Pearl.

It had not occurred to me, but fingers thick as bananas were a handicap when it came to picking up something the size of a boiled sweet. The Creeper scrabbled, rolling the pearl this way and that, unable to get a grasp.

I had a good two-handed grip on the scimitar. I judged the distance to the door.

The hostess took pity on the monster. She plucked the pearl in her delicate fingers and dropped it into the Creeper's cupped palm. He peered at it, content for the moment – but also perplexed. He didn't know what to do now. Then he saw Queen Tera. She stood up, magnificent. Her fluence struck the brute man like a bucketful of ice water. The Creeper's eyes glowed too, with fresh adoration. Could Margaret *cancan*? With her long legs and that costume, high kicks would be worth seeing.

Like a queen, Miss Trelawny extended her hand. She snapped her fingers.

Shyly, the Creeper gave away his precious and stood back in worship. Would the transference take? I'd not be surprised if from now on, the giant's heart beat to follow Queen Tera. If so, I was about to land myself in his bad books.

Margaret Trelawny again made a fist around the Borgia Pearl.

I ran towards her and scythed my blade down on her wrist, neatly lopping off her hand. She shrieked and blood gouted into the Creeper's face. I snatched up the hand – still shockingly warm – before its grip could relax, and bolted for the stairs.

The giant was temporarily blinded. Miss Trelawny was temporarily distracted. The Grand Master was permanently dead.

I ran through the hallway, naked but for a bandage loincloth, streaking past dazed houris – the gilt had mostly rubbed off – and a sticky law lord. I nearly tripped over a spine-snapped corpse.

Why didn't people just get out of the Creeper's way when they had the chance? Miss Trelawny's cringing staff would have to clear up more mess than usual. Mr Pears' soap is recommended for getting blood out of your Egyptian altar hangings, by the way.

Still clutching my gruesome prize, I bounded out of Trelawny House. My cab was still waiting. The Creeper hadn't done away with Chop on his way in.

'Conduit Street,' I ordered. 'Chop-chop, Chop!'

I laughed. Chop-chop, Chop! I'd only needed one chop. In my lap, Margaret Trelawny's hand opened like a flower. I took the pearl and the ring, and tossed the thing into the gutter for the dogs to fight over. If Queen Tera had all the powers she claimed, her hand might take to crawling after me like a lopsided, strangling spider. I could do without that.

It had been an interesting, eventful day.

XIV

I had a teeth-gnasher of a rage on. Often in the course of our association, I felt an overwhelming urge to box Professor Moriarty's ears. Or worse. He had taken me into the Firm because – not to put too fine a point on it – I had proven myself more than willing to gamble my skin on any number of occasions, just to feel the iron rise in my blood and cock a snook at death. So, by his lights, I had volunteered to be put repeatedly in harm's way and shouldn't complain about it.

However, that little trick with the Borgia Pearl – slipped into my supposedly undetectable secret pocket – was typical high-handedness. Admittedly, things had sorted themselves out in our favour. Equally admittedly, if the Prof *had* troubled to inform me of the stratagem, I'd have refused to go along with it. All for risk, disinclined to suicide: that's me.

Deep down, despite his genius, I couldn't help but think Moriarty threw the pieces up in the air and hoped for the best, then claimed it had come out exactly to plan. It'd have been the same to him if the Creeper had crushed my spine or Maniac Marge had mummified me or the Grand Master had done whatever it is Grand Masters do to those who annoy them. He wasn't notably upset by the fate of Runty Reg, and the lookout had been with the Firm longer than I.

Still, with a balloon of brandy and a fresh set of clothes, I calmed down and could even feel a pride of achievement. Every item on the shopping list was scored through:

~~1. The Green Eye of the Yellow God~~
~~2. The Black Pearl of the Borgias~~
~~3. The Falcon of the Knights of St John~~
~~4. The Jewels of the Madonna of Naples~~
~~5. The Jewel of Seven Stars~~
~~6. The Eye of Balor~~

Any one of these keepsakes would have been a premier haul, but six within forty-eight hours was a miracle.

The Professor stood in front of the glittering sideboard, hands out as if feeling the warmth of a fire. His head oscillated. Then, he clapped his hands.

'Nothing,' he said. 'No detectable supernatural power. These objects effect no change in temperature or barometric pressure. Miracles or malign mischances do not occur in their vicinity. They are simply *trouvées* men have arbitrarily decided to value.'

'I don't know, Moriarty,' I said. 'I've been feeling rum all day. I don't say it's the curses, but your Crown jewels have *something*. If enough people pray to the things, maybe they pick up juju the way a blanket gets wet if you empty a bucket of water on it?'

The Professor's lip curled.

'Whatever you or I think, plenty have invested so much belief in these prizes they'd kill or die to get 'em back,' I said. 'If that's not supernatural, I don't know what is.'

'Foolishness, and a distraction,' he said.

I conceded, with a shrug, he might be right. The wallahs who were after these pretties grew stupider as they neared their objects of desire. Even the Creeper, who was already an imbecile. At a glimpse of the sparklers, they lost habits of self-preservation. A fanatic flame burned in the lot of 'em. You could see it in their eyes.

'One thing puzzles me yet,' I admitted.

Moriarty raised a hawkish eyebrow, inviting the question.

'What has this collection got to do with saving Mad Carew's worthless hide? The heathen priests are still after him. After us, too, since we've got their Green Eye. Now, we've also to worry about the Creeper, the Templars, the Fenians, the Camorra and the Ancient Egyptian mob. We're more cursed now than when we started and Carew's no better off.'

Using a secret spyglass – which meant not presenting a tempting silhouette in the front window – Moriarty had kept up with the comings and goings in Conduit Street. Mostly comings.

We were besieged.

The gelato stand was open, well after the usual hours and in contravention of street trading laws. Don Rafaele Corbucci was at his post, though he'd dropped the tutsi-frutsi call. A gang of scene-shifters gathered around, including dark-eyed Malilella of the stiletto. They all stared up at the building, licking non-poisonous ice cream cornets.

The Pillars of Hercules had fallen ominously silent, but stout Sons of Erin loitered outside, whittling on cudgels. Among them, I distinguished a tall, better-dressed goon with a bright-green bowler hat and a temperance ribbon. Tyrone Mountmain, with a pocketful of dynamite. Aunt Sophonisiba was there too. No one quaffed from the flask she offered round, disproving the old saw that an Irishman will drink anything if it's free.

The armoured monks held their corner. Bereft of a Grand Master, they still had vows to uphold. Moriarty said a new Grand Master would be elected within hours. The Knights of St John openly held swords and crossbows.

We'd already had a bolt through the window.

A dark carriage was parked across the street. In it, a veiled woman with an alabaster hand sat alongside a grim giant. Margaret Trelawny and the Creeper remained, at least for the moment, an unlikely item. How had she got the hand so quickly? A few of her cult-followers stood about, fancy dress under their coats. Slaves, I suppose.

As for our original persecutors, the priests of the little yellow god… some of the rubbish heaps stood up on brown legs. A troupe of Nepalese street jugglers put on a poor show. Did they feel crowded by the presence of so many other groups of our enemies?

A pair of constables, on their regular beat, took a look at the assembled factions, about-turned and strolled away rapidly.

'I suppose we can only die once,' I said. 'I'll fetch out the rifle with telescope sights. I can put half a dozen bastards down before they take cover. Starting with Temperance Ty, I think…'

'You will do no such thing, Moran.'

The Professor had something up his sleeve.

The doorbell rang. I adjusted the spyglass to see which fanatic was calling. It was only Alf Bassick, with a large carpet bag, back from Rotherhithe.

I pulled a lever which – by a system of pulleys and electric currents – unlocked our front door. Moriarty had designed the system himself. Wood panelling over sheet steel, our entrance was more impregnable than the vaults of Box Brothers. Even the dynamite boyos would have trouble shifting it.

Bassick didn't immediately come upstairs.

Moriarty told me to go down and determine the cause of the delay.

When I reached the bottom of the stairs, I saw Bassick was stretched out on our hall mat with a Nepalese dagger stuck between his shoulders. If we'd sent Carne on Bassick's errand, he might have come through it – that fake hump at least protected his back. It was after midnight. The besieging forces were bolder.

I turned Bassick over and ignored his gasped last words – blather about his mother or money or the moon – to get the bag. Whatever Moriarty had sent him for, death was no excuse for failure.

Returning upstairs, I didn't need to tell the Prof what had happened. I assumed he'd taken it into account in his squiggle charts.

Moriarty opened Bassick's bag and took out six identical caskets. He lined up the boxes on his desk and flipped each of their lids open. Inside, each container was custom-made to contain a different treasure, with apertures ranging from a bird-shaped hole for the Templar Falcon to a tiny recess for the Borgia Pearl. Every Jewel of the Madonna had a nook. The Professor fit his acquisitions into their boxes and shut the lids.

'There should be keys,' he said.

I rooted about in the carpet bag and found a ring of six keys. Moriarty took a single key and locked all the boxes with it. He shuffled the boxes around on the table.

'Moran, pick any two of these up.'

They weighed the same.

'Shake them.'

They rattled the same.

'In addition to their respective jewels, each box has a cavity holding loose weights,' the Professor explained. 'Any would balance a scale exactly with any other. They sound alike. They look alike. Tell me, Moran, could an object-worshipper differentiate between them?'

'If they can, they're sharper pencils than me.'

'Is it possible some may be supernaturally attuned to the contents? They'll be able to pick out their own hearts' desires through magic?'

'If you say so.'

'I say not, Moran. I say not.'

I tapped a knuckle on a box. It was not just wood.

'A steel core, like our front door, Moran,' Moriarty said. 'The boxes will take considerable breaking.'

I still didn't know what he was up to.

He put the boxes back in the carpet bag. And pulled on his ulster and tall hat. He regarded himself slyly in the mirror, checking his appearance but also catching his own clever eye. Odd that someone so unprepossessing should be a monster of vanity, but life is full of surprises.

'We shall go outside… and surrender our collection. But, remember, only one box to each customer.'

'What's to stop us being killed six ways as soon as we open the door?'

'Confidence, Moran. Confidence.'

Terrifyingly, that made sense. I stiffened, distributed three pistols about my person, and prepared to put on an almighty front.

XV

Professor Moriarty opened wide our front door and held up his right hand.

It seemed everyone was too astonished to kill him.

He walked down our front steps, casual if a little too pleased with himself. I followed, my thumb-cocked six-shot Gibbs in one hand, a Holland & Holland fowling piece tucked under my other arm. If this was where I died, I'd take a bag of the heathen down with me.

Moriarty signalled for the interested parties to advance. When they moved en masse, he shook his head and held up his forefinger. Only one of each faction was to come forward. There was snarling and spitting, but terms were accepted.

Tyrone Mountmain, chewing a lit cigar. That meant he had dynamite sticks about him, with short fuses.

Don Rafaele Corbucci held back, and sent my old girlfriend. Malilella spat at my boots and I noticed inappropriately that she was damned attractive. Shame she was a bloody Catholic.

A Templar Knight unknown to me crossed himself and advanced.

Margaret Trelawny let the Hoxton Creeper help her down from her carriage. She was more modestly dressed than on the occasion of our last meeting, but her veil was pinned to the snaky headdress. She looked no fonder of me than the stiletto sister.

They stood on the pavement, wary of each other, warier of us.

'One more, I think,' Moriarty said.

A heap of rags by the rubbish bins stirred. A brown, lean beggar crept forth. He had a shaved head and a green dot in the centre of his forehead. The high priest of the little yellow god.

'You each wish something which is in our possession,' Moriarty said.

Mountmain swore and his cigar-end glowed. Malilella flicked out her favourite blade. Margaret Trelawny flipped back her veil with her alabaster hand – she must have been practising – and glared hatred.

'I intend to make full restitution…'

'Ye'll still die ye turncoat bastard,' Mountmain declared.

'That may be. I do not ask payment for the items you believe you have a right to. Nothing but a few moments' truce, so Moran and I might return to our rooms and set our affairs in order. After that, we shall be at your disposal.'

I held up the sack like Father Christmas. The boxes rattled.

Six sets of eyes lit up. I wondered again if the fanatics *could* sense which box held which desired, accursed object.

Don Rafaele gave the nod, accepting terms, binding the others to his decision. That made him the biggest crook in the assembled masses, if only the second biggest on the street.

'Moran, do the honours of restitution.'

I was at sea. How was I to know which box went to which customer?

'Do you await a telegram from the Queen, perchance?' Moriarty said.

He was enjoying himself immensely. I wanted to kill him as badly as anyone else.

Without fuss, I took out a box.

'Ladies first,' I said, and shoved it at Margaret Trelawny. She tried to take it with the hand whose fingers wouldn't close and it nearly fell, but then caught it with her remaining hand and clutched it to her ample chest.

'And you, big fellah,' I said, delivering a box to the Creeper. He considered it as an ape might consider a carriage clock.

'Malilella, *grazie*.' Giving her a prize.

'The gentleman from Nepal,' I addressed the little brown priest.

'Worthy Knight,' I said to the Templar.

'And you, Tyrone. Fresh from the pot at the end of the rainbow.'

Mountmain took his box.

Recipients examined their gifts and thought about trying to get into them. Suspecting trickery, not unreasonably, Tyrone handed his box to a follower and told him to open it with a cudgel.

Moriarty took a step backwards. I did too.

Eyes were on us again. I shot out a streetlamp as a diversion, and we whipped inside. The door slammed shut. A Templar sword thudded against it, splitting wood and scratching steel.

From the hall, we heard the commotion outside.

We went back upstairs and took turns with the spyglass. The Creeper had the wood off his box, but it was still shut. A long-fingered Camorra man worked a set of picklocks. Tyrone's cudgel man gave his box a good hammering.

'Let's make it a little easier,' said the Professor.

He opened our front window a crack, sure to stay out of the line of fire, and tossed six loose keys into the street.

The brown priest was first to pick one up. And first to be disappointed. He was the new owner of the Black Pearl of the Borgias.

The Creeper threw his own box into the gutter and strode towards the little man, arms outstretched. Nepalese jugglers got in the giant's way, but were tossed aside, twisted into shapes fatal even to a full-fledged fakir. Before the giant could get a grip on the pearl-clutching priest, another – larger – bundle of rags stirred. Something the acromegalic Neanderthal's own size, red-eyed and white-furred, barrelled across the road to protect its master. The Creeper and the *mi-go* locked arms in a wrestler's grip, then rolled out of sight.

Other keys were found. Other discoveries made.

The knight was rewarded. He opened his box and found what he wanted. The Falcon was at last restored to the Order of St John! He was shot by a blind-drunk Irishman anyway, setting off a Fenian–Templar scrap. Cudgels against swords wasn't an equal match, but when dynamite came into it, armour didn't hold up. Tyrone tossed fizzing sticks at the monks, who were hampered by heavy armour and confining robes.

The Camorra pitched in with knives and garrottes. Mountmain and Don Rafaele tried to throttle each other over a prize neither of them wanted: the Jewel of Seven Stars. Malilella and Margaret Trelawny circled each other, stiletto against scimitar. Maniac Marge had surprising left-handed dexterity with the blade, but shocked the Camorrista by lashing her across the face with her new, unyielding hand. Malilella responded with unkind words in Italian and a series of stabs which struck sparks off Tera's serpent crown.

Blood ran in the gutters. It did my heart good. My nerves were back. We settled in to enjoy the show.

There were alarums and a great deal of smoke. A few fires started. Even the police would have to show up soon.

The Templars, who initially got the worst of it, threw over the handcart from which they had been soliciting alms to reveal one of Mr Gatling's mechanical guns. Evidently, the mediaeval order kept up with the times. Fire raked the pavement, throwing up chips of London stone. Irishmen, faux Egyptians, Neapolitans and Nepalese scattered. Dead bodies jittered back into a semblance of life as bullets tore into them.

Half of me wanted to be out in the street, stabbing and shooting and scything with the rest. A more cautious urge, carefully cultivated, was that I should stay well out of this. Still, it was a jolly show!

The barrel organ of death chattered for a long minute, until an asp-venom dart from an Egyptian blowpipe paralysed the gunner. Then, things quieted a little.

The fight wasn't out of everyone, but few were in a condition to continue.

Moriarty took the speaking tube and ordered Mrs Halifax to bring him his nightly cocoa.

I was not surprised he could sleep.

This time, he really had thrown all the pieces up in the air just to see where they'd come down.

XVI

Most of the rest of it was in the newspapers. I can't give you a thrilling first-hand account because I wasn't there. However, here's a rundown of the outrages.

In the next two days, fifty-seven people were murdered. Irish, blacks, knights, innocent parties, Nepalese itinerants, well-regarded members of society with Masonic connections, scene-shifters, fences, fortune-hunters, policemen, a white hunter who set out to bag the *mi-go* for the Horniman Museum, and so on. Two members of the Castafiore clique fought a duel with antique pistols, and blew each other's chests out – tricky shooting with unreliable weapons, considered a draw. Some smiled the Italian smile. Not a few displayed the Killarney Cudgel Cavity. Others expired from wounds not associated with any particular region.

The ice cream parlour on Old Compton Street was destroyed by a supposed act of God. Don Rafaele returned to Naples, accompanied by Malilella – they came out of the wars with the best loot, though they didn't get back the Jewels of the Madonna. These days, the virgin of Naples is paraded about with the Jewel of Seven Stars and the Eye of Balor. An influx of Irish and Anglo-Egyptian tourists might not let that situation continue. Corbucci later got himself poisoned, to nobody's surprise. [11]

The Hoxton Creeper had vitriol dashed at his chest. He was seen falling into the Thames, clutching the Templar Falcon. I knew better than to think him dead.

With the Falcon lost, reputedly in the mud with the Agra treasure, the party of the late Grand Master Alaric Molina de Marnac had to gouge out their own eyes and flagellate for six days and six nights to atone. Rumours persist that the blackbird has turned up in Russia or China and the search goes on. There may be more than one flapping about on the market. The Templars aren't the only interested party. Fat Kaspar, who had never heard of the *rara avis* before the Professor mentioned it, was struck queer by an obsession and took off after the statue. He didn't believe it was in the river. Another promising career ruined. [12]

Margaret Trelawny's house was blown up, supposedly due to a gas leak. Found barely alive in the ruins, she's in hospital now, mummified in bandages and speaking a tongue not heard on the Earthly plane in thousands of years. The membership list of Queen Tera's Circle happened to be delivered to the *Pall Mall Gazette* with scandalous photographs. Resignations, retirements, suicides and scandal ensued.

Tyrone Mountmain expired from drinking poisoned ginger beer. His Auntie Soph was hanged for it. There are more Mountmains, though – so the Struggle goes on. Eternally.

XVII

Early the next morning, the Professor had me roused from Fifi's bed – all that killing naturally had my blood up, and there was but one handy treatment for that – and insisted we take a promenade across the battlefield.

Conduit Street was strewn with debris. Bullet pocks scarred walls and pavements. All the windows were broken. Don Rafaele's stand smouldered. Other residents were appalled, and complaining. Not all the corpses had been carted off. A Templar was crucified across the doors of the Pillars of Hercules. A pile of rags lay on our front step, brown hands outstretched and empty. A policeman – one of 'ours' – shooed away busybodies.

The street was full of trash.

Margaret Trelawny's white hand, all but two fingers broken off, lay in a pool of congealed, melted ice cream.

A few of the Jewels of the Madonna were about too, amid the crushed ruin of one of Moriarty's trick boxes. Their settings were bent and broken.

Moriarty spotted the Green Eye of the Little Yellow God and the Black Pearl of the Borgias, rolling together in a gutter like peas in a pod. Someone's real eye, red tangle of string still attached, lay with them.

'Pick those up, would you, Moran? We've still a client to service.'

'Just the Green Eye?'

'We'll have the Black Pearl, too.'

'We'd better hope the Creeper drowned.'

'I'm sure he didn't. Excessive lung capacity. An entirely natural, if freakish attribute, before you ask. But for the moment, there's little risk.'

Moriarty was pleased with his handiwork.

'This wasn't about Humphrey Carew, was it?'

'Not entirely, Moran. Very perspicacious of you to notice. I never get your limits. You have them, of course. No, the Green Eye was the least of our items of interest.'

'A lot of trouble for an item of little interest.'

'There is always a lot of trouble in situations like these. I can't abide a fanatic, Moran. They are variables. They do not fit into calculations. The mumbo-jumbo is infinitely annoying. Consider the Camorra – a perfectly sound criminal enterprise, poisoned by infantile Marianism. Really, why should a bandit care about a statue's finery? Likewise, the Fenians and their hopeless 'Cause'. They may free themselves from British rule, but for what? The Irish will still have priests to rob and rape them and bleat that it's for their own good, and they never think to shrug off the yoke of Rome. The Templars – who knows what they are for? They've forgotten themselves. At bottom, none are any better than the Creeper. Baby brains fixated on shiny things.

'It is best for us, for the interests of the Firm, that these cretins be taken off the board. The Italians and Irish and pseudo-Egyptians shall trouble us no longer. The Soho Merchants' Protective Society is smashed. Our tithes will be paid without complaint. Mrs Halifax will lose no further assets to Margaret Trelawny. Navvies and poets who might have been tempted to sink monies in the Irish Invincible Republicans will gamble and drink and whore in establishments we have an interest in. The wealthy and powerful who need to be blackmailed will not have to dress up as pharaohs to do it.'

For the only time I can remember, Moriarty smiled without showing teeth. This morning, as on few others, he was content. His sums added up.

'What about the little brown priests?' I ventured. 'They'll still come for us. We have the emerald.'

'If I do not pay the remainder of the purchase price today, ownership reverts to Major Carew. Moran, do you have a penny about you?'

'Why, yes, I…' I began, fishing in my watch pocket. I caught Moriarty's eye and my fingers froze. 'No, Moriarty,' I said. 'I'm short of funds.'

'Pity. We shall have to return Carew's property, with apologies.'

The man himself was in the street, blinking in the daylight. He took in the carnage and destruction.

'Is it over? Am I safe?'

'That's for you to decide. I can guarantee that you will not be murdered by the priests of the little yellow god.'

Carew laughed, still mad – but happy, too.

He walked down to the dead priest and kicked him. The Nepalese rolled over. He had been shot neatly through the dot in his forehead.

'That's what I think of your blasted yellow god,' he said.

Moriarty gave Carew back his emerald, and he waved it in the dead priest's face. A laughing daredevil again, he cast around for ladies to impress with his flash.

'I'll have this green carbuncle cut up in Amsterdam, and sold to the corners of the Earth. Then I'll have the last laugh! Hah!'

'My bill will be sent to your club,' Moriarty said. 'I suggest you settle it promptly.'

'Yes, yes, whatever… but, hang it, I'm alive and this blighter's dead. All the blighters are dead. You're a miracle worker.'

I knew – with an instinct that the Professor wouldn't call supernatural – Mad Carew would gyp us. He was that sort. Couldn't help himself. One

THE HOUND OF THE D'URBERVILLES

implacable foe was off his back – for the moment, at least – yet he was thoughtlessly on the point of making another.

Carew pumped my hand and pumped Moriarty's hand. The Professor gave our client's shoulder a friendly squeeze and pushed him away. Carew walked off with a bounce in his stride, whistling a Barrack-Room ballad.

We watched him leave.

'One thing, Moriarty,' I said. 'You promised Carew he wouldn't be murdered by priests of the little yellow god. Even if the London nest is wiped out and their hairy pet is on the run, there are others back home in the mountains. An army of them, just like this fanatic, sworn to get back the emerald. They'll know of this mess soon enough, and they'll send other priests across the globe for Carew and the Eye.'

'True.'

'So you lied to him?'

'No. I seldom lie. It spoils the equations. When I clapped his shoulder, I gave him a present...'

He opened his hand. The Black Pearl of the Borgias wasn't in it.

'It will take the next assassins months to get here from Nepal. It will take but hours for the Creeper to get out of the river.'

XVIII

So, now you know how it came out. According to Carew's will, he was to be buried at his last posting. They fit him in a coffin, face up but toes down, and some obliging Nepalese who happened to be visiting London transported him all the way there. The emerald went with him and was stolen from his body before burial. So, the poet had the truth of it, after all – with the exception that Amaryllis Framington married a tea trader and retired to Margate.

There's a one-eyed yellow idol to the north of Khatmandu,
There's a little marble cross below the town;
There's a broken-hearted woman tends the grave of Mad Carew,
And the yellow god forever gazes down.

CHAPTER SIX: THE GREEK INVERTEBRATE

I

'James,' the Professor said.

'James,' his brother acknowledged.

'You've not met my associate,' Moriarty said. 'Colonel Moran, Colonel Moriarty.'

'Colonel,' nodded the thin-faced cove.

'Colonel,' I responded.

I've seldom had cause to mention Moriarty's family. Read on, and you'll find out why.

Until that winter, I knew little of the clan. The parents had been lost at sea some years previously. The single odd thing my partner in crime – not just a turn of phrase – had let slip about his people was that Mr and Mrs Moriarty had such a liking for the name 'James' they gave it to each and every child of their union.

'It's James, James,' the Colonel said.

Yes, there was a third Moriarty brother. It was fortunate there were no sisters.

The triplicate nonsense would have been even more confusing if any of the three brothers could lay claim to a single intimate acquaintance who might wish to address them by their first name. You're feeling sorry for them now, aren't you? No love for the Jameses Moriarty, boo hoo hoo. Just goes to show you never met any of 'em. If you had, you'd suppress a shudder and nod sagely. Only one Moriarty is a villain in the public eye (though not, as it happens, a court of law), but if you ask me the Professor wasn't the worst of them.

Most of us are saddled with relations. I've touched on my own from time to time. Seldom happily. With regret, I discern traits passed down – though not anything useful, like the family loot – from old Sir Augustus to me. He was a terror, a bully and a cool shot in the service of Queen and Country. I've worked for myself – or the Prof – but otherwise carry on in pater's tradition. I've also attained that sorry point in life when I look into the shaving mirror after a heavy night in the tap-room and see the old man staring back at me with bloodshot orbs. The propensity for slipperiness with cards, believe it or not, I have from dear Mama, who showed me how to deal from the bottom while I was in velvet knickers and had ringlets.

Somehow, the notion that Professor Moriarty had parents – might have *been a child* – never sat right. A viper is a snake straight from the egg. I couldn't help but picture little Jamie as a balding midget in a sailor suit, spying Cook and the baker's boy rolling in flour on the kitchen table through his toy telescope, and blackmailing them for extra buns.

It had been a profitable season for the Firm. We'd done nicely out of the Mystery of the Essex Werewolf, come out of the lamentable business of the Four Lemon Drops with surprising credit, and salvaged more than could be expected from the disaster of Loki Tunnel. Lately, England was too confining a laboratory for Moriarty's experiments in crime.

We were expanding on the continent, tactfully skirting – for the moment – territories claimed by others and offering consultant services to blackguards in Spain, Holland and Poland. Moriarty had put his stamp on a series of coups – kidnappings, major thefts, an assassination – which

THE HOUND OF THE D'URBERVILLES

raised his stock as the premier criminal mastermind in Europe.

Queen Victoria could unroll a map of the world and take pride in the extensive red patches which mark the Empire; the Prof had similar ambitions for the globe in his study. Stuck with red-headed needles wherever a Moriarty crime had been accomplished, the globe increasingly resembled a pincushion.

I had recently greatly enjoyed murdering a Member of Parliament with a garrotte of red ribbon, then providing succor to his saucy widow, his blushing twin daughters... and, thanks to a fortuitous midnight encounter, his tweeny maid. I'd have done the prig for the bonuses alone, but that business put twenty thou in the coffers. You'd never believe who paid for that forced bye-election. My only regret was that I couldn't mount an honourable head on the wall. I contented myself with draping the ribbon on some antlers and keeping intimate trophies from the ladies of the deceased's household in a private drawer alongside like items.

It was a new year, a new decade: 1891. Life was fine. Crime was paying.

Then, early in January, Professor Moriarty asked me to accompany him to the Xeniades Club to meet with his brother, Colonel Moriarty.

Are you familiar with that breed of novel heroine who prefaces a chapter of awful experiences with 'had I but known...'? Well, had I but bloody known, I'd have stayed in bed with or without a tweeny foot warmer. But I didn't and got up. Cheerful as a goose-throttler the week before Christmas, I put on my hat, picked up my cane, and toodled along to Jermyn Street and Colonel Moriarty's club.

A few words on the Xeniades Club – what a horrible place! I'm a member of the Anglo-Indian and the Tankerville myself, though I tend to let niceties like paying annual fees slide for the odd decade. As a cardplayer, yarn-spinner, hero of the Empire, big-game hunting bore (I admit it) and devotee of manly pursuits, I've been in and out of every gent's club in London, from the Athaneum and the Beefsteak through the Troy Club and Boodle's to the Club of the Damned and the Mausoleum Club (pronounced Mouse-o-lay-um, if you ever get the invite). I'm also known at exclusive gathering places catering to fellows who are most decidedly not gentlemen but can afford to pay for their pleasures and the privilege of having those who provide them keep quiet afterwards.

The Xeniades Club was founded by whining bounders who'd been black-balled at any number of established London clubs and decided that at least one should have no barriers at all to membership. You can imagine the shower that let in: grubby-fingered tradesmen, monomaniacs and cranks of every persuasion; plain-speaking provincial aldermen; foreigners, even. Furthermore, the Xeniades encouraged 'lively debate', and was thus one of the noisiest big rooms I have ever been in... not excluding the mess hall at Sing Sing Prison during a riot in which twelve inmates and three guards were killed, or the auditorium of the Paris Opéra after a chandelier fell on the audience during (what else?) that bloody jewel song from *Faust*.

If I were in the habit of thinking things through, I'd have made these *deductions*: the Xeniades was for blighters so objectionable no other club would have them. Colonel James Moriarty was a member. *Colonel* James Moriarty. What kind of colonel can't even get into the Army and Navy, which is open to *any* serving officer on full or half pay? Any soldier who can rise to the rank of colonel – which is, admittedly, where they leave you when they tumble to what sort of a rotter or loon you are behind the medal ribbons and, yes, I am speaking for experience – ought to have distinguished himself in some manner which would at least get him into Stoats and Weasels.

No, Colonel James was in the Xeniades.

At least, we didn't have our awkward introductions in the Loud Room but rather in a draughty, underused annexe I gathered was called the Cold Room.

The Professor was vague as to which regiment his brother was a colonel in, but had let on that the fellow was still serving. Somehow – and, again, I of all people should have known better – that made me imagine a younger, straighter-spined, suntanned version of the James Moriarty I knew. More hair on his head and a set of fierce whiskers, in full uniform, bristling with martial fervour. I envisioned a cruel, canny Moriarty brain applied to devastating pre-emptive strikes against the foe (always best to get your reprisals in first, I say).

Instead, the Colonel was a sallow, slouching fellow with a sunken chest, the ill-cared-for clothes of a clerk who no longer has hopes of advancement, a perpetual cold which required odd poultices and compresses which afforded no appreciable benefit, and a little square of moustache like a patch he'd missed with his cutthroat three days ago. He was seven years younger than the Professor, but seemed nearer death.

From one whiff of him, I knew he'd never set foot on a battlefield. Asked what army line he was in, he bluntly said 'supplies' and left it at that. I assumed he was less a soldier than a wholesale orderer and deliverer of boots, tins of bully and those greased cartridges which make Indians mutinous. Again, I leapfrogged to a conclusion. Throughout this whole affair, I did that. I wish I could say I learned my lesson, but plainly I didn't.

So, minimal pleasantries aside, to the point: 'It's James, James.'

'My youngest brother is a stationmaster in the west of England, Moran,' the Professor stated.

'Fal Vale Junction, in Cornwall,' said the Colonel.

'Where he can't do any harm,' said the Professor.

'So you say, James.'

'I do say, James.'

At that, the Professor's head began its familiar oscillation. Unnervingly, the Colonel began to sway his head from side to side in mirror of his brother. It was a family habit! The two bobbed heads like Peruvian llamas working up to a spitting contest. My hands convulsed in a kind of terror. Was this a tussle of fraternal wills or some species of communication beyond other mortals? The brothers kept it up for several minutes.

I wondered if it was possible to get a drink in this place.

At length, they quit playing silly beggars.

'Through my influence,' the Colonel said, 'James has secured his present position...'

'He owes you his *station*, you mean,' I interjected.

'As I said... Colonel Moran, was that one of those, what are they called, jokes?... I have gone to no little trouble to put James where he is. I gather he is not satisfied, which will scarcely come as a surprise to you.'

'James is seldom satisfied,' the Professor said, addressing me as an aside.

I shrugged, unsure what was required.

'James will attempt to rope you in, James,' the Colonel said. 'He has ever tried to play us off, one against the other. You remember when he was expelled from Greyfriars?'

'An incident not one of us is liable to forget.'

'Indeed not. This time, I insist you stay out of it. No good can come of your involvement. James is hysterical and unreliable, again.'

'In that case, I wonder you troubled to use your influence in your brother's cause, Colonel,' I said.

The question of how a supply officer could 'influence' a railway company appointment did occur to me.

'Blood is thicker than vinegar, Colonel,' the Colonel said.

'True true,' I assented, like a pious idiot.

'James will approach you, James,' the Colonel continued, fixing eyes on his brother. 'You will ignore him. All will benefit. Have I made myself clear?'

'Admirably, James.'

'Good. Now, James, f--k off back to your blackboard.'

The Colonel turned and walked back into the noisy room. I gathered, with some astonishment, that we were dismissed.

My face burned. Professor Moriarty stood there, expression unchanged.

'Moriarty, does your brother... your brother, the Colonel... have any idea of your real business?'

The Professor cocked his head to one side, smiling unpleasantly.

'James is not the most perceptive of us.'

Moriarty was sensitive about defiance and discourtesy. The last man to tell him in so many words to f--k off was a cracksman who came across some jewels in a safe he was rifling for documents we had paid him to obtain, and foolishly decided no tithe was owed on them. After a week in our thick-walled basement, what was left of the poor sod was grateful to be tossed into the Thames.

'If you want me to kill him, I'll do it for nothing. As a favour, Moriarty. To repay your years of, ah, friendship. Bare hands?'

The Professor considered it.

'No, Moran. It's not yet time. And this matter is not ended.'

'Well, any time you want it done, it's done. You can count on me.'

'I have often said that, Moran.'

That was news to me. He laid a cold hand on my shoulder. From him, this was almost a singular gesture. Recalling that the last time he unbent so, he palmed the cursed Black Pearl off on me, I instinctively patted my pockets. If the Professor noticed, he was too lost in his own thoughts to pass comment.

I fancied he was in a melancholy humour.

Family reunions will do that to you.

II

When we returned to Conduit Street, a telegram awaited. From the third James Moriarty. The Professor read the wire, and passed it to me.

JAMES – FAL VALE TERRORISED BY GIANT WORM! – COME AT ONCE – JAMES.

I gave him back the telegram.

'A giant *worm*?' the Professor said. 'What, pray, does James expect me to do about it?'

I considered the matter.

'Tricky proposition, giant worms,' I said. 'Hard to know which gun to pack. Or which end to shoot. A good, sharp *kris* is your best tool. You have to chop the devil into slices rather than segments, or they all wriggle off separately and you've got a pack of little crawlers to deal with rather than the one outsize specimen.'

I knew what I was talking about. I've come across six-foot worms, mouths ringed with shark teeth, in South Africa. They look like pale, boneless pythons and can eat through solid rock, let alone a man's chest. You tend to mistake them for a thick rope or a draught-excluder, until you see a swallowing ripple run along their length or discern the disgusting brownish-pink core at the centre of the creamish translucent tube.

'James doesn't mean worm in that sense, Moran.'

'Is there another?'

'Archaic English, sometimes *ourm*. A synonym for dragon. The notion that such fantastic creatures breathe fire is associated with the English worm dragon rather than the Chinese lizard dragon.'

That was a different challenge.

'I've never stalked dragon, but I fancy an elephant gun would suffice.'

I was not entirely serious. I mean, I've heard of the *kuripuri* of the Amazon – degenerate survivors from the prehistoric age of reptiles – and I've shot the head off a Komodo dragon, which is merely an overgrown iguana and poor sport. If you've paid attention, you'll know I've tangled with several mythical species. Red Shuck and his pack turned out to be just dyed wolves, but the taxonomists were still out on the *mi-go* I'd run across in Nepal and Soho. Still, I wasn't prepared to swallow a worm unknown to science in Cornwall. Moriarty's head bobbed, though, so I knew there'd be trouble in it.

After furious oscillation, Moriarty crumpled his brother's telegram and tossed it into the fire. It went up with a puff, like a stage magician's flash paper.

'More urgent matters must be attended to, Moran,' the Professor declared, turning away from the fire. He touched fingertips to his pinpricked globe and gave it an idle spin. 'Soon, we must consider seriously the obstacles presented to our continental expansion by the entrenched interests of our *colleagues* in France and Germany.'

I'd known this was coming.

In Paris, a new Grand Vampire held office. He had displaced his predecessor after the Affair of the Six Maledictions – in which *Les Vampires* had been involved, not very happily. Having been forced (by us) into unprofitable battle with the Knights Templar, the Frenchies had cause to feel they'd not been dealt fairly. Reprisals were expected.

In Berlin, an ambitious pup was slavishly imitating the Moriarty Method by assembling his own criminal cartel. More adept at disguising his person than the Professor, this upstart seldom showed his real face. On our books, the kraut-eating swine was marked for an eventual seeing-to because one of his favoured impostures – a shock-haired, stooped alienist with mesmeric eyes – was an impudent caricature of the man whose act he had blatantly stolen. He even guyed Moriarty's side-to-side head wobble, which ticked off the Prof more than the arrant plagiarism of his Loughborough Diamond Coup in the Dusseldorf Marzipan Stone Substitution.

It wasn't just restlessness, a jaded need to expand an empire, which compelled Moriarty into border skirmishes with his continental rivals. In his mettle, he needed to be the best – which is to say, *worst* – in his field.

The Firm would go to war!

Not soon enough, said I. For I wasn't content to be content, to grow plump and pampered in a London rut – no matter how many blushing twins were thrown into the pot – when there were savage lands to be conquered, and desperate campaigns to be waged. The hunter's blood stirred and would not be quieted. View halloo, and into the fray...

Then, a railway messenger arrived. The lad was startled to be greeted on our doorstep by Tessie the Two-Ton Taff, in peignoir and straining stays. Mrs Halifax was off with one of her *filles de joie*, selling a healthy 'inconvenience' to thin-blooded, childless Americans, so the Great Lay of Llandudno was serving in Mrs H.'s stead for the day. The Welsh girl took the messenger by his ear and hauled him up to our reception room, where he presented a sealed envelope to the Professor. Having taken a shine to the railway lad, Tess then dragged him into the kitchens for what she referred to as 'a nice dollop of dripping'. I doubt the boy ever reported back to his office, though I don't credit the rumour spread by envious, bonier girls that Tess ate him.

This time, Stationmaster Moriarty enclosed a signed letter on the headed paper of the GS&W Railway Company. If presented to the conductor of the Fal Vale Special, which was to leave Paddington at two o'clock that afternoon, the document would entitle the bearer to accommodation gratis for himself and his party.

A wilful contrarian, Professor Moriarty was in a quandary. One brother had ordered him *not* to go to Cornwall. The other had summoned him *to* Cornwall. He could not disobey both equally. To defy one, he must satisfy the other. Besides weaving his head from side to side, he was grinding his teeth – a new habit, so far as I knew.

I tried to get him back to continental matters, asking his estimate of the Great Vampire's intriguing new protégée – a female who styled herself 'Irma Vep' and was reputedly the greatest man manipulator in the business since *that bitch* herself.

But he would not be distracted from family business.

'There's nothing else for it, Moran. We shall have to seek out this worm. Pack guns.'

'Your brother doesn't mention a fee.'

'He would not.'

'Family discount, eh?'

Moriarty's shoulders were rounder than usual. I saw my needling was getting through. Family can worry under the skin like a tick. The Professor was, in his way, a great man. Yet, despite what many who encountered him said, he was still a human man.

I'll warrant Gladstone, Palliser and Attila were the same – in command of their destinies and fixed on their great goals, but red-faced and sputtering when joshed by some sibling who remembered when nursie smacked their bottoms for making sicky-sicky on their bibs. Attila, of course, could have irritating relations thrown into a wolf pit. However, in the so-called enlightened modern age, such methods of easing domestic stress were frowned upon.

So, we were hunting dragons. With no payday in sight.

I consoled myself with the thought that this expedition was but an appetiser: a quick kill to warm up for the long, delicious hunt to come.

We were at Paddington Station in good time for the Special, which was ready to board at its platform. We passed through scalding steam to reach the steps to the single carriage. Other passengers were already in their seats, which made me wonder who else was invited on the Fal Vale Worm Express. A conductor stood by the steps, with a whistle and a clipboard. Folds of skin hung loose under his eyes and chin.

Moriarty presented his brother's letter to the official, who stated – in a tedious West Country drone – that no one had told him of extra passengers, opined that anyone could obtain a sample of the company's stationery and declared he had never heard of the supposed signatory.

'This b'ain't no good *yurr*,' he said. 'Only money or murder'll get yer 'board this train, or my name b'aint 'Ubert Berkins.'

Foolishly, we opted for money.

III

As the Fal Vale Special steamed out of London, the Professor sank into a deep quiet. He was thinking.

I'd known him not speak for a week, then arrange the removal of a human obstacle to one of his designs and become almost morbidly cheerful. I'd seen his crazes start up like a sudden summer storm, ending in ruination of one stripe or another for someone who had crossed him.

I need not mention again Nevil Airey Stent, the former Astronomer Royal. Even the Red Planet League business pales beside the fate of Fred Porlock, convicted in a court convened in our basement of a capital crime for selling information about the Firm's dealings to outside interests. What was done to the traitor made the Lord of Strange Deaths seem lenient, and stood as a serious disincentive to anyone else who might consider following his unhappy path of collaboration with the law.

I'd even been in the room while the Moriarty brain ticked as he worked over purely abstract problems. As a devotee of games of chance and calculation, I'm a fair hand at practical maths, but Moriarty's sums were well beyond my capabilities. He could have said 'ah-ha!' or 'eureka!' and chalked stickmen on the blackboard, claiming to have solved a puzzle which had baffled generations of clever clogs, and I'd be none the wiser.

But this was different. His head was not bobbing. His chin was clamped to his chest. He was still grinding his teeth. He would not be spoken to.

I'd never seen Moriarty like this. I concluded that only family could put him in such a black humour. His brothers set him equations for which there were no solutions, but which prompted endless, futile calculations. This was a new side to the Professor, and, I admit, I was uncomfortable with it. This forced me to a strange, giddying realisation that I had become *comfortable* with Moriarty's other sides, the ones which were terrifying to the rest of the world. What did that say about me? Through association, had I become as much a freak of nature – as much a monster – as the old man?

Moriarty wasn't in conversational mood and I'd not packed anything to read. Railway bookstalls tend not to stock *Mistress Payne's Rollicking Academy* or R.G. Sanders' *Natives I Have Shot*, my favoured perusing material. I was thrown back on eyeing up the other passengers.

Since this was a Special, the rest of the crowd must also have been invited.

I couldn't immediately see how they fit together. A young lady, travelling alone – always promising, rarely delivering – trim enough figure, but affecting pince-nez and a severe look. A funny little Frenchman with waxed moustaches, deep in the *Journal of the Society for Psychic Research*. A middle-aged parson with white powder in his hair and dusting his cassock; an old scratch on his cheek, a scar you'd be more likely to pick up duelling with sabres at Heidelberg than reading up *Acts of the Apostles* at Lampeter. A man-about-town type, who had clocked the lone young lady and was buffing his nails in an attempt to draw her attention. And a gaunt, floppy-haired gent, who ogled me balefully. I tossed him a jovial smile, and got a more penetrating stare for my pains. He produced, filled and lit an ostentatious pipe, wreathing himself in rings of pungent smoke.

'We're all for Fal Vale, then,' I ventured.

Yes, an extraordinarily stupid thing to say. It often helps to give an impression of extraordinary stupidity. Folk think so little of you they don't pay attention when you're standing behind them with a handy shiv.

'Indeed,' the parson said, in a high-pitched voice. 'The Special only stops there.'

'That is why it's called a "Special", don't you know,' drawled the man-about-town type. Too much hair oil for a proper Englishman. 'I'm Lucas, by the way. Eduardo of that ilk. I'm in it, too. Psychical research.'

The little Frenchman shrugged '*nom de*' something. He continued to make squiggly notations in the margins of an article on ectoplasmic manifestations.

'I suppose you've heard of the Fal Vale Worm,' I said.

Lucas nodded. 'I imagine we all have. It's why we're here.'

'I was not given to understand that this would be a tourist excursion,' the gaunt pipe smoker said. 'I took this for a serious investigation.'

'Who might you be, old bean?' Lucas asked.

'Thomas Carnacki,' the fellow replied.

The little Frenchman, impressed, muttered '*nom de*' something else.

'The Ghost Finder,' the parson observed. 'Celebrated investigator of the Whistling Room, the Horse of the Invisible and the Dwellers in the Abyss? This is quite a pleasure…' [1]

'Yes, indeed,' I said. 'I should like to shake the hand of the famous Mr Carnacki.'

'I imagine you would, ah…?' Carnacki asked, making no attempt to stick out a hand to be shaken.

'Sebastian Moran,' I said.

'Colonel Moran, the big-game hunter,' the parson said. Plainly, he was handily up on his *Who's Who*. I waited for him to list my medals, distinctions and tiger bags, but he didn't.

The celebrated psychic sleuth fiddled with his pipe.

'My name is Cursitor Doone,' the parson said, with a curt little nod as if acknowledging a salute. 'I am a ghost finder myself, in an amateur manner of speaking. Our friends the spirits are much misunderstood, I believe.'

'Sabin,' the Frenchman said. 'I take a sceptic's interest. All can be explained by the light of reason and logic. You will see – yes, you will – I am correct. There is no worm.'

The Reverend Doone seemed on the point of rebutting the sceptic, but Lucas spoke over him…

'Miss…?' he said, raising a hopeful eyebrow at the lady.

'Madame… Madame Gabrielle Valladon,' the woman said. 'I am Belgian zoologist.'

Which was odd, since she had a German accent.

But not as odd as someone who *wasn't* Thomas Carnacki claiming to *be* him. The hollow-cheeked, pipe-puffing lookalike might have fooled someone who'd seen a picture in the rotogravure, but I *know* Carnacki. I'd fallen asleep during one of the Ghost Finder's interminable tale-telling evenings in Cheyne Walk, and was booted out for having the temerity to snore during an account of his encounter with the Persistent Poltergeist of Penge.

During the Affair of the Mountaineer's Bum, a tale for which the world will never be ready, the Firm secured Carnacki's services to establish the supernatural bona fides of a public convenience in Tooting we wished to convince Inspector Patterson of Scotland Yard was haunted. Given his reputation as the least credulous of his profession – the dimwitted Flaxman Low, for instance, is eager to credit every twitching curtain and damp patch to phantoms from beyond the veil – a Carnacki verdict is respected. It is one of the Professor's greatest triumphs that he was able to pull the wool over such perspicacious eyes.

This gaunt stranger was someone else. A disguise merchant. That narrowed the field down a little, even if men of a thousand faces were becoming ten a penny. Sometimes – as on this train – you couldn't toss a bottle without beaning a detective made up as a ruffian, a crook posing as a toff, a swell larking about as a disfigured beggar, or a swindler in a dog collar and surplice.

But I couldn't put a name to this particular mask.

I didn't let on that I'd tumbled the imposter and kept smiling like a fathead.

'Oh,' I said, as if remembering there was one more introduction to be made. 'This is Professor Moriarty.'

Moriarty didn't come out of his thought fugue.

'The mathematician?' the parson said. 'Author of *The Dynamics of an Asteroid*?'

'No, the master criminal, author of ransom notes and blackmail demands,' I didn't say – though it did spring to mind.

'Yes. He's one of your cold fire of logic boys, too, Monsieur Sabin,' I said instead. 'Between the party of us, we'll soon have this worm in its place.'

'If place it has, Colonel,' the parson responded, as if that meant something. 'If place it has.'

There were two others with us. It was peculiar that a single-carriage Special should need two conductors, especially since one took the trouble to stay away from the passengers. The jowly Berkins, who had gouged us for our 'gratis' travel, passed regularly down the aisle, offering 'refreshments' which also turned out not to be complementary. While another person in the black, silver-trimmed tunic and cap of the GS&W line spent the journey sat at the rear of the carriage, peak pulled low over a face further obscured by several bandage-like strips of sticking plaster. Yes, another play-actor – though an uncommon shapely one. Despite a sparse moustache and thick eyebrows, this conductor was – as the swell of the tunic-front told my practiced eye – a woman.

'I say, let's pass the time with a hand or two,' Lucas said, producing a deck of cards from his top pocket and pretending to be clumsy as he shuffled. 'Six-penny stakes, to make it more interesting, eh what?'

That was blood in the water to this old shark.

By Fal Vale Junction, I would have earned back the train fare and more. I could feel it in my cracking knuckles.

IV

I arrived at Fal Vale a little poorer, but much wiser. Lucas was a lamentable cheat, almost ostentatiously... but lost, consistently. Sabin could have won most hands, but folded early... not bothered by winning or losing, and putting on a show as a distracted, exasperated logician. By the second deal, I knew Reverend Doone and Madame Valladon were playing as secret partners. I kept my losses down, resisting subtle suggestions that stakes be upped just when I held a surprisingly strong (but not winning) hand.

The fake Carnacki did not play with us, but took out a deck of tarot cards and laid out a patience I swear he invented on the spot just to look mystic. The real ghost finder wouldn't have wasted a captive audience, the whole carriage would have been regaled with his exploits. The Incident of the Boiling Kettle, The Mystery of the House of the Improbable, The Dreadful Affair of the Slug – I've heard them all.

The gaunt fellow watched the game through his tobacco fug. He couldn't have kept a closer eye on us if he'd produced a magnifying glass.

After rattling along the main line at speed – when an engine only has to pull a single carriage, it can beat timetabled trains by hours – we slowed down and chuffed along a Cornish branch which wound through deep cuttings and past tiny stations. Finally, we stopped at one of these neglected halts.

'Fal Vale Junction,' 'Ubert Berkins announced, needlessly. 'All change *yurr*.'

It was already full dark. The station was lit by three poor lamps.

I nudged Moriarty. He was suddenly alert.

'None of our fellow passengers are who they say they are,' he whispered. I'd worked that out for myself, thank you very much. 'Watch out for the Greek woman in the conductor's uniform. She has a throwing knife holstered between her shoulder blades.'

That was news. Later, Moriarty would explain how he knew her nationality from the way she buttoned her borrowed trousers or chewed her little fingernail, and I'd pretend to pay attention. It was an impressive parlour trick, but tiresome all the same. The throwing knife gen was useful info, though.

We busied ourselves collecting our belongings. I took care with my gun case, not letting Berkins 'assist' me, rather shooing the pest out of the way to try and cadge a tip from someone else. We all descended from carriage to platform.

The mysterious other conductor deigned to step down after us, but slipped into the steam cloud before anyone could try to talk with her. I watched her go, then noticed Madame Valladon also had an eye on her. In silhouette, the conductor's womanly gait was obvious.

The *echt*-Belgian zoologist looked away from me, casually. Lucas was still lingering about her, with the air of a near-sighted lion who doesn't realise the gazelle he's stalking has a revolver in her handbag. See, I can spot a concealed weapon too.

Sabin collared Berkins and issued instructions for the unloading of heavy trunks which supposedly contained delicate scientific instruments which should not be piled upside down. The conductor could have done with another pair of hands, but his distaff colleague was gone.

The Reverend Doone beamed, and announced, 'The emanations are strong here. I sense a presence. Discarnate, but welcoming. Can anyone hear me on the astral plane?'

I was more concerned with the earthly plane.

Especially when the Special pulled out of the station, steaming off with a shrill of its whistle. I wondered where the train was going, since this was its only stop – then guessed it had to loop about somewhere before going back to London. Nothing had been said about return travel arrangements.

The engine driver had made haste away from Fal Vale Junction, not lingering even for a pie and a cup of tea. It seemed someone who knew more about this stretch of country than I did was keen not to bide here long. At that, most people with a brain would take fright. I felt a thrill in my water.

In a moment of clarity, I felt every droplet of mist in the night air, heard every tiny sound from the trees. I anticipated danger with a half-sickened, half-excited craving which – I now admit – was close to the hateful love a dope fiend has for the pipe or a drunkard for the bottle. With potential death in the air, I was alive!

Berkins was gone with the Special. As far as I could tell, the woman conductor had not got back on board.

Moriarty strode along the platform, ulster flapping like bat wings, chin thrust out. I wondered if and when he would trouble to take me into his confidence. From experience, I knew he had an idea of what was going on. But frequently it suited him to keep it all to himself, and just tell me when to shoot someone.

Fal Vale Junction was not much of a station. There was a waiting room, with a welcoming open fire and a selection of periodicals on a rack... but it was locked. Out on the platform, without the benefit of the fire, it was freezing. The tearoom was open, in the sense that its door was wedged with a brick... but it was dark and cold. I touched the urn to see if there was still hot water, but it was like ice. Cakes and sandwiches from an earlier decade were on display. Something with teeth and a tail had been in among them and left chew marks and droppings.

'A warm welcome,' I commented. 'I was hoping for one of those famous Cornish clotted cream teas.'

'Can't get they *yurr*,' Lucas said, guying Berkins.

Outside, the Reverend marched about, sensing things of a spiritual nature. His boots clicked on the flagstones of the platform.

A branch veered off from the line and vanished into a hillside tunnel. A big wheel on the platform worked a set of points which could send trains into this hole. I'd looked up Fal Vale Junction in *Bradshaw's Guide*, and not been able to determine where this offshoot ran to. Probably a tin mine, clay pit or unloading dock in Poldhu Cove. Beyond the hill was the coast, which put me in mind of wreckers and smugglers. It wasn't like Bradshaw to be vague, though. The rails were shiny and well maintained, so the branch was obviously in use.

Moriarty walked nearly to the end of the platform, and peered into the dark as if through a telescope. Could he discern life on some far-distant star? Or was he just fixed on some theoretical point half a mile into the tunnel?

'I sense a visitor,' the Reverend said, and stood up straight as if for inspection.

We were all ignoring him now, but he was right. In the dark of the tunnel, a tiny flame burned.

'It is an apparition of fire,' Doone announced. 'We must be calm and receptive. Those who have passed beyond the veil are more frightened of us than we are of them.'

The flame was bigger. No, it was the same size… but coming closer.

Madame Valladon's hand was in her bag, curled around her revolver, no doubt. She could fire through the seam if she had to.

We watched the light. It bobbed slightly as it advanced.

'Well met, spirit,' Doone said, almost singing.

The fake Carnacki touched his fingers to his temples, as if doing a music hall mind-reading act.

'That is no spirit light,' Monsieur Sabin declared. 'It is a railwayman's dark lantern. There is always, you see, a logical explanation. Have I not proved this? Yes, I have.'

The Frenchman was right.

Now we could see the lantern, swinging from side to side, and make out the man carrying it. He wore a peaked cap, which flashed silver, and a long, black coat.

'James, is that you?' the Professor shouted.

'Yes, James,' came the answer.

'Hurry up,' Moriarty insisted. 'It's cold here on the platform.'

'I'm aware of that. It's cold here in Cornwall. On winter nights, those tend to be the climactic conditions throughout these isles.'

'Climatic. "Climactic" refers to a climax or culmination, not the weather,' the Professor said.

The newcomer shrugged off the correction.

Stationmaster Moriarty trudged along the gravel rail bed and up the incline to the platform, where the Professor waited impatiently. The brothers exchanged beak nods. They walked together towards the rest of us. They shared a stalking gait.

Young James was a Moriarty all right, with piercing eyes behind thin-rimmed spectacles and the beginnings of the family stoop. His face had not yet sunk to the vulture leanness shared by the Colonel and the Professor, but that would come in a few years if nobody hanged him. Walking up to our group, he set down his lantern and took off his cap. He had a fuller, darker head of hair than either of his brothers. He ran his fingers through his locks, probably a sly dig.

'James, you're not looking well,' he said, mildly. 'The country does not agree with you. You are a city bird.'

'I say, do you two know each other?' Lucas asked. 'I only just realised, same name and all that. Stationmaster Moriarty. Professor Moriarty. You must be father and son?'

At this suggestion, the Jameses made faces as if they'd bitten something sour.

'They are brothers,' Sabin said. 'I am surprised you failed to find that out when you researched our summons here.'

'Research? Oh I never bother with that. Prejudices the mind. Prods you to premature conclusions.'

'Tchah,' said the Frenchman, dismissing Lucas' *pensée*.

'I suppose James told you to keep away from Fal Vale,' Stationmaster Moriarty said to the Professor. 'He's made his position clear, as usual.'

'I thought *you* were James?' Madame Valladon said.

'No, *he* is James,' Doone said. 'Professor James Moriarty.'

Neither brother explained. Our fellow travellers were left in confusion.

Professor and Stationmaster smirked together, almost undetectably – a family expression which excluded the rest of us. I got a chill from more than the night air.

The brothers didn't much care for one another, but each knew the other well. I was on as intimate terms with the Prof as he would allow, yet I was often forced to admit I shared rooms with a stranger. Hitherto, it hadn't bothered me: Moriarty kept secrets from everyone, so why should I be any different? I was his employee, not his friend. We knocked about for mutual advantage, not hale-fellow-well-met nonsense. Sometimes, I despised him more than I hate my old man... with a similar, curious sort of hate commingled with admiration, passion and a sense they were impossible to get away from.

I broke with Sir Augustus to avoid becoming simply 'the dutiful son', only to become Moriarty's Number Two. In many things, the Professor had supplanted pater – whippings were less direct, but no less frequent. With the appearance of Moriarty's brothers, I realised there were those closer to his cold heart. Family by blood, not association. I'd thought the Professor invincible, beyond human hurt or harm, but it seemed the other Jameses could prick him.

Stationmaster Moriarty produced keys and opened the waiting room. We all pressed eagerly indoors. Thanks to Lucas lifting his hat and getting in the way, Madame Valladon claimed the chair nearest the fire. Sabin wasn't happy leaving his precious boxes on the platform, but reluctantly did so. Doone said he was sure the spirits wouldn't disturb Sabin's belongings.

Only the fake Carnacki kept away from the fire. I wondered if he was wearing a wax nose which would melt if he got too close.

The Stationmaster stood like a man in command, enjoying the company he had put together, anticipating fun and frolics. I've known society matrons take pleasure in seating next to each other people they know will quarrel before the fish course is done. 'Fireworks' are all part of the entertainment. I wondered if Young James had combined sceptics and believers in this party for similar reasons, then recalled none of this lot were who they said they were. Ergo, this ghost-worm hunt was nothing of the sort.

The Professor stood to one side, watching his brother.

One other thing: Young James Moriarty hadn't asked who *I* might be.

During the journey, I'd ferreted out that everyone else present had received a personal invitation. Though his note to the Professor referred to 'you and your party', the Stationmaster could scarcely have expected his brother – a maths master, so far as anyone knew – to show up at Fal Vale with a war-scarred, semi-notorious reprobate in tow. Most folk would be astonished that Professor Moriarty was even on a nodding acquaintance with the ferocious Basher Moran. So, I reckoned Young James already knew who I was. Unlike Colonel Moriarty, he had an idea what business the Prof was really in. Our Stationmaster hid his dark lantern under a bushel in the Cornish wilds, but some stratagem boiled in his Moriarty brain.

'Now, about this worm…' Young James began. 'What am I bid for its secrets?'

V

I had not expected to attend an auction in the waiting room of an obscure railway station. Apparently, the 'secrets of the worm' were on the block. I couldn't say whether Stationmaster Moriarty intended his brother to join the bidding or had invited the Professor to observe and be impressed.

None of the other Special passengers immediately stuck up paws, scratched noses or waved sheaves of banknotes. The game had changed quickly, and our pack of psychic investigators were still playing the last hand.

Young James looked pleased with himself.

'The legend of the Fal Vale Worm is well known,' he said. Stepping aside, he pointed to an indifferent, faded picture hung over the fireplace. It showed a creature slithering white coils among green Cornish hills. Hairless and earless, it had a catlike snarl and human eyes. A knight in armour raised a lance against plumes of flame pouring from the beast's nostrils. Rude peasants sensibly scattered away from the titanic combat. The creature had no legs, but from the peculiar way the unknown artist had depicted the running peasants I judged legs weren't his strong suit, so he might have been tempted to leave them out.

'The story is old as clay,' the Stationmaster continued. 'An undying beast, native to the depths of the ancient mine-workings, the worm emerges by night to exhale infernal flame. Every village hereabouts has an inn called The White Dragon where folktale collectors buy drinks for yokels who trot out their family legends. Always, someone claims their grandfather or great-uncle saw or met or fought the worm, and it's always some other man's grandfather who got burned or eaten. You have variations on this theme all over the country, in remote regions where a Beast of the Bog or a Wyvern of the Wold might hide away from the local hunt or the catchers from London Zoo.'

He produced another framed picture to spice up the narrative, a photograph of a canvas and papier-mâché worm with twelve human legs protruding from its body posing against a stone wall. It had a snarling, frilly eyebrowed, fanged head at either end.

Young James continued, 'Every year at the Padstow May Day Festival, a team of six Fal Vale men represent the worm. They skirmish in the street with rivals from other villages who dress up as 'obby 'osses.'

Evidently, lecturing was a Moriarty family trait. I wished Young James would hurry up and get to it.

'Uncommonly for its breed, the Fal Vale Worm has been active lately, and left evidence of its night work. You will have seen notices in the press of the fires which have troubled this area in the last few months; fires which will not be put out by buckets of water. Copses and haystacks turned to white ash. Fields brown and smoking after heavy rain. A farm at Compton Dando burned to the ground. A scarecrow caught fire two nights ago, and the black skeleton of a crucified man was found where the scarecrow had stood.'

The Professor nodded. If he had known about this incendiary outbreak, he hadn't shared the information.

'There is natural explanation,' Sabin insisted.

'You never know, though,' Lucas said. 'Not with a worm.'

'I doubt a spirit would cause such harm,' Doone said.

I was not immediately inclined to conclude that the Fal Vale Worm was the genuine article. My first suspect would be some sweaty, burn-marked little fellow with a box of lucifers, a jug of paraffin and a heart which skips whenever anything catches light.

We had a couple of firebugs on our lists; gents who go by names like Benny Blazes, Tim the Torch or Firebrand Sam. Even if there's a solid bit of profit, from insurance or otherwise, to be had, it makes sense to use someone who knows – and loves – fire to perform arson duties. They'll do it for nothing but jollies, for a start. The flame which burns when doused with water is a firebug tell. It's not magic, just a mix of chemicals: they all have favourite recipes and jealously guard their secret ingredients.

'The worm has been seen,' the Stationmaster said, 'zooming along the rail bed outside, disappearing into the tunnel faster than any train. I can produce sworn testimony. But sworn testimony will not, I believe, impress anyone in this room. I shall accept no bids until you've the evidence of your own senses.'

He smiled, readily. Not an expression I associated with his brothers. From his waistcoat pocket, he produced a railwayman's watch.

'If we forsake the comfort of this room for a few moments, we may bear witness to an, ah, occult phenomenon.'

'…Which runs on a timetable, James?'

'Yes, James. Punctually.'

'Many spirits are affected by cycles of the moon,' Doone put in.

I had the uneasy feeling I was the only one in the room completely in the dark. It was plain we were no longer hunting ghosts.

'I say,' Lucas said. 'Where's our Carnacki toddled off to?'

Madame Valladon swore in German.

The imposter had slipped out of the room when everyone else was paying attention to the Stationmaster. He had left his pipe propped by a stopped clock, so his smell lingered.

'This is not to be tolerated,' Sabin declared.

'Raw-ther,' Lucas agreed.

'Mayhap Mr Carnacki was an astral projection all along?' ventured Doone.

'An astral projection who left the door open?' I said.

The Stationmaster seemed to be thrown off his game by this distraction, but swiftly tried to re-establish order. He held up his watch and tapped it.

'I insist that agreed rules of conduct remain in force,' said the Frenchman.

Young James put his railwayman's whistle to his lips and blew a shrill toot.

'I suggest we follow my brother's direction, for the moment,' the Professor said. 'We shall see what is to be seen, then draw conclusions. Is that acceptable?'

Sabin nodded. The others fell in line.

Moriarty looked to his brother, like a headmaster who has shown a junior staff member how to quiet the boys. Our host, I fancied, was irritated. Of the three Jameses Moriarty, he was the least commanding... It seemed a comedown that a family which could produce a Professor Moriarty and a Colonel Moriarty should run to a mere Stationmaster. Now, I wondered whether Young James had not been promoted above his natural abilities.

The Professor lead us out onto the platform. His brother followed.

A thick mist had risen, turning the rail beds into rivers of white. I smelled something like sulphur... which I associate with firearms rather than hellfire. I could *taste* danger in the air. Fal Vale Junction felt like a fort just before the attack. While the others formed their observing party, I sauntered towards the pile of luggage and slipped a rifle out of my gun case. I carried it unostentatiously, barrel-down like a crutch. I felt much happier with a loaded gun at hand.

'What's through that tunnel?' Lucas asked.

'Tin mines,' explained the Stationmaster. 'In the daytime, ore trains run to and from Tarleton. The metals are cold at night.'

'The so-called worm, it abide in its mine by day, and emerge by night?' Sabin asked. 'This is your suggestion?'

'More than a suggestion,' Young James said. 'You can set your watch by it.'

Everyone turned towards the tunnel. All I could see was night and fog.

In a music hall, when the magician wants you to watch the pretty lady in tights or pay attention to his waving wand… that's the time to look everywhere else, to see how the trick's being pulled off. I let the ghost-finding brigade peer into the hole, and scanned the station and environs. The fake Carnacki was hiding somewhere. I'd not forgotten the lady conductor with the throwing-knife either. With all this mist, there were many places nearby where a person could lie low.

'Can you hear that?' Lucas asked, hand up to his ear.

From inside the tunnel, there was a sound. A shushing, wailing, rattling. Worms, as a rule, are quieter. Even giant ones. The gunpowdery smell was stronger.

'There are spirits…' the parson began.

'Shush, Hugo,' cut in Madame Valladon. 'You can stop play-acting.'

Doone shut up, crestfallen.

The noise grew louder.

'Something runs on the rails?' Sabin said. 'A train, *hein*?'

It sounded like no train I'd ever heard.

'Look…' Lucas pointed.

There was firelight in the fog. It barrelled towards us faster than something without legs or wheels ought to be able to.

I had my rifle up. Whatever came out of that tunnel would get one between its eyes, if eyes it had.

Stationmaster Moriarty was still brandishing his watch, grinning. He seemed to be enjoying the spell cast over his guests. The Professor hung back, tutting impatiently.

A cold, sharp point pricked under my chin. The rifle was firmly twisted out of my hands. A female person pressed close to my back, arm about my chest.

The Greek lady, of course. I stood stock still.

Then, in a rush, the worm was out of its hole…

…and rushing through the station past us, leaving only a swirling wake. The disturbed fog reformed over the rails.

The worm wasn't white and fires burned in its belly. A foul smell lingered behind: it was a mechanical thing.

Down the line a way, bright flame blossomed. For an instant, the countryside lit up as if it were daytime. I blinked away fire patterns burned into my eyes and watched as a burning wave swept across a field that inclined towards the rail bed. An old shed was instantly obliterated. Flaming sheep scurried, screaming, for the horizon. A butt of water exploded into fragments.

In the firelight, the worm was visible – it had soundlessly halted on the tracks. Liquid fire dribbled from hose-like cannons protruding from its sides. It was armoured, shield-like plates bolted together in a limber, flexible carapace – a big, bulletproof version of the May Day Festival worm costume.

The worm was a war train! A land dreadnought.

The bogus ghost finders chattered to each other, in several languages. I had an idea now of their true profession.

'England alone must not have this thing,' Sabin said. 'It would mean catastrophe for the civilised world.'

'So we hear from France,' Stationmaster Moriarty said. 'Can I take it that a bid is made?'

Sabin nodded.

'Thank you, Monsieur de la Meux. What of Imperial Germany? Fraulein von Hoffmannsthal, can you and Herr Oberstein make an offer?'

Madame Valladon – whose real name turned out to be Ilse von Hoffmannsthal – conferred with the parson – the notorious spy Hugo Oberstein – and gave a nod. They had abandoned their pretence of not knowing each other, let alone their fraying cover identities. I was relieved not to have to listen to any more prattle about spirits from the Reverend Doone.

'Mr Lucas. You are a free agent. Do you act, in this instance, for the Tsar of all the Russias?' Young James addressed the dandy.

'A little to the East, old top. A more humane mikado ne'er did in Japan exist, you know... and they have the railways too, very modern.'

This was a nest of damn foreign spies! I've played the Great Game myself, on several sides. Nothing crawls like as a patriot lying and sneaking for his country.

'So "Carnacki" represents the Tsar?' the Stationmaster asked.

'That one acts for himself, James,' the Professor said. 'If you troubled to use your brain, you should have seen that first thing. He is the imposter among imposters. The *real* fake Carnacki is trussed in a trunk in the left-luggage department at Paddington.'

'Come, come, James. Nothing is amiss.'

'No? Then why is Miss Kratides holding a knife to my man's throat?'

Now, everyone looked at us. I raised the paw not pinned by the lady's grip in an attempt at a cheery wave.

'Don't mind me,' I said. 'Play on. Though, apropos of nothing, Oberstein: when you're introduced to people, you start to click your boot heels then remember not to. Few English parsons have that habit. If you're to continue your, ah, theatrical career, you might try to get that seen to.'

Oberstein spat on the platform. That wasn't like a clergyman, either.

Ilse von Hoffmannsthal took out her revolver, as she had been dying to do all evening, and pointed it at people who didn't notice or care.

The fire down the way wasn't dying down. The worm wasn't moving. It had no funnel and wasn't expelling steam. I wondered in an academic sort of way why it was so bloody fast. I had more immediate concerns, though. Blood was dribbling into my collar.

Young James was off his stride.

'Sophy,' he said. 'Is that you?'

The lady pushed me away. I stumbled, but got my balance and clapped a hand to my throat. For a moment, I was worried this Sophy Kratides person had slit my throat. They say you don't feel it if the knife is sharp enough, though who 'they' might be who've lived to pass on this intelligence, I couldn't say. Everyone whose throat I've cut has only managed a minute or so of inarticulate gurgling before shutting up permanently. I let my wound go and saw only spots of blood on my fingers. She'd just administered an attention-getting scratch.

Turning, I saw Miss Kratides peel off her mask of sticking-plaster, taking off the moustache and eyebrows with it. Sophy had a handsome, if severe face, and held a knife like someone practiced in its use. She slid it between her fingers, wiping off my blood. The top three buttons of her uniform jacket were undone. A smaller knife was holstered in the front of her corset, handle nestled between prize plums. How many other blades had she concealed in out-of-the-way portions of her anatomy? It might be diverting, if dangerous, to discover the answer. Her flashing eyes and sharp edges reminded me of other exciting ladies of my acquaintance... Mattie Ball of Wessex, Malilella of the Stiletto, Lady Yuki Kashima, Mad Margaret Trelawny. Yes, I never learn. I like the dangerous ones.

'You're not supposed to be here,' the Stationmaster said to her. 'You're *supposed* to be on the *Kallinikos*. Keeping an eye on Lampros.'

'Miss Kratides is where I want her to be, James,' said a voice from the other side of the platform. 'Keeping an eye on you.'

'James?' sputtered Stationmaster Moriarty.

I looked at the Professor, who raised his shoulders in a 'not me' shrug.

'Yes, James,' said the voice.

Out of the fog stalked Colonel James Moriarty.

We had the full set.

VI

So this is what the Colonel meant by 'supplies'. Secret weapons. I should have known no Moriarty would spend his life on bully and boots. I still took him for a sickly desk-rider, but he could do damage enough while sitting on his arse.

'James,' the Colonel said to the Stationmaster, 'I gave you this position to perform one duty, and one duty *only*. To revive and disseminate the legend of the Fal Vale Worm. To keep prying eyes away from the *Kallinikos*...'

Just to show I paid *some* attention at Eton... the war train was named for *Kallinikos* of Heliopolis, inventor of 'Greek fire', as used by the Byzantine Empire against the infidel circa 672 AD. The secret of the weapon, a forerunner of arsonists' accelerants, was supposedly lost. It seemed it had been rediscovered.

'Not only have you failed in this, James. You have contrived to gather all the prying eyes in one party.'

'Yes, James,' responded Stationmaster Moriarty. '*On my own initiative*. You can round them up. Buy them off. Shoot them. Whatever you do, they won't be spying on your trials and reporting back to their masters. Isn't that more useful than leaving them at large?'

'Not cricket, eh what,' Lucas said. 'You've got to have *some* standards!'

'No, Mr Lucas, you do *not*,' Young James responded. 'Do you not understood your own profession? As a spy, you must have no standards at all!'

M. Sabin – Herbert de la Meux, Victor-Duc de Souspennier – tried to step back into the shadows. My new girlfriend was there behind him, two interesting little knives slipped out of her bracelets. She made symbolic slices in his jacket. He didn't try to escape again.

We were all going to have to play audience to this family discussion.

'James,' the Stationmaster appealed to the Professor, 'tell James about human nature.'

The Colonel blew his nose. 'I see you are in this too, James,' he said. 'Despite *express* instructions.'

'Your cover is outmoded, James,' the Professor told the Colonel, his voice dripping with scorn. 'Putting the spook story about to scare off the curious might have done for Dr Syn. In those days, a dab of phosphor on an old sack-mask could turn a smuggler into a marsh phantom frightening enough for ignorant folk to shiver under their bedclothes on nights when the ghosts rode. But this is a world of telephone and telegraph. *Entire societies* of busybodies chase ghosts with anemometers and Kodaks.

'Reviving the worm legend is not a sensible tactic for keeping people *away* from military secrets. Rather, it is an invitation to every crank in the land to crawl over your proving ground. Frankly, it's a wonder this party consists only of spies. It won't be long before someone hires the real Thomas Carnacki to poke about with his electric pentacle and plum-bob. If a circulation-chasing newspaper puts a bounty on the worm, you'll have to deal with Moran's game-hunting fraternity too.'

The Colonel was on the ropes, his brothers ganged against him.

All three heads oscillated as they stared at each other, like a convocation of cobra. It was hard to look away from, but harder to look at.

The *Kallinikos* was on the move, coming back this way. I glimpsed the Greek invertebrate's operators through slits in its hide. Like the Cornish worm, the war train had a head at both ends. Two engines. It could move at equal speed in either direction, so long as there were rails to run on.

Metal snail tracks were creeping all over the world. The machine was not made for my sort of war: putting down natives, chasing hill-bandits, looting dusky potentates' treasure stores. It was built to roll over Europe, pissing fire on uhlans, cathedrals and shopkeepers. The contraption stank of bloody cleverness. The representatives of foreign powers took mental notes. Which wouldn't do anyone's empire any good without the plans. It's always the plans spies are after.

The worm slid into the station.

I didn't swallow Stationmaster Moriarty's latest version of events, in which he'd selflessly rounded up the most dangerous spies in Britain. I judged young James had the cold, calculating self-interest of his eldest brother. No atom of patriotism stirred in his breast. He might have planned a double-cross – technically, a *triple*-cross – but, if not for the early arrival of Colonel Moriarty and Miss Kratides, he'd at least have tried to get *paid* for the secrets of the worm before turning his catch over to the mercies of the Department of Supplies.

Lucas considered the *Kallinikos* wistfully. I could imagine the riches the Emperor of Japan would bestow on the man who brought him such a dragon.

I just felt a kind of congealed disgust.

It was like the first time I saw a Maxim gun in action. Oh, for a minute or two, the rat-tat-tat is exciting, and it's quite amusing to see wave upon wave of spear-chucking, astounded natives jigging like broken marionettes as red chunks of their bodies fly off in all directions. Then, a battle which would once have raged for three days – and seen seven Victoria crosses bestowed (five posthumously) on the brave, foolish lads who defended some flyblown ridge just because a Union Jack fluttered above it – is over and done with inside two minutes. As the operator fusses about his overheated precious gadget, wiping grease off his spectacles and calling for tea and biscuits, it all seems terribly empty.

Anyone who can direct a hosepipe can turn the crank of a wonder-gun and murder more heathens in a single burst than a sharpshooter with clear eye, steady nerve and taste for the kill – which is to say, Basher Moran or the nearest offer – can pot in an entire campaign. I knew how handloom weavers must have felt when factory owners installed the spinning jenny. One thing about Mr Hiram Maxim's gun, though: a sock full of blasting powder and pebbles, shoved down a fat barrel and packed tight with a swagger-stick, makes for an amusing incident the next time the clerk in charge gives the machinegun a test-fire to impress the staff officers.

Professor Moriarty, who had science instead of a soul, was interested in the *Kallinikos*. He quizzed Colonel Moriarty, who – I saw – was not beyond wanting to impress his older brother.

'You have George Lampros, then?'

'This is a Lampros–Partington design,' the Colonel admitted.

Now, it was the Professor's turn to lecture. 'The formula for "Greek Fire" has been preserved since the Byzantine Empire by a family of alchemists and engineers. George Lampros is the last of them. Moran, you will recall I drew your attention to his obituary in *The Times* and listed the seven significant factors that suggested his death had been faked to cover a new, secret employment ...'

I did not recall. Quite often, I didn't pay attention when the Professor was off on one of his tears. I'd probably been waiting for him to hand over the paper so I could see how much I'd lost at the races the day before.

'Lampros is a Greek patriot,' continued the Professor. 'Why has he shared his secret with Britain?'

The Colonel made a *pfui* gesture. His face was dark red in the light of the still-burning fields. He responded, 'As a Greek patriot, Lampros envisions a coming war between Christian Europe and the Ottoman Empire, in which our island fortress will be the last redoubt. He is politically naïve, of course.

We have a contingency plan for modern crusades against the infidel Turk, but it is but one among many potential conflicts for which we must prepare. The *Kallinikos* is a prototype, the first launch of a land fleet which will take the rails against any threat to the interests of our Empire. One day, soon, half the world will be in flames thanks to the Lampros formula... I intend to make sure Great Britain is in the other half.'

Sadly, I had no sock of blasting powder about me.

'You disagree, Colonel Moran?' Colonel Moriarty said. 'Does the *Kallinikos* offend your sensibilities?'

Like the Professor, the Colonel could read my face. It's not such a trick. When I'm angry, I frown like thunder. When I'm enjoying myself, I grin like an ape. Only when I've got a better hand than the other fellow does the curtain come down and I present an aspect of stone. I was frowning, now.

'It does take the sport out of it,' I suggested mildly.

Three Moriarty brothers craned their necks to glare electrically at me.

'Sport!' spat the Stationmaster. 'Have you missed the last fifty years of history?'

'No, chummy, I've been in the thick of it, where the medals are won and the bodies are buried. I've had the fun, while you've been clipping platform tickets.'

'In a generation, you'll be obsolete,' Colonel Moriarty told me. 'The first time the *Kallinikos* sees off a cavalry charge, your type of soldier will be one with the dinosaurs. It may be less sporting, less fun, but we shall *win*.'

'You may be right, Colonel,' I told him. 'But you'll have the deuce of a battle first. Not with the enemy, with your own lot. You're still in the British army and they'll never stand for...'

'I'm not *in* the British army,' he said, with a Moriartian gleam in his eyes. 'I *am* the British army. Just now, in command of a single train, I outgun all the medal-laden idiots who rode into the Valley of Death but didn't learn from it.

'You think the Empire's war machine is still run by public school bullies who went into their father's regiment and had a commission warm and waiting? I admit there are all too many of that breed. You can find them guzzling brandy in deadly dull clubs or sweltering in Turkish baths, swapping yarns about the wily Pathan and Johnny Zulu. They're for show, Moran. For parades and guarding Buckingham Palace and skirmishing with brown bandits.

'When we go against, say, Kaiser Wilhelm – and, make no mistake, we will – the *Kallinikos*, designed by scientists and operated by engineers, will carry the day. We'll keep you on, of course. Your kind of soldier. We might call you a land captain and put you on top of the train like a figurehead. We'll give you medals when you get your head shot off. But soldiers in overalls, not scarlet uniforms, will carry the fight.'

Colonel Moriarty looked at me and saw the sort of men who sneered at his precious Department of Supplies and would never let him sit at the top table no matter how many battles his choo-choo juggernaut won. He couldn't even make or operate the *Kallinikos* – just fill in the forms to get it on the rails.

I took my revolver from my coat pocket and pointed it at the Colonel's head. That shut him up.

'Moran,' cautioned the Professor, mildly.

In that moment, I couldn't tell whether Moriarty would be grateful or furious if I killed his brother out of hand.

'I could have you burned where you stand, before you manage to fire,' Colonel Moriarty said.

I had noticed the nozzles of the flame-cannons swivelling to point at me.

Turning, I fired... and took off one of Oberstein's kneecaps. He was felled and the palm-sized compression pistol – disguised as a big pocket watch – rolled from his grip. He had been creeping into a position where he could have shoved the thing in the small of the Colonel's back and blasted his spine.

'Can I have another medal for that, chief clerk?' I asked. 'I seem to have saved your life.'

Sophy Kratides' face was burning. She'd been behind Oberstein and had not seen him reaching under his cassock.

At my shot, Lucas and Sabin had thrown themselves on the ground. Ilse von Hoffmannsthal, however, stood straight.

Oberstein swore in German.

Lucas and Sabin began to roll along the platform and – *in a flash!* – I perceived something not one of the brothers Moriarty had yet realised.

I can't sniff dropped cigar ashes and tell you the inside-leg measurement of the smoker. But I've come through numerous battles with skin relatively intact because I don't suffer from a maths teacher's need to dwell on my workings-out. I just *know* things, without really troubling with how or why I know them. It's a whiff in the air, sometimes; or a broken twig on the trail which is just too neatly snapped to be natural. Now, it was two men who – we had been told – acted for different masters moving in unison.

Stationmaster Moriarty thought he had summoned rival bidders, but his bogus psychic investigators were a spy ring. The card game which had tipped me off that Oberstein and Ilse were in cahoots was a double-bluff to convince me Sabin and Lucas *weren't* in it with them.

Sophy Kratides whipped out throwing-knives, and might have skewered both the rolling men but for von Hoffmannsthal, who stepped in front of her and launched a kick which would have done credit to a cancan dancer – it turned out her skirts were loose trousers tailored to seem like conventional feminine attire, until the wearer made a move like this – and planted a boot-heel into the Greek woman's sternum. I heard the thump of impact and Sophy staggered back.

Ilse then pulled a comb from her hair, which turned out to be a long, thin dagger. Sophy recovered her balance and thrust both of her knives toward the other woman's eyes, only for the blades to be struck aside – with sparks – by a sweep of Ilse's dagger.

Then, it was on… an expert knife-fight between fit fillies who whirled like dervishes and slashed at each other with well-matched precision and clinical malice. Their loose hair tossed as they hissed insults at each other in several languages. Both took minor cuts and sustained rents in their clothes, but avoided the other's would-be killing thrusts.

Entertaining, I admit, but a distraction. I rapped on the worm's metal hide with my revolver.

One of the plates of the *Kallinikos* slid aside, making an aperture in the carapace. An engineer – our old friend Berkins, in tailored overall and a peakless cap like a convict's – was puzzled by the sudden commotion.

'You can't do that *yurr*,' he said.

Lucas and Sabin had rolled away from the train, and stood up. They got busy with the big wheel which worked the points. Lucas struggled with the control. Sabin – whose walking stick was a disguised shotgun – kept us from interfering.

It wasn't them I was bothered with, anyway. Though I saw what they were up to.

The Professor spotted him first.

'Moran,' he shouted. 'Up there.'

On top of the train crouched a thin, spidery figure. He wore a black body-stocking and a tight-fitting hood with slit-holes for eyes. He must have been lying on the roof of the waiting room.

It was the double-fake Carnacki. Chief of the spy ring, it appeared.

I took a shot, which went true. It spanged against my target's chest, and he was pushed backward but not knocked down. He was armoured, just like the worm. The gaunt, lithe fellow made sure I hadn't another shot at him, stepping off the other side of the train and dropping behind it.

'All aboard,' I shouted, and barged past Berkins.

'You're not cleared for the *Kallinikos*,' complained Colonel Moriarty. 'You could be shot for treason!'

It wouldn't be the first time they'd tried.

The Professor held his brother back. Which showed a faith in me I'd come to expect. At least the Professor understood what I was doing. Neither of us could have said why, though. Oh, we wanted to slap down the false-face fellow who thought he could pull off a coup under our noses, but it's not as if we felt an obligation to preserve Her Majesty's secrets for the Department of Bloody Supplies. I've lived long enough with my impulse to hare off into dicey situations where death and danger lurk to know I could no more moderate this tendency than a tiger could decide to be polka-dotted for a change.

Moriarty, however, was usually more calculating.

The spy master would get into the worm somehow, and I'd face him in its belly.

The interior of the *Kallinikos* was cramped, certainly not designed for comfort. Also, stifling and malodorous. Canvas straps hung everywhere. I couldn't stand up straight without bumping my head on the ceiling. Gauges, batteries, dynamos and dials took up too much space. Charts and graphs were pinned to a draughtsman's table. Electric light bulbs hung from a thick central wire, pulsing with inconsistent current.

I pushed Berkins off the train, with some pleasure. He fell on his fat arse.

There was a shot. Sabin, firing at the ground as Lucas finally wrenched the wheel. With the points thrown, the *Kallinikos* could roll onto the main line – off the branch it had been using in the trial manoeuvres. If the spy master took command, he could burn the whole county to cover his escape and plunder the machine's secrets at his leisure.

All three Moriarty brothers crammed into the aperture like Siamese triplets, jostling to board the war train. The Professor established seniority with sharp elbows, and was inside the *Kallinikos* ahead of the Colonel and the Stationmaster. None of them needed to be on the worm, but no James could have borne it if another were on board and they were left behind. Brothers, eh?

In the present pickle, I'd have found Sophy the Knives more useful than the Moriarty boys, but she was still apache dancing with Ilse. There was a reason the Professor employed me to handle the rough stuff – it wasn't that he couldn't take care of himself when there was blood on the floor, but he saw the wisdom of delegating to experts. In battle, that meant me. Still, I could have done without worrying over an arithmetic tutor, a desk soldier and the family idiot.

'Keep out of my bloody way,' I told the brothers, 'and I'll find our bloody imposter.'

They showed identical, stricken faces. None cared to be told what to do. All chewed over any sleight with eventual retribution in mind. Scratch any of 'em, and there was Moriarty marrow underneath.

'Carnacki the Ghost Finder,' I shouted, 'is there anybody there? Do I sense a presence in the aether?'

Our spy master had got into the *Kallinikos*, I'd no doubt. One of the plates hung loose, showing a sliver of the outside through the hide of the worm. The hole didn't seem big enough for a grown man to squeeze through, but this customer had more than proved his slipperiness today.

I saw a shadow and fired. Something exploded. A cloud of sulphurous flame puffed, burning brighter than natural fire. A couple of canvas straps were incinerated. A wave of intense heat rolled at me. I nipped behind a bulkhead. If Greek Fire got on flesh, it would sizzle through to the bone. The puff burned out quickly, but left a residue of acrid fumes. They might be lethal, too. This contraption was as dangerous to the operators as the enemy.

'This is a delicate system,' the Colonel said. 'It's not advisable to use firearms in here.'

Heaven forbid anyone should shoot a gun in a war machine!

The Colonel's face and hands were soot-blackened. The Moriarty brothers were a music hall act. I supposed I could join in too. I'd lost my eyebrows to the flame.

Flares of light popped in my vision, even if I rubbed fists into my closed eyes.

Someone screamed further down the worm – inside one of its heads.

There was a lurch. The machine began to move.

VII

A whistle shrilled.

I found out what the canvas straps were for. The brothers Moriarty clung to the appendages, but still swung like human punching bags. I saw why the charts were pinned down and the equipment bolted to frames fixed to the interior walls.

'Who is this man?' the Colonel demanded. 'The one who isn't Carnacki.'

We all looked at Stationmaster Moriarty. He had issued the invitations.

'He's supposed to be Paul Finglemore, alias Colonel Clay, alias many others,' Young James admitted. 'The man who never wears the same face twice…'

The Professor pooh-poohed that. 'But he's not Finglemore, is he? This is an unknown, a shadow man, a ringer. He learned of your auction of secrets, James. Your net for spies, if you will. He saw a way to exploit it. A man who acts for himself.'

The Professor should know about that.

'He's a damned anarchist,' the Colonel declared.

At present, I didn't care who our shadow man was or what cause – if any – he espoused. I just thought it past time to stop him. He'd blacked all our faces. I was thirsty for a little evening up of the scores.

The *Kallinikos* picked up speed.

'Colonel,' I said, 'who else is on board?'

'That's not information I can share with anyone outside the Department of Supplies,' he replied.

'Don't be an ass, James,' said his brothers.

'Colonel,' Colonel Moriarty said, 'you're to swear on your honour not to reveal anything you might learn of this machine...'

It was all I could manage not to laugh in his face. I held my hand up as if pledging a solemn oath – which I'm breaking by writing all this down. Dearie me, I'll be sent to bed without supper.

'...there's Lampros, supervising the Greek Fire tests... Major Upshall... we call him the pilot, you might think he's an engine driver... Berkins – no, wait, you threw him out... two assistant technicians from the Royal Engineers, don't know their names... a recording clerk, Philip Gould... and Ram Singh, my immediate junior in Supplies.'

'They're all almost certainly dead.'

'That'd be a nuisance.'

The Colonel had the traditional Moriarty reverence for the lives of his fellow men. Not that I'm any different.

'Except Lampros,' said the Colonel. 'He'll need Lampros.'

'Your alchemist hasn't given you his formula, then?' I asked. 'He mixes up his own batches of Liquid Inferno, and your stinks profs can't work out the recipe?'

The Colonel nodded. 'Bright boy. Preserve a secret since 672 AD and it's hard to let go. Once you've shared, you're not special any more. Not essential to the program. And if you're not essential, you're surplus.

'We need that formula and we need Lampros,' the Colonel continued. 'More than the *Kallinikos*, it's what this project is about. The train is a moving platform for the fire weapon. A replaceable prototype.'

'I'll remember you said that,' I said.

The next compartment contained sighting and firing mechanisms for the fire nozzles. I found three dead men, trussed and hanging from the canvas straps. Not a mark on them, but faces twisted enough to indicate their last moments had been unpleasant. These were the two sappers whose names the Colonel hadn't bothered to learn and the recording clerk, Gould. All wore overalls and rimless caps. Gould had a green eye shade and an inky right hand. Whatever he'd been keeping records in – a logbook or ledger – was missing.

I peered through a periscope-like apparatus, and saw Cornish fields whiz by. Some sort of green-tinted, see-in-the-dark lenses were involved. Fiddling with the thing in the hope of sighting a road sign or landmark, I twisted the wrong knob.

A bright, burning stream arced across the countryside and scattered like twenty gallons of flaming puke. We sped on, so I don't know if I awoke some rustic by burning the thatch over his head or harmlessly set fire to a pile of rail-side gravel.

Beyond the firing compartment was the currently leading engine. Our shadow man must be at the controls. I had my revolver up, determined to put bullets into soft living flesh rather than dangerous combustibles.

My inadvertent test-firing of the flame cannon must have drawn attention.

The compartment door – a concertinaing, semi-transparent sheet of something chitinous like isinglass – was crinkled aside. A dark silhouette stood in the breach, eyes angry in mask-slits, gun in hand.

I shot first and a ragged red hole opened in his chest. My ears rang from the report. My kill collapsed, in a mess. No, not a kill. I'd plugged a decoy. Tumbling to the mistake, I threw myself to one side.

I heard a puff. A six-inch nail juddered in a bulkhead, a breath away from my ear.

'Nice bit of kit,' I said. 'But only at close-range. For a distance shot, an air rifle can match any gun. But air pistols are one-shot toys.'

The dead man's gun – empty, I'll be bound – was fastened skilfully to his hand with twine. His skin was white, so he wasn't Ram Singh. That made him Upshall. The shadow man had put his clothes on the pilot, but kept the chest armour which had saved him earlier.

I stepped through the door, into the worm's head.

The ringer hadn't had time to pump his pistol again. Of course, I'd have come a cropper if he'd had a brace of the things… but he hadn't. He carried a back-up gun, but that was tied to the late Major Upshall's hand.

There was a stench in the air, worse even than the foul smell elsewhere on the *Kallinikos*. A dead body lay across the floor, face smashed into a contraption of glass tubes, tanks and copper wires. Acid was eating through his head. So much for Ram Singh of Supplies.

In command of the train was the fake Finglemore, the fake fake Carnacki. The shadow man now showed another face. Beaky nose, high brow, hawk eyes. He could have been anyone. He wore Upshall's overalls.

He had one hand on what I took to be the throttle of the *Kallinikos*, and the other about the throat of a stocky, olive-skinned gent. This could only be George Lampros: Keeper of the Flame, Greek patriot, political naïf, valuable item.

'Stay back, Colonel Moran, or I'll kill him.'

His fingers squeezed the Greek's plump neck, thumb working up around the ear for a snapping grip.

'Let me take care of that for you,' I said, and shot Lampros in the face.

VIII

I'd just killed the only man in the world who knew the secret of Greek Fire. We'd have to make do with all the other ways of setting light to each other's houses. I recommend a bucket of coal oil poured through the letterbox, some rags shoved in afterwards to soak it up a bit and a slow taper to give you time to be somewhere else when the blaze catches. No doubt a new, even-more-devastating method of burning half the world would come along in a minute.

The shadow man was surprised, though. Hawk eyes a-goggle. I had a warm thrill – as if I'd lost every hand for an afternoon and evening, but a single turn of the cards had put me back in chips.

I took aim, again. It would have to be another head shot, since he still had armour under his overalls.

Forestalling his execution, he chucked Lampros at me.

He had a caber-tosser's strength. The heavy Greek landed on me like a sack of melons. A lot of blood from the grapefruit-sized hole in his face got in my eyes.

The ringer wrenched the throttle-handle loose and stood over me with the broken-off iron bar raised like a club. I tried my best to shift the dead Greek so I could kick the spy master in the shins. He brought the handle down, but I got Lampros' head in the way.

He didn't try that again, but turned his club to the controls of the *Kallinikos*. He battered a brass panel, smashing dials and knocking off switches. Sparks cascaded from a broken meter. Then he grabbed a canvas strap, pulled himself up like an acrobat and disappeared through a hole in the roof.

I freed myself from the corpse and assessed the controls. Even if they hadn't been ruined, I wouldn't know how to toot the whistle let alone throw the brakes. On recent experience, I'd be likely to yank the wrong chain and blast us all to flinders.

I peered through the green-tinted, eye-shaped portholes which studded the worm's head. The *Kallinikos* was making express time. It was also tipping from side to side alarmingly. I had doubts it was up to anything but a straight stretch. Lighter, and more flexible, than an ordinary train – those scale-like armour plates rattling against each other – it might come off the rails at any moment.

I went back to share the news with the Moriarty brothers and found them bickering. It might have all gone back to the unsettled matter of who scoffed the last picnic pastry on that outing to the Great Exhibition for all I knew.

'James, James, James,' I shouted. 'Everyone on the crew is dead. The ringer's on the roof. He wrecked the controls; I assume he took the brakes. The train's going to crash.'

'Lampros?' the Colonel asked anxiously.

'Moran said *everyone* on the crew, James,' the Professor said. 'Further elucidation is neither necessary nor, in the circumstances, desirable.'

That put Moriarty *medius* in his place.

'There's a swing bridge ahead,' the Stationmaster said. 'At this time of night, it'll be open. Boats come up the Ross for the china clay.'

'Thank you for that touch of local colour,' I said. 'Open – that doesn't mean open for railway traffic, does it? It means we're hurtling towards a bridge that won't be there?'

Young James nodded.

'Tell me something useful,' I said. 'How soon will we reach this open bridge?'

'How fast are we going?'

'No bloody idea. Fast.'

'Impossible to tell, then. Soon.'

Jumping off the *Kallinikos* was not an option. It would mean, at best, getting smeared along the side of the track like breakfast marmalade.

'Our present enemy does not strike me as bent on self-destruction,' the Professor said calmly. 'He will have a safe way out.'

'At this speed, he can't grab a low branch without breaking his fool neck,' I said.

'The *Kallinikos* has two engines,' the Professor responded. 'Two complete sets of controls. He will be making for the other set. Does he know how to drive the train?'

'He was making a fair fist of it before I barged in on him.'

'Then, he will reverse our direction.'

'That can't be done unless the other engine is disengaged,' the Colonel said. 'If its controls are smashed, then that is not possible.'

'Can the engine be decoupled?'

'Yes, of course.'

'Then, he will free himself from the *Kallinikos* and effect an escape…'

Young James spelled out the obvious '…leaving us to go into the river!'

The Colonel made his way, monkey-like, from strap to strap to the rear of the carriage. He tried to wrench aside the door. It was jammed shut.

The Professor went to the hole through which the shadow man had got onto the train, and set about enlarging it enough for me to get through.

I reloaded my revolver.

'He'll know you're coming,' Moriarty said.

'Of course,' I replied, handing him my hat.

I stuck my head through the hole. A rush of air hit me like a wave full of pebbles. The *Kallinikos* was racing through a deep cutting. A wall of banked-up earth was barely two feet away from the train. If I touched it, I'd be scraped loose and mangled. So I took care to hug the worm's metal hide as I crawled up on top.

I threw myself flat on the train roof and dragged myself towards the rear engine. By touch, I found the hole where the shadow man had got inside – a long cut made between plates. Typical of the Department of Supplies. For all its armour and revolutionary design, the war-worm was more pregnable than the average third-class carriage on the 8.15 to Dog-Walloper's Bottom.

I was not fool enough to plop through the hole, and get a knife in my ribs for my pains.

There was a porthole above the controls, offering a glow like a skylight. I made my way there, inch by thorny inch. I didn't let my head show, but got a glimpse below. The spy master was throwing switches and pulling levers. Electric lights burned. Dials came to life. He was getting his engine running before decoupling the rest of the train.

He kept looking around, alert.

I rose to a crouch, struggling to keep balance. The rushing wind would blow me off the roof if I presented too broad a back. Keeping steady, resisting an impulse to go too quickly, I stood. I let seconds pass, to get used to the slipstream. I took out my revolver and aimed at the porthole.

I fired, then stepped into the hole I'd made.

I intended to drop neatly down into the cabin in a rain of glass.

Instead, the train's impetus slammed me into the rim of the porthole at waist height. Jagged glass shards ripped through my coat. I fell badly, on top of the ringer.

He got a knife – something small, like a scalpel – in my side, but I smashed my revolver-butt into his nose. It squashed and bled. I didn't know how badly

I was stuck, but got up off him. I kicked the shadow man several times, in the head and kidneys. He rolled away from my boots, and sprang up – agile as a big cat.

I shot him in the chest again, knowing it wouldn't kill him. At close range, the impact must have broken some ribs. He yelled and fell again.

I saw the wedge – a wrench – that was keeping the door to the compartment shut, and kicked it free.

'In here,' I called to the Moriarty brothers.

I hauled the ringer up, took away his knife, and put my gun to the soft part under his chin. No chain mail there. Give him credit, he was already recovering from the equivalent of a sledgehammer blow to the chest. He was scouting for new means to vex me.

The Professor, the Colonel and the Stationmaster entered the cabin. The space was not really large enough to accommodate us all.

'Why haven't you killed him?' the Colonel asked.

'Can you drive a train, James?' I said.

'No.'

'Can you, James, or you, James?'

Twin headshakes.

'Then we need him alive, for the present. Can any of you at least decouple this locomotive?'

'That's simple,' the Stationmaster said.

Young James took the loose wrench and used it to open a hatch in the floor. He twisted a lever below. There was a ripping sound, as plates parted. We were free of the rest of the *Kallinikos*, but still travelling in the same direction – fast.

On a slight incline towards the bridge which wasn't shut, we gained speed and pressed against the other carriages.

I looked into the shadow man's angry eyes. 'Now, chummy,' I said, 'do you still want to be an engine driver when you grow up?'

I slightly relaxed the pressure on the pistol, without taking it away.

For a moment, I thought I'd misjudged the man. Plenty would die rather than give in. Some players see mate in two moves and kick over the board. I've never found out if I'm that sort myself, but rather think I am. If I'd been the one who knew how to drive the train, I'd have laughed at me and double-dared me to shoot my head off.

This was a more calculating person.

Someone more like the Professor. Cold-blooded, but practical.

Without saying anything, he rose and turned to the controls. A charge had built up in the batteries. I saw dynamos and what-nots whizzing. Acid bubbled in tanks. My impression was that all he had to do was engage this engine – whatever that meant – and we would be away.

The *Kallinikos* came out of the deep cutting and, miraculously, held to the rails as they took a gentle curve down a hillside towards the Ross Gorge. The other head smashed through a white wooden pole which hung across the line as a warning that the swing bridge was open.

'Toot-toot,' I said, darkly.

The shadow man threw a lever. A whistle did sound – not steam, but some indicator that the engine was working. Our wheels screamed as they were forced to turn the other way.

The rest of the train parted from us.

Through the open door which had lead into the previous carriage, now separated from our engine, I saw the rails leading to the edge of the precipice. Our lights showed what awaited us. Below was the River Ross. Not a raging, foaming torrent but a placid waterway. Ahead, useless, was the middle-section of the bridge, turned sideways on its pillar in the middle of the river.

The gap widened, but we were still travelling the wrong way.

If I shot the ringer now, it wouldn't make any difference. On balance, I decided I'd rather what happened to me happened to him, too.

The front engine breasted the edge, dragging its carriages – which twisted, flame-nozzles pointing upwards – into the air. The *Kallinikos* was going at such speed I thought briefly that it might leap the gap, but the bridge-section was in the way. The worm's head smashed against the pillar, and the whole contraption fell into the Ross with a scream of metal…

…there was an explosion, which left spots in my eyes for months. All the Greek Fire in the belly of the worm went up at once. A patch spread across the water like a floating island of flame.

I assumed we were going to fall into that.

But we slowed. The rails complained.

The brothers Moriarty held fast to canvas straps.

Through the open door, I could count the number of sleepers between us and the edge.

Then, there were half as many…

Then, none. Our wheels, I fancy, touched the lip of the gorge as we slowed to a stop. We all lurched, and Stationmaster Moriarty fell towards the door. Neither of his brothers tried to haul him back, but he got hold of the folding isinglass and didn't tumble into the burning river.

The engine still ran. The wheels got traction.

And we changed direction, drawing away from the drop.

The sleepers appeared again. The gorge receded. Without the rest of the train as an anchor, we got up speed quickly. We were back in the cutting, rolling towards Fal Vale.

With another gun-prod, I persuaded our reluctant pilot to moderate our speed. A fatal crash now would be beyond irony.

'How about a toot of the whistle,' I suggested.

He made no comment.

'Next stop, Fal Vale Junction,' I said, light-headed. 'All change *yurr*…' [2]

IX

The surviving head of the *Kallinikos* rolled into the station. I took care to watch the pilot as he threw the brakes and prodded him as he turned off the engine. A series of switches had to be thrown in sequence. The drone of the dynamos died.

Colonel Moriarty was trying to issue orders again. No one listened. Most of the folk who would have snapped to when he told them had gone into the river with the tail of his wonderful war-worm. The Department of Supplies wasn't an easy, safe commission any more. In the Colonel's coming wars, even file-clerk and engine-maintenance soldiers would be asked to pay the butcher's bill.

At Fal Vale, the fighting was over.

There was some precariousness in getting out of the engine. There was no side door, just an egress to the rest of the train… so, the Moriarty brothers had to clamber down onto the rail bed and then make their way up onto the platform. They could have walked to the far end of the station, and taken the gentle slope up, but Young James pulled himself up to the platform, tearing his uniform at the knees, to show how limber he was. After that, his older brothers grimly followed suit, despite aged bones, tight waistcoats and a seeming unsuitability for such physical action. The Colonel grunted, went red in the face as he lifted his feet off the rails, and had to be pulled up by Stationmaster Moriarty and Berkins. He lost some buttons, and the last vestiges of his commanding manner.

Both brothers stuck out hands to assist the venerable Professor, but Moriarty couldn't resist letting a card he rarely showed fall out into the open.

After taking a step or two back, the Professor rushed forward, and swarmed out of the rail bed up onto the platform with the agility of a young monkey. He might give the impression of being like a dry stick, with bent shoulders and fragile bones. In fact, he had a wiry, cultivated strength and physical aptitude which – on several occasions – proved a fatal surprise to people who thought he'd be easy pickings in a straight-up punching match. He had some Eastern tricks – nobody knows more about dirty fighting than the Chinese, who've made a religion out of pokes, kicks and gouges which would get you barred in disgrace from a British boxing ring – and held by a peculiar diet involving melon seeds and carrot shavings. You couldn't get me to eat that if it bestowed eternal youth and added six inches to your prick.

I shoved the shadow man out of the train, revolver aimed steadily at the back of his head, and – taking no chances – escorted him to the end of the platform and up the slope. I've nothing to prove and if there's an easy way to be had, I'll have it. We rejoined the rest of the party by the waiting room.

Berkins – not entirely the yokel I'd taken him for – had Oberstein, Lucas and Sabin tied to the points wheel. The Frenchman had been shot in the shoulder, making him a lopsided match for the German I'd shot in the knee. Lucas had been lightly tortured in a friendly, no-particular-information-required sort of way. They made a sorry lot of minions, and didn't meet the angry gaze of our un-humbled but bested master spy.

I hoped we could settle the matter of the ringer's true identity before dawn. I was prepared to peel off his faces, one by one, with a razor.

Berkins took over with rope, and knotted him to his fellows.

The war of the wildcats had to be counted a draw. Ilse von Hoffmannsthal was in the wind, but Sophy Kratides wasn't dead. The Greek fury, bodice interestingly in shreds, swore revenge against the German valkyrie.

As returning hero, it struck me that a kiss and a cuddle might be in order. Coming through battles alive always makes a body frisky. Yes, a healthy bounce on handy upholstery would see out the night nicely. However, one glimpse of Sophy's dark face, augmented by a cut along the jawbone, made me think better of the fancy. No one wants to barely escape a train crash and capture a dangerous spy, then get struck in the vitals by a hot-tempered foreign wench. When she found out what had happened to her countryman Lampros, she'd be well off me… even without the detail, which I was keeping to myself, that I'd done for him.

'There are few railways in South Africa,' Professor Moriarty said.

I didn't know where that came from, but the Colonel did.

'The Boers have no fight in them, James. They're well down the list. France or Germany, or France *and* Germany. Then, the Americans.'

The Professor said nothing more. I took his point – a war train was no use unless your enemy obligingly built rails straight into the heart of his territory and then didn't mine them when hostilities started. Even Greek Fire, if its secret could be recovered, wasn't suited to a ruck with scattered intransigents who knew the lay of their land. The *Kallinikos* might have been named the *White Elephant* for all the good it really was.

My sort of soldier would be killing foreigners for the Queen for the foreseeable. The Department of Supplies would have to lump it. The last whisper I heard was that they were sponsoring mechanical wings which kill every dolt who straps them on and jumps off a cliff.

'James,' the Colonel said, 'what is your association with Colonel Moran? I have made enquiries. He has a, shall we say, somewhat *mixed* reputation.'

I knew what that meant. Ask anyone who knew me in the army and you'll hear the same things about Basher. Tiger in the field, bounder in the mess. A good man to have your back, but a bad one to show your back to. Trust him with a fight, but not your sister, your wallet or a deck of cards.

Stationmaster Moriarty waited for the Professor's answer, too. 'Moran is my associate, James. I employ him.'

'For what? Wiping off the blackboard and collecting exercise books?'

'My business is numbers, James. You know that. Numbers and equations. You do not understand them. You never have. A fault in Supplies, I would have thought. Value is calculated in numbers. And chance. Morality does not come into it. That's the purity of mathematics. Nothing clouds the issue. Not religion, not politics, not sentiment. I have applied my methods to a well-established field of human endeavour. In this, I use Moran and men and women like him.'

He turned to the Greek hellcat.

'Miss Kratides, take my card. As bodyguard to a man who no longer has need of one, you are without a position. A place could be found for someone with your skills in my business. One day, James, you will work it out. You will see the solution.'

The Colonel was none the wiser. Young James was laughing.

'James,' he said, 'well spoken… and might I say that it's time I… ah, that I was given your card?'

The Professor looked his youngest brother square in the face, then inclined his head in turn to the truncated wreck of the *Kallinikos* and the tied-up collection of sorry spies. He gazed up to dark skies, already tainted by the seeping red of dawn. He lifted his shoulders, indicating the mess of the world in general and this worm business in particular.

'No, James. I have no place for you.'

'Not sentiment,' he'd said. 'Not *family*,' he'd meant.

Stationmaster Moriarty, least stony faced of the brothers, gulped as if he'd been slapped. I doubt if Colonel Moriarty was much impressed with his showing this night either. The Firm would not take him on and the Department of Supplies would have little further use for him. The GS&W Railway Company wouldn't be too happy with his record, either. Someone would have to take the blame for the flaming crash at the swing bridge.

'The Lizard to Newquay stopping train will be here in ten minutes, Moran,' Moriarty said, tapping his watch chain. 'We can change at Truro and be in London by midday.'

To the Stationmaster, the Professor said, 'James, you will issue travel documents for Colonel Moran and myself. You will also have Berkins refund the monies extorted from us to board your *Special*.'

To the Colonel, the Professor said, 'James, you will wish to remain here until your superiors arrive to have a report from you about this incident and take these gentlemen in hand. You will want to keep my involvement *sub rosa*.'

Neither of the Professor's brothers were happy, but both did as they were told.

Now, Moriarty turned to the shadow man – who had patiently followed all this.

'We have not met before, but you have been aware of me as long as I have been aware of you,' the Professor addressed the spy master. 'Your associates believe your intent was to deliver the secrets of the *Kallinikos* to a foreign power, simply for money.'

'Not money, Professor.' He smiled, thinly. 'Numbers.'

Moriarty nodded.

'You think yourself my mirror, I see. Well, then, numbers, if you will. You have traded secrets before, I know. You have stolen them simply to prove they can be stolen and sold them back to their original owners. But that is not your real interest, your passion. Which is for the game, the gamble. Now, you have crossed my path. I foresee a wearisome inevitability to future relations. I might tell you that you have learned your lesson, that you should from henceforth take care not to incommode me. I know you would take this as a challenge, and set out to inconvenience me. I shall, of course, counter your every move, and retaliate, hampering your larger plans. Neither of us will prevail, immediately. Our businesses will suffer in this, the true coming war. The situation will become impossible. There can be only one outcome.'

'Agreed.'

'Then you will withdraw?'

'I agree there can only be one outcome,' the ringer said. 'I imagine we disagree about what it might be.'

'Moran,' the Professor said. 'Kill him.'

I brought up my gun.

The Colonel began a protest.

I pulled back the hammer.

The shadow man remained calm. I've seen that before.

Again, I felt a knife at my throat. Again, my gun was taken. Again, Sophy.

Ah, Sophy, Sophy, Sophy.

'This man is a prisoner, James,' the Colonel said, with icy relish. 'The property of the Department of Supplies.'

The Professor's head oscillated. He was grinding his teeth.

Now, Colonel Moriarty – a punctured gasbag, filling out again – thought he was higher up the pole, and relaxed, confident in Sophy's blade. Stationmaster Moriarty – still sulking at the rejection, swinging back to cling to his other brother – backed him up, and made show of checking the prisoner's bonds.

'You will not keep such a property,' the Professor said.

I remembered the gun bound to Major Upshall's hand. Someone as good with knots as that wouldn't stay tied up long.

The shadow man's face – if it was his own – flickered with amusement.

'Catch your train, Professor Moriarty. We shall continue this match in due course. You will know where to find me.'

The Lizard to Newquay was puffing down the line. A whistle shrilled.

The Professor looked at the ringer, then at his brothers. No trace of expression all round.

Sophy gave me back my gun. I'd no doubt she'd kill me if I tried to use it. I still hoped she'd call on us in Conduit Street.

Berkins came up with tickets and a refund on our original fare.

No one said goodbye, so I did, cheerfully. It was a split decision as to whose expression was the most angry, miserable or murderous.

Moriarty and I boarded the train.

X

At Truro, we secured a first-class compartment on the Penzance to Paddington. Moriarty gave off such deadly emanations that – though the train was busy – no one dared to join us.

The Professor hadn't spoken since Fal Vale.

I beetled off to the dining carriage and had a large breakfast. I winked and twirled my moustache at three ripe, giggling country girls going up to the city for a day trip. The way I felt after the night's work, I could have ruined the lot of them before they had to catch their return train. Then, some hale fellows joined them and they giggled much more, pointing at me from behind tiny hands. I realised I was still soot-blackened, and repaired to the lavatory to scrub my face. The dirt came off, but the bruises were still there, and the cut to my throat. I also had a scratch in my side where I'd been stabbed. I felt ridiculously old.

I ordered a pot of coffee from the steward and went back to the compartment.

The Professor consented to drink. He was chewing over the night's events.

There was the question of the ringer's true identity, but that would keep. Instead, I asked the thing that had nagged at me ever since the meeting with Colonel Moriarty at Xeniades Club.

'Moriarty,' I said. 'Why did your parents give their three sons the same name? Why are you all James?'

'It was our father's name. He wished to pass it on.'

'To all of you?'

'To a son who pleased him. It is my understanding that, upon my birth, he was pleased. In the nursery, as I began to show aptitude… with sums… he continued to be pleased. My mother also, I believe, though she never said as much. She never said much of anything, I recall. Father would review each week with me and declare himself pleased. Then, when I reached the age of six, he found himself less pleased. Then, not pleased at all. I went over my sums again and could find no error in my workings. So I reasoned that the failing was not in me, but in Father. I did not tell him as much, for I knew he would not see it that way.

'Then, when I was seven, my brother was born. My brother James. Father was pleased with James. From the day of my brother's birth, I believe my father spoke not one word to me. I was fed and clothed and schooled, but in the house, I was a ghost. My brother did not know who I was, but eventually gathered he would not be punished if he visited trifling nuisances and afflictions on me. Father was still pleased with James. In the nursery, and for some while after, he continued to be. My brother was James. He would not believe that was my name too. He only truly realised who I was, what my name was, when our brother was born. Our brother James. I was fourteen and James was seven. He lost the name too.

'Young James was the only James. We were ghosts separately, James and I. Not together. That was not possible after what had passed between us when I was the only ghost. Young James was *the* James and Father was pleased with him. In the nursery, and afterward… He never became a ghost, and – as you can tell – lacks firmness of character, if not craft and cunning. Had Father and Mother not been lost at sea, they might have had another child, another James. That might have been the making of Young James.'

'How did your parents come to be "lost at sea", Moriarty?'

The Professor paused, and said, 'Mysteriously, Moran.'

I drank my coffee. Remember I said the Professor wasn't the worst of his family. Wasn't the worst James in his family. Neither were his brothers. The worst, so far as I could see, was James the first.

'James, James and I have taken different paths,' Moriarty said. 'We have never been fond, but we are family. I am not given to calculations with no outcome. But I have considered the question of how things might have differed if I'd been the only James born to my parents' union, or if my brothers were named, say, Robert and Stuart. Then, might I – the sole James Moriarty – have been different? Much of what I might have been was taken away, taken back with my name, and failed to survive successive attempts to transplant it to my brothers. James and James, also, are not whole, have had to share with me something that should be one man's alone. But there is a strength in that. Some qualities, some possessions, are distractions.

'Young James had a comfortable settlement from our parents, but it did him little good and is all gone now. He will never be more than a functionary. A poor one at that. James went into the army, to find an order, system and path. He is respectable. My first inclination was to join the clergy. That I see no mathematical proof whatsoever for the existence of God is no drawback. Rather, atheism is likely to help advance in the Church of England. No distracting beliefs. Then, I saw what could be done with numbers and have made my life's work the business which employs you and so many others. Had I been the only James Moriarty, I would not be what you see before you.'

I looked into his clear, cold eyes. His head was steady.

I had no doubt of what he had told me. No doubt at all.

In that compartment, it was cold. Around Moriarty, there would never be warmth.

We were well past Reading.

'We're nearing our final destination, Moriarty.'

'Yes, Moran. I believe we are.'

Chapter Seven: The Problem of the Final Adventure

I

You know how this ends. Someone goes over a waterfall.

A lot of rot has been spouted about what happened to Moriarty in Switzerland. One of his brothers and that medical writer in *The Strand* muddied the waters with a public row [1]. It was a surprise to me when Colonel Moriarty of 'f--k off back to your blackboard' fame put the Professor up for posthumous sainthood.

In letters to the press, Moriarty *medius* tossed off accusations about his brother's demise, which he laid at the door of 'an unlicensed, semi-professional adventurer'. This Watson oik piped up with a spume of 'most dangerous man in London' piffle to exonerate his long-nosed, trouble-making former flatmate. Lawsuits were threatened. Arguments raged in clubs, letter columns and the streets.

In a battle which might interest scholars of modern urban warfare, the Conduit Street Comanche whipped the tar out of an irregular band of crybaby destitutes who pledged allegiance to the Watson's departed mucker-wallah.

The third James Moriarty – with bloody cheek! – sold the *Pall Mall Gazette* personal, intimate memoirs of all the wickedness his brother the Professor was behind. Even with an Irish spinster scribbler as a ghost [2], Young James was unable to cough out anything publishable and became the only Moriarty ever convicted in court of anything. The *Gazette* had him up for breach of contract and reclaimed the advance fee.

Colonel Moriarty and the Fat Man of Whitehall – who turned out to be the brother of the Thin Man of Baker Street – exchanged cryptic, terse, bitter *communiqués* under the letterheads of the Department of Supplies and the Diogenes Club, respectively. No one outside 'most secret' circles will be allowed to read these until one hundred years after the death of someone called 'Billy the Page' [3].

Holding myself aloof from this hullaballoo, I found it expedient to continue a continental holiday with pleasant companions. I followed the controversy via week-old newspapers left in hotel lobbies. Always good sport on the French Riviera. You can see North Africa from there, which offers exotic game and fragrant souks.

My longstanding curiosity about whether those Mississippi riverboat gamblers were half as sharp with the pasteboards as their reputation has it, still pricked. And, not satisfied by two go-rounds with the yeti (home court advantage helped neither of us to better than a draw each time), I still felt honour bound to make a third attempt at bagging a big shaggy *mi-go* pelt from the Himalayas.

Many – indeed, most – surviving members of the Firm were, by then, in police custody. Only one, Charlie Vokins of the Royal Opera House, came close to naming the Prof – whom he called Macavity – in his statement. He was subsequently killed in his cell, bitten by a venomous spider hitherto unknown outside the tropics. Its presence in Holborn has set the world of arachnology afire. The rest of the gang took a sensible 'don't know nuffink' line from arrest to arraignment and beyond. Chop uttered only his name, which he shouted in response to every question – usually with a violent hand gesture.

It was said the Moriarty Firm was smashed completely, but you have to pay attention to who's saying it. To whit… Scotland Yard, who'd only just been forced by this nagging Thin Man to admit such an outfit even existed. On the whole, the Yard would rather not have known about it because (adopt the proper brandy-soaked drone), 'These things can't happen in London, don't you know, and if they can, they couldn't last out the week because Great Britain has the finest police force in the world.' Depressingly, this may be true – foreign rozzers generally make imbeciles like Lestrade, Mackenzie and MacDonald seem towering geniuses.

The only other person to declare the Firm defunct was a certain John H. – or *James* H., to cloud an already fogbound issue – Watson, MD, whose literary prospects had just washed over the Falls. I have it on good authority that *The Strand* doesn't care to run reminiscences about beastly bad backs, mysterious gammy legs or interesting appendicitis.

Oh, we'd had setbacks, but I wasn't the only one of the Firm in the wind. Parker the garrotter, for one, escaped notice. Simon Carne came up with another disguise, and posed as a private detective who swore to bring 'that scoundrel Carne' to book. 'PC Purbright' was working a scam with Filthy Fanny, shaking down monied toffs the faux waif accused of molesting her in Seven Dials. When the raid came, PCP mingled with the real coppers and 'arrested' Filth. He said he'd get her swiftly to the Yard for questioning. They hopped on the Brighton Belle and vanished from history. After a good wash and dressed in grown-up clothes, Filth would have been unrecognisable.

Mrs Halifax willingly confessed to crimes from gross indecency through baby-farming and living off immoral earnings to impersonating a Mother Superior, but swore up and down that the old gent and his military pal who rented her upper rooms were complete innocents and unaware of what went on at her now-notorious address. I like a trollop who knows her business – you don't pay 'em just for the tumble, you also pay 'em to keep their mouths shut about it afterwards. Her girls were all credits to the oldest profession. It brings a tear to the eye, a tickle to the loins and an irresistible urge to check the inside pocket to see if the wallet's still there when I think of any of 'em.

Polly Chalmers, 'the occasional maid', claimed she had just woken from a horrible dream and had no memory of the last seven years. Ceridwen Thomas, 'Tessie the Two-Ton Taff', put three constables in hospital (one permanently) during her arrest and swore no gaol cell could hold her (fit her, more like). Halina Staniewiczowa, 'Swedish Suzette', answered questions only in Polish, to the confusion of the Swedish interpreter Scotland Yard had brought in at great expense for her interrogation.

Wing Liu Tsong, 'Lotus Lei', was released after mysterious strings were pulled and got a job lighting joss sticks in Limehouse for the Lord of Strange Deaths... whom, truth to tell, she'd been working for all along; her new duties sound innocent enough, but you don't know what happens to the mandarin's guests if they don't comply with his polite requests for co-operation or information by the time the stick has burned down.

Molly Duff, 'the Ranee of Ranchipur', formed a Thuggee strangling sisterhood in Aylesbury Women's Prison and queened over the place for twenty years. Lady Deborah Hope-Collins, 'Mistress Strict', went up before a judge she recognised as one of her overgrown schoolboy regulars; she was given a good character by the court after all charges were dismissed. Marie-Françoise Lely, *ma belle* Fifi, slipped through the net by marrying Inspector Patterson, the plod in charge of the Conduit Street round-up, then disappearing with the wedding presents two days into the honeymoon... at that, Pie-Eye Patterson was lucky to have had forty-eight hours service from the finest truncheon-polishing lips in Europe.

Neverthehowsoever, the cat was at least halfway out of the bag.

During his long career as an evildoer, Moriarty shrugged off rumours about his true enterprise and maintained a respectable false front to the outside world. All through our association, even as he cut himself into crimes and netted one of the highest private incomes in the Empire, he kept at a dull teaching job which brought in just £700 *per annum*. The Devil knows where he found the time to give lectures, mark papers and expel slackers, but he did.

None of his former students or present colleagues spoke up in his favour when the press had a field day maligning him. I gather the inkies were as terrified of the dear old soul as anyone who met him in his criminal capacity – once, I know for certain, he slowly put a youth to death for misplacing a decimal point – even before it came out that he was, as the sensation papers have it, 'a diabolical mastermind'.

So, the world now knows – or thinks it knows – the truth about the terrible Professor James Moriarty.

Well, that's fair, so far as it goes.

Still, in Fleet Street terms, I've an 'exclusive'. Only two people really know how Moriarty died. One took that long plunge into the foaming torrent, and is in no position to reveal anything. The other is me. I've kept *schtumm* so far, but now it's time to tell the end of the story of the worst and wildest man I have ever known. Have I your attention? Good, let us continue…

II

On our return from Cornwall – early in January, 1891, for those who like to mark off the dates – Professor Moriarty bunged himself into his work. Oh, he was still in one of his moods... brooding on family matters, I'll be bound, redoubling his efforts to achieve abstruse goals in a triply vain effort to earn back his name. All he wanted was the recognition of a sire who was a) plainly an out-and-out maniac incapable of human feeling, b) unlikely to appreciate the Prof's high standing in any of his chosen fields and c) long since drowned.

After one glimpse behind the curtain, I knew better than to ask for more. I was on hand with the Firm for my sure eye, cold nerve and lack of scruple, not as sob shoulder or scratching post for an unknowable conundrum of a man. In those days, Moriarty spent more time with his wasps – remember them? – than his lieutenants, but popped out of his study periodically to issue orders and pass comment. I made sure his instructions were carried out, though even after long experience I was puzzled by some of his moves...

Dynamiting a pillar box on the corner of Wigmore and Welbeck Streets just after the post had been collected and it was empty...

Bestowing one hundred pounds upon a respectable solicitor in Taunton on the condition that he dash acid at the portrait of a former alderman which hung in the local assizes (respectable or no, the shyster went through with it)...

Contriving a delay of twenty minutes on the City & South London Railway to ensure a minor government clerk did not keep an appointment with an optician in King William Street…

Injecting minute quantities of a bacillus into every bottle but one of a case of port wine – tricky thing, using a hypodermic needle on the cork without leaving an obvious hole – presented to the Chief Coroner of Cardiff, ostensibly by a grateful widow lately exonerated of husbandicide.

Whatever that little lot was all about went over the waterfall, so your guess is as good as mine. The Professor was always doing things like that. Usually, there would come a moment when I could see the point of these preliminary moves, and a grand scheme would be apparent. In these cases, that moment never eventuated. I think of this as Moriarty's *Unfinished Symphony of Crime*.

In years to come, a mastermind as yet unborn might read this passage, see at once the design thick old Basher couldn't make head nor tail of, and set out to complete Moriarty's final coup. Good luck to you, mate. Post me my cut – care of Box Brothers Bank – if I'm still living.

The only profit to come from the Fal Vale excursion was a welcome addition to the Firm. Three weeks after the loss of the *Kallinikos*, who should present herself at Conduit Street but Miss Sophy Kratides, bearing the card Moriarty had given her. She sought employment suitable for her skills.

To reach our reception room, she had to climb the stairs past Mrs Halifax's establishment, uncommonly busy at that time of the morning. Swedish Suzette and Mistress Strict, *en deshabille*, were riding a publisher and a merchant banker across the landing. Not a few of their gentlemen callers liked the bit between their teeth and the lash on their flanks. At the last formal event, I'd won seven guineas wagering on the Librarian of Jesus College to best a muscular Christian poet by a full length. Coming across this sporting event gave Sophy the wrong idea about the line of work on offer.

She charged into our rooms het up, red in the face and knife out, intent on avenging any slur against her virtue. Since the Prof did not emerge from his study to investigate the commotion – which was mostly in Greek – I was responsible for calming the tigress with assurances that we only wanted her to stick her knives into people. Eventually, I persuaded her to put away the blade and share a divan with me for a proper job interview. I had Mrs Halifax send in tea, without her deadly biscuits. Mercifully, Polly remembered to wear the full uniform – not just mob-cap and apron – when she brought in the tray.

'Do you have references?' I enquired.

Sophy opened her pocketbook and handed me a newspaper clipping from an English language periodical published in Hungary. The news item involved Harold Latimer and Wilson Kemp, two dissolute Englishmen, who were reckoned to have quarrelled and stabbed each other to death [4]. Kemp, also known as Davenport, was a familiar if unwelcome face. Crooked as a corkscrew but not half so handy, he'd done a share of minor minionage about town, obtaining compromising letters for the blackmailer Charles Milverton or suborning young idiots onto the books of the shylock Dan Levy [5]. Moriarty had several times turned down Kemp's petitions to join the Firm, rating him unreliable, vile and inept. Getting stabbed in Budapest proved the Prof right again. Latimer was a new to me, but if he knocked about with Kemp it was a fair bet that he was a c--t of the first water.

Sophy claimed both for her bag. She'd been settling a personal score – avenging a murdered brother. One had to appreciate not only the dainty knife-work but the care taken to arrange matters so the Hungarian peelers had a cut-and-dried solution to the mystery and no need to trouble the lady said to be travelling with the deceased clots.

In finishing Kemp and Latimer, she'd discovered an aptitude for wet red work and had taken to it professionally. She had stabbed a French *juge d'instruction* through the lungs for *Les Vampires* on a freelance basis, but turned down the Grand Vampire's offer of a permanent position. She shrewdly reckoned the rising Irma Vep would not take kindly to competition for the title of deadliest woman in Paris. A bureau of the Greek government gave her employment, on the condition that she stay out of Greece, then contracted her to look after the late George Lampros – mention of whom prompted me to hem and haw somewhat – as a liaison with the British Department of Supplies.

'The death of Lampros counts as a black mark on your record,' I said, making sympathetic moon-eyes from the other end of the divan. 'I imagine you're motivated to do better in your next position.'

She spat out a mouthful of tea.

'You misunderstand my former commission, Colonel...'

'Call me Sebastian, or Basher even, Sophy, if I may...'

I own I might have twirled my moustache. I know it's a tiresome old look-at-me-I'm-a-roué stage gesture, but – dash it – I've got a moustache (a big one too), and it's there for the twirling. I'd lick my thumb and twirl my eyebrows if I thought it'd produce the desired results. I mean, I was on a divan, with a trembling young miss (and her knives) prettily arranged on the cushions, in need of tea and sympathy and a job... and the warm possibility she might accommodate to an obliging gent who saw his way to help her in this wicked world. If you don't twirl the old 'tache then, you might as well not have whiskers at all.

As it happens, the minx was all business.

'My orders were to keep Lampros alive, unless it seemed probable that he, and the secret of Greek Fire, were at risk of becoming the property of another power... in which case...'

She made an expressive pass across her throat with a barbed thumb and pulled an unmistakable grimace.

'I would have killed him myself, Colonel.'

That was a facer. Did she suspect what even Moriarty hadn't tumbled to, that mine was the bullet that had done for the oily inventor? There was no time to further discuss the matter. For, at this point, Moriarty emerged from his bolt-hole. He did not seem surprised to find Sophy Kratides in our parlour.

'Has Moran discussed terms?' he asked. '£4,000 per annum, payable in advance every quarter. An account will be opened for you at Box Brothers. This is acceptable, yes?'

She nodded. This was acceptable, yes.

Moriarty continued to talk at her, head bobbing as usual. 'Do you own a black dress and veil? You are to be a widow this afternoon. If you do not have such items in your wardrobe, Mrs Halifax will provide. You will be furnished with a wedding ring, photographs of your late husband, and keepsakes of your two children – who were lost in a boating accident on the Serpentine. Since I don't need to remember them but you do, you may choose their names. Your husband, Benjamin Thoroughgood, was English, so I suggest you do not choose Greek names.'

'Will and Harry,' she said.

Moriarty paused in his oscillation, elevating an eyebrow. He picked up the reference. Told you he memorised crimes from all over the world.

'Very apt. My condolences on your loss, Mrs Thoroughgood. Colonel Moran and I will accompany you to Kingstead Cemetery this afternoon for the funerals. I suggest you put something in your eyes. You will have been crying for days.'

Sophy set down her teacup, sat up straight and arranged herself neatly on the divan. She put her hands in her lap, took a deep breath, paused... and let out a banshee wail. She tore her hair, screwed up her eyes, and slapped her cheeks. Tears poured out in floods. Mrs Halifax and Polly looked in, startled... but backed off when they saw Moriarty impassively watching the show. Sophy clawed the air and howled. Her screech set the teeth on edge more than la Castafiore's high notes. I applauded and would have tossed roses if any had been to hand. Moriarty nodded approval and told our new employee to give Mrs H. her measurements.

III

Lot of rum doings in Kingstead Cemetery. The real Thomas Carnacki has a whole evening's worth of spook anecdotes about the place. The management have had to double the night guard since the Van Helsing scandal broke in the *Westminster Gazette*. An old Dutch crank was arrested for repeatedly breaking in, vandalising the tombs and desecrating the corpses. Especially young, relatively fresh lady corpses. No accounting for taste, but – *really?* – is there nothing foreigners won't sink to?

As it happens, we should have seen that coming. The degenerate quack was a regular of Fifi's in Amsterdam and London. His particular jolly involved his lady companion of the evening sitting in a bath of ice water for half an hour to get her temperature down, then lying still, cold, silent and unresponsive on a garlanded bier while he did something unmentionable with a length of wood. I suppose this performance was all very well to take the edge off, but in the long run it didn't quite slake the appetite. If I ever run into the johnny, I'll give him a length of wood all right… *and* fill his mouth with garlic.

The Thoroughgood funeral was at three o'clock.

From their crowded tomb in the cemetery's Egyptian Avenue, you'd reckon the Thoroughgoods must be the most unfortunate family in the land. Never were such people for dying. It seemed to be all they ever did. That was, indeed, the case. There was no Thoroughgood family. It was an account established with Bulstrode & Sons, undertakers. Said account was settled, generously and promptly, in cash.

Moriarty also supplied illicit and expensive materials to the senior Mr Bulstrode, an enthusiast of obscenity reckoned to have the finest collection of pornography in private hands in Europe. The Bulstrode Archive of Smut perhaps rivals the legendary section of the Vatican library at the personal disposal of the college of cardinals. I am proud that a presentation copy of *My Nine Nights in a Harem* reposes in a coffin-shaped bookcase in Bulstrode's private mausoleum between *The Secret Life of Wackford Squeers* and *The Intimate Encounter of Fanny Hill and Moll Flanders*.

The Firm was tied in with Bulstrode because, on occasion, we found ourselves inconvenienced by a corpse who would not do for the river. Those fortunates were entombed with all due solemnity, as members of the Thoroughgood family. After many an enjoyable funeral, Moriarty, Moran and party had popped into Jack Straw's Castle for pies, pints and ironic toasts to the dear departed. Not a few folk down on the lists as 'disappeared without trace' have 'Thoroughgood' in marble over their final resting places. If you ever wondered where to find Baron Maupertuis, the Belgian who tried to corner *quap*, you could have done worse than enquire after poor old Uncle Septimus Thoroughgood [6].

I wasn't aware of any surplus stiffs on the premises – though I'd not have been surprised if one or two decedents showed up under the sideboard or in the window-seat. That had happened before. I was given pause by the two smaller coffins sharing the second funeral carriage. To my knowledge, the Professor had only ever murdered one circus midget... and that was in the way of an experiment. He wished to determine whether a child-sized corpse 'burned beyond recognition' in a bread-oven could be proved in autopsy not to be a particular missing heir. Guess what? It can. It was back to the drawing board in the Finsbury Disinheritance Caper.

Moriarty and I, hats ringed with black crepe, sat either side of the faux widow in an open calêche, holding up black umbrellas against the drizzle. Sophy sniffled like Eleanora Duse upon learning her fiancé has been assassinated in *Fédora*. Chop, suitably top-hatted and dour, sat up on the box, holding the reins as two fine black horses, with plumed headdresses, drew us up Kingstead Hill. At least one of the nags from Bulstrode & Sons was dappled, but soot-blacked every morning to fit the mood. In the rain – and have you noticed how it always rains at funerals? – the blacking began to run.

Other mourners awaited in Egyptian Avenue. Select souls, mostly in crow black. Sombre faces, betokening the friends of bluff Ben Thoroughgood and poor little lost Willy and Harry. Even I was shocked to see who'd turned out. I didn't know 'em all straight off, but recognised enough faces to take a guess as to who else might be signing the condolence book. There were veiled ladies in the party, none making as much effort as Sophy.

I had, of course, brought my Gibbs side arm and pearl-handled pocket razor. In addition, a coil of piano wire nestled inside my hat – a trick I learned from the late Nakszynski, the Albino. In case of special circumstances, the ferrule of my umbrella came off to unsheath a needle which was envenomed by squeezing a bulb in the handle. Judging from the cut of everyone's mourning clothes at this send-off, I wondered if I'd not come underarmed.

Grimes, a well-paid sexton, had the tomb opened and berths cleared for the three newcomers. Coffins were stacked up like child's building bricks, suggesting that the Thoroughgood family would soon have to purchase another wing for their needs. I gallantly assisted the widow down, while Moriarty held the umbrellas. One or more of the mourners whistled.

A pair of Bulstrode sons shifted the coffins into the tomb. Mr Beebe, an entirely legitimate – if myopic in everything – clergyman, droned a sermon. We used to ask Mrs Halifax's girls to come along for a pleasant outing, but their giggles and rude remarks put the parson off his stroke. Now, only those who could remain 'in character' – like the estimable Sophy – were entrusted with invitations.

Several of the Thoroughgood men were interred anonymously by the terms of contracts they had signed with Mrs H. It was a service she provided to any clients who died of a coronary, asphyxiation or sheer exhaustion in the pursuit of their pleasures, and would rather disappear than have loved ones know the exact circumstances of their deaths.

Solemn duties done, the morticians tactfully withdrew. Beebe hung about soliciting donations to a restoration fund or home for indigent seamstresses or somesuch. A pay-off mollified him and he left too.

Inside the tomb, mourners stood around glass-topped coffins. Some doffed hats, some raised hankies, some lit cigars and muttered, impatient with the performance. The beloved dead looked like Madame Tussaud's waxworks, for the very good reason that the same artisans made both. Benjamin Thoroughgood was a spare head of General Gordon.

Moriarty told Grimes to seal the tomb doors behind us, and return in an hour. The sexton – who had never been able to account for the Dutch guilders he tried to pay for drink with on the night Van Helsing was arrested – had complied with stranger requests. I wish I could say this was the only time I'd heard the rasp and scrape of heavy stone tomb doors closing with me still on the inside and corpses for company.

'Gentlemen, ladies, I bid you welcome,' Moriarty addressed the mourners. 'You know why I've invited you here. Several of you have travelled great distances, at no little inconvenience to your continuing interests. Your presence betokens the seriousness with which you take this matter. Most of you are familiar with each other, but some are new to this rarely convened circle. We all know who we are. Do I need to make introductions? Some of us prefer titles to names... so, the Lord of Strange Deaths and the Daughter of the Dragon... the Grand Vampire of Paris and Mademoiselle Irma Vep...

Doctor Nikola of Australia and Madame Sara of the Strand... Miss Margaret Trelawny and the Hoxton Creeper... Doctor Mabuse of Berlin and Fraulein Alraune ten Brincken... Arthur Raffles of the Albany and his, ah, friend, Mr Manders... Théophraste Lupin and Josephine, Countess Cagliostro... Doctor Jack Quartz of New York and Princess Zanoni... Rupert, Count of Hentzau, and... Miss Irene Adler.'

One of the veiled ladies lifted her black gauze.

'Hello, boys,' said *that bitch.*

IV

So there you have it. The worst people in the world. All in the same tomb. If Grimes fell down a manhole and left us there to rot, or – more likely – eat each other, well… every detective, do-gooder and right-thinking prig in Christendom could get sloshed and break out their party hats.

I wouldn't know how to send a telegram to someone like Dr Nikola, who favoured Asian mountain fastnesses and Pacific island hideaways, and I'm not deranged enough to invite the Lord of Strange Deaths to tea. As the loyal reader knows, I'm afraid of very little, but if anyone gives me pause it's that dome-headed, bloody clever Chinaman. Being not afraid of death isn't the same thing as not caring about hours – in some cases, weeks – of preliminary discomfort. The cellars of the Si-Fan were known as places to avoid. The mad mandarin had a marmoset on his shoulder, if you can believe it. His Eurasian companion – supposedly his daughter, as if that spared her anything – occasionally fed the chittering beast nuts from a packet. The Celestial pair wore white robes, because they do everything sideways out East and that's the custom for attending the funerals of folks who aren't in your immediate family.

As for the others… by now, you've heard of most of them. Those you don't know you're better off for it, but I'll fill in the dance card anyway.

The second biggest surprise was the presence of my old friend Mad

Margaret – Queen Tera as was – and her pet goon. The bandages were off. She now wore a smooth white alabaster mask which matched her replacement hand – eyebrows and lips picked out in gold. God knew what she looked like underneath, though her luxuriant raven hair had either re-grown or was a wig left over from the Princess Theatre's last *Antony and Cleopatra*. She'd retrieved the Jewel of Seven Stars and wore it on her meat hand. The Black Pearl of the Borgias – which I happen to know Countess Cagliostro once coveted – winked from a brooch on her lapel. I doubted she'd forgiven or forgotten our previous encounter and she can't have felt kindly towards the Professor after the mêlée in Conduit Street and the dismantling of her Kensington Temple. If she was here, keeping her resentments to herself, then she must have a very good, or very insane, reason to join the circle.

I'd never seen Jack Quartz before. Can't say I was impressed. He sported an ostentatious cigar and the flashiest girlfriend. Princess Zanoni had more paint, powder and wax on her face than the fake heads in the coffins. The American mad doctor was tubby round the middle and running to jowls that made him look as if he were hiding cotton balls in his cheeks. Yanks never know when to stop, whether their passion is vivisecting beautiful women – which was how Dr Jack passed his leisure hours when running New York's criminal underworld became too burdensome – or eating yard-across slabs of beef with fried potatoes washed down with brown carbonated health tonic. Nikola sliced people and animals up alive too, with obscure scientific end – the Prof tried to explain it to me once – but Quartz played with scalpels just for larks.

Lupin and Raffles were just jumped-up thieves, useful enough if you wanted a diamond necklace abstracted, but essentially lightweights. Then again, next to Moriarty, Nikola or the Lord of Strange Deaths, I was just a jumped-up murderer, and only got to sit on a slightly higher chair than the burglars.

Title or not, Rupert Count of Hentzau – a Ruritanian Michaelist, if your memory goes back that far – was just like me. Call him a dashing rogue or laughing daredevil if you must, but he was your basic assassin in comic opera uniform. His moustache was waxed to points which could have your eye out and he seemed forever on the point of bursting out laughing. We were both all-rounders, though he was a sword and I a shot. I daresay if we met under different circumstances, we'd each cede the other supremacy with our favoured tools and look for a third weapon to settle the question of who was the deadliest man in Europe. The jaunty cad reminded me of a young version of myself, which naturally inclined me to hate the fellow. He further antagonised me by showing up with *that bitch* as an arm adornment.

More interesting to the connoisseur of criminal masterminds was the young German the Prof had called Dr Mabuse, though that was only one of his preferred names. I've mentioned him before. Remember, the ardent imitator who was wont to present a sham of Moriarty's own face and manner? He'd come to this party in his Moriarty costume, head bobbing atop an enormous fur collar, chalk on his cuffs and something in his eyes to make them glint. I had a sense I'd met him before, wearing another face or faces, and inwardly cursed this disguise craze… Simon Carne and Colonel Clay had started it, and now it was likely nobody was who they said they were or who you wanted them to be. Except the Hoxton Creeper – he could pass for a Stone Age Man or an Easter Island statue come to life, but otherwise had an extremely limited range. Others weren't so distinctive. Anyone could wear an alabaster glove and mask, shove footballs down her blouse and claim to be Margaret Trelawny. However, most of the women in the world twisted enough to pull it off were in the present company as their own saucy selves. Mabuse's moll – who looked no more than twelve, except for eyes that might have seen Babylon fall – was a strange duck, all angles and poses, with dramatic hair. I took her for another dagger-under-the-pillow damsel. It's a sign of this age of emancipation that so many girls take to the trade.

Countess Cagliostro and Madame Sara were senior adventuresses, who had attained their station by stepping over the corpses of dozens of men who'd not thought to take them seriously. Most women – bless 'em – try to take a couple of years off their age, but Jo-Jo Balsamo put it about that she was decades older than she looked, and privy to the alchemical secrets of le Comte de Saint-Germain and her supposed ancestor the mountebank Cagliostro. Over a long weekend in a Valparaiso boudoir in '63, she'd put my back out – nearly thirty years on, she seemed not a day older, while my back hurt more with every passing year. What was she doing with a perfumed lout like Lupin?

Sara, no last name given, ran a series of odd little rackets from a beauty shop on the Strand, and had her tithe to the Firm delivered in scented envelopes nestled in gift baskets of salves, unguents and creams the Prof had no use for. I'd tried her hair-restorer on a thinnish patch on my crown, but it hadn't helped. Lately, her envelopes had been so fat I wondered if she was paying us over the odds in an attempt to persuade us she was a more notable crook than we took her for. Moriarty assured me she really was raking in as much as her payments indicated, and could claim financially to be the most successful female criminal of the age. Though she had Nikola at her side, the Madame generally had no use for masculine company. She worshipped at the altar of Sappho; or, if Sappho were unavailable, a bloomers-wearing, monocle-sporting saleslady in the bicycle department of Derry & Toms.

This Grand Vampire was new to me, successor to the fellow we'd given Napoleon's brainbox and the fellow who'd retained Sophy's stabbing prowess. Bald as an egg, he took the gang's name seriously enough to have his eye-teeth filed to points. Showing up in Kingstead surely put him at risk of getting holy water dashed in his face. No Frenchman likes to wash, so it was just as well Van Helsing had been deported. His young companion – who stuck around as Grand Vampires came and went – was dressed and coiffed as a boy. No one was fooled. Even the light-fingered Raffles and the dimwitted Manders, queer as eight-bob notes, knew Irma Vep was no lad. Madame Sara must also have noticed her tight-cut black knickerbockers and shapely silk-stockinged calves. The ephebic, anagrammatical vampire bore watching… though in this company she had stiff competition, in both the general bounce-worthiness and deadly-as-a-mamba stakes.

Ah, yes, Irma, so sorry… also, profuse apologies to elusive Alraune, tempting Tera, experienced Jo-Jo, serpentine Sara (a cursory nod in her case), zestful Zanoni, and the by-no-means-hideous Daughter of the Dragon. Even Sophy Kratides, the woman I'd come with, would have to step aside.

'Hello, boys,' indeed.

So, here she was again. I knew I would forget everything I'd learned since Rosie the pot-girl in The Compasses told me she was 'with child' to get me to cough over the money I'd been sent from home for my fifteenth birthday. Which she then spent on gin and sailors before giving birth only to the bolster she'd shoved under her pinafore.

I'd rather have met Kali's Kitten again.

But, even in a tomb, surrounded by arch-fiends… that smile… those eyes… that twist of the end of the lip… that artfully stray curl…

Irene Adler. Damnation.

I'd have turfed Ben Thoroughgood out of his last resting place and stretched out in his stead if she'd asked me to.

I'd have garrotted the Lord of Strange Deaths' pet marmoset if she'd asked.

I'd have snatched the Black Pearl and swallowed it, daring the Creeper to cut me open to get it back.

I'd have… well, I'd have made a fool of myself. Again.

V

Hentzau offered round a hip flask, but his sardonic smirk did not inspire confidence in the gesture. With an 'oh well, more fool you' shrug, Rupert took a healthy draught, opened his mouth to show brandy sloshing about inside, gulped and pantomimed satisfaction. He opened his mouth again to show he hadn't shammed the swallow. The performance put off even those – like yours truly – who could have done with a stiff one. He might have dosed himself daily with minute portions of, say, arsenic, to build up tolerance. Such tricks have been known. Only Madame Sara took him up, taking a dainty swig. She'd probably rendered herself immune to every poison known to nature or science in the course of perfecting her 'beauty treatments'.

The Daughter of the Dragon made no attempt to share her packet of nuts with anyone but the marmoset. Quartz didn't hand out his cigars, though he had a fat case in his inside pocket. This prompted Raffles, who was puffing on a Sullivan, to show off his famous manners by passing round his cigarette case. I say *his* case – it had the crest of the Duke of Shires on it. *That bitch*, Irma and Hentzau accepted fags, and in no time at all the tomb smelled like a crematory. The snob thief waited for his Sullivans to come back – robbers always expect other people to steal from them, I know I do. Lupin didn't take a cigarette, but did hold on to the case for a moment, jokingly making a pretence of slipping it absent-mindedly into his coat pocket before handing it over. Raffles didn't look as though he found that funny.

So much for the social aspect of the gathering.

'We are the greatest criminal minds of the nineteenth century,' began Moriarty. Knowing we were in for a lecture, I settled my behind on a stack of Thoroughgood coffins. 'And yet, like the century, our days are numbered…'

No one voiced outrage. Closed-mouth crowd, of course. Deep thinkers, on the whole, disinclined to bluster until they'd heard the whole story. Still, I'd have expected an indignant yelp or two of 'I didn't come all this way from Kensington… or Pago Pago… or Berlin… to be insulted'.

'Really, we draw to the end of a golden age in our field of endeavour. Who has there been to oppose us, but ourselves? No police force constituted thus far has been more than a momentary inconvenience to our businesses, easy to thwart and easier to suborn. Not since Jonathan Wild has anyone at our level been brought to a court of law, let alone convicted and hanged. We have had an easy time of it – but it will not last. Already, some dilettantes have set about making war on us. Men – and a few women – of intellect, wealth, resource and character who have set themselves against us, not because they are *supposed* to, but because they *must*. We all know the species of law breaker who steals or murders or violates because he has not the strength of mind to resist the urge…'

The barest flicker of a glance at the Hoxton Creeper made his point.

'Such impulses exist also in those who will be our enemies. They have a perverse instinct, a compulsion if you will, to bring us down. Plainly put, they do not like what we do and are not prepared to let us continue without hindrance. At present, it's an easy matter to be rid of a stray honest prosecutor or police inspector. There are more than a sufficiency of *our sort* of public officials to thwart the efforts of such freaks. But, make no mistake, we see the dawn of a new era. Crime fighting is about to change. What will happen when civilised countries opt to devote as much to their police forces as to their armed forces? The sort of cool hand who once sought glory and fame fighting the foreign foe or discovering the source of the Nile will set out to become not a soldier or an explorer but a *detective*. Modern science will be turned against us. The detective of the future will be a thinking machine, as cold and effective as any of us. They will have capabilities to match, or better, our own. Let me give you an example...'

The Professor held up his hand, fingers splayed.

'The lines and whorls on your fingertips are unique to you. Touch any surface with your naked hand and you leave traces more distinctive than a signature. All of us, wherever we go, leave these calling cards. As yet, this fact is unknown to all but a few. Within twenty years, it will put an end to your kind of crime, Raffles. In terms you understand, rain will stop play. Could you open a safe while wearing gloves, or trouble to wipe clean every object touched in the process of breaking and entering a house? Even if *you* could, could Mr Manders? Fingerprints on windows, strongboxes, weapons... even human skin... will send to gaol or the gallows three-quarters of the professional criminals currently active – and *all of the amateurs*.'

That put the cricketer in his place. He wouldn't have looked half so startled if bowled out for a duck by a schoolboy.

'I have heard of zese fingerprints,' the Grand Vampire said. He had a high-pitched voice, and hissed through those teeth. 'A Frenchman 'as pestered ze *Sûreté* about using zem to identify ze criminalss. Also, ze *beumps* on a man's 'ead. Even ze shapess of earss.'

'I'm not prone to sticking my ears against anything in the course of a crack,' said Raffles.

'Except safes, old boy,' put in his friend. 'Sometimes you do, to listen to the tumblers. Leave a perfect impression of the lugholes, I'll be bound, eh what? If jolly old Mackenzie of the Yard had a cast of your ear, he'd nab you in no time, don't you think?'

'Shut up, Bunny,' Raffles said, irritated. 'I've known clever crooks undone by devotion to imbecile girlfriends. Raffles and Manders showed it was the same story among bumboys.'

'Phrenology – the bumps on a man's head, as you say – has its place, too,' Moriarty said. 'Dr Mabuse, you can change many things about your appearance, but the shape of your skull, even under crepe and wax, will be apparent. The *squama occipitalis* is distinctive and unmistakable. *I would know you...*'

The two stared at each other a moment.

'And I would know *you*,' responded the German, exaggeratedly bobbing his head. I've seen fighting cocks look at each other like that, just before the squawking, pecking, clawing and killing flurry. I was put in mind of the Moriarty family reunion I'd attended.

Good Lord, could Mabuse be some long-lost Moriarty bastard! If not the Professor's, then the Colonel's? No, such twists only happen in three-volume novels. Besides, well, really...!

'I have considered fingerprints too,' Dr Nikola said, breaking the moment. 'Such things will first take hold in Europe and America, but will reach my quarter of the world in time. I agree we must pay attention to developments in detection, must not underestimate the scientific method. Moreover, we must not ignore the quality I think you do not fully appreciate, Moriarty. Idealism. Altruism. To label such things a mere compulsion is to simplify dangerously. Heroism is not susceptible to mathematics. It is not a condition to be cured, like a fever. Like all faiths, it is mysterious and strong. I daresay we shall have to get used to it. If we do not understand, appreciate and admire idealism, we shall lose.'

Hentzau got his cynical snort in before I did. Like me, he could show off a chestful of medals, mentions in dispatches and fancy write-ups in the press. We've both been called heroes by our nations and adoring multitudes, but we couldn't scrape up a jot of idealism between us. What we had wasn't heroism, but daring. Not the same thing, though it's an easy mistake. In the army and the bush, I'd sneered at heroes – mostly at their wakes – but I'd moderated my opinion at about the time Jim Lassiter put a gun to the back of my head. That gun-fighter had something. Diggory Venn, too, dash his red skin and stout heart. Even the real Carnacki was a different breed. Men like that were out there, and would always be tough nuts for men like Bloody Basher and gallant Rupert.

Moriarty just looked blank at Nikola's speech. Quartz was bored and impatient. The Lord of Strange Deaths was inscrutable, as if that were a novelty. Countess Cagliostro was counting her pearls. If you've heard anything about the later careers of all these individuals, you'll know they should have paid more attention to the little dark chap who warned against heroes. All of our masterminds had a Jim Lassiter – or nearest offer – in their future. Not everyone in the circle got tossed off a waterfall, but we all got bloody noses. Some of us went to prison.

'Heroism is an *attractive* quality,' Irene said, mischievously.

'Everyone can be bought, sister,' Quartz snarled. 'Or intimidated. Or dropped in the East River in a sack. Cut into an idealist and you find they bleed and die like all undermen.'

'I disagree, Mr Quartz,' Nikola said, warmed to the subject and pointedly not recognising the Yank's academic qualification. 'Idealism exists, as surely as terror, greed and lust. We deny it at our peril.'

'Are you a tiny bit of an idealist yourself, Doc?' Irene asked.

The minx was flirting with Nikola, who was – under the manners, clothes and intellect – still at bottom just a native. I squeezed my umbrella handle involuntarily, filling the ferrule with poison.

'Not at all, Miss Adler,' he responded. 'I am a pragmatist, in search of enlightenment. I am not a romantic.'

That was a cup of cold water in her flirty face. Was Nikola one of Raffles' lot? Didn't seem likely. Exquisites, in my experience, tend to be randy sods, not 'thinking machines'. In the end, the cracksman who stayed three steps ahead of Mackenzie of the Yard while burglarising the best houses in London had to flee to South Africa and get himself shot in one of those coming wars to avoid ending up jugged on charges of sodomy like Oscar Wilde. Those who sat at the top table, like the Prof and the Lord of Strange Deaths, seemed practically sexless. No one ever mentioned the *mother* of the Daughter of the Dragon. Would Mabuse's need to emulate Moriarty extend to sawing off his own pecker? It was put about that Alraune, his present consort, was grown in a petri dish from mandrake root and protoplasm. That was one scientific way forward for the breed, though it takes a lot of the fun out of it to my thinking.

'At the highest level of our calling,' went on Moriarty, back to his memorised lecture notes, 'most of us are scientists, even if we call it alchemy or vivisection or pursuing the secrets of the ancients...'

Sage nods from doctors, professors, sorceresses and quacks. The Lord of Strange Deaths got his degree from Edinburgh University, and both Moriarty and Nikola were pukka qualified brains. However, like Nikola, I was sure Jack Quartz had got his doctorate by collecting coupons from fudge tins and posting them off, with a dollar handling fee, to an outfit in Oklahoma who sent back the fancy sheepskin he had framed in his laboratory.

'Unencumbered by morality, unhindered by Dr Nikola's bugbear idealism, science has shown us the way,' Moriarty continued. 'Advances in warfare, medicine, engineering, transport, communications and economics have all contributed to the modernisation of crime. We have built upon the achievements of our predecessors. Where once a Dr Syn, a Dick Turpin or a Blackbeard had smuggling rings, outlaw bands or pirate ships, we have armies, businesses and fleets. My Lord of Strange Deaths, you are more truly an emperor than your ancestors who styled themselves as such. Dr Quartz, your operations extend from the Canadian Northwoods to Tierra del Fuego, an entire *hemisphere*. Monsieur le Vampire, wherever French is spoken, half of every *louis d'or* stolen passes into the coffers of your group. I am not flattering any of you. We could do better. The nations of Europe have carved up Africa, but – aside from the Si-Fan's presence in Palestine and the Queen Tera Cult's limited operation in Cairo – an entire continent is not represented here. As yet, sub-Saharan Africa has produced no one like us. That will come – ten years hence, should we gather again, there will be a black face among us.'

…and it'd be my job to shoot him, I didn't add.

'Like the other empires of the world, we do not always rub along. Countess, you have murdered two previous Grand Vampires that I am aware of. Dr Nikola, you oppose the interests of the Si-Fan in Northern India…'

'…and you did me dirt in Panama, Prof,' Quartz said. 'Don't think I didn't know about that!'

'You sent me Jasper Stoke-d'Urberville,' Moriarty countered, coldly. 'I have not convened this meeting to hash over old scores.'

Margaret Trelawny gave a slow handclap, flesh against alabaster. She was less chatty since she retreated behind the mask.

'Good job too,' Irene said. 'Or we'd all need coffins.'

'Thank you, Miss Adler…'

'I heard you'd another term of endearment for me, Prof…'

She winked, and a string in the old vulture's cheek went tight.

'To move on,' Moriarty insisted, 'many thinkers believe the old powers of the world are marching towards a cataclysmic conflict which will bring ruination to established order and further only the cause of revolution.'

It surprised me that Professor Moriarty was quoting from Colonel Moriarty's copybook. As we knew from the *Kallinikos* affair, the Department of Supplies was busy preparing for the coming wars.

'We too risk such a world war.'

'Some of us might welcome it,' Dr Mabuse said. He even did Moriarty's voice. 'It is the way of empires to fall, and leave ruins.'

'…and new outfits take over,' Quartz said.

'This is of no concern to my father,' the Daughter of the Dragon suddenly piped up. 'In the East, the Si-Fan is eternal.'

A snort came from behind Margaret Trelawny's mask.

'Ladies, ladies…' I put in. 'Play nice.'

It struck me that I'd never heard the Lord of Strange Deaths actually called 'the Dragon'. That was another of those questions no one asked. He discouraged even trivial curiosity.

'None of us have reached our present position without struggle,' Moriarty said. 'You know how Miss Trelawny came to be in her present position. She and I – and several other factions not represented here – had differences of opinion about how the business of crime might be conducted, particularly in London. *Les Vampires*, also, were involved, at one remove, in that battle. Alone of those who stood against me then, Miss Trelawny has made treaty, and been willing to adjust her methods to serve under me as regents of crown colonies serve under queens or emperors. She has seen the advantage. She is, for all the set-dressing, a reasonable woman.'

That was news to me. Which stung. Mad Margaret might be happy to throw in with the Firm if it meant she could return unhindered to her high old pharaonic life of blackmail and extortion in Kensington. But I would bet tuppence to a silver tiara she was less happy that the fellow who had chopped off her favourite hand was walking about unpunished. Moriarty must have offered her *something* while negotiating the 'treaty' which brought her into the fold. If that secret clause turned out to be my head on a dinner salver, I'd be steamed about it – especially if she was lining up the bloody Creeper to take my job.

While in the mood to brag about his status as Fagin to a band of grown-up pickpockets, Moriarty declared, 'Madame Sara and Mr Raffles, among many others who have profitable endeavours in Great Britain, may also attest to the benefit they derive from operating under my umbrella.'

'You've never offered little me a position under the bumbershoot, Prof...' Irene said.

'I can think of several,' I put in.

'Ah-hah, the organ-grinder's monkey *can* speak,' she said. 'How're your wounds, Basher Boy? Still sore? So, Jim, why haven't you come to me to make a treaty as you did with Queenie here? My fizzog didn't get burned off, so I might be even more disposed to take a proposition seriously.'

'You are not to be trusted, Miss Adler,' the Professor said.

'*And you are?*' she snapped back.

For an instant, I thought Moriarty would throttle her there and then. His fingers opened and closed, as if he were wringing the necks of invisible chickens. His head stopped moving, and he stared fire at the Jersey nightingale. She did something pretty with a handkerchief and smiled sweetly. Hentzau's fingers drifted to the pommel of his dress sword – Ruritanian funeral gear runs to full honours and a sabre – and I saw why Irene had brought the lad along. Our Miss Adler had got about the world a bit since we'd met, not exactly leaving satisfied customers in every port. I'd guess most of the men present – and all of the women – wouldn't mind leaving her locked inside one of the handy Thoroughgood coffins. Since infatuation is passing, even without poison or picked pockets, her present protection wouldn't last. In six months, or six *minutes*, Rupert would knock along with prevailing opinion and join the queue of frustrated former partners who'd like to sheath steel in whatever *that bitch* had in place of a human heart. Just now, however, he was favoured in her eye and befuddled enough to put his sharp sword at her disposal. Could I slip inside his guard with a thrust from a poisoned brolly? In confined space, best not to chance it.

Moriarty, with a force of will greater than mine, answered Irene politely.

'None of us is to be trusted, Miss Adler. At the risk of stating the obvious, we are criminals. To the world, we are villains.'

'My father does not accept that Western definition,' said the Daughter of the Dragon.

'"To the world", I said. Not to me. Not among ourselves. I hope that, here, in this tomb, we can be honest at least with each other. For, if we are not, then we shall fail and fall. We must find common cause.'

'With you as chairman of the board, of course,' Quartz said.

'I have no interest in such a position. Only the insecure would need a title. I do not suggest we become one combine. Such would be unwieldy, and as prone to internal rifts and failings as, say, the British Empire. I merely suggest we divide the world, not simply according to geography and politics, but race and creed. We shall have a commonwealth of criminal empires. To have hope of victory, ultimately of survival, in a world where the police aren't corruptible fools, we must be more than robber barons. Make no mistake, the world has always been against us. For an age, we have thrived because the world was divided between those who were afraid of us and those who didn't believe in us. We cannot rely on that situation persisting much longer. We will stay in our shadows. We cannot operate openly, no matter how much some of us might like the limelight, Count Rupert. Name a famous criminal, and you'll name someone who got caught. Light will be shone at us, but we shall have to remain invisible. Quartz, if you wish to be, as you say, Chairman of the Board, be my guest. You have my vote. If such a chair existed, I should not care to sit in it. To the *Übermenschen* of the law, the holder of such an office would be a challenge. And knights errant can't resist a challenge.'

Quartz puffed more smoke. '"*Übermenschen* of the law"? That's putting the case a bit strong, ain't it, Moriarty? Pinkertons and vigilantes and flatfeet…'

'They are coming, Quartz. We will face them. Agencies are being constituted in all our countries. In America, more than anywhere else. Individuals will hear a call. Detectives, adventurers, superior policemen, prosecutors. Men with unique abilities. Men who have badges, men who wear masks, men who are – and I do not exaggerate for effect – *a match for us*. Some will rise to fight for abstract notions of justice… some to protect the downtrodden… some to seek revenge. The *most dangerous* will be dispassionate thinkers for whom solving a mystery will be reward enough. We have all been setting puzzles which are to the scientific investigator what an unclimbed peak is to a mountaineer.'

'Moriarty, you truly think the barbarians are at our gates?' Raffles asked. 'Is there nothing that can be done?'

'We have to strike *now*,' Moriarty insisted. 'We must not wait to be crossed, inconvenienced, incommoded, hampered or persecuted. We must single out our enemies and smash them before they make their first moves. We must find these heroes… yes, Nikola, *heroes*… in their cribs and strangle them or beat their brains out. Kill their parents, assistants, comrades, sympathisers in the police or the press. They must *never come to be*. If we are to enjoy a utopia of crime, we cannot allow our adversaries to rise. Do you understand?'

A pause. Goggle eyes all around. People who impressed, hypnotised and terrified everyone they met were impressed, hypnotised and terrified. I felt the chill of the grave, but then again I was sat on a coffin in a tomb after a funeral. As always, I'd had no idea what had been going on in Moriarty's brain.

Unsurprisingly, it was Irene who dared speak first.

'Prof, I take it all back. That thing they call you. I always took it for a joke, but you're the silver dollar. Rupe, gimme that jug, I want to – no, I *have to* – raise a toast. To Professor James Moriarty, *the Napoleon of Crime*!'

She took Hentzau's flask and drained it at a gulp.

VI

Grimes let us out of the Thoroughgood tomb, in case you were worried he'd forget. We emerged, veils lowered and hats back on, into afternoon gloom. The rain had stopped, but the bushes were dripping, the slate tombs slick and black.

The original plan for Kingstead Cemetery was to offer four distinct styles of funerary pomp. Patrons could select the Egyptian Avenue, Roman Avenue, Grecian Avenue or Gothic Avenue. Three of these imperial modes didn't catch on, but a lasting craze for all things pharaonic prompted a proliferation of obelisks, animal-headed gods and columns etched with hieroglyphs. Marble angels, a faun or two and the odd hooded skeleton relieved the monotony, but these rare items were crowded into neglected corners.

Dominating Egyptian Avenue was a sphinx which was alarmingly stamped with the distinctive whiskered face of a certain dead banker. I knew his eternal riddle: when will you pay me? I had my own answer – which was why said moneybags was now mummy-wrapped in a gilt-covered sarcophagus under fifty tons of statuary built to thwart tombrobbers. It was not entirely pleasant to be confronted with the weathered features of a recent customer, five-times life-size, on a lion the length of a London omnibus. I blame Mad Margaret Trelawny's fancy dress party, and not being able to forget that they'd toyed with making a mummy of me. Actually, like a great many foul things, the

Egyptian rot started with that little Corsican oik – the Napoleon of Being Napoleon as we might say, if we were drinking a toast out of his brain-pan in the den of the Grand Vampire.

Founded in 1839, the cemetery had been built to seem ancient. Its artisans had skimped on materials, so there was more crumbling, cracking and moulding after fifty years than the bereaved might care for. It was one thing to want your forebears to rest in picturesque semi-ruins, yet another to find out they were interred with shoddy workmanship at an inflated price.

'Fresh air and sunlight, eh?' Rupert of Hentzau declared, filling his lungs. Like a lot of sword-wallahs, he had the prancing gait of an acrobat or a *ballerino*. He was practically jumping up and down to be out of the confined tomb. A natural show-off, he needed space and freedom to move – which was worth jotting down mentally. 'Professor, I owe you an apology,' he continued. 'Irene and I idly considered that you might have some scheme in mind whereby you slipped out of the tomb alone, then shut the door on your guests, leaving us without even a cask of sherry to make our few remaining hours more pleasant. Eliminating your competition altogether. It's not as if you've no history of such… amusing stratagems.'

He tossed his head towards Mad Margaret and the Creeper. Behind a veil, her white mask looked almost natural, while an outsized funeral hat and giant morning coat – bespoke tailoring was clearly among the benefits of hooking up with the Cult of Queen Tera – did not make him stand out less. Both wore scars which served as advertisements for distrusting Professor Moriarty.

Word of the Battle of Conduit Street had got round the world's rogues and villains. Rupert's amusement was doubtless sincere. Everyone who was in the game for thrills and boodle wished they'd thought of it first. Stamping down the fanatics, however temporarily, made for a more convivial, profitable, worry-free life of crime.

Meanwhile, I was none the wiser. Proving once again that Rupert was just a younger version of me with more hair oil, I'd also suspected the Prof intended a coup to wipe out his peers at a stroke. It's not as if I'd be let in on the blessed great design, even when it came to pointing and telling me to shoot. Moriarty hadn't taken me into his confidence when invoking the Six Maledictions, ensuring an enfeebled lunatic benefited from the Bermuda Tontine, or impersonating a broken-necked lady ghost in Wessex (his best acting role, by far). He burdened me with no more information than he deemed necessary for me to perform as a cog in contraptions conceived in the coils of his swollen brain. Sometimes I ruminated darkly that I wasn't paid enough for the grief, though I kept my grumbles to myself. I knew what happened to crims who quibbled with the Professor about their cut of the take – in fact, *I* was what happened to them.

That bitch was smirking and cooing in German with her dashing Count – useless language for love-making, German, but she made it sound obscene enough to get what she wanted. I felt my colour rising. To my mind, there'd been too much clever talk lately… and not enough blood. Much of Moriarty's lecture in the tomb was above my head. I was no diabolical mastermind. In this company, I got lumped in with knife-women, bag-carriers, bodyguards, sneak thieves and fast swords. When Moriarty knocked heads with the Lord of Strange Deaths, Countess Cagliostro and Dr Nikola – even the upstart Mabuse, the crass Quartz and whoever this Grand Vampire was – I might as well sit in the kiddies' corner with imbeciles like 'Bunny' Manders and the Creeper.

Normally, at this juncture, I would have suggested a pie and a pint at the Spaniards. Maybe a round or two of whist. This company could surely boast other practiced hands with the pasteboards.

But it hadn't been that sort of Thoroughgood funeral. Bulstrode & Sons were paid and gone, and Old Mr Bulstrode had graciously accepted rubbings from brasses found in a section of Barchester Cathedral definitely not open to the public. Everyone wanted to get away as swiftly as possible.

'Houses don't burgle themselves,' Raffles said. I suspected he'd said it before and would say it again. 'Let's do this again soon. Another Thoroughood must be on his deathbed somewhere. Toodle-oo.'

All our colleagues had crimes to get to.

Our carriages lined up outside the cemetery. Chop and the other coachmen stood in a silent knot, out-staring each other, hands casually near concealed weapons. A word or a gesture could spark a fuse, and they'd pull guns, hatchets and long knives and go to work. Soldiers all, the coachmen were almost disappointed that the party broke up without bodies strewn on Kingstead Hill.

Some of the company left with ceremony, in ostentatious coaches. Quartz had hired something bulletproof and enormous, prompting me to ponder two or three different ways someone riding in such a secure monstrosity could be murdered. Others made a point of vanishing without trace when no one was looking. Mabuse and Alraune: there one moment, gone the next. Irma Vep only pretended to leave, bless her. She slid behind a lichen-pockmarked angel, keeping an ear out for fresh developments.

As host – theoretically nearest and dearest of the imaginary deceased – Moriarty remained while the rest were beetling off. Sophy, of course, was with us, dabbing a hankie under her veil. Irene lingered a while and tried to tweak the Prof by flirting with him. She'd have got more of a rise from the statue of Weary Death at the door of the Forsyte tomb. As ever, *that bitch* was after something but wouldn't say what it was. If the hussy wanted to know the time, she'd make suggestive gestures with an unlit cigarette then half-inch your watch while you were striking a lucifer.

Finally, she gave up and fetched Rupert away to the Café Royal.

Moriarty, head oscillating, was deep in thought again. With him, it was either a lecture lasting for pages and pages or pin-drop dead silence. He had no chit-chat in him.

Sophy lifted her veil and cut off the waterworks.

'I wish I'd snaffled one of Raffles' Sullivans,' I said.

Sophy produced the cracksman's cigarette case from her widow's weeds. For the first time, the Greek woman smiled broadly.

'I take… for practice,' she said.

I laughed out loud. Raffles would be *livid*.

'Did you haul anything else out of him?'

'Yes,' she said, handing me back my wallet. The French postcards were all there, including the one I swore was Irene Adler wearing a domino mask and little else. I'd not felt a thing and could swear I'd not let the cricketer near me.

'Cheeky bugger,' I said, admiring the deftness of the lift. 'Hah, that's funny, you know, because Raffles is…'

'One of those. Yes. We have them in Greece.'

'Of course you do. Practically invented it.'

'His friend, though. "Bunny". Him… not so much. He like the French girl. Irma Vep.'

Another reason for Raffles to blow his top. When they got home, Manders would get an old-fashioned thrashing. The duo had been in it together since school, when the soppy new bug had fagged for the captain of the eleven. At Eton, they made me slave to a prefect, supposedly to build 'character'. It worked, but not the way they wanted. After I stabbed Timkins with a letter-opener, he polished *my* boots and cooked my breakfast. Goes to show how folks take differently to the old school tie.

I doubted Irma would be interested in the Manders clot, but didn't shout out to ask. She could look after her own love-life.

While I was gossiping with Sophy, Moriarty kept thinking.

Eventually, he snapped out of it and had Chop drive us home – with a detour to call at the Hospital for Sick Children in Great Ormond Street. There, the Professor approached a matron to ask after three particular patients. These unfortunates had been wasp-stung during a picnic in Crystal Palace, hosted by a charitable society with a mania for getting unwashed slum tykes into the open air for healthy living and physical jerks. With practiced tact, the woman gave the sad news that one urchin had succumbed, another gone blind and the third wouldn't stop shaking. Quietly pleased with himself, Moriarty noted the results of the experiment in a little book. A delicate girl, being discharged after being cured of fainting spells, took one look at the crow-black Prof, head bobbing like a vulture and hands knotted like a praying mantis, and had a relapse. Some brats – like some dogs and one or two horses – have the knack: they know a wrong'un straight off. Moriarty should have been more worried about common children than phantom heroes.

VII

Back in Conduit Street, something was up. My hunter's instincts pricked and my whiskers twitched. Mrs Halifax was queerly excited by our return, and a peculiar air of conspiracy prevailed among the tarts. A long parcel had arrived, from Germany, and sat on my desk. Not something I was expecting.

'It is the custom, I believe, to include a card with such presentations, Moran,' Moriarty said, suddenly too close to me. 'In this case, it would be contrary to my ruling on not leaving an evidentiary paper chain. Furthermore, no sentiment is required, for I believe – though others have argued the matter – you would not welcome such were it to be extended…'

I'd no idea what he was waffling about. One of us might have gone mad, but I'd be hard pressed to say which. First, a gathering of the world's premier criminals for a summit. Then, experiments with wasp stings. Now, what…?

Moriarty trailed off, and gave Sophy the nod. She turned down the gaslights. It was evening dark out, and the room became a jungle of shadows. I tensed, prepared for attack. Had the Prof hired the woman to murder me and then replace me? Was I to be driven from the tribe like an old, broken-tusked elephant who can no longer trumpet? I'd not go without a scrap. Reaching for the pistol holstered in the small of my back, I discovered someone – Raffles, you bounder!? – had lifted it. So, it was just teeth and claws! If this were how it ended, I was ready to give an account of myself which would not be forgotten.

Then Mrs Halifax entered the darkened room, proudly bearing a cake – solid, brandy-saturated stodge under an inch of lemon cream – surmounted by a forest of thin candles. Little flickering flames lit up the room and the faces of the girls of the house – well, those who weren't presently *occupée* – as they trouped in after the Madame. Fairy Mary Purbright, Throttler Parker, Filthy Fanny and other faithfuls of the Firm were also in the procession. Chop brought up the rear, pushing a trolley which bore ice buckets full of champagne bottles and a tray of Waterford crystal glasses.

Raggedly, the company sang 'For He's a Jolly Good Fellow'. To me.

I was less surprised the time I spotted the Bishop of Bath and Wells using the kink-wrist Mississippi shuffle and dealing from the bottom of the deck.

'Happy birthday, Colonel Basher,' Mrs H. said. 'And many more of 'em.'

I was less surprised the time the Pirate King of the Lepers turned out to be my old Eton whipping boy Porky Sourbright, duffer of the second eleven.

The Madame passed the cake off to Two-Ton Tessie – not someone I'd have trusted it with – and lurched up to me. Harriet Halifax administered a ginny kiss which left powder on my cheeks and lip-rouge in my moustache. She still had the eight-inch tongue that made her name in her Stepney youth.

I was less surprised the time the Burmese Python Lady turned out to be a bloke.

In the ten years – god, ten years! – I'd been with the Firm, Professor Moriarty had given no indication he was even aware I had a birthday, let alone knew when it was (it's in *Who's Who*, of course). Since being fleeced of my birthday money by Rosie at fifteen, I'd not made much of the day myself. I bagged a white tiger on my thirty-fifth birthday after all the bearers had fled. Captain Jellinek served nicely as tethered kid, having hobbled himself by twisting his ankle. I personally skinned my cat, thinking a white winter coverlet would be my fine present to myself. That fur went missing, stolen by dirty natives, and Jammy Jelly died without settling his gambling debts, so the day was a curate's egg. The look in the tiger's eyes, though, as she raised her head with Jellinek's heart in her jaws and saw me sighting on her… that was an exquisite moment. Not a day goes by that I don't think at least once of those magnificent tiger eyes, the ropes of blood dangling from her maw, that contemptuous snarl of kill-me-if-you-must-but-you'll-never-come-close-to-knowing-what-I-am [7]. If I were back in school again, perish the thought, that would be my 'Most Memorable Birthday' essay topic. Otherwise, while I was out of the country, Augusta and Christabelle – the blessed unmarriageable – annually dispatched knitted socks or scarves to my postings. I'd neglected to inform them of my London address. Really, I had meant to dash off a postcard, but just hadn't got round to it… for ten years. It had been a busy decade, I supposed, and it was now a trifle late to tell my sisters I'd returned to Merrie Olde England. I imagined I'd worn out my heroes' welcome at their rented hearth, if I'd ever have had one.

Somehow, even I had forgotten my birthday.

'Blow them out, blow them out,' chanted the girls and Purbright. If he kissed me, I'd knock his bobby's helmet off.

I puffed and extinguished all but three of the candles. Mrs Halifax pretended I'd managed the clean sweep and earned my wish. She pinched them out while the Ranee of Ranchipur distracted me with a peck on the cheek.

Purbright turned up the gaslight again. I winced at the details which sprang up when the room was properly lit. There were mirrors.

'Fifty years old,' Mrs Halifax said, as if commiserating with a sufferer from a deadly disease. 'It comes to us all, or at least all of us as is fortunate not to get killed off otherwise…'

Fifty! At that age, old Sir Augustus – for whom I was now a veritable twin – died of apoplexy. His once-iron constitution was weakened by the lingering effects of the brain fever which cut short his appointment as

Minister to Persia in the forties – my first spoken language was Fārsi, have I ever mentioned that? But in the end a towering rage did for pater. He was set off by something snide Lord Palmerston's undersecretary said when Prime Minister Pam was too busy dealing with Gladstone's latest resignation to bother with a petition from a diplomatic corps warhorse who felt he should have been made ambassador to somewhere more important and less fly-blown than Paraguay. Sir Augustus had been in a bate for years, probably his whole life – certainly, I can only remember him in states of dudgeon ranging from high to stratospheric – and his lid was forever on the point of boiling over. He was red in the face and steaming from the ears when he booted me out of the family home after I was sent down from Oxford for boxing a bursar's ears and throwing the oik through a leaded Elizabethan window. He threw a threepenny bit in my eye and said it was the last coin I'd ever get from him. On the day of his funeral, the 19th of October 1864, I lost seventeen quid at Ascot, got drunk on Scotch whisky I couldn't pay for and was jugged for the night on a drunk and disorderly. In Windsor clink, I roomed with Prince Stanley, a gypsy who later taught me how to thieve like a champion but took a knife to my face when he found I'd tupped his sister from behind. I first let my moustache grow to cover the scar Prince gave me; that, I realised now, was what had begun my slow transformation into a double for my father.

The convention is that drowning makes your life flash past your eyes… now, at this surprise party, my life flashing past my eyes made me feel as if I were drowning. Blowing out candles had taken more out of me than it should. I lit a Joy's cigarette. No Sullivans in my case – they're for ponces, poofs and parvenus. I filled my lungs with smoke, which ought to have made me feel better, but didn't [8].

So, fifty years and still alive. Half a century, not out – though I did feel knocked for a six. Three-quarters of the lads I was at school with were bones on battlefields, rotten in fever pits or stuffed under marble in Kingstead. Most of those who were alive had white hair, if they'd kept it… false teeth… and grandchildren. I suppose I have grandchildren. If you run into a scamp in Kathmandu or Amritsar or Zula who looks a quarter like me, a quarter like some dusky tart and a half like an unknown personage, then kick his or her arse before he or she robs you or rooks you. The Basher blood will run true.

Almost as an afterthought, I did the sums. Born 1840. Mrs H. was wrong. I was past fifty-one. F--k me for a French tart, that was older than Old Sir Augustus got to be!

The cake was sawed into chunks. Moriarty didn't trouble to conceal his impatience with this social occasion. It was my birthday, but Mrs Halifax followed the chain of command and offered the Prof a slice of cake first. Brusquely, he turned it down. The attentions of the girls who were there – Fifi was 'busy', with some damned subaltern due to ship out for parts East in the morning who wanted to be up all night before departure – were welcome, but palled as quickly as the cake. Corks popped – I didn't think to scrabble in the corners for them, and check for hypodermic needle punctures – and champagne was poured. The fizz was passed around. I couldn't taste mine.

I looked at Sophy, my most promising recent acquaintance. She avoided my gaze. I fancied that passing this milestone made me of less interest to her in my cranky old age than I might have been in my roaring forties. I watched her drink champagne and talk with Lotus Lei. The girls warmed to their subject, trading the whereabouts of spots in a man's body where a long needle or a stiletto can slide in unnoticed then produce the most excruciating pain.

As a birthday treat, I wondered if I could ask for that bloody subaltern to be hauled up here in his drawers, then turned over to the Greek and the Celestial as a sort of dressmaker's dummy. They could stick needles into his balls for an hour or two. After that, I might relax by punching him in the face until it looked like meat. Then, on the morrow, it might be amusing if the young terrier's cronies came to see him aboard the ship, which was supposed to bear him off to the Empire to make his name and fortune, and he didn't make an appearance until the anchor was pulled up with him tied to it upside down.

'Moran, get to it and open that, would you? Before we all die of old age.'

Moriarty reminded me of the parcel. His birthday present to me, I realised.

I had my penknife to the string before it occurred to me there might be a trick. It would be just like the Prof to test out some new explosive device – a bomb, sent through the mail! – on whoever happened to be handy, i.e. me. That would make way for Sophy the Knives to take my berth.

There was a bit of a hush, and folks – chewing their cake like cows chew the cud – gathered around to see what I found inside the wrapping paper.

It was a locked wooden case. Varnished cherrywood. Moriarty handed me a key. The custom-made lock had a left-hand turn – you'd be surprised how many people don't even try to twist the key the 'wrong' way before giving up – and lifted the lid. Nestled in velvet recesses were the components of a device which distantly resembled a gun. Barrel and breech were conventional, but the stock was swollen to accommodate a rubber lung. Also included were a pump-handle and some lengths of rubber tube.

Sophy was interested, but it was too manly a contraption to enthral the other girls. They drifted away. A bell tinkled, and Mrs Halifax sent Polly and the Ranee to take care of gentlemen callers. Party or no, there was a business to run.

'I had Von Herder make this,' Moriarty explained. 'It is an air rifle.'

'I know, Moriarty,' I said. 'The shadow man on the *Kallinikos* had a toy pop-pistol like it.'

'That was a Straubenzee, an inferior piece. For precision, the Von Herder will match your Gibbs, Moran. It is silent, has no recoil and fires revolver shells. Imagine… a man falls dead with a soft-nosed pistol ball in his head. He can't have killed himself, for he has no gun in his hand. He is alone in a room or in an open space. No one is within pistol range. How can this be? The murderer is half a mile away, in a place of concealment. Who then shall take the blame? What a puzzle that will be, Moran. A challenge to the scientific detective, I should say.'

Of course, it would be me up a tree pumping like a loon to get the thing ready for a second shot. The Von Herder was for someone reasonably sure he'd shoot true the first time. Fair enough, I'm known for clean kills. I've almost always brought down the cat or the elephant or the barrister with a clean shot. But there are always *circumstances*. At long range, the wind plays tricks. Too many animals have a habit of resting still long enough for you to line up sights, then making sudden movements for no good reason except to avoid being shot in the head.

I assembled the air rifle, which fit together as neatly as a child's model ship. On another birthday I recollected – my ninth or tenth – I was given a model ship, though I'd asked for a real gun. In a pet, I launched the ship in the ornamental ponds of the *khanum*'s palace at Mazandaran, and bombarded it with pebbles until it sank with all hands. I thought I was alone in the courtyard, but something made me turn round and I saw a raised trapdoor which had been concealed in a mosaic. A ghost poked his skull face up through it. Now, I realise it was just a white man with no nose and lips, but then I was convinced it was a genuine spook. Even at that age, I knew terrible deeds were done beneath the palace. It was then, with those fried-egg eyes staring and the exposed teeth snarling, I realised a curious thing about myself: I was brave. The ghost did not frighten me. I was excited, yet calm. Annoyed, but purposeful. Time slowed and I was its master. I still had some pebbles, and pitched one at the apparition, plonking him straight on the bony bonce. The trapdoor dropped shut and that was the last of my ghost [9]. The women of the palace said no such spirit walked here, and Mama told me to shut up about it – though Augusta and Christabelle were agog for details, the more hair-raising the better – lest our quixotic hostess be offended and urge her suggestible son to trade agreements with the wicked Tsar instead of our good Queen.

All these birthdays on, it was the model ship again. I still didn't have *a real gun*, no matter how deadly this puff-rifle might be. Moriarty missed the point. The *bang*! Herons startled from the reeds! The echo, resounding in my ears! The animal keeling over, dropped and dead before the sound has died down. The pull of the bolt and the *ting* of the ejected cartridge case! All part of the *moment* of a perfect shot. Lost with the limp *phut* of this toy. A telescope sight was also included in the box. I looked through it, sighting on Moriarty's globe. Before using the air rifle, I'd want to fire it in. I had confidence in Von Herder's sensitive fingers when it came to mechanical parts, but knew better than to trust a blind engineer with optical jiggery-pokery, even if he did get his lenses ground in Venice.

I held the assembled airgun – it was light – and got the feel of it. It would do, I suppose. It would have its bag. Tradesmen and club bores and Australians and rats and detectives. Not tigers. Not wolves. Not sporting men. Not even natives. This was a tool for a job. No pleasure in it at all, really.

The company looked at me. Mrs Halifax said, 'Aren't you going to thank the Professor?'

Moriarty looked sour and turned away.

Something was called for, something needed to be said. No words came.

'I shall be in with my wasps,' he announced, and abandoned the party for his private study, the windowless room.

The champagne ran out, but there was beer and gin and Scotch. Purbright got squiffy and attempted to sing 'The Boy I Love is Up in the Gallery' in imitation of Marie Lloyd. Two-Ton Tessie, a fervent admirer of Miss Lloyd, sat on him to shut him up.

I disassembled my present and fit the parts back into the case. Sophy Kratides cast a sceptical eye over it.

'I prefer knife. For to get up close. To see eyes,' she said.

Those tiger eyes came back to me. I thought of telling Sophy about it. I had never mentioned how that moment stayed with me to anyone. There had never been anyone to whom I *could* mention it. I didn't. It might have made me seem, I don't know, *weak*.

'How old are you, Sophy?' I asked.

I know, I know… you never ask a lady her age, but it was my party and I had privileges and, lady though she was, Sophy Kratides was *foreign* and they have other standards.

'Twenty-seven,' she said. Her eyes were clear.

It was important to me, in that moment, that she was *more* than half my age. If only technically.

Of all the women in the room, Sophy was the one who wouldn't want paying. I know, I know… I've said it before: you always end up paying, and with tarts at least you know that beforehand and can be cheerful about it. Sometimes you need the *illusion* of a thing freely given.

I claimed a birthday kiss. But we fit together wrong.

Another moment passed. Throttler Parker set his Jew's harp twanging – he's a virtuoso on the noise-making nuisance, so I'm told by experts – and Mistress Strict hauled Polly about in a regimented foxtrot.

Sophy, kindly if wet-lipped and moustache-scratched, asked me if I'd care to, but I've had too many evenings end with women smashing crockery to be tempted by Greek dancing. She was taken away by Simon Carne, nimble and limber despite his fake hunchback.

A while later, I left the party to avail myself of the lavatory on the first-floor landing. I was steady on the stairs, though I'd a lot of drink in me. It's a Bangalore Pioneer point of pride to be ready for inspection (indeed, for battle), no matter how much firewater was downed in the mess. On my way back, I lingered at the door of Fifi's boudoir. I heard the rattle of a bedstead and her famous screeches of abandon – louder, I fancied, than ever – all to a rhythmic pulse. The subaltern gasped as if the life were being yanked out of him.

I should have wrenched the door open, dragged the young pup off the girl, tossed him into a corner, and told him to sit quietly and take notes as I demonstrated the Basher Moran Special. I'd make Fifi scream, all right. Scream like the Mountmain banshee having her toenails pulled out. I'd rattle the bedstead till it flew apart, and we were rutting on springs.

I should have.

Instead, I succumbed on the stairs. I sat down for a moment's rest, and fell asleep. I woke hugging the airgun case like a hard pillow. For some reason, I'd taken Moriarty's present with me from party to *pissoir*. Well past midnight, the house was quiet except for someone sobbing in a distant room. It wasn't my birthday any more.

VIII

After several dozen gins, Mrs Halifax finally cornered Throttler with a demand the little man put his Jew's harp skill to lower purpose. The next morning, the Madame was indisposed, so Polly brought in breakfast. When bending over to polish the silver and 'surprised' by a caller who fancied himself Master of the House, Poll was frolicsome and saucy. Obliged to do actual drudge work, she was sour-tempered and tended to clatter.

I wasn't fresh as a daisy. I could hardly look at my kedgeree. Moriarty, emerged refreshed from his wasp den, set to decapitating boiled eggs as he looked over a sheaf of telegrams. Some were strings of numbers. His plans proceeded well, I gathered. If thwarted, he'd be in a mood to torture his eggs before topping them. His oscillation was almost cheerful. He cut his toast into soldiers, for dipping in yolks.

The air rifle was on the table, locked in its case.

I was still astonished the Professor had thought to get me a birthday present, even if it was a tool I'd be expected to use in his service. I supposed I should show gratitude, or even interest.

'The Von Herder, Moriarty... is it to be used in your pre-emptive strikes?'

His head stopped moving and he looked at me queerly.

'What do you mean?'

'To dash down the heroes before they set out on their quests. I assume you've a list of coconuts for the shy. Which budding genius of detection will first present a target for a silent potshot?'

Moriarty laid down a half-eaten soldier. He had yolk on his lips.

'Moran, you should know better.'

'You've lost me,' I said, perplexed. 'Your lecture to your peers, about the threats we face...'

'Real enough and we'll deal with them in time, but what I said in the tomb was mostly *yarning*. A distraction from the true purpose of the gathering.'

Even for Moriarty, this was rum.

'You mean you do not propose "a commonwealth of criminal empires?"'

'Of course not. Can you imagine such a thing operating for more than a week? Would you care to be in business with Jack Quartz? The man's insane, for one thing. An habitual, compulsive betrayer. They all are. Things we might do for expedience, they do out of habit. The Lord of Strange Deaths despises the white races and would always seek primacy. To that Chinaman, you and I and General Gordon and Queen Victoria are all the same barbarian breed. *Les Vampires* are French, no more need be said of them. Any arrangement such as I seemed to propose would lead to internecine wars and ruin us more swiftly than a dozen police forces acting in concert.'

'"*Seemed* to propose"?'

'A diversion, Moran. A serious enough proposition to be listened to for a short while. None of our guests will have considered it past nightfall. Even the Creeper. No, that was not the purpose of the summit I convened. I had to be sure one man would attend. An invitation to him alone would have been too obvious a trap. His flaw is vanity, you know. He wanted to look me in the face again and feel he had the measure of me... but, even more than that, he wants to be of our party, on a level with Professor Moriarty and Dr Nikola and the Countess Cagliostro. He does not lack ambition.'

'Who are you talking about?'

'Mabuse, of course. Dr Mabuse, or whatever else he may call himself. He likes "the Great Unknown". The man without a real face. The master of disguise. The fake fake Carnacki. The shadow man of the *Kallinikos*.'

'Dr Mabuse was the ringer?'

Moriarty clapped, once. 'Enlightenment dawns. Yes, Moran. Dr Mabuse was the master spy who tried to steal the secret of Greek Fire. Oh, he's had me marked for some while, observing at a distance, learning my methods. He was in the audience at Stent's Red Planet League lecture. The droll student who shouted, "I say, Stent, is that the sick squid you owe me?" In the business of the Bensington Rejuvenator, he was one of the researchers in Cologne who falsified the experimental logs. Then, he assumed the guise of a London rough called "Frog Junkin", and was even – at two or three removes – on our payrolls for a month, doing odd jobs in the East End. The Frog stood lookout when Parker garrotted the Reverend John Jago during the Spitalfields Anti-Vice Crusade. After that, he became a Neapolitan for a year, in the Camorra under Don Rafaele Corbucci. He was at the Battle of the Six Maledictions, and pretended to die with a Templar sword through him. All the while, he has been maintaining multiple lives in Berlin – as an alienist, a financier, a rabble-rouser, a rabbi, a washerwoman, a card shark, a policeman. Plagiarising my methods, he has built up his own gang. I do not know where his mania comes from, for mania it is. He wishes to steal everything from me. He wants to *be* me.'

My jaw was slack, and I dribbled tea.

Why on earth would anyone want to be Moriarty? Of all the people to idolise, to envy, to imitate... Professor James Moriarty! I honestly think the Grand Vampire got more enjoyment out of his calling, and his life expectancy could be calculated in months. Moriarty was what he was because his nature gave him no other option. He had grown crooked from stony ground, leeching what water he could from deep roots. To set out to become such a solitary monster was beyond understanding.

This kraut plainly couldn't bear to be whoever he originally was. Else, why try on all the other faces? Great impersonators are all the same. Simon Carne and Paul Finglemore were just as cracked – ditchwater dull as themselves, but alive when they could hide under crepe hair, wax noses and trick corsets. Even *that bitch* dressed up for character parts and flung herself about to put clear blue ocean between Miss Irene Adler, international adventuress, and Mrs Irene Norton, New Jersey bourgeoise.

'Surely, if the picklehead's barmy, he's liable to wake up one morning frothing at the mouth claiming he's transformed into a giant beetle. You know what these disguise wallahs are like, Moriarty. It's a short hop, skip and hysterical fit from padded cheeks to padded cell. No need to worry about competition from inside the madhouse.'

'In the end, you are right, Moran. The strains of living so many lives are too much for one man. Yet, in the short term, Dr Mabuse will prove troublesome.'

'You've only just found this out?'

'I had to be sure Mabuse was the mastermind of the *Kallinikos*. Only face to face could I determine beyond doubt he was the creature who interfered with us in that business. Hah! The cheek of it! Playing Finglemore playing Carnacki, and running all those other agents as if they were rivals not minions. He uses mesmerism, of course. Symptomatic of a need to control what cannot be controlled. Very German. He's no spy, not through conviction or calling. He set out to steal Greek Fire not for profit, though I daresay he could have turned a penny selling the secret on an exclusive basis to five or six governments. No, he took an interest because he knew my brothers – my cursed brothers! – would pull me into the affair. He came at me through my *family*, Moran.'

'Low, I admit… but he *is* a foreigner.'

The Professor thumped the table, rattling the silverware. By his standards, he was impassioned.

'I cannot tolerate such impudence. It's to the death, now. There can be no other outcome. Mabuse must fall that Moriarty can endure.'

'He's no hero, no *detective*…'

'Try to keep up, Moran. At present, we've little to fear from bloodhounds and magnifying glasses. My would-be doppelganger is a direct threat. Mabuse was the most likely, but the Grand Vampire and Hentzau were possibilities. I had to include them to rule them out. Even Théophraste Lupin was suspect. Only a scheme as vast as my balloon about a "commonwealth of criminal empires" could justify the guest list necessary to flush out our foe.'

My head span. It was not yet ten o'clock, and I could have done with a lie-down. The most outrageous aspect of what the Professor had done – the most inadvisable, to my feeble mind – was daring to summon the deadliest men and women on Earth as set-dressing.

It was all about some bloody German.

The likes of the Lord of Strange Deaths and Countess Cagliostro would not care to be 'also in the cast as courtiers, gentlemen, sailors, gondoliers, etc.' If they ever found out, they'd seek redress from the Professor. And, by association, everyone in the Firm – including me. These creatures didn't last as long as they had – and the Lord and the Countess had, by some accounts, lasted for centuries – by being the sorts who don't find things out. If his scheme went wrong, Moriarty would have his commonwealth of criminal empires all right – an alliance of evil geniuses, master crooks and deadly assassins directed against his oscillating head! Mabuse would only have to hold the others' coats while they dismantled us piece by piece!

'So, we hit Mabuse?'

'How, Moran? He won't look like he did yesterday.'

'You said you'd know him however he was disguised.'

'So I would. But I'd have to see him to know him. He won't show himself now until he chooses to.'

'Why didn't we shoot him yesterday?'

He looked at me, piercingly. I recollected an alligator whose eye I caught while dropping off a New Orleans friend in a bayou. I half thought Moriarty would take up nictitating some day.

'Moran, I would back you against Rupert of Hentzau, though you are twice his age… I would give you even odds against Irma Vep or Princess Zanoni… and you could best Arthur Raffles despite his boxing blue. But the Daughter of the Dragon? Dr Nikola? The Creeper? All of them together? I fear you would not survive a scrap like that. Which is why I took this from you…'

He returned my small-of-the-back revolver.

'You do have a plan, Moriarty?'

'Several.'

He went back to his breakfast and his telegrams. I was not reassured.

IX

What happened over the next three months was in the papers. Oh, the press didn't make the connections. But the facts were noisy enough.

In the middle of February, someone with a Clontarf accent called Inspector Lukens on the telephone and told him a dynamite outrage was imminent in North London. That night, a terrific explosion in Kingstead Cemetery destroyed the Thoroughgood tomb. So many bodies – and parts of bodies – were flung about Egyptian Avenue that it was four days before they were sorted out. Then, the Special Irish Branch announced this 'Fenian atrocity' was not mere vandalism, but foul murder. Walter Grimes had been caught in the blast, prompting amusing 'man found dead in graveyard' headlines. The sexton's widow couldn't say why he was at the cemetery well after normal service hours.

Of more concern to the Firm, especially when Patterson of the Criminal Investigation Division took an interest, was that examination of supposed Thoroughgood corpses turned up one or two recognisable heads. The senior Mr Bulstrode sweated it out when called in to explain how he had come to mistake the absconded Belgian financier Maupertuis for Uncle Septimus. The undertaker acted befuddled, more concerned that the CID not examine the contents of the coffins in his private parlour than with trifling accessory to murder charges. Inspection of the ruins by those police laboratory bods the Prof had got his peers all steamed up about disclosed some curious facts. The dynamite had been smuggled into the tomb in the coffins of young Will and Harry. The trigger was a very slow-acting fuse, an ingenious – indeed, scientifically admirable – gadget. Acid took weeks to dissolve a metal catch, whereupon two chemicals rushed together in a glass chamber to produce a sudden flame and set off the bomb. It was a very *Moriartian* device, though I knew better than to say so in his presence.

If the bomber had hoped to provoke yet another sweep against London's Irish poets and navvies, his purpose was achieved. More Mountmains were roughed up and tossed into cells. Lukens announced that the Invincible Republican Irish were now known to have been behind the cornering of quap, and Baron Maupertuis just the front man. Inspector Patterson counter-announced that the Fenians would have been pretty foolish then to draw attention to the fact with a bombing which returned the Baron to the public eye (so to speak) and reopened the old case. Lukens agreed that the Fenians, on the whole, were pretty foolish. In which case, Patterson idly wondered, why did Scotland Yard need a whole well-funded department to do battle with a bunch of inept clods who thought dynamiting a sexton advanced the cause of Home Rule? This public row did not convince me that the police were ever going to hamper the business of the Firm.

Then, a form of pox caught fire in Conduit Street. Every female person in the house came down with it – the symptoms were angry red blotches over the face, persistent voiding of bodily wastes from every orifice, and sleeping spells which lasted from twenty to thirty hours. With Mrs Halifax and every one of her girls out of commission, customers had to be turned away. Those few persistent enough to barge in and insist on regular appointments encountered swollen, puking, shitting, spotted *filles de joie* and beat a hasty retreat.

Dr Velvet, the quack on hand for the girls' little female complaints, didn't know this pox, but said it was not venereal in character. He thought it might be an allergic reaction, but really couldn't say – though he charged his usual fee for not saying. Velvet was especially puzzled that only the women in the house were affected – the sole exception being Slender Simon, the catamite Mrs H. kept on hand for those bucks whose tastes ran to tossing a pretty boy into the mix when taking 'em on two or three at a time.

Chop and Purbright brought up some girls from South of the River – savages with tattoos and bone earrings, to hear the men talk about them – and put them in the empty house across the way, taking care not to let them get anywhere near our sickening tarts. The new soiled doves came down with the pox too, and were disappointed in any hopes they had of meeting a gent from up West.

At the risk of incurring a debt no one wanted to think about, we secured a consultation from the Lord of Strange Deaths – who would, in other years, have been our number one suspect. As the world's greatest expert in exotic poisons and subtle plagues, he saw straight off how it had been done. A mixture of Peruvian boomslang venom and Tanzanian desert rose sap had been smeared on soap used in the laundry where the bed sheets were washed. The Lord was, in his inscrutable way, irked that the attack against us had been made from a Chinese establishment in which he, naturally, had a controlling interest. By way of apology, he had the laundry manager crushed in his own steam press. An outsider, of course, was responsible.

A sudden rash of efficiency erupted in police forces across the nation. A crime Moriarty had carefully planned for an Edinburgh mob – the theft and ransom of a collection of horrible Highland landscape paintings which happened to be favourites of the Queen – was a fizzle. The lay was cracked exactly as the Professor dictated, but a posse of jock constables lay in wait with truncheons. In several towns, bought-and-paid-for coppers were mysteriously reassigned to menial duties and replaced by newly appointed hotheads with private incomes and a burning zeal to fight crime.

A long-standing blackmail operation in Leeds was smashed when a dozen worthies simultaneously grew spines and took their lumps by owning up to indiscretions, misappropriations and other sins to wives, employers or the petty sessions court. Thus rendering an extensive archive of letters, photographs and statements gathered over a decade entirely valueless. Five myopic customs officers in Dover were given a choice between resignation or arrest, shutting down a handy black-market trade route to and from Europe. An all-comers bare-knuckles contest in Epping Forest was raided. Some of the greatest sports in the land, who liked a flutter on the pugilists, had to be politely reminded such pursuits were technically against the law. A courier was arrested in Amsterdam. When punched in the gut, he sicked up a lavender bag of uncut diamonds. Three ringleaders of the Conduit Street Comanche were seized from their dens, scrubbed with lye and packed off to schools in remote rural areas run by muscular Christian brothers with gruel, the lash and compulsory prayers at four in the morning.

All this was inconvenient. The next phase was more bothersome, and struck closer to home. We were hampered.

I've not dwelled much on the day-to-day business of the Firm. My duties were elevated, and as a consequence I had little to do with the collection of tithes from outfits operating under our aegis. Various London businesses – public houses, restaurants, sweet shops, opium dens, theatres, music halls, casinos, dog tracks, pie stalls – paid handsomely for the privilege of not having their premises raided by the Comanche. They also allowed the Firm the use of services from time to time, and provided household necessities and luxuries gratis. A great part of the economy of the city, even the *legitimate* economy, depends upon criminal custom, and Moriarty had painstakingly spun his web so we profited from our associations. Then, there was a hiccough.

Nathaniel Rawlins, a solicitor with only one client, came reluctantly to

Conduit Street to announce that his collectors were coming up short. It was his duty to oversee collections, pay out salaries and bank profits with Box Brothers. He was terrified of earning the boss' opprobrium, so let the shortfall go unreported for several vital days before bringing the matter to us. The Professor was busy with his wasps and his plans, so I had to deal with the matter. Rawlins assembled his tallymen, and I listened – with growing fury – to their complaints. Some formerly cowed proprietors were withholding payments, claiming that if they were paying for protection they should get it. Windows had been smashed, pot-boys roughed up, some obscene public displays shut down by the police, and a café in Tite Street closed after an outbreak of food poisoning caused by something less exotic than boomslang venom in the soup. Folk who'd been happy to pay and tell themselves that they were subdivisions of the Firm rather than victims of extortion were bleating loudly.

As assassin-in-chief, I was expected to eliminate a plague of minor officials, vandals, constables and annoying customers to pay back all those sovereigns we'd squeezed out of Soho. I was not about to put my new airgun – tested and sighted in, but not yet fired in the field – to such low use, and told the collectors to collect harder. Rawlins wouldn't have recruited them if they weren't capable. Over the fat years, they had got too used to an easy life, and let their saps go soft and knuckle-dusters get rusty. For a while, more insistent demands restored the flow of money… but then the Tite Street waiters, unemployed and crotchety, set about Bruiser Downes with table legs and saw him off. New faces sprung up in the street, eager to offer the protection it was whispered that the Firm could no longer deliver. Several of Rawlins' collectors took beatings, set up in business for themselves (very unwise) or scarpered on long-planned seaside holidays. The Professor shrugged this drip-drip-drip problem off as not sufficiently interesting, and told me to take drastic measures. Unable to think of anyone else who could do the job, I negotiated with Margaret Trelawny – not a lady I was overly keen to dine with *á deux* – to borrow the Hoxton Creeper. His looming presence made the average publican or shop manager find cash they didn't know they had to make arrears payments, but the Creeper was not subtle. Witnesses tended to remember his face, and couldn't help giving good descriptions of him. Mad Margaret demanded a greater degree of autonomy for her Temple of Tera, which I was forced to grant her. At that, I fancied her mask smiled nastily.

The Firm was trembling.

Most of the Thoroughgood funeral party had hied back from whence they came – Dr Nikola was rumoured to be in the Congo, perfecting surgical procedures on gorillas – but *that bitch* was still in town. I considered setting the Creeper on her for my peace of mind, but the giant was a mug for a pretty face and I didn't fancy having a spine-snapping juggernaut lobbed straight back at me. Irene and her beau were everywhere… at the opera, at society balls, giving charity concerts, visiting missions in the East End, dining with cabinet ministers. I wondered what had become of Colonel Sapt, the Ruritanian Secret Police Chief. When *that bitch* first plagued us, he was her companion and secret confederate. Sapt was a Rudolfite and Hentzau a Michaelist, so she'd hopped the fence in the Ruritanian succession debate. I assumed that, as ever, she was on nobody's side but her own.

I discerned no obvious link between Irene Adler and the troubles besetting us, but she was up to *something*. Even if she was just in London to see the fireworks, she was a nagging pain. In a move which, even if I say so myself, was exceptionally clever, I assigned Sophy to discover *that bitch*'s secrets. Naturally impervious to the diva's charms, our knife-woman also had experience enough with handsome scoundrels to see through Rupert's hand-kissing insouciance.

Sophy came back and reported, with a cold smirk, that Irene's main reason for staying in London was a secret course of beauty treatments at Madame Sara's – touching up her hair colour, ironing out tiny wrinkles around her eyes. Sophy took great delight in this. Picking up Moriarty's pet name for Irene, she amended it to *that* old *bitch*. I should have been reassured... but was struck with melancholia. Irene Adler, too, was not as young as she'd once been. Only Jo-Jo Balsamo was eternal, and she looked more marble statue than woman.

A week after Sophy's intelligence, we received a formal letter from Madame Sara, severing all ties – financial and otherwise – with the Firm. Damn me, but I should have seen it coming. All the while she was having cream worked into her temples, Irene had worked her spell on the Sorceress of the Strand. The Derry & Tom's androgyne was furiously pedalling off heartbreak on a bicycle tour of Wales while Sara worshipped at the altar of Adler. My instinct was to order an explosive reprisal against the Madame's premises, prefaced by telephoning Lukens with a begorrah or two, but the papers announced Sara had temporarily shut up shop and would be travelling on the continent with friends. She had been invited to Ruritania to 'do' the Princess Flavia's hair for an upcoming coronation. There might be time to nobble her before she boarded the boat-train, but what with all the other grief the Firm had only a skeleton staff on hand. Sophy volunteered to do the deed, but I didn't want to chance such valuable asset on a mere pettish killing. A mad vitriol-chucker would do, but they were in short supply that season.

The Professor, uncharacteristically, said we should let Sara go and be glad to be rid of her if she took *that bitch* off the table. I hoped the pair of she-cats tore Rupert of Hentzau to pieces. When word got out that Moriarty had accepted letters of resignation and declarations of independence – hitherto unthinkable – there was a queue of messengers from ship-deserting rats of all colours. It was Decline and Fall to the letter, and the Goths and Vandals overrunning our empire sported size-nineteen boots and knob-end helmets.

X

The Firm ran a printing press in Wapping, running off snide [10] good enough to pass in Threadneedle Street. Not an Archie Stamford botch, but prime quality forgery. In April, the plant was subtly sabotaged. Paper with a face value of £7,000 had to go in the furnace. The rag was excellent, the engraving exceptional and the ink mixed to the proper recipe. Our plates matched the genuine article, down to the rubric 'For the Gov.r and Comp.a of the Bank of England, Frank May', but our five-pound notes came out signed 'James Moriarty'.

This prompted me to a *deduction*: our 'Great Unknown', the intelligence behind the strikes against us, couldn't be Dr Mabuse, or – at least – not Mabuse solo. The nose-tweak with the chief cashier's signature betrayed that most un-German characteristic: *a sense of humour*. I barged into the Prof's study with this profound insight, but he'd already worked it out through wear on a vanished night-watchman's left-behind trousers or the depth rat turds had sunk into the dripping pan on a hot day or somesuch.

'Mabuse needed only to prick us,' I was told. 'He has put blood in the water. To alert the sharks. He himself has left the country. He is not at any of his Berlin addresses, which are watched constantly. He wears a new face. He is gone to earth. But he pays attention, follows the feeding frenzy.'

Moriarty had nervous energy now. For months he had accepted each blow and merely oscillated, *thinking thinking thinking*… I hoped we were at the point of *doing doing doing*.

The Professor wiped wasps off his long canvas gloves, brushing them into the funnel of the glass and wood nest-maze he had constructed. He took down his best hat and pulled on his coat.

'I have a call to pay, Moran,' he said. 'In Baker Street. A minor nuisance on the point of becoming a middle-sized obstacle must be bent to our purpose...'

Ah-hah, I thought, the Thin Man! He'd been a bother a time or two. The Birdy Edwards foul-up, for once. The Maupertuis fiasco, for twice. He'd also nabbed a couple of the Firm's sometime clients: Grimesby Roylott was dead and John Clay gaoled thanks to his unwanted intervention. And… well, he was just a shit… a puffed-up, hectoring, tiresome beaky shit. With a halfway decent line in publicising himself, as witness: all those back numbers of *The Strand* piled up in the jakes.

This brothel-creeping keyhole bandit had popped up at the edges of the picture all spring. In Leeds, just before the smashing of the blackmail ring. At Scotland Yard, in conference with Inspector Patterson. Disguised as a trainer at the Epping Forest tourney. Delivering a box of papers to the Crown prosecutor in Dover. Treating himself to a celebratory beefsteak at Simpson's in the Strand. He was one of the toothiest of the sharks tearing into our flanks.

'This is his handiwork, then?' I said, waving the funny money.

Moriarty allowed it was. 'Most droll, Moran. Our *consulting detective* has the fingers of a forger. He has my signature to the curlicue. He could cash a cheque at Box Brothers.'

My fire rose. Larks like this got under my skin. I was heating up, and – after all these months of frustration – ready to 'go off' like Krakatoa.

'Hang a dartboard on the fiddler's back, Moriarty. The Von Herder's fired in. This pestilential sleuth c--t would make a decent first kill for its bag!'

'Not yet, Moran. I've a use in mind for the Thin Man.'

This surprised me.

'I know the blighter's *in trade*, but surely he wouldn't take you as a client.'

'I have, through proxies, hired him three times. We couldn't get shot of that homicidal lunatic Bert Stevens until I persuaded him to carry his carcass to Baker Street. Mabuse can do us more injury than Stevens ever did. And he is in hiding, where he thinks he cannot be found. We need a bloodhound, and the Thin Man has a reputation. It will be a simple matter to draw the attention of the Great Detective to the Great Unknown. He believes he serves abstract reason, but has been manipulated into this persecution of our Firm. With all his cleverness, the Thin Man cannot realise the full extent of our organisation. He has us in his sights now, but would not know our names – would not be scribbling details on his index cards, would not be in cahoots with Patterson of Scotland Yard – were it not for information gifted him by Mabuse. You remember "Fred Porlock"?'

I did. All too well. It was the alias of someone inside the Firm who leaked titbits to all sorts of wrong people: policemen and detectives and journalists. We found him out, and Moriarty... well, let's just say a culprit was duly tried, convicted and punished.

'We were given the wrong man. "Frog Junkin" was "Fred Porlock". Mabuse himself, sowing the seeds of our ruin.'

We were beset on all sides. The spectres the Professor had invoked in the Thoroughgood tomb were manifesting. I wondered if we'd ever be rid of these parasites. Napoleon hadn't survived concerted attacks by lesser men. We had our Blucher in Mabuse, and now it seemed we had our Wellington in the Thin Man.

Just remember, when that sycophant Watson credits him with the fall of the Firm, the Great Detective had to be told about us. Our real arch-enemy was 'Fred Porlock'.

XI

While Moriarty was in Baker Street, I arranged murder attempts. The bloodhound needed pepper on his tail, so *near misses* were to be contrived. As I've said before, it's too easy to misjudge and put a warning shot in someone's fool head.

The Professor returned to HQ and gave a report of his meeting with the Thin Man. He was especially full of himself.

'His nerves are shot, Moran. He hides behind curtains. He knows about the Von Herder, and is terrified to show a silhouette at the window. He takes precautions when out and about, changing directions like a compulsive, suspecting any who might approach. Yet he leaves his doors unlocked. His lodgings are open to any who might wander in. In his present state, *failing* to assassinate him will be a challenge. We'll have to shield him from harm he might do himself. I intended to present my card and confront him in his hallway. But I was un-greeted and unopposed. I climbed the stairs to his flat but held back at the doormat. Surely, the extraordinary lack of security was a lure for an ingenious trap…? But, no, he offers open invitation. I found the Great Detective shrinking in his study, surrounded by scribbled notes. He has an untidy mind, reflected in his surroundings. There is no logic to the clutter. His interests are higgledy-piggledy. He is not an impressive specimen.

Startled at my presence on his threshold, he reached into his pocket as if caught doing something unmanly by a schoolmaster.

'"You have less frontal development than I should have expected," I said. "It is a dangerous habit to finger loaded firearms in the pocket of one's dressing gown."

'He wasn't even dressed for the day. At eleven-thirty in the morning. His hair a rats' nest, he was in pyjamas under that vile grey gown. He took out a revolver and put it on the table.

'"You evidently don't know me," I said.

'"On the contrary," he answered, "I think it is fairly evident that I do. Pray take a chair. I can spare you five minutes if you have anything to say."

'"All that I have to say has already crossed your mind," I said.

'"Then possibly my answer has crossed yours," he replied.

'"You stand fast?"

'"Absolutely."

'I took out my memorandum book, which startled him into making a grab for the gun. He almost shot himself, Moran. Or shit himself. One or the other – or both. That such a creature should esteem himself capable of destroying me! I allowed him the comfort of the weapon. I enumerated dates upon which he had meddled in our affairs, emphasising occasions when he thought his part unknown to me. You should have seen his eyes. He has a drug addict's eyes. He uses cocaine, and lies to his doctor about the dosage. Thirty-seven per cent solution, I should say. I told him he must drop the case.

'"After Monday," he said.

'"I am quite sure that a man of your intelligence will see that there can be but one outcome to this affair," I told him. "It is necessary that you should withdraw. You have worked things in such a fashion that we have only one resource left. It has been an intellectual treat to me to see the way in which you have grappled with this affair, and I say, unaffectedly, that it would be a grief to me to be forced to take any extreme measure. You smile, sir, but I assure you that it really would."

"'Danger is part of my trade,' he remarked, sweat on his brow.

'It was not danger I offered him, I said, but inevitable destruction. Having flattered him with weasel words about his intellect, I crushed him. He must stand clear or be trodden underfoot. I hinted, Moran, at matters I knew would run through his brain – even if he chooses to keep them private from his closest confidantes. I let him know he did not yet perceive the extent of the forces he was meddling with. For the sake of what he took to be a smart retort, he had come out and told me when the axe would fall. We are to expect raids on Monday. That is when Scotland Yard will swoop, will attempt to net our entire organisation. They will knock before dawn, as usual, kick in doors, roust felons from beds, and slap the darbies [11] on us. This honest, unimaginative soul has not the wit to keep back vital intelligence. If I were to tell a man I would murder him on Monday, it would be a ruse. I'd strike on Sunday, before he was prepared, or Tuesday, while he congratulated himself on besting me. The Thin Man is so confident in his victory, he cannot help but celebrate the win before the race is finished.

'I did not tell him about Dr Mabuse, but talked up the "duel between us" in such a way as to let him *glimpse* the possibility he was acting in another's interests. I could see him pick up the clues I scattered like spittle on the carpet. He thinks slowly, Moran. He forges chains of reason, link by link. It is a simple matter to nudge, to steer his course. I know his every move, his every thought. I saw a realisation dawn that there was a Great Unknown in the game… that this shadow man might not be an abstract servant of justice, but a subtle criminal. I let him see that the smashing of Moriarty would create a vacuum, inviting in a successor who would credit him, the servant of justice, with clearing the way for a lasting empire of crime. I gave him the scent, Moran. The merest whiff. I named no names, though "Fred

Porlock" hung in the air. He has had report of the *Kallinikos*. He has file-cards on major European criminals. Little notes to himself. On yours, he has scrawled "the second most dangerous man in London". Under "Dr Mabuse", he has written a question mark. My visit has underlined that question mark.

"'You hope to place me in the dock," I said. "I tell you that I will never stand in the dock. You hope to beat me. I tell you that you will never beat me. If you are clever enough to bring destruction upon me, rest assured that I shall do as much to you."

"'You have paid me several compliments, Mr Moriarty," said he…

"'*Professor* Moriarty," I corrected him.

"'Let me pay you one in return when I say that if I were assured of the former eventuality, I would, in the interests of the public, cheerfully accept the latter."

'There is no reason with such a man, Moran. "I can promise you the one, but not the other," I said calmly, and left him to his funk. A morning's work. I trust you have done as well.'

Moriarty's smug air of having effected a major coup rubbed me the wrong way. All he'd done was exchange schoolboy 'yah boo to you' taunts with the Thin Man in his den. In contrast to his gloating, I merely gave a statement of what had been arranged for the afternoon's entertainment.

The rule of three applied. This afternoon, our man would survive convincingly serious encounters with a runaway van, falling masonry and Bruiser Downes. The bandages were off and the wounds healed, but Downes was broken – his reputation would never recover from the Tite Street rout. If the Bruiser were taken in on an assault charge, it would be no loss. These trifling gestures should chivvy along the detective. Moriarty said he'd scurry for his doctor like a maiden aunt with the sniffles. Just to put a cherry on top, Benny Blazes was due to set light to the Thin Man's digs that evening. Those damned index cards, the Persian slippers full of shag and the dusty back-editions of the *Police Gazette* – I'm sure the Great Detective said he subscribed for the articles and ignored the illustrations – had the makings of a fine old bonfire, though our reliable arsonist was under orders not to do too much damage.

'Now, *we* have played the part of "Fred Porlock", Moran. We have fed the dog scraps. He will pick up the trail, I've no doubt. He's not unintelligent and his brain will be spurred by the shame. He'll never tell his Boswell how Mabuse has used him against me. But he'll need to know the truth. I've spoiled his coup, Moran. He'd intended to be in at the kill on Monday. In his head, he had composed the modest comments he intended to make to the press. Now, he knows he wins only a phantom victory. He will leave the prosaic business of making arrests to Inspector Patterson, and go in search of the Great Unknown. The bloodhound is off his leash. We may follow him at our leisure.'

Moriarty was the shark now, scores of teeth in his smile.

I did not raise the matter foremost in my mind as these subtle, cruel, cunning, logical madmen entered into the final phase of their protracted dance. Whichever mind mastered the others, the Firm would – unless drastic measures were taken – be practically extinct come Monday morning.

And since when was I only the *second* most dangerous man in London?!

XII

So, to Switzerland...

I have no idea how the Thin Man tracked Mabuse to Meiringen. Thanks to the bloodhound's (if I might say) *Moriartian* habit of not telling his number two anything important, J.H. Watson, Medical Dolt, is in the dark too. In his scandal sheet write-up, Watson presents his friend's bizarre decision to hare off across Europe, rather than stay in London to close his greatest case, as a spur-of-the-moment decision to take a pleasant holiday. Of course, this is from the man who claimed he hadn't heard of Moriarty until that week... then later 'remembered' he'd been made aware of the Professor, 'Fred Porlock' and the Firm much earlier [12]. As I've said, the detective was in that bad business at Birlstone Manor. Not to do speak ill of the annoying, but note: when the Thin Man cracked the case, he announced the supposed victim was still alive. I'm sure Birdy Edwards, when thrown into the sea, found time to thank the sleuth for deigning to solve the mystery of his fake murder so Moriarty could commit his real one.

As then, the Thin Man was flushing out our quarry for us. We really should have bunged him some cash for services rendered.

Moriarty told me to pack the Von Herder for a hunting trip. He had spies at all the transport terminals and, after supper, a message came in from Victoria

Station that our bloodhound had reserved a carriage on the next morning's boat-train to Paris. The Prof seized on this intelligence with a troubling glee. I'd seen it on tiger hunts: some idiot is so high on the idea of bagging a prize cat, he doesn't much care if he comes back from the jaunt in one piece. The lives of native bearers – even other white guns – become a currency to be spent freely for a chance of a clean shot. On occasion, I have *been* that idiot. Now, I found myself thrust into the unwanted role of sensible companion.

All the while Moriarty was playing silly beggars, the Firm was coming apart. Our lieutenants were assailed by summonses to appear in court, notifications of legal action, constables brandishing fresh search warrants, and the sudden refusals of bought-and-paid-for officials to lose paperwork. When Patterson of the Yard showed up in his outer office, Nathaniel Rawlins squeezed through a tiny rear window. After wandering the streets in a tizzy, he hanged himself with his college scarf in a stall in the Theobald's Row conveniences. Opinion differed as to whether Rawlins took the easy way out to avoid disgrace or knew that turning Queen's Evidence to get off would earn him the 'Fred Porlock' treatment.

As it stood, I don't know if the Prof had attention to spare for keeping the help terrified. He was busy giving a bewildered Polly instructions for the care of his wasps while he was away. He was most insistent the inconvenience of a police raid should not disturb the insects' routine, and assured her that she'd be out on bail in time for their midday feed. I didn't mention that our brief was dangling in a public bog and might not be at his best when delivering bonds.

Sophy was to be included in our party. It turned out, in one of those small-world-isn't-it?-type things, she had cause to blame the Thin Man for failing to prevent her brother's murder. Another instance of his habit of curing the disease only for the patient to die anyway. The Great Detective hadn't even bothered to bring the killers of Paul Kratides to book, which is why Sophy had to do for Latimer and Kemp herself. I told her that the Prof wanted the boob alive for the moment. A disappointment, I fancy. I said it was probably all right if she wanted to cut Watson's throat, but she shrugged that off as a distant second best. Women, eh?

If you want railway timetables, you'll have to dig out *The Strand*. I've not the patience. The next day, the Thin Man and the Fat Head tried to shake us off by sending their luggage on to Paris while they hopped off the boat-train at Canterbury and took the Newhaven ferry to Dieppe. Moriarty saw through the trick, but decided our hound would sniff better if he thought he'd lost us. The Professor and I followed the trunks to Paris and spent a few days there as guests of *Les Vampires*. Sad to report, the Grand Vampire who'd come to Kingstead had just died in a fall from the Eiffel Tower, but his replacement was suitably hospitable. He only tried to murder us once, and then with little conviction, merely as a formality.

We all drank champagne out of Napoleon's skull. I squired Irma Vep to the Moulin Rouge, where I merrily purloined the evening's take as she performed a service for one of the first families of France. Jewels were abstracted from a dressing room before they could fall into the dainty clutches of a dancer who'd worked for a month to seduce a young vicomte to get them. Of course, Irma switched the sparklers and gave the old comte fakes, then whisked me off to after-hours *anis* in a den of apache.

While we were enjoying *la vie Parisienne*, the Thin Man spent two days in Brussels. That's something of a record: I don't know another Englishman who's stuck Belgium for more than a single day without getting drunk on their beer, sick on their chocolate or in trouble with their schoolgirls. We knew what he was up to because Sophy, who'd stuck with him quietly while we ostentatiously lost his trail, sent telegrams every few hours. We also had word from London, via Simon Carne: Patterson had made his raids, most of the Firm were locked up, Margaret Trelawny was en route to Egypt, Mrs Halifax's house was shuttered, the Creeper was reported drowned (a likely story) and Raffles found it expedient to spend some time in the nets. All this put me in an ill-humour. I know I was only an employee, but I'd put a great deal into the enterprise. I'd been on Moriarty's rolls longer than I served with the bloody Bangalore Pioneers. I'd killed more people for him than for the Queen. The Firm meant more to me than f--king Eton! Since Sir Augustus turfed me out of the family pile, I'd messed temporarily all over the show. That brothel in Conduit Street was the nearest thing I'd had to a home. I didn't care to think that was all over and ashes.

Moriarty betrayed no trace of feeling. He asked after his wasps, but that was all…

Seeing my concern, he set out his position.

'When I return to London, Moran, I shall start again. From nothing. Free and clear. Unimpeded by fallible subordinates. Without clutter. This time, I shall follow strict mathematical formulae. I have involved myself in matters superfluous to the equation. This is an opportunity to wipe the blackboard clean. Within a year, I shall be able to *concentrate*. All possible threats to me will be eliminated. The work will continue, in a purer sphere. Then I shall get real results.'

All nice and neat and dandy, I supposed. I still didn't see what was so wrong with the clutter. Fifi was part of the clutter. Come to that, so was I.

The next telegram informed us the Thin Man was in Strasbourg.

'Mabuse has a face in Strasbourg,' the Prof explained. 'As proprietor of a *salle à manger*. He was wearing that disguise a day after his visit to London. Many a courier of diplomatic pouches has been drugged and searched in that humble hostel by the main railway station. Our bloodhound has the scent!'

It was time to quit Paris. Our hosts knew what had happened in London, and we must have seemed like wounded beasts, fleeing. If ever there was a chance to kill us off without fear of reprisal, it was now. Irma invited me to dine in a private salon, more or less promising intimacies… even on the slim chance this was a genuine offer rather than a trap, I was inclined to make the play. Moriarty told me not to be a fool and produced tickets to Geneva.

It was our turn to leave luggage behind, but I carried the Von Herder with me.

XIII

Ever been to Geneva? It's a *clean* city. The gutters are swept three times a day. On the streets the cobblestones are individually polished. The public conveniences are the most hygienic in the world. The tarts are scrubbed, efficient and copulate like the mechanical girl who comes out of the cuckoo clock. Even the rats have neat whiskers. The only thing dirty is the money.

If the Thin Man was following the money, the trail led here.

As we checked into the Hotel Beau-Rivage, Moriarty was handed a telegram. It fell to me to tip the bellboy – a French *franc*, hard Swiss cheese for him – while the Professor decoded the numbers and Greek letters he'd worked up as a special cipher for Sophy.

We had come to town ahead of the Thin Man, but he was on his way from Germany. Sophy reported that the detective, picking up clues found in that Strasbourg café, was interested in a Swiss banker, Adolphe Lavenza.

Without even looking at our suite, Moriarty hired a carriage to take us to the financial district – which, in Geneva, is three-quarters of the city. Zurich is worse, or better if you've an urge for that most overrated of criminal endeavours, bank robbery. That's either out-and-out bandit foolishness which leads to getting shot by well-paid vigilante officers (if any institution can afford hired killers, it's a bank – I've taken that shilling myself) or involves as much digging, blasting and carrying as any other kind of prospecting, with a consequent high risk of perishing in a cave-in or a mistimed detonation. Swiss banks don't even have much negotiable loot on the premises: they bury their gold, and keep ledgers and IOUs to prove how rich their customers are.

From a coffee house across the road, we watched the Lavenza Bank for an hour. People came and went, most so respectable it was plain to the practiced eye that they were crooks, a few as close a *Genevoise* could be to low and shabby.

A clerical fellow took a seat at the next table, gulped a cup of molten dark chocolate, and departed without acknowledging us. I recognised Ueli Munster, the Swiss representative of Box Brothers. Whenever business brought him to London, Munster called upon Mistress Strict for a chastisement earned many times over in his financial dealings. The naughty banker left behind a copy of yesterday's *Times*, which I snaffled as any Britisher curious for news from home might have. I turned with leaden heart to a notice of the Patterson raids, while the Professor slit open a packet of documents which had been concealed in the folded newspaper.

'Adolphe Lavenza is Mabuse's Swiss façade,' Moriarty said, looking over Munster's report. 'His bank is the Great Unknown's treasury. It played a part in the collapse of Baron Maupertuis. My disciple has ambitions to influence the economies of nations. He envisions a great bubble and crash after crash, an apocalypse of money. He sees further into the future than my brother, and marks out the real battlefields of the twentieth century: brokerages and banking houses. No armies or wonderful engines of war, but *numbers*. He has taken my methods, Moran. But he does not respect them. I see order. He wants chaos. Irreconcilable formulae.'

'Bastard's a damn anarchist!'

'A poor label for what Mabuse is becoming. It will be almost a shame to stifle the monster in the crib. He might achieve a new kind of mathematics. But he is on the slate, Moran. The slate we shall wipe clean.'

'Where's the bloodhound? We've got to the quarry before him.'

'I calculate the Thin Man will call on this address – *without* his travelling companion – in fifty minutes. We will cheat him of the kill.'

The Von Herder – our only luggage – was at the Beau-Rivage. I had my Gibbs pistol with me, though. And bare hands. *The Times* had put me in the mood to strangle a banker.

First, we needed to secure entry.

A respectable burgher, all pinstripes and pince-nez, emerged from the bank and strolled smartly round the corner. I held him against a wall by his throat while Moriarty determined which language to question him in. He spoke precise English. An Afghan tribal trick persuaded him to explain that a distinctive *carte de visite* was necessary to get past the front desk and secure audience with M. Lavenza. The card was surrendered by the caller, so he no longer had his pass. He said he could help us no more. Moriarty disagreed. We hauled him back to the main thoroughfare.

Within a few minutes, fortuitously, two men approached, carrying a wardrobe between them. One was fat, one thin. Our unwilling informant admitted he knew the men to be in Lavenza's circle… then unwisely cried out for help. By the time the carriers had set down their burden to come to his aid, he was dead. Seconds after that, so were they. I broke the burgher's neck and was stuck with a dead weight. Moriarty scientifically killed the workmen with his penknife. They were finished before they started bleeding. The Professor went through the fat man's pockets and found two plain white cards punched with different queer-shaped holes.

This was all accomplished on a busy street, inside a minute. Passers-by paid no attention as we hustled slack bodies into the wardrobe – which was large and empty enough to accommodate them. Of different stations in society, they would not have sought or wished such intimacy in life. I reckoned them equals now.

A policeman marched up and I feared we'd have to cram in another, but his only interest was in making sure we did not leave furniture on the street.

'It is untidy, an obstruction,' he insisted.

I nodded to the Swiss constable and we hefted the wardrobe – not without difficulty, for obvious reasons – up to the entrance of the Lavenza Bank. The doors were opened by a liveried colossus. Moriarty presented the cards to a smart young lady, who posted them into a slit in a small, mechanical box. Gears ground and a red electric lamp flashed. We were told to leave the wardrobe and pass through a green-baize door.

In a small antechamber, we found upholstered chairs and a selection of German, French, Italian and English periodicals. All dull and financial. Nothing spicy. A voice boomed from the room beyond an inner door. Instructions were being issued in deep, rasping German. Someone – Mabuse as Lavenza, I supposed – outlined a plan for a daring robbery. Jewels from the Royal Collection of Ruritania, kept in Swiss vaults, were to make a rare public appearance at the coronation. An opportunity existed to seize them in transit from Geneva to Strelsau. Language aside, it could have been Moriarty talking. I sensed the Professor steaming. I was affronted on his behalf – Mabuse was plagiarising a classic Moriarty gambit. The sooner the copycat was in a bag and drowned, the better.

At the end of the speech, auditors were dismissed. Three men and a woman came out of the inner room, purposeful. They had taken no notes, but apparently committed the plan to memory. Paying us little attention, they left about their business. After a moment's pause, the voice addressed 'Operator number six and operator number fifty-one'. We were ordered to come in.

We had only moments before Mabuse saw we were not his delivery men.

Moriarty opened the inner door and I went through, with my Gibbs up. The room was dim. The only source of light was hidden behind a thick gauze screen which hung over an alcove. A silhouette was presented: a man sat at a desk. I shot him in the head and he keeled over. The kill made, I turned about-face and levelled my gun at the green baize door. No one came to investigate. This section of the bank was built like a vault. Soundproof.

The Professor tore away the curtain.

Triumph died. The voice of Dr Mabuse told his operators to come in, again. And again, repeating.

The dead man wore a gagging hood and a straitjacket. In falling, he had set an Edison phonograph revolving. Mabuse's voice was on wax and came from a trumpet. I lifted the needle and shut the contraption up.

Moriarty unstuck the dead man's hood from the mess of his head, and peeled it off.

I'd shot Ueli Munster.

'F--k,' Professor Moriarty said.

I agreed.

The bastard had tweaked our noses again, properly. Mabuse had sat wearing another face – after Moriarty had said he'd always recognise him if he saw him! – and enjoyed his chocolate at the next table.

The green-baize door was locked, but easily kicked open. The uniformed giant and the smart young lady had cleared off. So far as we could tell, the premises were untenanted but for the two of us and four corpses.

We got out of the Lavenza Bank quickly.

XIV

The Thin Man acquitted himself no better than us at the Lavenza Bank. I presume he found the bodies, noted an irregular curl of apple-peel in the waste-paper basket as significant and picked up a fresh scent. He didn't alert the clean, efficient Swiss police of any crimes or mention the Mystery of the Four Dead Swiss Bankers, the Phonograph and the Wardrobe to his tag-along biographer. Claiming to be weary of cities, he proposed a bracing schedule of hiking, sightseeing and scrambling up mountains.

This is what Watson said: 'For a charming week we wandered up the valley of the Rhone, and then, branching off at Leuk, we made our way over the Gemmi Pass, still deep with snow, and so, by way of Interlaken, to Meiringen. It was a lovely trip, the dainty green of the spring below, the virgin white of the winter above.'

Back at the hotel, we found Sophy waiting. After recent events, I was minded to look at her teeth to make sure she really was herself. I doubt Mabuse could have pulled off the imposture, despite seemingly supernatural abilities, but a female disguise merchant was floating around Europe. I'd not forgotten what a nuisance Irene Adler could be if she put her mind to it. In theory, she was in Ruritania with Rupert. There was a god-awful mess about the succession, with Rudi, Michael and a red headed dark horse named

Rassendyll making bids while the crown was in play [13]. Still, I'd not put it past her to visit Switzerland to see the endgame out. At this point, I didn't even know who *that bitch* was betraying. She'd done us dirty by winding around Madame Sara, but I never found out if she was a paid Mabuse confederate or just kicking our teeth on the principle that we were smiling and she had on her steel-toed pumps. We had the real Miss Kratides, though she had nothing fresh to report.

Moriarty was in a cold fury. I was in a hot one. We'd bagged a brace of Swiss apiece, but were no better for it. I imagine murder charges could have been involved. Worse, according to Swiss *mores*, we'd left an untidy mess. Adolphe Lavenza was a shed snakeskin. All we could do was mark the Thin Man while he sniffed over the countryside. I was no longer confident he had a hope of running down Mabuse.

Geneva is not Paris. There's nothing to do at night.

Sophy was packed off on her travels again, following the Thin Man's traipse through verdant snowiness or whatever. She sent back mostly incident-less reports. The only thing that suggested we might have a trail left was that some lederhosen yodeller tried to shove her out of a boat on the Interlaken. She got a knife into his neck several times, and pitched him overboard. He sank through wonderfully clear waters, ribbons of red unrolling from the gills she'd put in him. Tedium had got to her and she was waxing poetic. Not a healthy thing for a woman or a murderer. An early sign of the vapours or a perverse impulse to confess.

To remind our bloodhound of his duty, we had Sophy roll a rock off a ridge at him as he ambled along the shore of the Daubensee. His deerstalker soaked by the splash, his nerves showed. She said he jumped like a grasshopper. Moriarty was not in a much better condition. In those days, he oscillated so badly I thought he'd do himself an injury. He ground his teeth and his vertebrae creaked. He covered sheets of hotel notepaper with numbers and symbols.

The staff at the Beau-Rivage were afraid of him. He was showing his skull too much. I was just red-faced and irritable. Day-old numbers of *The Times* and the *Gazette*, with further revelations from Inspector Patterson, did nothing for my humour. The Yard was clearing its books, pinning decades of unsolved crimes on 'the Conduit Street Ring'. I admit most of the ones from the last ten years were ours, but the 1809 disappearance of Benjamin Bathurst was almost certainly not Moriarty's doing since he'd not yet been born. Constance Kent killed her brother without our help, though the Professor owned a mosaic – Perseus, brandishing the head of Medusa – the young murderess executed while doing her stretch in Millbank.

On the 2nd of May, Sophy's regular cipher telegram came from the Englischer Hof in Meiringen, a small Alpine village. The Thin Man was expected to arrive on the morrow and travel on to Rosenlaui, an even smaller Alpine village, going a little out of the way to visit a tourist attraction, the Reichenbach Falls. Not one of her more interesting *communiqués*. On the same tray was a telegram from Peter Steiler, who represented himself as landlord of the Englischer Hof. He broke sad news. Miss Kratides had been found dead in her locked room, a knife in her breast. She was believed to have taken her own life. In her papers was found our address in Geneva. He trusted we would accept his condolences and wondered in a polite Swiss way whether we would make (i.e. pay for) funeral arrangements. He assured us there was no urgency: even at this stage of the year, there was plentiful ice for the staving off of decay.

Ah, Sophy. I considered the loss. Dead, and never the recipient of a Basher Special.

'The Thin Man must have tumbled her,' I said. 'He knew she blamed him for her brother and got his blade in first. I'd have done the same. I'd not have tricked up that locked-room mystery, though. Damn ostentatious. Detectives can't resist going melodramatic when they turn murderer.'

'No, Moran,' Moriarty said, eyes shining. 'The Thin Man won't be in Meiringen until tomorrow. Another hand did this.'

'Not that cretin Watson!'

Moriarty breathed the name, by now an incantation: 'Mabuse'.

He was already paging through *Baedeker's Guide to Switzerland and the Alps*, calculating the fastest route by scheduled train and hired trap. He was obsessed, again. Moriarty didn't take kindly to nemeses.

'What about the detective?'

Moriarty was impatient with details. 'A minor matter. His usefulness is at an end. It would be untidy to leave him alive, though. Once business with Mabuse is concluded, we shall pitch him off the waterfall. A frothing torrent at its base will make a suitable last resting place for the Thin Man of Baker Street. What say you to that, Moran?'

I laid a hand on the Von Herder case. It was long past time the air rifle saw use.

XV

Two days later, just after dawn, we entered Meiringen, a stopover for alpinists on their way to Trollenberg, waterfall aficionados on their way to Reichenbach and consumptives on their way to the grave.

The Professor called a halt just inside the village limits, and got down from the trap. He would rouse the local constabulary to enquire about the Grecian lady's death – Moriarty going to the police! – while I was to look up this Steiler at the Englischer Hof. The Thin Man and the Thick Head were likely in residence, and Moriarty had to avoid the detective. It was less likely I would be recognised, though I'd not forgotten than impertinent index card.

'What about Mabuse?'

'He is either here, or he has gone,' said the Professor, not being much help. 'Be wary, Moran. He has proved himself incalculable.'

You can't be as fond of dangerous pursuits as me and keep your skin *without* being habitually wary. Bravery is not the same as stupidity. Indeed, if you've the nerve to dance with the big cats you must always be *alert*. I resented Moriarty giving written instructions, with fifteen separate diagrams, on how to suck eggs. He should know Basher Moran better by now.

Leaving Moriarty to trudge towards the *polizei*, the trap rattled up the steep main road of Meiringen. Even this late in the season, snow piled on the pavements. It had been there since last autumn. The dirty, grey banks were studded with lumps of dog shit. *Baedeker*'s misses that detail.

Every building in sight was a *hof* of some sort. They competed for custom with themes and gimmicks. The Englischer Hof hoped to attract visitors from our shores with a Union Jack hung upside down, conveniences labelled 'Victorias' and 'Alberts' and a menu offering such British fare as 'fish and chits', 'squeak and bubble' and 'plump duff'.

After the night's travel, I was hungry. But not enough to risk Swiss chits for breakfast.

Leaving the trap, I realised another reason why Moriarty had got off first: he had stuck me with paying the coachman. Funds were becoming an issue. We'd left England with bandoliers full of sovereigns under our combinations. Unavoidable expenses had mounted. We'd skipped out of the Beau-Rivage, where we were registered as 'Gilbert Smyth' and 'Sullivan Jones', without settling the bill. Our London accounts (and cash stashes) were beyond reach. Our line of credit with any continental Box Brothers associate was cut off when someone shot Ueli Munster in the head. We were in danger of running out of money. If this holiday went on much longer, I might have to resort to picking pockets, getting up card games with strangers in hotels or lifting the wallets from any corpses we might leave in our wake.

Warily – yes, more than usually so – I did a recce. No assassins hidden in the snow piled up against the back of the Englischer Hof.

I entered the lobby, which adjoined the breakfast room, and assumed a downcast, solemn air. I was under orders to examine the body, then disclaim Sophy, leaving funeral costs to whoever might be stuck with them. More penny-pinching. Still, when you're dead, you don't care whether you're under marble or in a sack...

However, when you're alive, you eat breakfast.

Just as I was about to ring the desk bell, I happened to glance into the dining room. Among the tourists – several with limbs in plaster from skiing – sat Sophy Kratides, tucking into a kipper. The dead don't, on the whole, have appetites.

Sophy saw me and was surprised. She coughed up a bone, delicately, into a napkin.

I couldn't put the pieces together.

Then, I could. Meiringen was a killing box. A tiger pit.

For us.

I saw faces. English tourists, local guides, busy waiters, a smiling Swiss who had popped up behind the desk like a jack-in-the-box. Any could be Mabuse.

Anyone could be anyone.

I reached into my coat for my Gibbs.

'I am Peter Steiler,' said the Swiss, who hadn't sent a telegram to Geneva. 'How may I serve you, sir?'

I was calm. 'I am joining that lady for breakfast,' I said. 'Bring me anything on the menu that isn't English. And coffee.'

'Certainly, sir.'

Smiling broadly, I sat down at Sophy's table. Loudly, I said, 'Hullo, old thing –' not risking a name, since I didn't know what she'd given at the *hof* – 'sorry I'm late and all that. Bit of bother with trains. Too used to travelling in France and Italy, don't you know? Swiss trains actually leave according to the timetable, would you believe it? Funny kind of foreigners, eh, what? Have you heard the cricket scores?'

'Crick-et?' she said, equally loud, eyes wide.

'Yes, old thing. Raffles out for a duck against the Australians!'

Coffee arrived.

Under her breath, Sophy asked, 'What are you doing here?'

'Waltzing into a trap, I think. You'll note who isn't here with me and probably saw this coming.'

Sophy took a grip on her toast knife.

All around, people were convivial. Conversation, clattering, someone trying to learn to yodel, noisome gustation. A bit too normal and busy. Then, I really saw the faces.

One of the young English lady tourists was Chinese, the Daughter of the Dragon. The dirndl-and-clogs maid who brought the coffee was Alraune, Mabuse's odd companion. Irma Vep peeped out from behind a *Times* held upside down. She was sharing a plate of croissants with Princess Zanoni. Leaning on a broom and trying in vain to look inconspicuous was none other than the Hoxton Creeper, dressed in lederhosen and a sou'wester. A waiter trundled a trolley bearing a covered plate to our table. He lifted the cover and took up a revolver. It was Rupert of Hentzau.

'Come down in the world, Rupert?' I asked. 'I hear the succession went badly for the Michaelists. A proper conspirator knows not to kill his favoured claimant in a fit of pique before the crown is on his head. Still, I didn't think you'd have to go into service.'

Hentzau laughed, showing teeth. Sophy stuck her knife through his hand and he dropped the gun. He was still laughing when he got a look down the barrel of my Gibbs, but there were tears in his eyes.

All noise in the room had stopped.

'Sebastian,' said a familiar, feminine American voice. 'Put the pistol away. One of these days, it'll go off and you'll do yourself an injury.'

'Good morning, Irene,' I said, not lowering the Gibbs.

Irene Adler was not dressed for the mountains, but for an opera set in the mountains: trim Norfolk jacket, tight britches, polished boots, dear little hat with a feather in the band. She sat herself down opposite Sophy and me. My companion reached for the pot, to fling scalding coffee at the New Jersey nightingale's face. It was empty.

'I thought of that, Miss Kratides,' said *that bitch*, sweetly. 'Rupert didn't see the cutlery coming, though.'

The rascal was levering the knife out of his hand. I hoped marmalade would make the wound go septic. He came at Sophy, intent on cutting her nose off with her own knife.

'Stand down, boy,' Irene said. 'Heel.'

Reluctantly, he stopped.

'It's just hired guns, then,' I said. 'No Jack Quartz or Nikola or Mabuse. This is below stairs.'

'No Moriarty, either,' she said.

I knew I could shoot Hentzau. His swordsmanship would avail him little with that injured paw, though he was a left-hand-dagger-in-the-clinch sort of fellow. With mixed feelings, I could pot Irene from where I sat. Sophy had more knives. And forks and spoons – people forget you can do damage with them too. She could take Alraune, probably Zanoni. But we'd go under. Force of numbers. Irma Vep. The Daughter of the Dragon. The Creeper. Younger, stronger, less vulnerable – plain *better*.

If this was Basher Moran's last stand, come on and let it be…

'We want to talk about Professor Moriarty and Dr Mabuse,' Irene said. 'We want to talk about *diabolical masterminds*, in general. Are you prepared, Sebastian, to talk with us?'

There was a fuss at the door, which was locked.

'I am sorry, sir,' Peter Steiler said, out in the lobby. 'A private party.'

'This note says an Englishwoman needs a doctor,' said a fatuous British voice.

Dr Watson had arrived.

Irene cocked her head. It seemed Watson had been halfway to Reichenbach with his chum, when he was recalled to Meiringen by a bogus summons to the bedside of a lady in distress. Watson was as partial to the bedsides of ladies in distress as I am to the beds of ladies who'll probably end up in distress but won't care about it for the next hour or two. He exchanged gasps of astonishment with Steiler as he tumbled that he'd been rooked. He used language in person that he'd never put in the *Strand*.

Throughout this performance, the 'private party' was silent. Rupert wrapped a towel around his hand to stanch the bleeding. Irma stood up and – showing nursing skill surprising in someone who kept failing to keep her chiefs alive – made a good field dressing out of the towel. She licked her lips at the sight of blood and her eyes shone. *Les Vampires* was just a name, though – right?

Eventually, Watson cleared off.

'We should have let him join us,' Irene said. 'He's properly of our party, too. In thrall to… well, we could hardly say an *angelic mastermind*, could we? Not of someone who ditches his own sidekick as he goes to confront his destiny.'

XVI

What of Moriarty and Mabuse?

I wasn't there, so I can't tell you of their last encounter. And neither left a record.

Mabuse had a face in Meiringen, of course. The police captain – captain of two constables and a carthorse, at least – Moriarty had called on. Alraune, Mabuse's date at the Thoroughgood funeral, told Irene that much, though she was as in the dark about his stratagems as we all were about those whose standards we flew. Ties of blood, bed, tradition and terror did not entitle us to be in the know.

Not all of those present at breakfast in the Englischer Hof were declaring independence. The Daughter of the Dragon, though she later set herself against her father for the love of some white fool, thought a thinning out of the lesser mastermind population would benefit the Si-Fan. It was a Moriarty trick: the Battle of the Six Maledictions all over again. This time, only two – three, if we counted the Thin Man – players were to take each other off the board.

Moriarty knew who he was facing.

Mabuse knew what to expect.

Theirs was a brief meeting, over by the time Irene sat down at our table. It left Mabuse naked in the face – layer upon layer of make-up flayed away

– and broken in mind. I don't know how Moriarty did it, or at what cost to himself. I fancy he just uttered a formula, forcing into his pupil's mind an addictive, insoluble equation Mabuse was compelled to devote all his intellect to working out, but which opened up vast chasms of uncertainty. The man who was no one was condemned to a world where nothing was anything. Babbling in several languages, the nameless man was found by the bewildered constables, and taken away to an asylum… Later, he was let out, and returned to Berlin and his old tricks. However, he was never the same again, and was eventually defeated by his own madness.

If no one stopped them, bested them or killed them, the clever ones all drive themselves mad in the end. They look for nemeses, and – if none are available – make them up. I've heard it said that Moriarty *was* the Thin Man. I understand why people jump to that conclusion, for the one *needed* the other. In the way neither needed anyone else, not Dr Watson… and not Colonel Moran.

That was what Irene wanted to talk about.

I don't know if any of the big brains put her up to it – the ones who are so clever they can put an idea into another person's head without them knowing it – or if it was something she'd come up with on her own one-tier-down level of cunning and self-interest. A lot of it came, I think, from trying to get close to men – or a man – who would not let her in. That's above my level, though.

She knew how to put it to me.

'Hunter and hunted,' she said. 'You say in your book – which could afford to lose the chapters about guns, by the way – that the world is divided between the two types. To avoid becoming one, you must become the other. Do you still believe that, Sebastian?'

'Yes, of course.'

'The hunter and the hunted. Predator and prey. Alive and dead. The guns and the bag.'

'At present, I have a gun. Aimed at you, Irene.'

'It hasn't escaped my notice. But, Sebastian, you miss a category. Native bearers. Guides. Orderlies. Hounds. Where do they fit in? Neither hunter nor hunted. Of the party of the hunter, but not the hunter. Small lives. To quote you, "a currency to be spent freely for a chance of a clean shot". In this coming world Moriarty outlined, of very great villains and equally magnificent heroes, are you – are *we* – not such a currency? Are we not native bearers?'

I might have shot her. My finger tightened, involuntarily, on the trigger. It would have been only fair, for she had shot me. With the worst, most deadly ammunition. Purer than a silver bullet.

The truth.

Steiler came into the breakfast room, with another of his notes. This time, for me. From Moriarty.

Mabuse broken. Come to the Falls. The hide we scouted. Bring the Von Herder. On my signal, take the shot.

M.

On the journey, we had discussed this. The hide he mentioned was a perfect lay, marked on a tourist map Moriarty had given me.

'Sebastian,' Irene said. 'Your master whistles.'

XVII

So, we come to it. Above the Reichenbach Falls.

I had my lay. I set out well after Watson, who was rushing back up the mountain, but was at the Falls comfortably before him. Forward planning, you know. Always a good idea. Moriarty was a master at it. From my snug nest in the snow, I had a good view. The roar of the torrent was muted. I saw the narrow path, and judged where the antagonists might meet. A ledge, cropping out, with a grassy patch. No easy way to avoid a determined enemy there.

The Thin Man thought a few Japanese wrestling tricks would serve him in a fight with an old maths tutor. He'd not seen the Professor kill two Swiss wardrobe-carriers – the only souls I ever saw him personally murder, by the way – with a letter opener. If it came to a grapple, it would be a more even contest than the detective knew. With dead-eye Moran in hiding to ensure the outcome, it was no contest at all.

The Von Herder was assembled, loaded and primed. It took twenty minutes' vigorous pumping for a single shot. Once the gun was discharged, I'd be reduced to chucking rocks. As I said, I usually only need a single shot. I had a small pile of rocks ready, though. More planning.

I was flat out, on a blanket of fresh snow. Not the foul stuff back at the village, but a white, crisp, cold virgin fall. The air was thin and I was quite merry. Your brain gets like that in the mountains. You can hear bells and birdsong and voices in the waterfall if you let yourself.

I had the stock to my cheek, the telescope sight to my eye.

There was no more Firm. It was smashed and scattered. In his talk of starting anew, Moriarty had spoken in the singular person. There was no 'we' in his world.

I had prospects. Even without funds, I had my wits. And Sophy was handy. I had not been netted by Scotland Yard and even had the last of my reputation as a hero of the Empire and a cool hand in a crisis. In time, London would welcome Basher Moran. I could always get up a hand of high-stakes whist at the Bagatelle Club.

Tiny figures were struggling down the mountain path.

Through the telescope sight, I saw the antagonists come face to face. They had words. They broke off. One scribbled a note he left on a rock – a notice of the cancellation of milk delivery in Baker Street?

I saw two masterminds, two hunters, two tigers. From my perch, above them, they were small boys playing fight. A red and a white ant. Bacteria.

Then, it was on.

Professor Moriarty and Sherlock Holmes rushed at each other.

Moriarty raised his arm – the signal!

I took my shot.

ENDNOTES

PREFACE

1. …and reputedly, as Montacute Blore Box (1896–1953) was wont to boast, 'in Hell!'

2. 'Regardless of other crimes, anyone who founds a UK-based white rap label and signs up Danny Dyer should have his head kicked into an Essex marsh.' – Charles Shaar Murray, Facebook update, November 16, 2008.

3. London: Virago and Emeryville, CA: Shoemaker and Hoard, 2004.

4. An expansion of my article 'Mrs Warren and Mrs Halifax: Controlling Male Desire and Female Economic Emancipation', *Victorian Studies*, 41 (2), 1998. Considering the mentions, *passim*, of Mrs Halifax in the Moran manuscript, further research into this remarkable woman is a priority.

5. Victoria Gorse, *Gender in Asylums*, 1890–1914. Ms Gorse's thesis remains incomplete, and the student's whereabouts unknown… though odd text messages purporting to be from her are received to this day. The last I had was 'cha0s ra1nz!'.

6. In his introduction to an otherwise valuable edition of this long-suppressed work (University of Brichester Press, 2004), Dr Paul Forrestier dismisses Moran's candidacy and settles on Lord John Roxton as the author. As I pointed out in a review (*History Today*,

February 2005), the editor's 'conclusive evidence' boils down to a scattering of big-game hunting terms throughout the text – which equally supports the case for Moran. We await a retraction from Dr Forrestier.

7. Box Brothers offered their clients discreet secretarial services in the interwar years. Looking over their employee lists from the early 1920s, it is probable that the typist of the Moran manuscript was either Miss Kathleen Greatorex, later popularly known as the 'Penton Street Poisoner', or Mrs Elsa Shank-Goulding, who was shot as a spy in 1943.

CHAPTER ONE

1. Henry James Prince (1811–99), excommunicated from the Church of England for 'radical teachings', founded a pseudo-religious order, the Agapemone (Abode of Love), in Spaxton, Somerset, in 1845. His most fervent disciples were women with money. The Agapemone was one of several nineteenth-century communions run along the lines of the groups later established by Sun Myung Moon or L. Ron Hubbard. The circumstances of Moran's encounter or encounters with Prince are not known at this time. See: *The Reverend Prince and His Abode of Love* (Charles Mander, EP Publishing, 1976).

2. A more balanced account of these incidents can be found in *Riders of the Purple Sage* (Zane Grey, Harper & Brothers, 1912).

3. See *A Study in Scarlet* (John Watson and Arthur Conan Doyle, *Beeton's Christmas Annual*, 1887).

CHAPTER TWO

1. 'bread and honey'. Yes, the slang expression 'bread', usually associated with American crooks or hippies, is Victorian cockney rhyming slang: 'bread and honey – money'.

2. Past and future exponents of this long con include the explorer Allan Quartermain (H. Rider Haggard, *King Solomon's Mines*, Cassell & Co., 1885) and the journalist Tintin (Hergé, *Le Temple du Soleil/Prisoners of the Sun*, Casterman, 1949).

3. According to 'A Scandal in Bohemia' (John Watson and Arthur Conan Doyle, *The Strand Magazine*, 1888), Irene Adler was a coloratura soprano. None of these are coloratura roles.

4. For more on the Ruritanian succession, see *The Prisoner of Zenda: Being the History of*

Three Months in the Life of an English Gentleman (Rudolf Rassendyll and Anthony Hope, J.W. Arrowsmith, 1894) and *Rupert of Hentzau* (Friedrich von Tarlenheim and Anthony Hope, *The Pall Mall Magazine*, 1895). For a revisionary view of Ruritania in the 1890s, see 'The Ruritanian Resistance: How and Why' ('Doc M', http://www.silverwhistle.co.uk/ruritania/).

5. In the original manuscript, the allusion is followed by a parenthesis which has been heavily scored through. From the few discernible words, the redacted section seems to be a homophobic rant. Other passages in the memoirs, especially those concerning his time at Eton, indicate Moran shared his era's prejudice against homosexuality, but didn't despise gays more than he hated anyone else. Equally, his bile against 'natives' and foreigners is tempered by general misanthropy. Sebastian Moran *especially* loathed straight white male British Christians.

6. Ruritania is a German-speaking country, though Rudolf II tried to make French the court language.

7. Crusher: Police constable.

CHAPTER THREE

1. Joss: Luck.

2. *Ally Sloper's Half Holiday* (1884–1916). A weekly comic newspaper built around the popular comic strip character of Ally Sloper, created by Charles Henry Ross and Marie DuVal.

3. I could use this footnote to reveal the identity of the holder of this title – or at least the name he most commonly used – but Dame Philomela assures me that, even after a 120 years, this would not be advisable: 'You'd be risking a lot more than getting your pussy's ear clipped!'

4. The Si-Fan: A Chinese criminal-political faction, active throughout the nineteenth and early twentieth centuries.

5. See: John Watson and Arthur Conan Doyle, 'The Speckled Band', *The Strand Magazine*, 1892.

6. See: John Watson and Arthur Conan Doyle, 'The Red-Headed League', *The Strand Magazine*, 1891.

7. The draper's clerk was H.G. Wells, who evidently learned something about this business. See: *The War of the Worlds*, *Pearson's Magazine*, 1897, and 'The Crystal Egg', *The New Review*, 1897.

8. Less well remembered than rival cinema pioneers the Lumière Brothers, Georges Méliès or Thomas Edison, Paul Aloysius Robert (1870–1944) was a significant contributor to the early days of the motion picture. He directed *What Happened to Maisie Under the West Pier* (1895), the first British film to be seized and suppressed as pornographic, and *A Fight with Sledgehammers in Rottingdean* (1902), labelled the 'original kinema "nasty"'. On the strength of Moran's memoirs, it seems he could have laid claim to the invention of special effects techniques later associated with Méliès.

CHAPTER FOUR

1. See Thomas Hardy, 'Tess of the d'Urbervilles: A Pure Woman Faithfully Presented', *The Graphic*, 1891.

2. The American jurist Roy Bean (c. 1825–1903) dismissed a case against Paddy O'Rourke because – after close examination of the Revised Statutes of Texas – he declared 'homicide is the killing of a human being, however I can find no law against killing a Chinaman'. At the time, Bean's saloon-cum-court in Vinegaroon, Texas, was surrounded by 200 Irish labourers who declared they would lynch the judge if O'Rourke were convicted. This might have influenced the decision. By the standards of his times, Bean was a lenient judge. Most of those he found guilty were fined the amount of money they had about them at the time of arrest and set free; he only sentenced two men to hang, and one of those escaped.

3. Colonel Thomas Blood (1618–80) talked his way into the jewel house of the Tower of London, posing as a clergyman, and made off with the Crown jewels. He and his confederates were caught on Tower Wharf. Charles II, supposedly taken by Blood's roguish daring, pardoned him. In preparation for the raid, Blood befriended Talbot Edwards, master of the jewel house, and cajoled a private viewing, whereupon – presumably with roguish daring – the elderly man was struck with a hammer, knocked down, bound and gagged and stabbed. Blood's gang forgot to bring suitable swag-bags and had to improvise: Blood hammered flat St Edward's crown, his brother-in-law sawed

the sceptre into two parts and a man named Parrot stuffed the orb down his trousers.

4. See Frederic Van Renssaelaer Dey, '3,000 Miles by Freight; or, The Mystery of a Piano Box', The Nick Carter Library, 1891.

5. Written between 1115 and 1142.

6. Smith, Elder & Co., 1865.

CHAPTER FIVE

1. For a more detailed account of the Vermissa Valley Scowrers and the attempted murder at Birlstone Manor, see John Watson and Arthur Conan Doyle, 'The Valley of Fear', The Strand Magazine, 1914–15.

2. 'The Green Eye of the Yellow God', J. Milton Hayes, 1911. Moran's quotation of the once-popular monologue establishes this section of his memoirs was written at least twenty years after the event. Internal evidence suggests chapters one, two and six were written much earlier.

3. See: John Watson and Arthur Conan Doyle, 'The Sign of the Four', Lippincott's Monthly Magazine, 1890.

4. See: James Malcolm Rymer and Thomas Peckett Prest (attr.), 'The String of Pearls: A Romance', The People's Periodical and Family Library, 1846–7. Sweeney Todd and Nellie Lovett (or Lovat) are remembered for gruesome crimes – throats cut in the barber's chair, corpses recycled as meat pies – but they were, at bottom, mere thieves. The string of pearls, property of Mark Ingestre (or Ingestrie), was stolen from a sailor, Lieutenant Thornhill, who was supposed to convey it to Ingestre's sweetheart, Johanna Oakley. Ingestre's enquiries into Thornhill's disappearance lead to the exposure of Todd and Lovett.

5. See: Wilkie Collins (ed.), The Moonstone, Tinsley Brothers, 1868.

6. When they first met, Moran was under the impression that Moriarty 'kept no notes, no files, no address book or appointment diary'. It seems the Professor was vain enough to foster that impression, though Moran eventually learned this was not the case. This is more evidence that 'The Six Maledictions' was written as much as thirty years after 'A Volume in Vermilion'.

7. See: Malcolm Ross and Bram Stoker, *The Jewel of Seven Stars*, Heinemann, 1903.

8. Ermanno Wolf-Ferrari's *I gioielli della Madonna* (libretto by Carlo Zangarini and Enrico Golisciani) is drawn from news reports of these events. The opera premiered in Berlin in 1911 under the title *Der Schmuck der Madonna* but did not play in Italy until 1953.

9. In 1881, the *Fenian Ram* – a submarine designed by John Philip Holland – was constructed by the Delameter Iron Company of New York for use against the British. Rather than pay Holland, the Fenian Brotherhood stole the vessel from him, then realised none of them knew how to pilot it. Holland refused to give instructions in its use, and the IRB were stuck with something they could neither steer nor sell.

10. Edgar Allan Poe, 'The Purloined Letter', *The Gift for 1845*, 1844. The secret hiding place of the stolen letter is in plain sight – in the letter rack of a hotel.

11. See: Harold Manders and E.W. Hornung, 'The Fate of Faustina' and 'The Last Laugh', *The Black Mask*, Richards, 1901. Note that Manders, unlike Moran, accords A.J. Raffles credit for arranging the killing of Corbucci. It is not clear from the memoirs whether Moran disliked Raffles on principle or had a specific beef with the gentleman cracksman.

12. See: Dashiell Hammett, *The Maltese Falcon*, Alfred A. Knopf, 1930.

CHAPTER SIX
1. See: William Hope Hodgson, 'Carnacki the Ghost Finder', *The Idler*, 1910.

2. The Fal Vale swing bridge was the site of a later, famous railway disaster – which gave rise to another ghostly legend. See: Arnold Ridley, *The Ghost Train*, St Martin's Theatre, 1923.

CHAPTER SEVEN
1. See: John Watson and Arthur Conan Doyle, 'The Final Problem', *The Strand Magazine*, 1893; and 'The Adventure of the Empty House', *Collier's Weekly*, 1903. It is evident that Moran wrote his memoir after both these reminiscences – which offer differing accounts of the incident at Reichenbach Falls – were published. In 'The Final Problem', the narrator writes that 'the best and wisest man I have ever known' died at the Falls; in 'The Empty House', it is alleged that Watson's friend survived but, for reasons no else has ever found convincing, decided to let the world think him dead for a few years. Moran barely touches

on the many other theories which have been advanced as to what actually happened… that Moriarty was merely an alternate personality of a mentally ill man who threw himself alone off the mountain… that Moriarty survived to take his dead opponent's place in the world, and thereafter fought against crime as he had previously fought for it… that Moriarty evaded death by mentally projecting himself into a succession of other bodies and has lived on as a series of masterminds; the names of Carl Peterson, Gregory Arkadin, Alexander Luthor, Arnold Zeck, Professor Marcus, Peter Cornelius, Ernst Blofeld, Justin Sepheran, Derek Leech, Hannibal Lecter and 'Count Jim Moriarty' have been mentioned – and some of those aren't even real people… that Moriarty was never in Switzerland and faked his death so he could rebuild his just-shattered criminal empire. He also reveals nothing which will comfort the many theorists who have advanced the notions that Moriarty was a total innocent persecuted by a paranoid cocaine fiend, an alien invader (this might arise from dim rumours associated with The Red Planet League), a vampire, one of his brothers in disguise, a multiple personality (in this scenario, the Professor, the Colonel and the Stationmaster are aspects of the same person), a self-aware hologram, a giant rat (either from Sumatra or somewhere else), a woman, a clone from the future, gay, or (like every eminent Victorian from Alfred Tennyson to Vesta Tilley) Jack the Ripper. It's unlikely that Moran was blithely unaware of this feverish speculation, which was well underway during his later life.

2. As the author of *Katie Reed: A Turbulent Life* (Virago, 1988), I am satisfied that Moran here solves a significant mystery about the identity of the person with whom the feminist writer attempted collaboration in the summer of 1891. At some point, she – or another party – went through her journals and filleted the pages which cover this thorny business. We only know she was working as a ghost from the letters of her friend (and, later, lover) Charles Beauregard – to whom she complained extensively about her collaborator's 'uselessness, unreliability and octopus hands'. The assignment was thrust on Katharine Reed by Edward Tyas Cook, editor of the *Pall Mall Gazette*, on the still-commonplace principle of 'do one for me now and I'll give you something you want to do later'. Since 1988, a great deal of material about Reed – one of the most interesting women of the late nineteenth and early twentieth centuries – has come to light. It's my hope that an enlightened publisher will eventually enable me to issue a comprehensively revised edition of my biography. Paul Forrestier's *What Kate Reed Did* (University of Brighton Press, 2003) and Kim Newman's 'The Gypsies in the Wood' (*The Fair Folk*, SFBC, 2005) are, respectively, inadequate and fanciful.

3. This would seem to refer to William Houlston (1882–1973). It took seven months of enquiries to find out which government departments presently fulfil the functions of the

nineteenth-century Department of Supplies and the Diogenes Club. A D-notice prevents me from revealing even their current acronyms, though I have been given special leave to say that the Diogenes Club traded as Universal Exports in the 1950s which – at this stage of paranoia – inclines me to question whether this is true. Needless to say, attempts to ascertain whether either hold a bundle of red-taped documents marked 'Sealed until 2073' – let alone requests for premature access on academic grounds – have been unrewarding. A minor puzzle arises: if the exchanges were secret, how did Moran know they were 'cryptic, terse, bitter'? Had he read them?

4. See: John Watson and Arthur Conan Doyle, 'The Greek Interpreter', *The Strand Magazine*, 1893.

5. Both Kemp's employers subsequently came to bad ends. See: John Watson and Arthur Conan Doyle, 'The Adventure of Charles Augustus Milverton', *Colliers Magazine*, 1904; and Harold Manders and E.W. Hornung, *Mr Justice Raffles*, Smith, Elder & Co, 1909. From the records of Box Brothers, where Charles Milverton and Daniel Levy both banked, it is evident that the master blackmailer and the rapacious moneylender tithed significant portions of their incomes to the Professor. He allowed them to conduct their businesses, and his influence granted them a measure of protection. While Moriarty was alive, no one murdered Milverton or Levy; when he was off the scene, ruined former victims queued up to take their shots. Neither case was solved and the murderers went free. Milverton, Levy and other criminal or semi-criminal figures ran their particular rackets only because Professor Moriarty didn't find such enterprises stimulating or useful, unless for a specific purpose connected to larger schemes. Indeed, it is quite likely Moriarty used his pet blackmailer and usurer to ensnare or pressure officials or members of society he wished to make use of.

6. *Quap* is a form of pitchblende (uranium-rich sludge) found in some quarters of Africa. Around the turn of the century it was reportedly used in patent medicines. Since there are no recorded cases of patients succumbing to radiation poisoning, it's unlikely that tonics which claimed to derive from *quap* contained any. What Baron Maupertuis – who was reputed to have 'colossal schemes' – intended is unknown, but he met Henri Becquerel, the discoverer of radioactivity, in Paris in 1885 and is mentioned obliquely in Madame Curie's journals. Little is known about Maupertuis beyond his involvement in the Netherland-Sumatra Company, which failed in 1887.

7. The incident of the white tiger is not recounted in either of Moran's published books about his big-game hunting experiences. Curiously, of all the animals (and men) he shot, he seems to have held this kill sacred… and touches on it only in these unguarded pages. Uncertain about the passage, he experimented with a false name (Jammyfoot) to conceal the identity of his hunting companion before setting down the real one. Matthew Jellinek (1842–1975) is not mentioned at any other point in the papers, though *Three Weeks in the Jungle* is perhaps significantly dedicated to 'the tethered kid'. Jellinek was in Farrer House with Moran at Eton, then served with him in the Bangalore Pioneers. The archives of the Pioneers contain a report by Colonel Henry Patience, commanding officer during the regiment's secondment to Abyssinia for the 1868 punitive expedition. Addressing a sentiment that then-Major Sebastian Moran should be 'mentioned in despatches', Patience explains that Moran effected a single-handed rescue of then-Lieutenant Jellinek from an irregular force loyal to Emperor Tewodros II (they would now be called a 'Death Squad') known for torturing Englishmen to death. Patience notes this 'jape' proved popular in the officers' mess and made the young Major 'cut a dash as a hero to the men', but was executed against direct orders and constituted 'a serious breach of discipline for which a court martial would not be an inappropriate response, though no plans for a prosecution are held at this time'. This affair is not elucidated in any of Moran's memoirs – a mystery in itself since he is happy to go on at length about matters which do him far less credit. Upon Moran's arrest for attempted murder in 1894, John Watson said of him, 'This is astonishing, the man's career is that of an honourable soldier.'

8. According to an 1894 advertisement for 'Cigares de Joy' issued by the manufacturers Wilcox & Co., 'JOY'S CIGARETTES afford immediate relief in case of ASTHMA, WHEEZING, WINTER COUGH and HAY FEVER, and, with a little perseverance, effect a permanent cure. Universally recommended by the most eminent Physicians and Medical Authors. Agreeable to use, certain in their effects, and harmless in their action, they may be safely smoked by ladies and children. Box of 35, 2s 6d.'

9. Though he may never have realised the fact, Moran encountered this 'ghost' again in later life. In chapter six, he mentions he was in the Paris Opera House on the night in 1881 that a chandelier fell on the audience. This was the most famous crime committed by Erik de Boscherville, popularly known as the Phantom of the Opera. At the time Sir Augustus Moran was British Minister to Persia, Erik was employed by the family of the shah as an architect. For the *khanum*, the mother of Nasser al-Din Shah Qajar, Erik designed a torture labyrinth at Mazendaran which to some extent prefigured the famous maze he created

under the cellars of the Paris Opera. Accounts differ, but contemporary historians believe Erik congenitally disfigured rather than a victim of abuse or accident. See: Gaston Leroux, *Le Fantôme de l'Opéra, Le Gaulois, 1909–10*; Susan Kay, Phantom, Doubleday, 1990.

10. Snide: forged currency.

11. Darbies: handcuffs.

12. Scholars have long noted that Watson and Doyle set out contradictory versions of Watson's introduction to Moriarty in 'The Final Problem' and *The Valley of Fear*. Since these accounts can't *both* be true, the veracity of one or the other must be challenged. A similar, 'no, what *really* happened' discrepancy exists between 'The Final Problem' and 'The Empty House'. It should be noted that, though made *aware* of Moriarty, Watson never met him.

13. History says Prince Rudolf of Elphberg was crowned King of Ruritania in 1891. Shortly after the coronation, it was rumoured that Rudolf's cousin, the Englishman Rassendyll, occupied the throne in his place. Any argument was ended when Prince Michael was murdered by the Count of Hentzau at Zenda Castle, reputedly in an argument over a woman.

Notes and Acknowledgements

My parents, Julia and Bryan Newman, named me after a character in a Victorian popular novel. My mother's second favourite book was *Gone With the Wind*, so I narrowly escaped Rhett. I imagine this has shaped the course of my life.

The Hound of the d'Urbervilles has been percolating a long time, so I must own up to many debts. First off, to state the obvious, this book would not exist without Sir Arthur Conan Doyle. Every time I went back to the source, I found minor characters he made up and dropped who could sustain an entire series (if you want more Sophy Kratides, so do I). Primary secondary influences (as it were) are Zane Grey, Anthony Hope, H.G. Wells, Thomas Hardy, J. Milton Hayes and Arnold Ridley. Other elements crept in, so shout-outs are due to Guy Boothby (creator of Dr Nikola and Simon Carne), Frederic Van Rensselaer Dey, H.H. Ewers, Louis Feuillade, John Gardner, William Gillette, Dashiell Hammett, Hergé, William Hope Hodgson, E.W. Hornung, Norbert Jacques (and Fritz Lang and Thea von Harbou), Michael Kurland, Maurice Leblanc, William LeQueux, Gaston Leroux, Peter Lovesey, L.T. Meade, Nicholas Meyer, Bertram Millhauser (and Roy William Neill and Rondo Hatton), Spike Milligan, Jamyang Norbu, Sax Rohmer, Bram Stoker (and Christopher Wicking and Valerie Leon), Mark Tansey, Dudley

D. Watkins, Billy Wilder and I.A.L. Diamond, Carlo Zangarini and Enrico Golisciani (and Ermano Wolf-Ferrari), and others.

My grandmother Miranda Wood – who introduced me to Marvel Comics and *MAD Magazine*, without realising how important things she picked at random would become to me – gave me a hardback of *The Complete Sherlock Holmes Short Stories* for my twelfth birthday. I still have it. Later, the first thing I bought when I got a cheque guarantee card (remember them?) was W.S. Baring-Gould's two-volume *Annotated Sherlock Holmes*. The first Holmes novel I read was, oddly, *Sherlock Holmes vs. Jack the Ripper* by Ellery Queen (actually, Paul W. Fairman), a canny novelisation (and expansion) of Donald and Derek Ford's screenplay *A Study in Terror*. I was aware of Peter Cushing in the 1968 BBC-TV series, but the first media Holmes I remember is Carleton Hobbs in a BBC wireless production of *The Hound of the Baskervilles*. I should acknowledge the screen's great Moriartys (some in not-great Holmes films and shows), all of whom have filtered into my version of the Napoleon of Crime: Gustav von Seyffertitz, Ernest Torrence, Lyn Harding, George Zucco, Lionel Atwill, Henry Daniell, John Huston, Laurence Olivier, Viktor Yevgrafov, Eric Porter, Paul Freeman, Anthony Higgins and Vincent d'Onofrio. There are fewer Morans to choose from, but Patrick Allen is fine opposite Jeremy Brett in *The Return of Sherlock Holmes* and Alan Mowbray is suitably duplicitous opposite Basil Rathbone in *Terror By Night*.

The too-good-to-resist notion of Holmes co-existing with characters created by other people has been around since his heyday (in Boothby's *Prince of Swindlers* and C.S. Lewis's *The Magician's Nephew*, for instance, Holmes is mentioned as a real person) but took hold in my mind thanks to Philip José Farmer's 'biographies' *Tarzan Alive* and *Doc Savage – His Apocalyptic Life*, which mean more to me than anything by Edgar Rice Burroughs or Lester Dent. A comedy sketch TV series of the early 1970s starring a forgotten Welsh double act (Ryan and Ronnie) had Holmes pursue Dracula; this may be what started me thinking along lines which would lead to the *Anno Dracula* and *Diogenes Club* books, and now this Moriarty-Moran effort. The 1971–3 ITV series *The Rivals of Sherlock Holmes*, based on Sir Hugh Greene's anthologies, introduced me to the likes of Simon Carne and Carnacki the Ghost-Finder; both seasons of the show are now out on DVD (thanks to Luciano Chelotti and Grace Ker of Network Releasing) and worth your while. Would that there had been spin-off series starring Roy Dotrice and Donald Pleasence as Carne and Carnacki. In this book, it's been hard to avoid the long shadow of George Macdonald Fraser's *Flashman*, so I should especially mention *Royal Flash* (and Richard Lester's film), the *Prisoner of Zenda* pastiche, and *Flashman and the Tiger*, in which Flashman meets Moran. Doyle's Sebastian Moran and Fraser's Harry Flashman have much in common: they're both amoral rogues with a shelfload of medals, but at least Moran actually *earned* his gongs.

Besides other writers' novels, collections and short stories, I wouldn't have been able to write *The Hound of the d'Urbervilles* without reference books. Baring-Gould's *Annotated Sherlock Holmes* and *Sherlock Holmes of Baker Street: A Biography* are still the best place to start, but Leslie S. Klinger's more recent *New Annotated Sherlock Holmes* and *Annotated Dracula* are just as essential. In addition, I kept turning to Jess Nevins' *The Encyclopedia of Fantastic Victoriana* (Dr Quartz and M. Sabin wouldn't be here without it), Matthew E. Bunson's *The Sherlock Holmes Encyclopedia*, Leonard Wolf's *The Annotated Dracula*, David Kalat's *The Strange Case of Dr Mabuse*, Sally Mitchell's *Victorian Britain: An Encyclopedia*, and more reference sites on the internet than I can list, inevitably including Wikipedia (how did writers get by before they could instantly to look up whose signature was on British banknotes in 1891 or find out where the Astronomer Royal lives?).

Doyle invented Professor Moriarty to kill off Holmes in 'The Final Problem' and, ten years later, invented Sebastian Moran to bring him back in 'The Empty House'. This circumstance means Moriarty and Moran, supposedly partners in crime, share no scenes in the canon. Given that, like many arch-nemeses, Moriarty is a dark doppelganger for the hero, hints at the notion that Moran might be his 'Watson' – which is present in several early plays and films. In *Silver Blaze, aka Murder at the Baskervilles*, which tips the villains into an adaptation of the Moriarty-free short story (and sets it at Baskerville Hall to boot), Moran (Arthur Goullet) is plainly a sounding board and fetch-and-carry man for Moriarty (Lyn Harding). When reviewing this minor 1937 film for Nathaniel Thompson's *DVD Delirium*, I noted the Moran-as-Watson angle and mentally filed it away. Later, Ann Kelly of BBC Online asked me to write a Holmes story (something I've strictly avoided doing) and I returned to the Moran-Moriarty idea for 'A Shambles in Belgravia', which became a template for a series (one Doyle 'guest star', one other Victorian literary source, a parody title, a 'case' that doesn't turn out well). Subsequently, Marvin Kaye commissioned 'A Volume in Vermilion' for *Sherlock Holmes' Mystery Magazine* and Charles Prepolec solicited 'The Red Planet League' and 'The Adventure of the Six Maledictions' for his anthologies *Gaslight Grimoire* and *Gaslight Arcanum*. Thanks to these editors for their input into something I knew would be a novel disguised as a collection as soon as I wrote the meeting of Moran and Moriarty and realised how this relationship would end at the waterfall. Thanks also to David Barraclough, who suggested me for Titan's fiction line just before leaving the company, and Cath Trechman, my stalwart and intrepid editor. My agents, Antony Harwood, James Macdonald Lockhart and Fay Davies were involved.

Thanks as ever to people who helped out with emotional support, random kindness and odd bits of information or inspiration: Pete Atkins, Eugene Byrne, Susan Byrne, Meg Davis, Pat Cadigan, David Cross, Alex Dunn, Val and Les Edwards, Jo Fletcher, Christopher Fowler, Christopher Frayling, Neil Gaiman (who has also written a Moran-as-narrator story – and came up with the 'Professor Moriarty retires to Essex to keep wasps' joke), Mark Gatiss (who parallels the 'consulting criminal' premise, but added a *Jim'll Fix It* joke I wish I'd thought of), John Courtenay Grimwood, Maxim Jakubowski, Rodney Jones, Stephen Jones, Yung Kha, Jean-Marc Lofficier, Tim and Donna Lucas, Paul McAuley, Maura McHugh (who maintains my website at johnnyalucard.com), Helen Mullane, Sara and Rita Paço, Sarah Pinborough, Chris Roberson, Russell Schechter, Dean Skilton, Brian Smedley, Tom Tunney, Stephen Volk and the members of the 'Kim Newman's Anno Dracula books' Facebook group.

Kim Newman, Islington, 2011

AVAILABLE NOW:

ANNO DRACULA
KIM NEWMAN

It is 1888 and Queen Victoria has remarried, taking as her new consort Vlad Tepes, the Wallachian Prince infamously known as Count Dracula. His polluted bloodline spreads through London as its citizens increasingly choose to become vampires.

In the grim backstreets of Whitechapel, a killer known as 'Silver Knife' is cutting down vampire girls. The eternally young vampire Geneviève Dieudonné and Charles Beauregard of the Diogenes Club are drawn together as they both hunt the sadistic killer, bringing them every close to Britain's most bloodthirsty ruler yet.

Anno Dracula is a rich and panoramic tale, combining horror, politics, mystery and romance to create a unique and compelling alternate history. Peppering his story with familiar characters from history and fiction, Kim Newman explores the darkest depths of a reinvented Victorian London.

"Politics, horror and romance are woven together in this brilliantly imagined and realised novel. Newman's prose is a delight, his attention to detail spellbinding." — *Time Out*

WWW.TITANBOOKS.COM

COMING SOON:

ANNO DRACULA: THE BLOODY RED BARON
KIM NEWMAN

1918 and Dracula is commander-in-chief of the armies of Germany and Austria-Hungary. The war of the great powers in Europe is also a war between the living and the dead. As ever the Diogenes Club is at the heart of British Intelligence and Charles Beauregard and his protegé Edwin Winthrop go head-to-head with the lethal vampire flying machine that is the Bloody Red Baron...

A brand-new edition, with additional unpublished novella, of the critically acclaimed bestselling sequel to *Anno Dracula*.

"...stunning follow-up to his inventive alternate-world fantasy, *Anno Dracula*..." — *Publisher's Weekly*

"Gripping... superbly researched... Newman's rich novel rises above genre... A superior sequel to *Anno Dracula*, itself a benchmark for vampire fiction." — *Kirkus Reviews*

ANNO DRACULA: DRACULA CHA CHA CHA
KIM NEWMAN

Rome 1959 and Count Dracula is about to marry the Moldavian Princess Asa Vajda. Journalist Kate Reed flies into the city to visit the ailing Charles Beauregard and his vampire companion Genevieve. She finds herself caught up in the mystery of the Crimson Executioner who is bloodily dispatching vampire elders in the city. She is on his trail, as is the undead British secret agent Bond.

A brand-new edition, with additional unpublished novella, of the popular third instalment of the *Anno Dracula* series.

"Newman's latest monster mash is the third in a series of fiendishly clever novels… Like the blood gelato lapped by the undead demimonde, this novel is a rich and fulfilling confection." — *Publisher's Weekly*

WWW.TITANBOOKS.COM

ANNO DRACULA: JOHNNY ALUCARD
KIM NEWMAN

1976 and Kate Reed is on the set of Francis Ford Coppola's *Dracula*. She helps a young vampire boy, Ion Popescu, who leaves Transylvania for America. In the States, Popescu becomes Johnny Pop and attaches himself to Andy Warhol, inventing a new drug which confers vampire powers on its users...

A brand-new *Anno Dracula* novel taking the series to Andy Warhol's New York and Orson Welles' Hollywood. This long-awaited new book should not be missed.

SHERLOCK HOLMES: THE BREATH OF GOD
GUY ADAMS

A body is found crushed to death in the London snow. There are no footprints anywhere near it. It is almost as if the man was killed by the air itself. This is the first in a series of attacks that sees a handful of London's most prominent occultists murdered. While pursuing the case, Sherlock Holmes and Dr Watson find themselves traveling to Scotland to meet with the one person they have been told can help: Aleister Crowley.

As dark powers encircle them, Holmes' rationalist beliefs begin to be questioned. The unbelievable and unholy are on their trail as they gather a group of the most accomplished occult minds in the country: Doctor John Silence, the so-called "Psychic Doctor"; supernatural investigator Thomas Carnacki; runic expert and demonologist, Julian Karswell...

But will they be enough? As the century draws to a close it seems London is ready to fall and the infernal abyss is growing wide enough to swallow us all.

A brand-new original novel, detailing a thrilling new case for the acclaimed detective Sherlock Holmes.

THE FURTHER ADVENTURES OF SHERLOCK HOLMES

Sir Arthur Conan Doyle's timeless creation returns in a series of handsomely designed detective stories. The Further Adventures of Sherlock Holmes encapsulates the most varied and thrilling cases of the world's greatest detective.

THE ECTOPLASMIC MAN
BY DANIEL STASHOWER

THE WAR OF THE WORLDS
BY MANLEY WADE WELLMAN & WADE WELLMAN

THE SCROLL OF THE DEAD
BY DAVID STUART DAVIES

THE STALWART COMPANIONS
BY H. PAUL JEFFERS

THE VEILED DETECTIVE
BY DAVID STUART DAVIES

THE MAN FROM HELL
BY BARRIE ROBERTS

SÉANCE FOR A VAMPIRE
BY FRED SABERHAGEN

THE SEVENTH BULLET
BY DANIEL D. VICTOR

THE WHITECHAPEL HORRORS
BY EDWARD B. HANNA

DR. JEKYLL AND MR. HOLMES
BY LOREN D. ESTLEMAN

THE ANGEL OF THE OPERA
BY SAM SICILIANO

THE GIANT RAT OF SUMATRA
BY RICHARD L. BOYER

THE PEERLESS PEER
BY PHILIP JOSÈ FARMER

THE STAR OF INDIA
BY CAROLE BUGGÈ

COMING SOON:

THE WEB WEAVER
BY SAM SICILIANO

THE TITANIC TRAGEDY
BY WILLIAM SEIL

WWW.TITANBOOKS.COM